Sweet Caress

The Many Lives of
Amory Clay

William Boyd

B L O O M S B U R Y
LONDON · OXFORD · NEW YORK · NEW DELHI · SYDNEY

Bloomsbury Publishing
An imprint of Bloomsbury Publishing Plc

50 Bedford Square	1385 Broadway
London	New York
WC1B 3DP	NY 10018
UK	USA

www.bloomsbury.com

First published in Great Britain 2015

British Library Cataloguing-in-Publication Data
A catalogue record for this book is available from the British Library.

ISBN: HB: 978-1-4088-6797-6
TPB: 978-1-4088-6798-3
ePub: 978-1-4088-6800-3

2 4 6 8 10 9 7 5 3 1

Typeset by Integra Software Services Pvt. Ltd.
Printed and bound in Great Britain by CPI Group (UK) Ltd, Croydon CR0 4YY

MIX
Paper from
responsible sources
FSC® C020471

To find out more about our authors and books visit www.bloomsbury.com.
Here you will find extracts, author interviews, details of forthcoming
events and the option to sign up for our newsletters.

Quelle que soit la durée de votre séjour sur cette petite planète, et quoi qu'il vous advienne, le plus important c'est que vous puissiez – de temps en temps – sentir la caresse exquise de la vie.

(However long your stay on this small planet lasts, and whatever happens during it, the most important thing is that – from time to time – you feel life's sweet caress.)

Jean-Baptiste Charbonneau, *Avis de passage* (1957)

Amory Clay in 1928.

PROLOGUE

What drew me down there, I wonder, to the edge of the garden? I remember the summer light – the trees, the bushes, the grass luminously green, basted by the bland, benevolent late-afternoon sun. Was it the light? But there was the laughter, also, coming from where a group of people had gathered by the pond. Someone must have been horsing around making everyone laugh. The light and the laughter, then.

I was in the house, in my bedroom, bored, with the window open wide so I could hear the chatter of conversation from the guests and then the sudden arpeggio of delighted laughter came that made me slip off my bed and go to the window to see the gentlemen and ladies and the marquee and the trestle tables laid out with canapés and punchbowls. I was curious – why were they all making their way towards the pond? What was the source of this merriment? So I hurried downstairs to join them.

And then, halfway across the lawn, I turned and ran back to the house to fetch my camera. Why did I do that? I think I have an idea, now, all these years later. I wanted to capture that moment, that benign congregation in the garden on a warm summer evening in England; to capture it and imprison it forever. Somehow I sensed I could stop time's relentless motion and hold that scene, that split second – with the ladies and the gentlemen in their finery, as they laughed, careless and untroubled. I would catch them fast, eternally, thanks to the properties of my wonderful machine. In my hands I had the power to stop time, or so I fancied.

BOOK ONE: 1908–1927

1. GIRL WITH A CAMERA

THERE WAS A MISTAKE MADE on the day I was born, when I come to think of it. It doesn't seem important, now, but on 7 March 1908 – such a long time ago, it seems, threescore years and ten almost – it made my mother very cross. However, be that as it may, I was born and my father, sternly instructed by my mother, placed an announcement in *The Times*. I was their first child, so the world – the readers of the London *Times* – was duly informed. '7 March 1908, to Beverley and Wilfreda Clay, a son, Amory.'

Why did he say 'son'? To spite his wife, my mother? Or was it some perverse wish that I wasn't in fact a girl, that he didn't want to have a daughter? Was that why he tried to kill me later, I wonder . . . ? By the time I came across the parched yellow cutting hidden in a scrapbook, my father had been dead for decades. Too late to ask him. Another mistake.

Beverley Vernon Clay, my father – but no doubt best known to you and his few readers (most long disappeared) as B. V. Clay. A short-story writer of the early twentieth century – stories mainly of the supernatural sort – failed novelist and all-round man of letters. Born in 1878, died in 1944. This is what the *Oxford Companion to English Literature* (third edition) has to say about him:

Clay, Beverley Vernon

B. V. Clay (1878–1944). Writer of short stories. Collected in *The Thankless Task* (1901), *Malevolent Lullaby* (1905), *Guilty*

3

Pleasures (1907), *The Friday Club* (1910) and others. He wrote several tales of the supernatural of which 'The Belladonna Benefaction' is best known. This was dramatised by *Eric Maude* (q.v.) in 1906 and ran for over three years and 1,000 performances in the West End of London (see *Edwardian Theatre*).

It's not much, is it? Not many words to summarise such a complicated, difficult life, but then it's more than most of us will receive in the various annals of posterity that record our brief passage of time on this small planet. Funnily enough, I was always confident nothing would ever be written about me, B. V. Clay's daughter, but it turned out I was wrong . . .

Anyway, I have memories of my father in my very early childhood but I feel I only began to know him when he came back from the war – the Great War, the 1914–18 war – when I was ten and, in a way, when I was already well down the road to becoming the person and the personality that I am today. So it was different having that gap of time that the war imposed, and everyone has since told me he was also a different man himself, when he came back, irrevocably changed by his experiences. I wish I had known him better before that trauma – and who wouldn't want to travel back in time and encounter their parents before they become their parents? Before 'mother' and 'father' turned them into figures of domestic myth, forever trapped and fixed in the amber of those appellations and their consequences?

The Clay family.

My father: B. V. Clay.

My mother: Wilfreda Clay (née Reade-Hill) (b.1879).

Me: Amory, firstborn. A girl (b.1908).

Sister: Peggy (b.1914).

Brother: Alexander, always known as Xan (b.1916).

The Clay family.

★

THE BARRANDALE JOURNAL 1977

I was driving back to Barrandale from Oban in the evening – in the haunted gloaming of a Scottish summer – when I saw a wild cat pick its way across the road, not 200 yards from the bridge to the island. I stopped the car at once and switched off the engine, watching and waiting. The cat halted its deliberate progress and turned its head to me, almost haughtily, as if I'd interrupted it. I reached, without thinking, for my camera – my old Leica – and held it up to my eye. Then put it down. There are no photographs more boring than photographs of animals – discuss. I watched the brindled cat – the size of a cocker spaniel – finish its pedantic traverse of the road and slip into the new conifer plantation, promptly becoming invisible. I started the engine and drove on home to the cottage, strangely exhilarated.

I call it 'the cottage', however its true postal designation is 6 Druim Rigg Road, Barrandale Island. As to where numbers 1–5 are, I have no idea, because the cottage sits alone on its small bay and Druim Rigg Road ends with it. It's a solid, two-storey, thick-walled, mid-nineteenth-century, small-roomed house with two chimney stacks and one-storey outbuildings attached on either side. I assumed somebody farmed here a hundred years ago, but all that's gone, now. It has mossy tiled roofs and walls of concrete cladding that had aged to an unpleasant, bilious grey-green and that I had painted white when I moved in.

It fronted the small, unnamed bay and if you turned left, west, you could see the southern tip of Mull and the wind-worked grey expanse of the vast Atlantic beyond.

I came in the front door and Flam, my dog, my black Labrador, gave his one glottal bass bark of welcome. I put away my shopping and then went through to the parlour, my sitting room, to check on the fire. I had a big stove with glass doors set in the chimney recess in which I burned peat bricks. The fire was low so I threw some bricks on it. I liked the concept of burning peat, rather than coal – as if I

The cottage on Barrandale Island, before renovations and repainting, c. 1960.

were burning ancient landscapes, whole eons, whole geographies were turning into ash as they heated my house, heated my water.

It was still light so I summoned Flam and we walked down to the bay. I stood on the small crescent beach, as Flam roved around the tide rack and the rock pools, and I watched the day slip into night, noting the wondrous tonal transformations of the sunset on its dimmer switch, how blood-orange can shade imperceptibly into ice-blue on the knife-edge of the horizon, listening to the sea's interminable call for silence – *shh, shh, shh.*

★

When I was born – in Edwardian England – 'Beverley' was a perfectly acceptable boy's name (like Evelyn, like Hilary, like Vivian) and I wonder if that was perhaps why my father chose an androgynous name for me: Amory. Names are important, I believe, they shouldn't be idly opted for – your name becomes your label, your classification – your name is how you refer to yourself. What could be more crucial? I've only met one other Amory in my life and he was a man – a boring man, incidentally, but unenlivened by his interesting name.

When my sister was born, my father was already away at the war and my mother consulted with her brother, my uncle Greville, on what to call this new child. They decided between them on something 'homely and solid', so family lore has it, and thus the Clays' second daughter was called 'Peggy' – not Margaret, but a straightforward diminutive from the outset. Perhaps it was my mother's counter to 'Amory', the androgynous name she didn't choose. So Peggy came into the world – Peggy, the homely and solid one. Never has a child been so misnamed. In the event, when my father returned home on leave to greet his six-month-old daughter the name was firmly established and she was known to all of us as 'Peg' or 'Peggoty' or 'Peggsy', and there was nothing he could do. He never really liked the name Peggy, and was never wholly loving to Peggy as a result, I believe, as if she were some sort of foundling we'd taken in. You see what I mean about the importance of names. Did Peggy feel she had the wrong name because her father didn't like it, or her, particularly? Was it another mistake? Was that why she changed it later?

As for Alexander, 'Xan', that was mutually consented to. My mother's father, a circuit judge, who died before I was born, was called Alexander. It was my father who shortened it instantly to Xan and that stuck. So, Amory, Peggy and Xan, there we were – the Clay children.

My first memory of my father is of him doing a handstand in the garden at Beckburrow, our house near Claverleigh, in East Sussex. It was something he could do effortlessly – a party trick he had learned as a youngster. Give him a patch of lawn and he would stand easily on his hands and take a few steps. However, after he was wounded in the war he did it less and less, no matter how much we implored him. He said it made his head ache and his eyes lose focus. When we were very young, though, he needed no urging. He liked doing handstands, he would say, because it readjusted his senses and his perspectives. He would do a handstand and say, 'I look at you girls hanging from your feet like bats and I feel sorry for you, oh, yes, in your topsy-turvy world with the earth above and the sky below. Poor things.' No, no, we would shriek back, no – you're the one upside down, Papa, not us!

I remember him coming back on leave in uniform after Xan was born. Xan was three or four months old so it must have been towards the end of 1916. Xan was born on 1 July 1916, the opening day of the battle of the Somme. It's the only time I recall my father in his uniform – Captain B.V. Clay DSO – the only occasion I can bring him to mind as a soldier. I suppose I must have seen him uniformed at other times but I remember that leave in particular, probably because baby Xan had been born, and my father was holding his son in his arms with a strange, fixed expression on his face.

Apparently he had left precise instructions about the naming of his third child: Alexander if he was a boy; Marjorie if a girl. How do I know this? Because sometimes when I was cross with Xan and wanted to tease him I called him 'Marjorie', so it must have been common knowledge. All family histories, personal histories, are as sketchy and unreliable as histories of the Phoenicians, it seems to me. We should note everything down, fill in the wide gaps if we can. Which is why I am writing this, my darlings.

During the war, the man we saw most of, and who lived with us at Beckburrow from time to time, was my mother's younger brother, Greville – my uncle Greville. Greville Reade-Hill had been a photo-reconnaissance observer in the Royal Flying Corps, and was something of a legend owing to the fact that he had stepped unscathed from four crashes until his fifth crash duly broke his right leg in five places and he was invalided out of the service. I remember him in his uniform limping around Beckburrow. And then he transformed himself into Greville Reade-Hill, the society photographer. He hated being called a 'society photographer' even though that was exactly and evidently what he did. 'I'm a *photographer*,' he would say, plaintively, 'impure and not so simple.' Greville – I never called him uncle, he forbade it – set my life on its course, unknowingly, when he gave me a Kodak Brownie No. 2 as a present for my seventh birthday in 1915. This is the first photograph I ever took.

In the garden at Beckburrow, spring 1915.

Greville Reade-Hill. Let me call him to mind then, just after the war, as his career was beginning to take off, unsteadily but definitely upwards, like a semi-filled hydrogen balloon. He was tall, broad-shouldered and good-looking, real handsomeness marred only by a slightly too large nose. The Reade-Hill nose, not the Clay nose (I have the Reade-Hill nose, as well). A slightly large nose can make you look more interesting, both Greville and I have always agreed – who wants to look 'conventionally' handsome or beautiful? Not me, no, thank you very much.

I can't remember a great deal about that first photograph – that momentous first click of the shutter that was the starting pistol that set me off on the race for the rest of my life. It was a birthday party – I think my mother's – held at Beckburrow in the spring of 1915. I seem to recall a marquee in the garden, also. Greville showed me how to load the film into the camera and how to operate it – simplicity itself: look down into the small limpid square of the viewfinder, select your target and press down the little lever at the side. Click. Wind on the film and take another.

I heard the laughter in the garden and ran to find my camera. And then scampered across the lawn and turned the lens on the ladies in their hats and long dresses strolling down towards the beeches at the garden's end that screened the pond.

Click. I took my photograph.

But my remaining memories of that day are more to do with Greville. As he crouched by me showing me how the camera worked what has stayed in my mind more than anything else was the smell of the pomade or Macassar that he put on his hair – a scent of custard and jasmine. I think it may have been 'Rowland's Macassar' that he wore. He was very fastidious about his clothes and grooming, as if he were always on show in some way or, now I come to think of it, as if he were about to be photographed. Maybe that was it – as someone who photographed people in their finery he became particularly aware of how he was looking, himself, at any hour of the day. I don't think I ever saw him tousled or dishevelled, except once ... But we'll come to that in good time.

Beckburrow, East Sussex, our home. In fact I was born in London, in Hampstead village, where we lived in a rented two-floor maisonette in Well Walk just a hundred yards from the Heath. We left Hampstead when I was two because my father became temporarily rich as a result of the royalties he received from Eric Maude's dramatisation of his short story, 'The Belladonna Benefaction'. He used the financial windfall to buy an old house in a four-acre garden half a mile from the village of Claverleigh in East Sussex (between Herstmonceux and Battle). He had a new kitchen wing added with bedrooms above and installed electric light and central heating – all very newfangled in 1910. Here is what *The Buildings of England: Sussex* had to say about Beckburrow in 1965:

CLAVERLEIGH, a small village with no plan but considerable charm below the South Downs. One winding street ending at a small church, ST JAMES THE LESS at the S end (1744, rebuilt in 1865 in a limp, mongrel version of the classical style) ... BECKBURROW ½ m. E on the lane to Battle, a good capacious C18 tile-roofed cottage with attractive materials – brick, flint, clunch – and remains of timber framing at one gable end. The small mullioned windows of the old facade give an air of immense solidity. Sober neo-Georgian additions (1910) with a heavy-hipped roof. Inoffensive, a home to be lived in rather than an exposition of taste. A good weatherboard BARN.

That was what I always felt about Beckburrow – 'a home to be lived in'. We were happy there, the Clay family, or so it seemed to me as I was growing up. Even when Papa came home after the war – thin, irritable, unable to write – nothing really seemed to have changed in the place's benign enfolding atmosphere. We had a nanny, two housemaids, a cook (Mrs Royston who lived in Claverleigh) and a gardener/factotum called Ned Gunn. I went to a dame school in Battle, driven there and back by Ned Gunn in a dog cart, until we acquired our own motor car in 1914 and Ned added 'chauffeur' to his list of accomplishments.

When my father came home, in those early years after the war, the only real pleasure he seemed to take in life was long walks to the sea, over the Downs, to the beaches at Pevensey and Cooden. He strode out, leading his children and whatever friends and relatives we had with us, like some slightly demented Pied Piper, urging us on. 'Step we gaily, on we go!' he would shout back at us as we dawdled and explored.

My mother joined us later with the motor and we would be driven home at the end of the day to Beckburrow. However, once we arrived at the beach, it was immediately obvious how my father's mood changed. The high spirits of the walk gave way to taciturn moodiness as he sat there smoking his pipe staring at the sea. We never gave it much thought. Your father was born moody, my mother would say, always brooding about something. He's a writer who can't write and it's making him fractious. And so we put up with his interminable silences punctuated by the odd demonic rant when his patience finally snapped and he would stalk the house shouting at everyone, bellowing for 'Just a bit of peace and quiet, for the love of Jesus! Is it too much to ask?' We simply made ourselves scarce and Mother would calm him down, leading him back to his study, whispering in his ear. I've no idea what she said to him, but it seemed to work.

Your parents, however strange they may be in actual fact, always seem 'normal' to their offspring. Indeed, the slow realisation of your parents' defining oddness is a harbinger of your developing maturity — a sign that you are growing up, becoming your own person. In those early years at Beckburrow, from our move there until the mid-1920s, nothing seemed much wrong with our little world. Servants came and went, the garden flourished; Peggy appeared to be some kind of infant prodigy on the piano; baby

Xan turned into a somewhat self-contained, thoughtful and almost simple boy who could amuse himself for hours creating elaborate patterns with a handful of sticks and leaves or damming the stream at the bottom of the south lawn, conjuring into being a little empire of rivers and lakes and irrigation channels, setting small balsa-wood rafts off on minuscule voyages of discovery. It would keep him occupied an entire day until he was called in for supper.

What about our Amory? What about me? So far, so run of the mill. After the dame school in Battle came the secondary school in Hastings. Then in 1921 it was announced that I was going away – to be a boarder at Amberfield School for Girls near Worthing. When I left for Amberfield (Mother accompanying me, Ned driving) and we pulled away down the lanes from Beckburrow it was the first time in my life that I registered the full level of hurt, injustice and disappointment that amounted to a betrayal. My mother would hear nothing of it: 'You're a lucky girl, it's a wonderful school, don't make a fuss. I hate fuss and fusspots.'

I came home in the holidays, of course, but, as the one absentee, felt I was something of an outsider. The barn had been converted into a music room for Peggy, wainscotted, painted, a carpet on the floor and furnished with a baby grand piano, where she was taught by a Madame Duplessis from Brighton. Xan mooned about the garden and the lanes around the house, a solemn boy with a rare, transforming smile. My father appeared to be spending most of the week in London, looking for literary work of some sort. He was given a part-time job as an editor and contributor to the *Strand* magazine and was a reader for various publishing houses. The pot of money from 'The Belladonna Benefaction' was running out. A 1919 production in New York closed after a month but cheques continued to arrive in the post, the mysterious enduring legacy of a once successful play. My mother was quite content, it seemed to me, running her big house, or sitting on the bench of the magistrate's court in Lewes, or initiating and organising charitable works in the East Sussex villages around Claverleigh – fetes, tombolas, bring-and-buy sales.

And Greville would come down occasionally from London. Only Greville was my friend, I felt, and he taught me how to take better photographs, changing my Box Brownie for a 2A Kodak Jnr, with an extending lens on a concertina mount and, one mysterious afternoon, he blacked out the pantry, unpacked his trays and pungent bottles, and showed me the astonishing alchemy involved in taking images trapped on film and, through the application of chemicals – developer, stopper, fixer and washes – turning them miraculously into negatives which could then be printed into black and white photographs.

I still felt this nagging sore of resentment at my banishment, however. One day I generated enough courage to confront my mother and asked her why I had to go away to school when Peggy and Xan could stay at home. My mother sat me down and took my hands. 'Peggy is a genius,' she said, breezily, 'and Xan has problems.' And that was that, an end to the matter until my father finally went totally insane.

★

THE BARRANDALE JOURNAL 1977

I feed Flam, my loyal and loving Labrador, and, as the summer night slowly comes on, light the oil lamps. I use my diesel generator to power the small refrigerator, the washing machine and my radio and hi-fi. I don't want electric light or a television set – and, anyway, I won't be around much longer, so what's the point of more home improvements? I live in a comfortable technological limbo, a halfway house: on the one hand laundry, music, the world's news and ice cubes for my gin and tonic; and, on the other, a peat fire and the particular glow that the oil lamp gives off – the subtle waver of the incandescent wick, the lambent marshmallow, generating that subtle shadow-shift that makes the room more alive, somehow – breathing, pulsing.

Barrandale doesn't really deserve to be called an island. It's separated from the mainland of the west of Scotland by a narrow 'sound', maybe fifty or sixty feet across at its widest. And the sound is bridged, the 'Bridge over the Atlantic' as we locals grandiosely like to term it. There's another island with another more famous, grander, older, stone bridge (ours is made of girders and railway sleepers but is ten feet longer, which makes us feel ever so slightly more superior: we cross a larger portion of the Atlantic). Still, Barrandale is irrefutably an island, and driving over the bridge – over the sound – establishes, almost unknowingly, an island mentality.

My separate schooling, it turned out – so I learned later – was the result of a will. The death of a great-aunt (Audrey, on my mother's side) conferred on the Clay family a sum of money for the education of Amory, great-niece and firstborn. My father's steadily diminishing and erratic income couldn't have coped with the termly fees demanded by Amberfield, but, if I hadn't been sent there, or somewhere similar, the benefaction wouldn't have been forthcoming. Completely strange, unknown currents can shape our lives. Why didn't my parents tell me? Why did they pretend it was their decision? I was taken away from the familiar comforts and securities of Beckburrow and I was meant to be grateful, the privileged one.

My mother was a tall, bespectacled, somewhat cumbersome woman. She managed to conceal whatever affection she might have felt for her children with great success. She had two expressions she used all the time: 'I don't like a fuss' and 'Put that in your pipe and smoke it'. She was always patient with us but in a way that seemed to suggest her mind was elsewhere, that she had more interesting things she could be doing. We always called her 'Mother', as if it was a category, a definition, and didn't reflect our relationship, as if we were saying 'ironmonger' or 'historian'. Here's the sort of exchange that would ensue:

ME: Mother, could I have another helping of blancmange, please?
MOTHER: No.
ME: Why not? There's plenty left.

MOTHER: Because I say so.

ME: But that's not fair!

MOTHER: Well you'll just have to put that in your pipe and smoke it, won't you?

My mother on Cooden beach in the 1920s.
Taken with my 2A Kodak Jnr. Xan is laughing behind her.

I never saw any real expression of affection between my mother and my father – and at the same time I have to admit I never saw any signs of resentment or hostility.

My father's father, Edwin Clay, was a miner from Staffordshire who went to night classes at a Mechanics' Institute, educated himself, qualified himself, and ended his career as a director of Edgeware & Rackham, the publishers, where he eventually became the managing editor of five trade magazines that served the building industry. He grew wealthy enough to send his two sons to private schools. My father, a clever boy, won an exhibition to Lincoln College, Oxford, and became a professional writer (his younger brother, Walter, died at the Battle of Jutland, 1915). The one-generation jump was remarkable, I suppose, and yet I always sensed in my father that familiar mixture of pride at his achievements combined with – not shame, but a diffidence, an insecurity: an English social insecurity. Would anyone take him seriously, a miner's son, as a writer? I believe that part of the reason for buying Beckburrow and enlarging it and living the county life must have been to prove to himself that those insecurities were now worthless and wholly cancelled out. He had become thoroughly middle class; a successful writer of several well-received books married to a judge's daughter, with three children, living in a large and covetable big house in the East Sussex countryside. Yet he was not entirely a happy man. And then the war came and everything went wrong.

I think tonight I might begin to sort out all those old boxes of photographs. Or maybe not.

★

It is 1925. The Amberfield School for Girls, Worthing. My best friend Millicent Lowther stuck on the false moustache and smoothed it down with her fingertips.

'It was all I could find,' she said. 'They seemed only to have beards.'

'It's perfect,' I said. 'I only want to get an idea of the sensation.'

We were sitting on the floor, our backs to the wall. I leant forward and kissed her gently, lips to lips, no great pressure.

'Don't pout,' I said, not pulling away. 'Men don't pout.' The contact with the false moustache wasn't unpleasant, although, given the choice, I'd always prefer a clean-shaven top lip. I moved slightly, changed the angle, feeling the prickle of the bristles on my cheek. No, it was tolerable.

We older girls regularly practised kissing at Amberfield but I have to say the experience wasn't much different from kissing your fingers or the inside of your upper arm. Having never kissed a man, and I was now seventeen years old, I wasn't sure what all the fuss was about, as my mother would have said.

We broke apart.

'Any moustache pash?' Millicent asked.

'Not really. It's just that Greville's grown one and I wanted to see what it might feel like.'

'Gorgeous Greville. Why don't you invite him to visit?'

'Because I don't want you specimens ogling him. Did you get the fags?'

We bought cigarettes from one of the young Amberfield gardeners, a gormless lad with a harelip called Roy.

'Oh, yes,' Millicent said and fished in her pockets, producing a small wrap of paper and a box of matches. I liked Millicent a great deal – she was smart and sardonic, almost as sardonic as me – but I would have preferred her to have fuller lips, the better to practise kissing – her upper lip was almost non-existent.

I screwed one of the small Woodbines into the ebony cigarette holder that I had stolen from my mother.

'Just Woodbines,' Millicent said. 'Very infra dig, I'm afraid.'

'You can't expect a poor proletarian like Roy to smoke Craven "A".'

'Roy, the hoi polloi. I suppose not, but they do burn my throat, rather.'

'While your head spins.'

I lit Millicent's cigarette and then my own and we puffed smoke up at the ceiling. We were in my 'darkroom', a broom cupboard outside the chemistry laboratory.

'Thank the Lord your chemicals pong so,' Millicent said. 'What *is* that smell?'

'Fixer. It's called hypo.'

'I'm not surprised no one's ever descried cigarette smoke in your little cubbyhole.'

'Not once. Is "descried" the *mot juste*?'

'It's a word that should be used more often,' Millicent said, a little smugly, I thought, as if she had invented the verb herself, spontaneously.

'But correctly,' I admonished.

'Pedant. Annoying pedant.'

'Apart from us, only the Child Killer comes in here, and she loves me.'

'Is she a femme, do you think, the Child Killer?'

'No. I think she's sexless . . .' I drew on my Woodbine, feeling the head-reel. 'I don't think she really knows what she's feeling.' The Child Killer was in fact called Miss Milburn, the science teacher, and I owed her a great deal. She had given me this broom cupboard and encouraged me to set up my dark room in it. She had dense unplucked eyebrows that almost met over her nose, hence her nickname.

'But aren't we femmes?' Millicent asked. 'Kissing each other like this?'

'No,' I said. 'We only do it to educate ourselves, to see what it'd be like with a man. We're not bitter, my dear.' 'Bitter' was Amberfield slang for 'perverted'.

'Then why do you want to kiss your uncle? *Eugh!*'

'Simple – I'm in love with him.'

'And you say you're not bitter!'

'He's the handsomest, funniest, kindest, most sardonic man I've ever met. If you were ever in his presence – not that you'll ever be – you'd understand.'

'It just seems a bit odd to me.'

'Everything in life is a bit odd, when you come to think of it.' I was quoting my father – it was something he'd say from time to time.

Millicent stood up, cigarette between her lips, and squeezed her small breasts.

'I just can't imagine a man doing this to me . . . Rubbing my bosoms. How would I feel, react? I might want to punch him.'

'That's why it's just as well we try everything here, first. One day we'll get out of this jungle, we'll be free. We need to have some idea of what's going to be what.'

'It's all right for you,' Millicent said, grudgingly. 'The world you move in – writers, society photographers . . . My father's a timber merchant.'

'Your secret's safe with me.'

'Minx! Queen of the minxes!'

'I'm not a snob, Millicent. My grandfather was a Staffordshire miner.'

'I'd rather my father was a writer than a timber merchant, that's all I'm saying.' Millicent carefully removed her false moustache and stubbed out her Woodbine.

'Any more kissing?' she asked. 'We haven't tried it with tongues.'

'Bitter woman! You should be ashamed of yourself.' I clambered to my feet and went to look at my photographs drying on their line of string. A bell rang in a distant corridor.

'I think I'm meant to be supervising some of the younger specimens,' she said. 'See you later, darling.'

She left and I carefully unpegged the photos. I didn't print every negative I developed as I didn't want to waste paper on contact sheets. I would scrutinise the negative with a magnifying glass and was often very confident of the choice I eventually made. The decision to print was somehow key to what I felt about the photograph and each one that I selected would be given a title. I don't know why I did this – some vague painterly connection, I suppose – but in bestowing a title the photograph lived on in my mind more easily and permanently. I could recall almost every photograph that I'd printed – a memory archive – an album in my head. I think also that the whole process of photography still seemed astonishing at that stage of my life. The abidingly magical process of trapping an image on film through the brief exposure of light and then, through the precisely monitored agency of chemicals and paper, producing a monochrome picture of that instant of time still possessed its alluring sorcery.

Now, Millicent having gone, summoned by her bell, I took down my three new photographs – stiff, dry – and laid them out on the small table at the end of the box room. I had called the three photographs 'Xan, Flying', 'Boy with Bat and Hat' and 'At the Lido'. I was pleased with them all, particularly 'Xan, Flying'.

One hot day the previous August we'd gone down to the Westbourne Swimming Club Lido in Hove where they had a one-acre, unheated salt-water pool with a twenty-five-foot diving board at one end. It took Xan three jumps before I was happy that I'd truly captured him in mid-air.

I wrote the titles on the back of the prints in a soft pencil, added the date, and slipped them into my loose album. All three photographs were similar in that they were candid shots of people in movement. I liked taking photographs of people in action – walking, coming down steps, running, jumping and, most importantly, not looking into the lens. I loved the way the camera could capture that unreflecting suspended animation, an image of somebody halted utterly in time – their next step, their next gesture, next movement, forever incomplete. Stopped just like that – by me – with the click of a shutter. Even then I think I was aware that only photography could do that – so confidently, so effortlessly – only photography could pull off that magic trick of stopping time; that millisecond of our existence captured, allowing us to live forever.

Two days later I was in the sixth-form study room taking part in a staring match with Laura Hassall. It was her challenge but I knew I would win – I always won staring matches. We were allowed to speak to each other, deliberately to provoke a lapse in concentration or to distract so eye contact was broken.

'Stanley Baldwin's been assassinated,' Laura said.

'Poor. Very poor.'

'No. He has.'

'Good. Horrible man.'

'Xan, Flying', 1924.

'At the Lido', 1924.

'Boy with Bat and Hat' (Xan Clay), 1924.

We kept staring at each other, faces two feet apart, chins propped on our hands, eye to eye. Everyone else at the room was working at their prep, not bothering remotely with our contest.

'Laura?'

'Yes?'

'Romulus and Remus. Heard of them?'

'Ah ... *Yeshhh.*' She said it as a dullard would, irritated.

'Then, imagine,' I said, in a speculative tone, as if the idea had just occurred to me, 'imagine that Rome had been founded by Remus – and not Romulus.'

'Yes ... So what?'

'In that case, the city would be called Reme.'

Laura thought about this, instinctively, and lost. Her gaze flickered.

'Damnation! Shit and damnation!'

There was a knock at the door and a junior specimen appeared. She looked straight at me. Junior specimens were not allowed to talk unless spoken to.

'What is it, you odious child?' I said.

'God wants you.'

'God' was our headmistress, Miss Grace Ashe. I was wary of Miss Ashe – I suspected that she saw through me, saw my very nature. I knocked on the door of her office and waited, conscious that I was a bit on edge, that I was feeling nervy, not at my best. Such an evening summons was rare. I heard her say 'Come!' and I checked my uniform, smoothed the creases from the knees of my beige lisle stockings, and pushed the door open.

Miss Ashe's 'office' did not live up to the name – it was a sitting room, with a large burr-walnut bureau covered in papers and files set in an alcove. I could have been in a country house. The carpet was a navy blue with a scarlet border; a sofa faced two armchairs, all in white linen loose covers, across a long padded tapestry stool with books placed on it. The wallpaper had a cream and coffee-coloured stripe and the room's paintings were real and modern, stylised landscapes and still lifes painted by Miss Ashe's brother, Ivo (who had died in the war). Pale blue hessian curtains were allowed to bulk their hems on the floor and the table lamps burned dimly behind mottled parchment shades. Taste was being exhibited here, I realised, confident yet understated.

Miss Ashe was in her early forties, so we had calculated, pale and slim with her dark auburn hair combed tightly back from her brow to be gathered into a complex knotted bun. We all agreed she was 'chic'. Millicent and I had decided she looked like a retired prima ballerina. We were all, in truth, rather frightened and in awe of her and her elegant, impassive demeanour, but I made it my strategy never to show this. I tried to be uncharacteristically breezy and gay with her and I think she was consequently rather annoyed by my attitude, aware it was feigned for her benefit. She was always rather short and stern with me. No smiles, as a norm.

But she was smiling now as she waved me to a chair. I was disarmed, for a second or two.

'Evening, Miss Ashe,' I said, trying to regain the upper hand. 'That's a beautiful bracelet.'

She looked at the heavy silver and Bakelite bracelet on her wrist as if she'd forgotten she'd put it on.

'Thank you, Amory. Do sit.'

She sat down herself and reached for a cardboard file and opened it on her knee. She was wearing an emerald-green afternoon frock, trimmed with a lemon-yellow scarf at the neck. She flipped up the lid of a silver cigarette box on the table beside her chair, took out a cigarette, searched for a lighter, and lit her cigarette, all the time keeping her eyes on the open file. We'd noticed how Miss Ashe pointedly smoked in front of the older girls – it was a provocation. Thus provoked, I spoke.

'I suppose that's my dossier.'

She looked up. 'It's your *file*. All pupils have a file.'

'All the facts.'

'All the facts we know ...' She cocked her head, as if she were taking me in better. Pale blue eyes, unblinking. I didn't want to start a staring match with Miss Ashe, so I lowered mine and picked invisible fluff off my skirt.

'I'm sure there are many more "facts" we're unaware of.'

'I don't think so, Miss Ashe.' I smiled, sweetly. 'I've nothing to hide.'

'Really? You're an open book, are you, Amory?'

'For those who can read me.'

She laughed, seeming genuinely amused at my remark and I felt the beginnings of a blush creep up my neck and warm my cheeks and ears. Stupid Amory, I thought. Say as little as possible. Miss Ashe was scrutinising my file again.

'You passed all subjects at School Certificate with distinction.'

'Yes.'

'And you decided to drop maths, science and Greek.'

'I'm more interested in—'

'History, French and English. What's your subsidiary?' She turned a page.

'Geography.'

She made a note and then closed the file, looking at me directly again.

'Are you happy here at Amberfield, Amory?'

'Would you define "happy" for me, Miss Ashe?'

'You're answering a question with a question. Playing for time. Just be honest – but don't say you're bored. I don't care if a girl is stupid or bad but to be bored is a defeat, *un échec*. If you're bored with life you might as well die.'

Something about Miss Ashe's absolute assurance stung me. Without thinking I blurted out an answer.

'If you want me to be honest, then I feel I'm disintegrating, here. I'm not a groaner, Miss Ashe – I know you hate groaners as much as you hate boredom – but I feel . . . lifeless. Everything's insincere, sterile and spineless. Sometimes I feel inhuman, a robot—' I stopped. I was already regretting abandoning my usual poise.

'Goodness me. I'd never have guessed.' Miss Ashe very carefully stubbed out her cigarette.

You fool, Amory, I said to myself, angry. You've let her win. I stared at a book on the stool between us: *The Way of All Flesh* by Samuel Butler.

'Interesting language you use,' Miss Ashe said.

'Sorry?'

'Disintegrating, lifeless, spineless, inhuman, robot. It's just a school, Amory. We're trying to teach you, to equip you for your adult life. We're not some kind of autocratic regime trying to crush the life from you.'

'I feel I'm stagnating. Trapped in this gutless, antisocial jungle—'
I stopped for the second time. I'd run out of words.

'Well, you can certainly express yourself, Amory. Which is a gift.
Very colourful. Which brings me to the point of this delightful
encounter.' She stood up and went to her desk to pick up a slip
of paper.

'I'm very pleased to tell you,' she said with a certain formality,
turning and crossing the carpet towards me, 'that you've won the
Roxburgh Essay Prize. Five guineas. I'll make the announcement
at prayers this evening. But you may tell your closest friends in
the meantime.' She handed me the slip of paper – that turned
out to be a cheque. I failed to conceal my surprise as I took
it from her. I wasn't sure why I had spontaneously decided
to enter the competition. Perhaps it was because this year's
subject had intrigued me: 'Is it really "modern" to be modern?'
In any event I had entered, written the essay, and here I was,
the winner.

Miss Ashe sat down and studied me. I stared at the cheque,
realising I could now buy the new camera I coveted, the Butcher
'Klimax'.

'I was thinking, Amory, about Oxford.'

'Oxford?'

'After Higher School Certificate, you come back for a term and
prepare for Oxford entrance. The Senior History Scholarship at
Somerville, to be precise. I think you'd stand an excellent chance,
judging by your work – and the essay you wrote.'

Miss Ashe was a graduate of Somerville College. I was aware that
I was about to become a protégée, now this suggestion had been
made.

'But I don't want to go to Oxford,' I said.

'That's a very stupid remark.'

'I don't want to go to any university in particular.'

'You want to "live", I suppose.'

I could sense Miss Ashe was now quite irritated. The tide in this confrontation was turning my way.

'Who doesn't?'

'It's entirely possible to "live" while you're at university, you know.'

'I'd rather do something else.'

'And what do you want to do, Amory?'

'I want to be a photographer.'

'An intriguing and rewarding hobby. Miss Milburn has told me about your darkroom.'

'I want to be a professional photographer.'

Miss Ashe stared at me, as if I were mocking her in some abstruse way. As if I'd said I wanted to become a professional prostitute.

'But you can't do that,' she said.

'Why not?'

'Because you're a—' She managed to stop herself saying 'woman'. 'Because it's not a reliable profession. For someone like you.'

'I can try, can't I?'

'Of course you can, Amory, my dear. But remember that going to university doesn't preclude a career as a "photographer". And you'll have a degree, something to fall back on. Give Somerville some thought, I urge you.' She stood and crossed the room again to place my file on her desk. The meeting with God was over. I made for the door but she stopped me with a raised palm.

'I almost forgot. Your father telephoned me this morning. He asked if he could take you out for tea tomorrow afternoon.'

'He did? But it's Wednesday tomorrow.'

'You can have an exeat. I'll gladly waive the usual rules. Consider it as a bonus to the Roxburgh Prize.'

I frowned. 'Why does he want to take me out to tea?'

'He said he had something to discuss with you, face to face. He didn't want to put it in a letter.' Miss Ashe looked at me, almost with kindness, I felt, sensing my puzzlement shading quickly into alarm. 'Have you any idea what he wants to talk to you about?' she asked, her hand briefly on my shoulder.

'It must be some sort of family matter, I suppose. I can't think what else.'

Miss Ashe smiled. 'He sounded very positive and cheerful. Maybe it's good news.'

2. FAMILY MATTERS

I STOOD AT THE front door of Gethsemane, my boarding house at Amberfield, waiting for my father. I was in the full humiliating walking-out uniform: the long black gaberdine raglan coat with attached cape trimmed with cherry-red piping, the straw bonnet, the sensible buckled shoes. Half Jane Austen spinster, half Crimean War veteran, we thought. The rude boys of Worthing had great scurrilous fun with us whenever we walked in phalanx through the town.

I saw the family motor car, the maroon Crossley '14', sweep through the gates at the end of the south drive, and waved, trying to ignore my apprehension, feeling my mouth dry and salty all of a sudden. It was a cool September day with an erratic breeze pushing little gaps of blue between the bulky bright clouds – grey-white, slatey – streaky, pied skies.

The car pulled up and my father stepped out. He was wearing a navy blue double-breasted suit and his green and gold regimental tie. He looked handsome and confident – I remembered what Miss Ashe had said about his mood on the telephone and relaxed, somewhat. Perhaps there wasn't going to be any awful news about a separation or divorce or a mistress or some fatal illness after all.

He put his hands on my shoulders and kissed my forehead.

'Ah, Amory, Baymory, Taymory. Don't you look strange in that outfit? What can they be thinking of? Take that ridiculous bonnet off at once.'

'I have to wait until we leave the grounds. Are you all right, Papa?'

'Never been righter.' He thought about what he had said, then smiled. 'For a writer.'

'Why've you come in the middle of the week?'

'I needed to see you, my darling, to talk about something.'

'What's wrong? Is it mother? Peggy, Xan?'

'Everything's perfect. I've some interesting news, that's all.'

I relaxed again and opened the passenger door to climb in but he suggested I'd be more comfortable in the back.

'There's a spring about to come through the front seat. You don't want to be stabbed.'

So I slid into the back while he took up his position behind the wheel, turning to smile at me.

'I thought we might head up to West Grinstead.'

'But that's miles away. I've got to be back for prayers, Miss Ashe said.'

'There's a lovely little tea house I know – very cosy. We'll have you back in time for your devotions, don't worry.'

We drove north away from Worthing and the coast, over the Downs on the road for Horsham, Papa talking about Peggy and her unending flow of achievements, her bursary, her acclaim at the Royal Academy of Music – my sister, the prodigy.

'How's Xan?' I asked, keen to hear less of Peggy.

'Oh, you know Xan. Mooning about, talking to himself. He's breeding guinea pigs – he's got dozens. Keeps him busy.'

'How's he doing at school?'

'Very badly, by all accounts. Thank goodness for you two girls. I think my son's a goner.'

'That's an awful thing to say, Papa! Xan has real . . .' I thought. 'Xan sees the world differently to the rest of us.'

My father glanced at me over his shoulder for a moment.

'We all see the world differently from each other. There's nothing unusual in that. That's the whole point – we all have unique vision.'

It made no sense to me so I looked out of the window as we motored through Findon and Washington.

'What did you want to talk to me about?' I asked, after a while.

'My novel,' he said. 'I'm halfway through. It's going terribly well.'

'What's it about?'

'The war. I'm telling the truth. The unvarnished truth. Nobody's ever written anything like it. I'm going to call it *Naked in Hell.*'

'I don't think people want to read about the war. They want to look forward.'

'You can only look forward with confidence if you know the truth about your past.'

'There's the sign for West Grinstead!'

But, rather than turn right, my father turned left, down a narrow lane between dense hawthorn and elder hedges that led towards a beech wood.

'Where are we going, Papa?'

I saw a fingerpost that said 'Hookland Castle' and then, through the trees, caught a glimpse of a silver expanse of water, a long thin lake. The lane we'd taken led us directly to its southern edge, curving round into more woodland up ahead that partially screened the castle with its battlemented tower. Maybe there was a tea room at the castle, I thought, as we arrived at the lakeside. It was man-made, I could now see, part of a vast landscaped park, the water grey and corrugated by the breeze. There was some sort of classical Greek temple-folly on a small round island. We seemed to be going faster all of a sudden and my father glanced back at me, his face contorted in a strange grimace, as if he were fighting to keep back tears.

'I love you, my darling girl. Never forget that.'

And then he turned the wheel abruptly to the right and we swerved off the metalled road with a bump, roared across a thin strip of grass and the car fell headlong into the lake. The impact with the water flung me forward against the front seat, blasting the air from my lungs. I screamed as the light darkened as we plunged beneath the water and a monstrous whooshing and gurgling noise filled the interior of the car.

Then, almost instantly, the Crossley hit the bottom, our fall stopped, and the car canted over a few degrees. Water was rising through the floor and small jets sprayed in from the window mountings. My father had fallen sideways, away from the wheel, and seemed unconscious, his head leaning against the window at an odd angle. I felt the seconds slow to minutes. I crouch-stood, now knee deep in water, screaming – Papa! Papa! – but he didn't respond. I kicked off my shoes and shrugged myself out of my heavy coat. I wrestled with the door handle but I couldn't push it open. It gave only an inch or so as the water pressure from outside was too powerful. I unwound the window and a great torrent rushed in, bitter cold, the level rising almost instantly, it seemed, to my waist. But now the door would open and I fought my way out and swam my way up and emerged, choking, gasping, in a second. The Crossley was barely submerged, its roof just two feet below the surface. I clambered on to it and stood up, sucking in huge lungfuls of air. I could see the tracks we had made on the turf before the car had leapt over the stone banking of the lake edge and dived. Our momentum had driven us twenty feet or so into the body of the lake. A few strokes would take me to safety. Man-made lake, therefore not very deep, I thought, with preposterous rationality. Then I remembered my father.

I jumped back in and ducked under the surface to see that the interior of the car was now full of water. My father was floating in the space between the front seat and the windscreen, his eyes open, bubbles rising from his parted lips as his lungs emptied. I opened the front door – it opened easily – and grabbed the waving end of his regimental tie and pulled. He slid buoyantly out and I pushed him up to the roof before crawling on to it myself, grabbing him round the neck with an armlock like a wrestler, and raising his head so he could breathe.

This was all I could do, I reasoned. He had only been underwater a few seconds – surely he wouldn't have had time to drown. So I sat there and waited, holding him up and, on cue, he coughed, water dribbled from his mouth and he opened his eyes.

'What happened?' he said, and coughed again, vomiting more water.

'We're safe,' I said. 'What were you trying to do to us?'

'Oh, God. Oh, God, no!' he shouted. He shrugged off my arm and stood up. For an awful moment I thought he was going to fling himself back into the water.

'Papa! No!' I stood up and grabbed the sopping front of his jacket. He looked at me with awful intensity, putting his hands on my shoulders.

'It wasn't meant to be like this, Amory.' His voice sounded calmer, almost reasonable. 'I didn't want to go on my own, you see. I wanted you to come with me.'

A car had stopped in the lane – the driver no doubt arrested by the sight of two people apparently walking on water, and tooted its horn. I turned and waved and shouted that we'd crashed into the lake.

'I'll call the fire brigade! Up at the castle,' the driver shouted through the open window. 'Two minutes!' He drove off at speed.

My father shifted his position on the Crossley's roof, and the car beneath us wobbled slightly. He ran his hands through his dripping hair.

'What a mess,' he said. He put his arm round my shoulders and smiled at me, a strange little smile. A mad smile, his eyes dead.

'I thought the lake was deeper,' he said. 'Thought I'd read somewhere that the lake here was exceptionally deep.'

'Lucky it wasn't.'

'You've saved my life, Amory,' he said. Then he began to cry, suddenly, almost howling like an animal. I hugged myself to him and begged him to stop – which he did, quickly, sniffing and coughing, breathing deeply.

'I'm not well, Amory,' he said quietly. 'You have to remember that. You have to forgive me.'

'I forgive you, Papa. We're safe, unharmed, that's the main thing.'

'Just wet through.' He kissed my forehead. 'Amory, Faymory, Daymory . . . Shall we head for the shore? It seems ridiculous to be waiting here, standing on the car roof.'

'You won't do anything silly. Promise?'

'I have a feeling I won't do anything silly ever again. Promise.'

We slid into the water and swam to the shore.

★

THE BARRANDALE JOURNAL 1977

I drink gin at lunch, whisky in the evening. One large gin seems to do me fine in the middle of the day but as night falls I find the whisky too alluring. I drink it diluted with a little water in a heavy-bottomed tumbler – just standard blended whisky, whatever I can find in the shops in Oban (I'd never buy on the island, in Achnalorn, too many curious folk) – but I think I'm addicted to it, all the same. Three glasses, sometimes four. I sit reading, smoking, listening to the radio or to music and let my senses tilt steadily over into mild and delicious inebriation, hearing the wind-thud, the hoarse sea-heaving outside. It sends me to an easeful sleep and, I believe, calms and soothes my disturbing dreams. The few nights I haven't had my whisky anaesthetic are too haunted by the past, too febrile to be endured. I leave my bed, throw more peat bricks on the fire, watch the flames sway and flicker and wait for dawn to arrive, the dog Flam curled up on his blanket watching me, uneasy, troubled.

The immediate consequence of our headlong drive into the waters of Hookland Castle Lake was that my father was certified insane and sent to a 'posh loony bin', as my mother termed it. I had what I now suppose was a form of nervous breakdown. I seemed unable to stop crying and would even experience a kind of fit – body-wide tremors and copious sweating – that seemed epileptic but in fact was psychotic, catalysed by sudden and spontaneous memories of those frantic seconds in the car with the water rising, the fight to open the door and, always, the image of my father's impassive floating face, the bubble-beads streaming upwards from his mouth as if the few moments of consciousness left to him were being transformed into those buoyant quicksilver pearls of air, slowing visibly as his lungs filled with water.

I missed the rest of that Trinity term at Amberfield, and Michaelmas, following, confined to bed, subject to ever-changing regimes of boiling baths and poultices on my back – as if something could be drawn out of me – broths and teas and drugs of some sort, no doubt. I returned in the spring of 1926 to prepare for my Higher School Certificate. The other girls were kind to me – I was an almost mythic figure, once the story of the car in the lake and the rescue of my father emerged. Even Miss Ashe, every time we crossed paths, would make a point of stopping and chatting and solicitously enquiring after me: 'How are you, dear Amory . . . ?' I did badly in my exams – three passes and one failure – but was never blamed. There was no further talk of Somerville College and the Senior History Scholarship.

Curiously, I took no photographs for months and my darkroom was abandoned. That summer, after my exams, I searched my father's study looking for his novel 'about the war', rummaging through the drawers in his desk and his bookcases looking for *Naked in Hell*, thinking it might give me some sort of clue as to why he'd tried to kill us both, but found nothing. My mother, when I asked her what Papa had been working on, said that he hadn't written a word for two years at least, as far as she was aware.

I was correct in one thing, however: the war did have something to do with my father's madness. The clue wasn't to be found in the novel he never wrote but, many years later, I did try to discover what had happened to him in France that had brought him home so changed. It was in the history of his regiment, the East Sussex Light Infantry, the 'Martlets', and it did help me understand a little what it might have been that had turned his mind against himself. And, thereby, me.

Events of March 1918

After the withdrawal to the position fronting the edge of the Bois de Vinaigre outside Saint-Croix the 5/1 service battalion occupied the new front line. Owing to the nature of the ground the enemy was never closer than 400 yards and sometimes on occasion over 800 yards distant. It was the widest stretch of no-man's-land that the ESLI had encountered since 1915 at Loos and posed particular problems; lack of clear information regarding the German forces' dispositions being the most significant.

The short lull in the fighting allowed the new trenches to be strengthened and there were few casualties over the following days (two dead, seven wounded). Colonel Shawfield, commanding the 5/1 battalion, ordered a raid to be sent out on the night of the 26th to determine the nature and preparedness of the forces opposite in advance of the 5th Army's counteroffensive scheduled for the 30th.

The raiding party (led by Captain B. V. Clay DSO) was composed of twenty men, including two signallers who were to run a telephone line out to the ruined farm of Trois Tables, formerly battalion HQ before the retreat. The raiding party left our trenches at 2 a.m. A diversionary artillery barrage took place at 2.30 a.m. to the left of the German line at Lembras-la-Chapelle. Captain Clay's raid met heavy resistance and at 4 a.m. only ten men had regained the ESLI lines. Captain Clay himself was missing.

Three days later, during the 5th Army counter-attack, Trois Tables farm was retaken and Captain Clay was discovered hiding in a deep cellar beneath the ruined farm building, barely clad in a few shreds of his uniform. The bodies of Corporal S. D.

Westmacott, Private W. D. Hawes and Signaller S. R. Thatcher were recovered from the same cellar. Captain Clay was starved and semi-conscious and could give no coherent account of what had happened in the three days since his raiding party had left the ESLI lines. He was sent to the base hospital at Saint-Omer where he slowly regained his strength though his memory of those three days never returned. He was awarded a bar to his DSO. The citation read that his example 'was a monument to the strength and survival instinct of the human will under the most distressing and alarming conditions of warfare'.

The Regimental History of the East Sussex Light Infantry,
Vol. III, 1914–1918

3. High Society

I WAS PLEASED WITH the way I looked. Greville said that the key thing was that I should 'blend in'. He himself was always impeccably smart. He looked me over before we went off to Lady Cremlaine's reception – to celebrate her daughter's twenty-first birthday – walking around me, frowning and nodding, as if I were about to go on parade. I was wearing a floor-length silver satin dance gown with a little maroon velvet coatee over it. Hair up to one side, a diamanté clip holding it in place. My shoes were gold calf with the highest heels I could find. Heavy make-up: kohl on my eyelids, lurid crimson lips.

'Very good, darling,' Greville said. 'You'll be fighting all the young blades off.' Greville had reduced his wide and luxuriant hussar's moustache to thin pencil lines of clipped bristle – a little chevron above his lips. It made him look quite different, I thought, more sophisticated and mysterious.

We left Greville's apartment and went round to the mews behind the building, where the studio and the darkroom was, to find Lockwood Mower, Greville's apprentice, loading the backdrops, the lights, the tripods and the leather cases containing the heavy plate cameras – the Dallmeyer Reflex and the Busch Portrait – and belting them securely on the luggage rack at the rear of the motor.

'You look a proper film star, Miss Clay,' Lockwood said. I gave a demure little stage-bow. Lockwood was a tall, burly lad, about my age, I suppose, with tar-black hair and a very dark complexion, as if he were a gypsy or very heavily suntanned, like a Mediterranean sailor or olive-picker. His even features were spoiled by a slightly undershot jaw and the fact that his eyes were set a little too far apart. He looked both pugnacious and somewhat surprised, 'like a boxer who's just received bad news' was how I'd described him to Greville, who found that very amusing.

Lockwood was softly spoken and diligent and I'd noticed, in the weeks I'd been working with Greville, how Greville relied on him more and more. Lockwood did not have to blend in. He would rig up the room set aside to be used as an impromptu studio in whatever house or venue we happened to be working in and stay there. Tonight he was in his usual outfit: a black three-piece serge suit, navy blue flannel shirt and cerise tie. He had begun to copy Greville by putting some sort of pomade in his hair and there was always a pungent odour of cheap cologne about him.

Greville and I sat in the back seat and Lockwood took the wheel.

'*Allons-y, mes braves,*' Greville said and we set off. I felt a little boil of excitement in my stomach as we pulled on to Kensington High Street and headed to Mayfair. Off on a job – as if we were going on a mission of some kind – ready to storm the redoubts of high society.

Greville took out his cigarette case and offered it to me. I selected a cigarette and he lit it, before lighting his own.

'Who's this for, tonight?' I asked, blowing smoke at the car roof. 'The *Illustrated*?'

'*Beau Monde.*'

'Oh, dear, *Tatler* will be cross with you.'

'Good,' he smiled at me. 'We've got some real scalps tonight. I might need you to ferret them out.'

'My pleasure.'

I sat back in my seat as we drove up Knightsbridge. I had always thought it highly likely that I should fall in love with my uncle – and once I had gone to work for him that likelihood became irresistible, as far as I was concerned. To sit beside him like this, smoking a cigarette, our elbows touching as we were driven to

40

Lady Cremlaine's party, seemed the very apogee of bliss. We were already partners, working together, and I knew how much he liked me, how fond he was of me – he kept on saying it – it could only be a matter of time.

I checked that everything was ready. Lockwood had set up in a ground-floor reception room off the hall. Lights rigged, backdrop in place – hanging in carefully arranged folds from its frame – assorted potted plants carefully positioned, and the two big cameras on their wooden tripods, lenses receiving a final polish from Lockwood's lint-free duster.

'All shipshape, Miss Clay. Who's up first?'

I looked at my list. 'The Honourable Miss Edith Medcalf. Is she important? Have we done her before?'

'Not by me. Maybe Mr Reade-Hill knows her.'

'I'll ask our hostess.'

I found the Hon. Miss Medcalf – a lumpy-faced and offhand youngish woman reputedly in her late twenties, but who appeared much older (her dress looked like it had been run up from a pair of discarded curtains). She was one of those people who wouldn't age: she'd look the same at twenty-five or sixty-five. She turned out to be very pleased with herself and her new engagement ring and I delivered her to Lockwood. Then I went in search of Greville. He had to be there to take the photograph even though all that was involved was a few seconds' chit-chat and a click of the shutter release. Lockwood and I had done all the work, but society ladies wanted Greville Reade-Hill to take their photographs, not his niece or, heaven forbid, his apprentice.

I swept back upstairs to the ballroom where a sizeable dance band was playing 'Ain't She Sweet' and on the wide landing outside I saw Greville chatting to a diminutive slim man and two women in billowing lace. I sidled round to catch Greville's eye; he spotted me, excused himself and came over.

'Miss Medcalf awaits,' I said.

He handed me another list of names.

'Track this lot down,' he said. 'We should be out of here within an hour.'

'Who was that little chap you were talking to? I thought I recognised him.'

'That "little chap" is the Prince of Wales. Our future king.'

I looked round but he'd gone.

'Second thoughts,' Greville said, 'I'd better chase after him. You snap Miss Medcalf. Then I'll find Lady Foster-Porter.'

'Me?'

'I think you're more than ready to open the batting,' he said, and gave me a swift kiss on the cheek.

Miss Medcalf was not at all pleased to discover that her photograph was to be taken by Miss Amory Clay and initially refused, demanding Greville's presence.

'He's with the Prince of Wales,' I said, and that both calmed and impressed her but she strode off after the photo had been taken without a word of farewell or thanks.

The Hon. Miss Edith Medcalf at Lady Cremlaine's ball, 1927.

'Charming,' Lockwood said. 'Glass of champagne, Miss Clay? I snaffled a bottle from downstairs.' Lockwood poured us both a glass, we toasted my first 'society' photograph and I then went in search of the Countess of Rackham and the Marchesa Lucrezia Barberini.

Greville was right, we had nabbed our trophies in just over an hour and Lockwood drove me and the equipment back to Falkland Court. Greville was following later, continuing his wooing of the prince – a royal photograph would put him squarely in the elite and ensure a consequent rise in fees and clients. He'd already taken Prince Aly Kahn and was after Mrs Dudley Ward and Marmaduke Furness. The Prince of Wales would unlock many doors.

Lockwood pulled up outside the mews and began to unpack the motor – he lived in a small room under the roof with a tiny dormer window – while I made sure all the film and plates were properly stored and safe and returned to the flat. Greville's apartment was on the top floor of a large mansion block just behind the High Street and from the drawing-room windows there was a good view of Kensington Gardens and the palace. Greville's bedroom, dressing room, bathroom and study took up most of the rest of the space. I was in the maid's quarters behind the kitchen – a little room with a WC and a basin in a cupboard – but otherwise I had the run of the flat. I had painted the walls of my room emerald green and had hung red sackcloth curtains at the small window. I'd had some of my photographs framed and hung on the wall ('Xan, Flying', 'Boy with Bat and Hat' and 'Running Boy'), laid a second-hand Persian rug on the floor and a patchwork quilt on the bed. There was too much colour and too much busyness for such a small room but I felt snug and secure. I was living in London – and Falkland Court was my first home away from Beckburrow – and I was earning a living (seven shillings and sixpence a day) – and I was going out to parties with all the swells at least three times a week if not four.

I slipped out of my smart dress and hung it in the cupboard, putting on my new 'Zemana' – house pyjamas – with its floral appliqués. I wandered through to the drawing room, poured myself a small brandy and soda and lit a cigarette, waiting for Greville to return.

He really did have excellent taste for a man, I thought to myself. The drawing room had lacquered red walls and a polished near-white parquet floor with silk rugs scattered here and there. A painting of a naked Negro boy dancer hung above the mantel and the occasional tables were clustered with silver- and tortoiseshell-framed photographs of his biggest social prizes. I stood at the window with my cigarette looking over the roofscape toward the palace. Life was indeed good. You're only nineteen, I said to myself, look how well you're doing, a year out of boarding school. Laura and Millicent would sell their souls to the Devil to be where I was now. And who would have thought? I was meant to be at Somerville College, Oxford, reading history. *Non, merci.* Let life come to you, my father always said, don't rush about looking for it. Then I heard Greville coming in the front door and I felt myself tense with warm anticipation.

'You still up, you naughty girl?'

'Well . . . ?' I said, queryingly, as he came in. 'You have to tell me.'

'He didn't say yes – and he didn't say no. I think he's genuinely interested – he wants to see how I've taken some of his set. Have we got those portraits of Lady Furness? That'll swing it. We'll look them out in the morning.' He undid his tie and headed for the drinks table where he poured himself a whisky.

'A perfectly acceptable evening was marred by a rather unpleasant row with Lady Foster-Porter.' He drained his glass and topped himself up. 'There's no other word for it but I'm afraid Lady Foster-Porter is a ghastly old cunt.'

I wasn't shocked. Greville swore all the time in private, arguing that we owed it to the English language to exploit the full range of forceful expressions it offered. He went on to explain why the disagreement had arisen with Lady Foster-Porter – her refusal to honour the fee he'd demanded for her son's wedding.

'Very tiresome woman,' he said. 'She actually said her chauffeur could have done a better job.'

'Sourpuss bitch!' I threw in, loyally. 'How dare she?'

'Well, I was fuming by then, you can imagine. Boiling. I said her son's wedding merited exactly the treatment I'd given it. And reminded her I'd done the Earl of Wargrave's wedding the very next day. And he'd been delighted.'

'Did she shut up?'

'She called me a snob. Fucking old trout. She—' He stopped. 'Why're you staring at me like that?'

'You look very handsome, all of a sudden, cursing away. Swearing like a trooper.'

He came over, took my hand and gave me a kiss.

'Greville and Amory versus the world,' he said.

'Easy winners.'

'Lockwood sort everything out?'

'Yes, I'll give him a hand developing and printing in the morning – send everything off to the magazine.'

'Sit down, darling. There's something I have to discuss with you.'

He led me over to a chair in front of the fireplace and sat me down then knelt in front of me and took both my hands. This is it, I thought – it's going to happen, now.

'Your father,' he said. 'You have to go and see him.'

I hadn't seen my father since that day at Hookland Castle Lake when he was taken away by the police. I said to Greville – keeping my voice steady – that I couldn't bear to be in a room with my father, that it made me ill, unstable.

'I can't, Greville. He tried to kill me.'

'He wasn't well – he was deranged. He's much better now and he asks for you every time he wakes up, it seems, so your mother tells me. The doctors say it might help if you went down and saw

45

him. Each week, each month that you don't see him, you know, sort of agitates him more.'

I closed my eyes. Why was I being so foolish?

'I'll come with you,' Greville said. 'There's nothing to be frightened of. He's making good progress. And it might help you, as well. Catharsis and all that.'

He was right. But some tears flowed and I gave a little sob. As I hoped, Greville took me in his arms and rocked me gently to and fro. I breathed in, content in the moment, my head filled with the scent of custard and jasmine.

4. Cloudsley Hall

CLOUDSLEY HALL, near Rochester in Kent, was the asylum where my father had been taken after the Hookland Castle Lake incident. It was an ugly early neo-Gothic Victorian manor house built on the site of a grand eighteenth-century farm and consequently flattered by its ancient landscaped park dating back to that era. Cloudsley Hall had battlements, corner towers and an unlikely belvedere and there were two lodges at the gate leading to a gently winding drive through sheep-cropped, hillocked and wooded meadows to the hall itself. One might have been visiting a hotel or a private school.

Greville drove me there in his Alvis. My mother, Peggy and Xan had decided not to join me as they had seen Papa on numerous occasions and it was felt it would be more effective if I went to meet him alone. We were taken to the office of the medical director, a Dr Fabien Lustenburger, who was Swiss, Greville told me, an expert on the latest treatments for 'mania'.

Dr Lustenburger was a huge, portly young man, well over six feet, already quite bald but with a wide dense moustache that acted as a counterbalance to his almost indecently burnished pate. He was welcoming and warm, very pleased that I had come, and eagerly took me upstairs to my father's ward. Greville said he would wait in the library.

'Your father will seem completely well to you,' Dr Lustenburger said as we reached the landing of the first floor. 'I warn you. You will be surprised. You will say, why is he in this institution?' He had a barely noticeable accent. 'Maybe he will be a bit sleepy. When we rouse the patients they find the state of "waking" a little strange and hard to cope with. They spend so much time sleeping, you see.'

He led me through a ward of a dozen beds, most of them occupied by sleepers, in fact, men and boys, as far as I could tell from a quick glance to either side. The atmosphere was suitably hushed. Dr Lustenburger showed me in to a glassed-in balcony area that looked over the wide rear lawn of Cloudsley Hall – and the thin oblong of its ornamental lake, I was rather alarmed to see. The place was full of lush potted plants – palms and aspidistras – and overstuffed armchairs with leg rests. My father was sitting on one of them, wearing pyjamas and a quilted scarlet dressing gown. He looked very well, fresh-faced, his hair longer than usual, untrimmed, almost boyish, it seemed to me. He kissed and hugged me enthusiastically – entirely naturally, also, as if nothing had happened between us.

'Amory, Baymory, Taymory! Look at you, sweetheart. Isn't she the height of modern fashion, Dr Lustenburger?'

Dr Lustenburger, smiling, backed away without comment.

I launched into a somewhat hysterical prattle about my life in London, working with Greville, the parties I went to and the people I'd met. I felt very uneasy being alone with him. It seemed at once wholly normal and quaveringly tense. My father appeared to be listening, a vague smile on his face, and from time to time nodded and said, 'Wonderful,' and 'What larks, Amory,' and 'Goodness me.' Then he lay back in his armchair and closed his eyes.

I sat there for a few seconds watching him.

'What happened, Papa?'

He woke up at once and swung his legs off the chair.

'I can't remember,' he said abruptly. 'It's all gone, that's the problem. The medicines they give you in here, you know . . .' He took my hand and studied it. 'I know something awful happened – and I can remember you and me standing on the top of a car in a lake of some sort . . .' He gestured out at the vista through the glass, indicating Cloudsley Hall's lake. 'Bigger than that. And then I remember police, a police station, then doctors coming and then ... here.' He paused, then leant forward and lowered his voice. 'You know, when I first came here and I woke up the next morning I said, "My, I slept well last night!" And the nurse said, "You've been asleep for two weeks, Mr Clay."' He frowned. 'They put you to sleep here, Amory, for days and days at a time. Weeks. I've no idea how long I've slept. Months. I'm hardly ever awake, it seems to me.'

'Well, as long as it's making you better.'

'I did something bad to you, didn't I?'

'It doesn't matter now, Papa. Everything's fine. You'll be all right.'

'All the righter, for a writer. Send me a photo, sweetness. That'll make me well – I'll be able to look at you every day.' He fell back in his armchair again and closed his eyes.

There was a polite cough behind me and I turned. Dr Lustenburger had arrived silently to take me away. My father was fast asleep so I kissed his forehead and followed Dr Lustenburger down to his office where he explained something of his methods to me. They practised 'somnitherapy' at Cloudsley Hall. Dr Lustenburger was convinced that all aberrant and antisocial manias came from unhappy memories. Deep sleep, profound sleep lasting many days, was, he believed, the way to suppress the power of these memories. 'And in your father's case,' he went on, 'all these memories originate in the Great War.' He smiled confidently. 'However, slowly but surely, we are erasing them.'

Greville drove me to a pub just off the London Road, the Grenadier, near Gravesend, where we each had a whisky and soda. I expressed some optimism about the visit.

'Did Dr Lustenburger mention anything about the drugs, et cetera?' Greville asked.

'Papa did say medicines – but he wasn't specific.'

'It's a drug that makes them sleep so long. Knocks them out for days.'

'Sounds wonderful!'

Greville gave a knowing smile. 'It's called "SomniBrom" – a mixture of a barbiturate and a bromide.'

'Maybe not so wonderful, then. How do you know about all this?'

'Darling – "deep sleep therapy". DST. It's *so* fashionable. Anxiety removed by narcosis.' He made a face. 'With the help of a few electric shocks while you're snoozing.'

'My God! No!'

'My God, yes! Are you surprised he can't remember anything, anything at all? Electrodes attached to the head and all that. But you don't feel a thing. Quite benign, I suppose.'

'Poor Papa . . .' I felt suddenly sad, thinking of my father. 'It was the war, wasn't it?' I said vaguely. 'The war did this to him.'

Greville agreed with my platitude and we talked on, ordering another round of whiskies and soda. As he brought our drinks over the thought came to me that, as we sat there in a booth in the corner of the saloon bar of the Grenadier, somebody coming in and glancing casually over at us chatting away so earnestly might have thought that we were a couple, out courting.

★

THE BARRANDALE JOURNAL 1977

I walked over to Inverbarr – a good two-mile hike – for lunch with Calder and Greer McLennan, my best friends on the island. It was a fresh, breezy day, the wind tugging at my jacket and hat, the sun unusually brilliant, almost alpine in its clarity, when it appeared between the ranks of clouds. As well as going for lunch I was returning a book Calder had lent me called *The Last Year: April 1944–April 1945* by Dennis Fullerton. It was an account of the war in Europe during its tumultuous endgame and I was trying to chart my own progress through those twelve months and had been somewhat enlightened. At least I now had the big picture to go with my small precise one – where my meandering journeys had fitted into the great march of military history.

I walked up to the hogback ridge that connected Barrandale's two biggish hills, Beinn Morr and Cnoc Torran, that formed a crude spine to the island and, once on the ridge, could see Inverbarr below me, set back on the edge of its small cove with a view of the southern tip of Mull and the hammered silver plate of the Atlantic beyond.

Greer welcomed me at the back door, gin and tonic in one hand, cigarette in the other. She was a handsome tall woman whose snowy white hair was cut in a severe bob with a razored fringe that brushed her eyebrows. She was ten years younger than me but her white hair sometimes made her look older, I thought. She and Calder were retired academics from Edinburgh University. Calder had been a professor of economics while Greer was a cosmologist, 'of no eminence at all', she would add. Calder – small, wiry, bearded – was an overactive adult and a hiking, hill-walking obsessive. Greer was more sedate and was writing a book on molluscs, so she claimed. An odd job for a cosmologist, I had remarked when she told me. She had smiled and said simply that she felt the urge to focus on something closer to home.

Calder had pretensions as a cook and we ate a pearl barley broth and a peppery venison stew. We had coffee and cigarettes in the library. I spotted a large atlas on a low shelf and asked if I could borrow it. The atlas was too cumbersome to carry home on foot – as big as a paving stone – so Greer offered to drive me back round the island to the cottage. She had things to pick up in Achnalorn, she said.

In the village we parked outside the small supermarket and I took the chance to buy a newspaper, the *Glasgow Herald*, and two packs of cigarettes. Greer had done the same and we sat in the car park and smoked, flicking through our newspapers, watching the fishing boats come and go in the small harbour.

I pointed to a story on the front page of the *Herald*. A new galaxy had been found at some far corner of the known universe.

'Make your heart beat faster?' I asked.

'Not really my field,' Greer said. 'I was concentrating on what happened before the Big Bang. When there was nothing.'

'Stop right now,' I said with a laugh. 'I can't understand these concepts: "Nothing", "Infinity", "Timelessness". My brain won't go there.'

'That's why I retired early,' Greer said, with a rueful smile. 'I realised that what I was doing was meaningless to the entire human race apart from about six people in distant universities.'

'I need boundaries,' I said. 'I can't get to grips with "nothing". That once upon a time there was nothing and time didn't exist and that "nothing" was infinite . . .' I smiled. 'Or maybe I'm just stupid.'

'That's why I'm studying small molluscs in tiny rock pools,' Greer said, tossing her cigarette end out of the window and exhaling. 'We're just a certain kind of ape on a small planet circling an insignificant star. Why should I be fretting about what might or might not have happened thirteen billion years ago?'

'A certain kind of ape. I like that.'

'So I decided to chuck it in. It just seemed pointless, all of a sudden.'

'Good for you,' I said, then added, with more feeling than I meant, 'It's not as if the here and now isn't problematic enough.'

'Exactly,' she said, starting the car and pulling away.

'Talking of which. How's Alisdair?' Alisdair was their son, a diplomat, recently messily divorced. Two very young children involved and a bitter ex-wife.

'He's being posted to Vietnam,' she said dryly. 'That should keep him out of trouble.'

'Vietnam,' I said, not thinking. 'Well, it got *me* in serious trouble.'

Greer looked at me sharply.

'My, you're full of surprises, Amory,' she said. 'You dark horse. When were you in Vietnam, for Christ's sake?'

'What? Me? . . . Oh, years ago. When the war was in full swing.'

We had arrived at the cottage. Greer stopped the car and turned to me, keen to talk further, I could sense. I didn't want to linger and opened the door.

'Thanks so much for lunch.'

'Don't forget your atlas,' Greer said.

I opened the rear door and hefted it out.

'I'll tell you all about Vietnam one day,' I said.

'Promises, promises,' she said.

That night I drank too much whisky to stop myself thinking about the wars I'd known. In bed I felt ideally drowsy and when I closed my eyes the room tilted slightly, agreeably. Whisky – my deep sleep therapy.

★

Greville opened the bottle of champagne, poured us each a glass and we toasted each other.

'Got to be a record,' he said. 'Three balls in one evening. What's happening to London? It's unprecedented.'

I lit a cigarette, watching him throw off his jacket and fall into an armchair. I knew that tonight had to be the night.

'Couldn't have done it without you, darling. Thanks a million,' he said.

'And Lockwood.'

'Locky's a Trojan. But I think we might need another assistant if this goes on.'

I sat down opposite him.

'But it can't go on like this, surely. It's some sort of a mad exception. Everyone's out of control.'

'And it's not even the season ...' Greville thought. 'I know. Divide and rule. What if we split up? Do you think you could do one on your own? You take Lockwood. I'll find someone new.' He stood up and paced around the drawing room, thinking. 'We could do four events a night. Two each.'

'It sounds logical,' I said. 'But people only pay attention to me because they know I'm with you. They don't want to be photographed by Amory Clay. They won't *pay* to be photographed by Amory Clay, more to the point.'

'But they will.' He wandered back across the room towards me. 'Wait till they see your work.' He picked up my right hand and kissed it. 'My right-hand girl. I'm exhausted. Sweet dreams.'

In my little bedroom I slipped out of my gown and underclothes and put on a filmy silk shift that came to my knees. I touched a little perfume behind my ears and unpinned my hair. I felt very calm, I was surprised to note – this was no inebriated, wild decision. Matters had to come to a head. Then I paused and thought, as coldly as I could, about what I was about to do and the risks attached. It could all go horribly wrong, of course, but, I told myself, you could have died a few months ago, trapped in a car beneath the waters of Hookland Castle Lake. Don't let your life go by you, thinking of what might have been. Live for yourself, for what you truly want.

Live for yourself, I repeated as I padded through the dark flat towards Greville's bedroom. There was no light shining under the door. I knocked.

'Greville? Can I have a word?' I pushed the door open as he switched on his bedside light. His hair was tousled, a thick lock falling over his forehead. I'd never seen him so uncombed.

'Amory? What's happening? Is there anything wrong?'

I slid into bed beside him.

'I'm cold,' I said and, putting my arms around him, tried to kiss his lips.

Very gently but firmly he pushed me off.

'What're you doing? Are you out of your mind?'

'I've fallen in love with you.'

'Don't be fucking stupid, I'm your uncle!'

'So what? It doesn't matter.'

He sat up and ran his fingers through his hair, smoothing it back. He climbed out of bed and picked up his dressing gown. He was wearing taupe pyjamas with a darker piping, I saw. He threw the dressing gown at me.

'You're practically naked, you silly girl. Put that on. Why're you trying to seduce me? Have you had too much to drink?'

'Because I'm tired of being a "girl"!' My voice was shriller than I meant it to be. 'Tired of being a "silly" girl, even worse! And I love you. And I don't want anyone else to love me, or to . . .' I couldn't think of the right word. 'To possess me.'

He laughed and then walked to his dresser, found a cigarette and lit it.

'You have got a hell of a lot to learn, my dear.'

'I'm nineteen years old. I could have died. My father tried to kill me. I can't just wait for—'

He put up his hand to silence me and shook his head incredulously. I could hear him making little popping noises with his lips.

'The thing is, I'm not interested in girls, Amory. Can't you tell?'

'Tell what?'

'I'm interested in men. And boys . . . I'm what the smart set would call a "queen".'

I looked at him.

'Jesus. My God . . . I didn't . . . I don't know what to say.'

'Don't be embarrassed, darling. In fact I'm rather flattered you should think I'm appropriate material. The disguise is working very well.'

I yanked on his dressing gown, suddenly absurdly conscious of my tiny skimpy slip, of the light shining on my bare arms and shoulders. My breasts seemed, all of a sudden, preposterously white and large. I hugged the gown to me, feeling a chill shudder up my back. Cold shame, not hot shame, even worse. I wasn't going to cry but I'd never felt so stupid. Like a vast block of cast iron, tons of insensate metal.

He sat down beside me and took both my hands in his, just as he'd done when he'd urged me to go and see my father. In another world.

'Do you really want to stop being a virgin?'

'That was the plan. Now I'm not so sure. As you say I've got a lot to learn. Maybe I'll become a nun instead.'

Greville scrutinised me.

'You're incredibly impetuous, Amory, you know. Very headstrong.'

'Very stupid.'

'Yes, that's a way of putting it. It could get you into trouble in life.'

'It already has.' I retightened the belt on the dressing gown, feeling tears salty in my eyes. I wasn't going to cry. 'It's my problem. My curse.'

'Which means I don't think you'd be a very good nun, I'm afraid.'

I had to smile. 'Probably not.'

He looked at me searchingly, but in a kindly way.

'You know, if I thought I could, I'd help you out. You're a very pretty girl. But it would be awful – for us both. Too ghastly and embarrassing. Might ruin you for life. I'm just not made that way, darling. The machinery wouldn't work, if you know what I mean.'

'I'd better go. I think I'm going to die of shame. I'm so sorry, Greville, I never—'

'Why don't you seduce young Lockwood?'

'What? Lockwood?'

'He's obsessed with you. Shines out of his eyes. He adores you. Can't you tell?'

'I'm afraid I've only been thinking of you.'

'You'd be much better off losing your virginity with strapping young Lockwood than an inefficient pansy like me.'

We only see what we want to see and that's how mistakes are made. Greville suddenly came into focus for me, like a lens being turned.

At breakfast the next morning I crept into the kitchen but he was already there, spruce in his morning suit, ready for the wedding we were to photograph at the Brompton Oratory. He looked like an illustration from *Tailor & Cutter*.

'You're not going to jump on me, Amory, are you?'

'Very funny.'

But of course it was exactly the right thing to say. He made light of it. We could joke about it and therefore it was possible for me to be with him again, to function, at ease, even though everything was different. In a strange way I felt closer to him, now I knew about him. Now we had our secret.

'Any luck with Lockwood?' he said to me one day.

'Greville! Please!'

'He's a nice lad. Strong but gentle.'

'You make him sound like a shire horse.'

'You know what they say about shire horses don't you, darling?'

'No, I don't. And I don't want to know.'

But because Greville kept talking about him, kept introducing Lockwood and his charms into our conversation, I became aware of Lockwood in a way I hadn't before. I realised he was in fact always looking at me, covertly; I began to notice how he would take every opportunity to stand as close to me as propriety demanded. I saw that Greville was right: Lockwood *was* obsessed with me.

We were closing up the darkroom one evening, a few weeks after my fiasco with Greville. The red light was on and we moved about our business limned by its unreal thick luminosity. I was hanging up strips of developed negatives and I could feel Lockwood's eyes on me, like an invisible beam through the redness, playing on me. I thought – why not? It has to happen sometime – and the sooner the better. And having allowed the thought to enter my head I felt the concurrent physical consequences: that bowel-stir, that bone-weakness of pleasant anticipation.

Lockwood reached to turn on the main light but I caught his wrist before he could. We stood there looking at each other.

'What is it, Miss Clay?' His voice was dry, hushed.

'Would you like to kiss me, Lockwood?'

BOOK TWO: 1927–1932

1. LIFE IS SWEET

I RAISED MY CAMERA – my little Ensignette – and took a photograph of Lockwood Mower lying on the bed, sleeping, naked. He was hot, he'd thrown the sheet and blankets off and his pale long flaccid penis, lying over his upper thigh, was both pliant and semi-engorged. The pinched bud of his thick foreskin made his penis look tuberous, vegetal, somehow – not like his sex, his member, at all. It was a great photograph – so I say, my 'Sleeping Male Nude' – and I kept a print of it for years, secretly, in a seldom-consulted English–Portuguese dictionary, where I could easily look at it and think back, remembering him and those many months of our affair. And then I lost it, annoyingly, when I moved house after the war.

I put my camera away in my bag, slipped on my coat and left quickly without waking him. I had a job that afternoon and had to make my way to West Sussex for a garden fete hosted by Miss Veronica Presser – daughter of Lord Presser the iron-ore millionaire – at the village of North Boxhurst, which the Presser family owned, every brick and hanging tile, part of their vast Boxhurst estate which lay between Chichester and Bognor Regis.

I took the Tube from Kensington High Street to Walham Green, trying to concentrate on the job ahead and stop thinking about the last few hours I'd spent with Lockwood. Greville had passed on the Presser commission to me – it was for *Beau Monde* – and I knew it could prove to be a significant moment in my erratic career as a professional photographer. 'Do this Presser job well,'

Greville had said, 'and all my *Beau Monde* work will come your way. Guaranteed.'

I now lived in a shabby one-bedroom flat in a converted house on Eel Brook Common. No bathroom, just a small kitchen and a lavatory off the long, thin bed-sitting room. I still used the Falkland Court mews as my darkroom; Greville had given me my own set of keys, an arrangement that suited me as I was able to see Lockwood as often and as discreetly as I wanted. Which was quite often, so it turned out.

I packed up my two cameras in my leather grip (the 'Excelda' quarter-plate and the Goerz), stuffed a dozen business cards in my handbag, hoping for further commissions, and headed for Victoria station. Change at Hayward's Heath for Amberley and then a taxi to North Boxhurst. It was going to be a long day.

Miss Amory Clay

Professional photography

Tel: DUK 366

★

THE BARRANDALE JOURNAL 1977

I suppose we all – men and women – remember our first lover, like it or not; good, bad or indifferent. However, I've a feeling that women remember more, remember better. I can still bring to mind that first night I spent with Lockwood, after we'd kissed in the darkroom, with near-absolute recall. Lockwood had been both kind and controlling. Once the future course of the encounter was clear – that this was to be no simple kiss – and as soon as we were naked in his narrow, pungent bed upstairs, all lights switched off, he asked me if this was my 'first time around the houses'. Yes, I said. Then he asked me if I used sanitary towels or 'them tampon things'. Sanitary towels, I said. But why? Then I felt his finger inside me, pressing, and a sudden sharp pain that made me yelp. 'That's that sorted,' he said. He spread my legs and positioned himself. 'Wait a second,' he said, and left the bed. I heard him go into the little kitchen at the top of the stairs, then he returned and slid back in beside me. I felt him rubbing something on me. And then he entered me with a small wheeze and grunt of effort but I didn't feel much. 'I won't go mad, Miss Clay,' he whispered in my ear as he began to push rhythmically at me, 'seeing as it's the first time.' Right, I said, clenching my fists on his back. 'I can't rightly believe this is happening, Miss Clay. Happening to me, Lockwood Mower. Like I'm dreaming a dream.' He was as good as his word. He exhaled noisily and rolled off me after about five seconds and we lay in each other's arms.

I was expecting to feel more pain – all the speculative talk at Amberfield had been of blood-boltered sheets and agony. Carefully I reached down and touched myself – some sort of clotted waxy substance was there. Lockwood's emission? 'What's this, Lockwood?' I said, holding up my gleaming coated fingers. 'Just lubrication,' he said. 'It's an old trick. I remembered I had some soft lard in the kitchen. That's why you never felt a thing.' Have you done this before, I asked? 'Well, you know, once or twice,' he said. I could sense his grin widening. He kissed my cheek, gently, and whispered, 'My chum slid in like a greased piston, Miss Clay. Feel it. Go on.' He took my hand and placed it on his 'chum'. Now it was my turn to smile to myself in the darkness, feeling not sensual pleasure – that had never really arisen – but relief, enormous happy relief. It was over; it was done; everything had changed, now. 'You can call me Amory,' I said, kissing him back. The bed smelled rank and I felt my back itching. Lockwood had a reek of sweat and his cheap pomade about him. I breathed in, filling my lungs, telling myself to remember everything. I've never forgotten – and I've never cooked with lard since.

★

Miss Veronica Presser was entirely happy to be guided by me. She was a big enthusiastic girl with a gummy smile. I met her by the lawn tennis courts at Boxhurst Park where there was a one-game, knockout charity tennis tournament going on. I said that something casual and sporty would look so much more interesting than the usual bland portrait shots we'd all seen a thousand times before.

'Absolutely,' she said. 'Whatever you say.' For someone already reputedly worth several million pounds she was very easy-going.

'Make it as natural as possible,' I said, focussing the Goerz. 'Be yourself. Pick up another racquet. Yes, that's it! Perfect.' Click. I had her.

'What fun!' she said and gave a loud neighing laugh.

The next day, in the darkroom of the Falkland Court mews, I printed my portrait of Veronica with her two tennis racquets. I liked it a lot. It was high time, I thought to myself, that we moved away from the standard images of these society girls – the beauties and the fiancées, the debs and the heiresses. Let's make my first *Beau Monde* commission a photograph to remember, not just so much forgettable social wallpaper. However, I decided to lie when I sent it in to *Beau Monde*, such was my enthusiasm: I told them it was Miss Presser's personal choice, her favourite – and it was duly published, the following week, as a full-page lead to the society gallery.

'Good Lord,' Greville said, when he saw the magazine. 'Are you sure this was her choice? She looks like she's got wheels. Not really *Beau Monde* at all.'

Miss Veronica Presser at the North Boxhurst fete,
© *Beau Monde Publications Ltd, 1928.*

'She did say "What fun!" when I took the picture.'

'And you chose to interpret "What fun!" as "That's my favourite."'

'It seemed implicit. You know: the message she was trying to convey.'

'You can be very impetuous, Amory. I warned you.'

'True. Still—'

'Still, it's the best photograph I've seen in *Beau Monde* for a year. Very natural-looking. Better than mine.'

'Thank you, Greville. I've learned everything from you. Everything.'

We were in the drawing room of his flat. The evening sun was blazing obliquely in and a misty amber light seemed to fuzz and blur the windows overlooking the gardens, casting everything in the room in a golden fantastical hue.

'Still seeing young Lockwood?' Greville asked.

'From time to time.'

'He seems much – I don't know – neater, cleaner. Altogether more presentable.'

I had made Lockwood bathe – I supervised the first bath, I scrubbed him down – bought him some decent brilliantine (Del Rosa's 'English Musk') and several changes of shirts and, Greville was not to know this, thrown out his grey greasy sheets and provided him with freshly laundered ones that I brought with me when I stayed and took away to re-launder when I left.

'I never liked that blue flannel shirt of his,' I said. 'I think he'd wear it a week at a time.'

Greville laughed – his rare baritone boom that erupted when he found something genuinely funny.

'Amory Clay, what have I done to you?'

Beau Monde sacked me a week later, the result of a vehement litigious complaint from Lord Presser himself. His daughter was a laughing stock, he claimed, she was mortified, humiliated. The entire print run of the June 1928 issue was recalled and pulped at the cost of several hundred pounds. I was sacrificed instantly, in the hope Lord Presser would be mollified. Furthermore the editor of *Beau Monde*, one Augustin Brownlee, made it clear that they would spread the word amongst *Beau Monde*'s competitors. My perfidy would be made plain, my abject unprofessionalism everywhere advertised. I would never work for a society magazine again.

'I think it's a good photo, like a real person, not some stuffed doll,' Lockwood said, loyal to the end. I had sought solace with him for a night above the darkroom. He was sitting on the narrow bed, naked, watching me dress.

'I'm unemployable,' I said. 'All because some stupid fucking heiress lost her sense of humour.' I was picking up Greville's bad habits.

'Surely Mr Reade-Hill can—'

'He got me the *Beau Monde* job. I was his special recommendation. They're not exactly wildly happy with him, either.'

I buttoned on my brassiere and, as I reached for my slip, I felt Lockwood come up behind me, take me in his arms, his hands cupping my breasts, squeezing.

'I love your bobbies, Amory, so round and—'

'They're my *breasts*, Lockwood! Don't use these expressions. You know I don't like them.' He favoured strange slang words for body parts and types of lovemaking: bobbies, chum, the path, butter-churning, Jack and the beanstalk ... He was from St Albans and I wondered if it was some arcane Hertfordshire patois that he used.

He returned to the bed, unperturbed. Very little ruffled the even, placid surface of his nature. He loved me with unusual intensity, that I did know.

'I'm out of a job, Lockwood. I'm jobless.'

'You'll get a job. Nothing's going to stop you, Amory. Nothing.'

My mother looked at me blankly, unpityingly. From the barn I could hear Peggy playing endless scales on her piano. It was beginning to give me a headache.

'Why don't you meet a nice young man?' my mother said. 'Then you wouldn't need to be a photographer. Meet a lawyer or a soldier or a – I don't know – even a journalist. Or ...' she thought, 'or a vicar. An alderman, a brewer—'

'No thank you, Mother. No more professions.'

I wandered out into the garden, thinking. Greville had said I could always come back to work as his assistant, but, when I had left to set up on my own, he had hired a replacement, a young

Frenchman called Bruno Desjardins (whom I think Greville rather lusted after) and there really wouldn't have been much for me to do. Apart from *Beau Monde* all my work was for other society magazines – the *Young Woman's Companion*, *Modern Messenger*, the *London Gazette*, and so on – and all those doors would be closed to me now. There were newspapers – but I could hardly present myself as a photo-journalist. And there was portrait work – but you needed a studio for that and clients didn't exactly rush to your door if you had no reputation at all.

I saw three guinea pigs scurry under a laurel bush. Yes, I could always take photos of people's pets. I felt sick: I would never stoop so low. And anyway, there were no good photographs of animals. Photography wasn't about taking pictures of animals, it was about—

'Oh. It's you.'

'Hello, Xan.'

Xan came round the edge of the shrubbery with a guinea pig in each hand. He was tall for his age, twelve, and had a distinctly watchful air about him as if he didn't trust you, or was expecting you to make some kind of violent movement towards him. He looked grubby, needing a long soak in a bath.

'What're you doing?' I asked.

'Freeing some guinea pigs. I've got too many.'

'How many?'

'Over a hundred. But they don't seem to want to leave the garden.' He walked to the boundary hedge and set down his two newly liberated rodents. They sat there, noses twitching. Then he kicked earth at them and they ran into hiding.

'Why don't you sell them to a pet shop?' I said. 'Make some money.'

'That would be immoral.'

'Oh. Right.'

He looked at me with hostility.

'Why are you here?' he said.

'Aren't I allowed to come and see my family?'

'I suppose so.'

'How very gracious of you, Marjorie.'

'Don't call me Marjorie.'

He wandered off back to the garden shed.

I crossed the lawn to the barn. Peggy had stopped playing scales and the door was ajar. When the door was shut no one was allowed to disturb her. I knocked and went in. Peggy was sitting at the piano doing exercises with her hands, making fists and shooting her fingers out.

'Hello, Peggoty.'

She turned and smiled – at least one member of my family was pleased to see me. We kissed and I noticed how pretty she was becoming – dark-haired and big-eyed with a perfectly straight thin nose. My father's nose, the Clay nose, not the Reade-Hill nose that I had. She fitted a cut-down ruler between her thumb and little finger of her right hand, stretching them apart, painfully.

'What're you doing? That looks like torture.'

'My hands are too small. I haven't a full-octave spread. Madame Duplessis says I'll never make a successful concert pianist if I can't cover an octave.'

'You're only fourteen, darling. Still growing.'

'I can't wait for nature to take her course.' She smiled. 'Time waits for no woman.' She was wearing a forest-green jumper, tight against her small pointed breasts, and fawn slacks. She looked more like eighteen than fourteen.

'Have you got a cigarette?' she asked, and removed the ruler with a wince. 'Ouch.'

She shut the door and we both lit a cigarette and, clearing away piles of scores, sat down on the sofa at the end of the room.

'Does Mother know you smoke?'

'God, no. Xan steals her cigarettes for me. Madame Duplessis smokes so we're safe in here.' She looked shrewdly at me. 'Everything all right, Ames?'

'No.' I told her about the *Beau Monde* fiasco.

'Stay here for a few days. Do. Have a holiday.'

'I've got to earn some money.'

'Mother says we're poor, now. Papa's hospital is costing a fortune. We may have to sell Beckburrow, she says.'

I tried to take in these two pieces of news. Poor. Selling.

'My God, how awful . . . How is Papa?'

'He seems fine, pretty much. When he's awake, that is.'

'What about my legacy from Aunt Audrey? Can't we use it for Papa?'

'It was only for your education, Mother says.'

'I should have gone to Oxford. I knew it.'

Peggy pursed her lips, looking thoughtful. 'Once I start doing concerts and recitals we'll be fine. I can begin playing professionally next year, Peregrine says.'

'Who's Peregrine?'

'Peregrine Moxon, the composer.'

'Oh, yes.' I'd heard of Moxon. 'Does he really let you call him Peregrine?'

'He insists on it.'

'How do you know him?'

'He's a visiting professor at the Royal Academy. I've rather become his protégée . . .' She stood, went to the stove, lifted the lid and dropped in her cigarette butt. Fourteen going on twenty-four, I decided.

'Staying for tea?'

'Yes,' I said. 'Then I'd better get back to London. Try and resuscitate the corpse that is my career.'

We walked across the lawn to the house, arm in arm. I felt a kind of panic sluice through me, knowing that Beckburrow might have to be sold, feeling – illogically – that it was somehow my fault, that I was in some way enmeshed and inculpated in my father's illness and the price we would all have to pay.

'We'll be all right, won't we, Pegs?'

70

'Oh, yes. We just have to get through this year. Before I start earning.'

Ridiculous, I thought as we entered the house, to put your trust in your fourteen-year-old sister, musical prodigy or not. I had to do something.

Greville took me out to dinner at Antonio's, an Italian restaurant on the Brompton Road that we both liked. We ordered *vitello al limone* and a bottle of Valpolicella.

'I threw my weight around,' Greville reported. 'The *Illustrated* and the *Modern Messenger* will give you work, but it has to be strictly anonymous.'

'That's hardly going to help my reputation.'

'At least it's money. Bruno's going back to Paris for a week. You could work for me while he's away.'

'Dribs and drabs,' I said. 'My rent's going up. And we may have to sell Beckburrow.'

'You can always move in with me, my dear, as long as you don't try to seduce me again.'

'Ha-ha. Well, thank you. I may have to. But I'm going backwards, don't you see? How am I meant to make my way like this? How can I even make the most modest living? It's impossible.'

Greville topped up our glasses to the brim, nodding to himself, as he thought.

'What you need to do is change the way the world sees you.'

'Oh, yes. Of course,' I said with perhaps too heavy sarcasm. 'Easy.'

He was still thinking and hadn't noticed. 'You need to become . . . notorious. Disgraceful – even better.'

'Take more photos like Veronica Presser.'

'No, no. Something far more outrageous. You need a scandal.'

'A scandal? How do I create a scandal?'

He smiled. He was pleased with his idea, I could tell.

'If I were you, darling, I'd go to Berlin.'

★

THE BARRANDALE JOURNAL 1977

I stood and looked at the boxes that I'd lugged down from the attic. Five cardboard cartons filled with other boxes and old manila envelopes, dozens and dozens of them. Prints, negatives, Kodachrome slides – the photographic record of my life, all that I'd managed to hold on to. Some of the boxes were damp and mildewed, others wore layers of ancient dust. Was it worth it, I asked myself? Was it worth trying to sort this lot out in the time I had left, however long that might be? I picked a few boxes up at random and saw one that had a scribbled address on the front: 32b Jäger-Strasse, Berlin 2. I lifted the lid. It was empty.

2. Berlin

'IT SEEMS EXTREMELY RESPECTABLE,' I remarked to Rainer. 'Very sophisticated.'

Rainer looked at his watch.

'We have to wait until midnight.' He smiled, showing his small, perfectly white teeth. 'Then the fun is starting.'

We were sitting in a booth at the rear of the Iguana-Club somewhere in North Berlin. We had crossed Oranienburger-Strasse and I had seen a sign for the Stettiner station but otherwise I had yet to get my proper bearings in this city, the third largest in the world, so Berliners kept reminding me. I sipped at my drink and waited for midnight to arrive. In the meantime there was a small jazz band on a semicircular stage playing 'It Happened in Monterey'. South of the border, I thought, that's where I want to be, somewhere louche and very, very indiscreet. A few couples danced but without real enthusiasm, it seemed to me, as if the clientele were waiting for some signal to be given so they could really begin to enjoy themselves. Almost all the men were in evening dress with white ties.

Rainer offered me a cigarette and lit it for me. Rainer Nagel was his full name and he was an old friend of Greville. I wondered how they had come to know each other – and how well – but Rainer gave nothing away. He was a small stocky man, with a square face – handsome in a fit, muscular way – but he had an agitated fussy manner as if he were constantly trying to keep his

73

energy levels under control, always patting his pockets, tapping ash off his cigarette, checking the knot of his tie. I had asked him what he did and he said, 'Oh, a bit of this, a bit of that. A bit of buying, a bit of selling.' He spoke excellent English and was almost over-polite.

Now he snapped his fingers to attract a waiter's attention and, when the man came over, he whispered in his ear, for a good minute, it seemed. I was wearing a black crêpe dress with a velvet collar and a fur stole, also black. I had pinned up my hair under a felt cloche hat with a small ultramarine feather, the aim being to look both smart and unobtrusive. When Rainer had collected me at my hotel – the Silesia Hospiz, on Prenzel-Strasse, near Alexanderplatz – he had said, 'You look very à la mode, Amory,' with a kind of charming insincerity that almost made me laugh. I wondered if Rainer was a 'queen' like Greville, one of the many *Schwulen* that you could see all over the city, if you looked hard. I didn't think so, somehow, but I could hardly trust my intuition given how badly it had failed me with Greville.

At midnight, the band took a short break and I noticed a crowd of men and women heading for the lavatories that were reached by a corridor leading off the main club-room by the bar, indicated by an electric sign saying '*Klosett*'. Rainer glanced around the room as it slowly emptied – this was odd, I thought, as I knew that clubs in Berlin stayed open until three in the morning. Then the band returned and began playing again, though it was apparent that no one was much interested in dancing any more. Waiters began to clear the unoccupied tables.

'Are they closing?' I asked.

'No. We are opening.' Rainer stood up and I did so too, taking the opportunity to quickly snatch a photograph or two of the room with my little Ensignette. So much for the celebrated decadence of Berlin, I thought. Where was I going to find my scandal?

The Iguana-Club, Berlin.

Rainer guided me through the tables and we made for the corridor that led to the lavatories.

'Welcome to the Klosett-Club,' he said.

There was a door – it looked like the door to a broom cupboard – between the *Damen* and *Herren* toilets, and a tall moustachioed man in a gold-frogged greatcoat that came down to his ankles stood there guarding it. Rainer gave him first a card, then some money and the door was opened for us revealing a steep flight of stairs that led down to a thick leather curtain. As we descended I could hear the excited chatter of conversation and could smell cigar and cigarette smoke. Rainer held the leather curtain open for me and I stepped into the Klosett-Club. Now, this was more like it, I thought.

It was a dark, narrow, low-ceilinged room – I wondered if it had been an underground garage in a previous life. Clustered tables and chipped gilt chairs faced a tiny stage with a backdrop of shimmering sequinned curtains. All the tables had small stubby lamps on them like mushrooms, with domed crimson shades that gave forth the dimmest glow. I could hear American, French and Dutch voices amongst the chatter. A few waiters squeezed through the tables, trays of drinks held aloft. It was warm and there was a curious underlying smell in the room – below the perfume and smoke. Oil and grease? Maybe it had indeed been a garage, once.

I turned to find Rainer in conversation with a skinny man in a pistachio-green satin jacket and a yellow bow tie. Rainer beckoned me over.

'This is Benno, the manager,' he said. 'This is Fräulein Clay, the famous English photographer.'

We shook hands. I saw that Benno had painted eyebrows as he leant forward, confidentially.

'You may take any photos you like – but just of the show. You must only mention the Klosett-Club when you publish them, please.' He pointed. 'See – we have another photographer here tonight. We are making good publicity.' He laughed and gestured across the room at a young man in a dark suit lounging against the far wall. His collar seemed too large for his thin neck – almost affectedly large – and his straight blond hair fell down in a lock in front of his right ear. He turned to look at us, almost as if he knew he was being discussed, and I saw a thin, big-eyed, starveling's face. A beautiful waif. I noticed he had a Rolleiflex over his shoulder. Damn, I said to myself, feeling my disappointment weigh on me like a heavy rucksack. Another photographer – another fucking photographer, as Greville would have said. It was like a tourist trail.

'Thank you very much,' I said to Benno, who kissed my hand and sped off towards the stage. 'We can go,' I added, turning to Rainer, 'this place is obviously too well known.' I inclined my head at the other photographer. 'Hardly exclusive.'

Rainer shrugged. 'We might as well see the show,' he said, undauntedly cheerful. 'Have a few more drinks. Benno's getting us a good table at the front.'

I saw Benno beckoning us over so we went to join him and he sat us down at a table one row back from the little stage where a man was setting up a microphone on a stand. We took our seats and I asked for a gin and orange, leaving my camera in my handbag under the table. I glanced over at my rival who was now talking to Benno, himself, and I saw Benno point us out – Fräulein Clay, the famous English photographer. Then the lights dimmed and a couple of spots hit the stage. A Negro with a trumpet in his hand emerged through the sequinned curtains wearing a white suit dotted with black discs like a Dalmatian dog. The crowd roared their approval.

'Ladies and gentlemen!' he said into the microphone in English with an American accent. 'Ingeborg Hammer will dance "Cocaine Shipwreck"!'

Whoops and cheers greeted this news. Rainer leant over.

'Sometimes she is dancing with a man but tonight she dances alone. We are very lucky.'

'What's her name again?'

'Ingeborg Hammer. Very famous here in Berlin.'

The Negro began to play his trumpet – an improvised jazzy wail – and, slipping out from the curtains, a tall wraith of a woman in a filmy black dress appeared, its neckline slashed to the waist. Her face was a white death-mask of face powder, her eyes smoky with kohl and her lipstick was a purple gash. She stood for a moment as the applause died down, arms spread, hands fluttering, as the trumpet solo continued its free-form extemporisation. She was indeed very tall, I saw, almost six feet – and then she started to move in a series of jerky, impressionistic dance steps and, inevitably, her décolletage gaped to reveal her hanging flat breasts, the prominent nipples purpled like her lips. She lurched and swayed, stooped and staggered, her white arms flailing, looming over tables and recoiling dramatically. Sometimes she would stand immobile for ten or twenty seconds while the trumpet riff continued. It was, I thought, at once ridiculous and completely mesmerising.

At one moment in the dance she passed near our table, walking on tiptoe with tiny bird-steps, and I became aware, at the edge of my vision, of my rival photographer, head bowed over his Rolleiflex, snapping away. Ingeborg Hammer struck her pose by our table and a waft of a curious perfume came off her – of camphor, I thought, or formaldehyde – the smell of a mortuary or dissection laboratory. I looked up into her white face, completely expressionless, her body trembling as the trumpet's screeching began to crescendo, telling you that the 'Cocaine Shipwreck' was about to reach its fatal encounter with the rocks. Ingeborg took three steps back, ripped off her dress and fell to the floor, naked, her pudenda shaved clean, one hand twitching for a few seconds before there was a final demonic scream from the trumpet and the lights went out. When they came back on seconds later she had gone. She took no bow; the trumpeter mopped his glossy face with a handkerchief and accepted the plaudits on her behalf.

'*Das ist fantastisch, nein?*'

I turned. I hadn't heard anyone approach but here was the rival photographer, crouching by my chair.

'*Ich spreche kein Deutsch,*' I said, realising instantly that the thin-faced waif with the flopping lock of hair was a woman.

'I'm Hannelore Hahn,' she said in near-accentless English. 'Benno told me you were a famous English photographer. Where's your camera? You missed a real—'

Rainer stood up, interrupting her. 'I'll leave you to talk about lenses and exposures and all that stuff,' he said. 'Give me a telephone call tomorrow, Amory. I take you somewhere else.'

He kissed me goodbye, shook Hannelore Hahn's hand and sauntered off. Hannelore slipped into his seat. She was wearing a black and red striped tie with her big-collared shirt and I could see, now that she was opposite and lit by the glow of the mushroom lamp, that she was lightly made-up – and eerily beautiful in a vague manly way. Which was the point of the outfit, I supposed.

'It's better when she dances with her partner, Otto Deodat,' she continued. 'It's more ... More sexual. He's very handsome, Otto, with head shaved, you know, and often naked with his body painted. Very tall like her.' She smiled showing her uneven teeth, overlapping at the front as if too crowded for her narrow jaw. 'I've many photos of them both. I can show you if you like.' She took out her cigarette case and selected a black one from the multicoloured row that was lined up inside. 'Is that gin? Could I ask you to buy me one? I've no money left.' She smiled, holding up her camera. 'I spent everything on my Rollei.'

I recognised that I was fairly drunk by the time we left the Klosett-Club and I decided I should head back to my hotel. Hannelore seemed none the worse for all the gins she'd consumed and offered to share a taxi with me. The sky was like grey flannel – early summer dawn heralded – and the air was cool. I shivered as we headed out on to Arkonaplatz looking for a taxi.

But the streets we wandered through were empty, as the light gathered and the darkness began to thin. We cast about us here and there – I was completely lost – vainly waving and shouting at any passing vehicle in the hope it would miraculously transform itself into a cab. After half an hour I was sober again. Hannelore checked her watch.

'We might as well walk,' she said. 'Your hotel is only twenty minutes or so from here.'

And so we set off through the monochrome streets, the sound of our heels echoing off the facades of the apartment blocks, a few neon signs glowing in the clearing gloom, street sweepers and night workers returning home were our only companions. We walked past a small hotel – there was a waiter standing outside with a grubby tailcoat. Thick yellow light shone from the half-open door behind him. Should we go there, I asked Hannelore? No, no, she said: that place isn't for us.

We saw the young men before they saw us, as we turned on to Oranienburger-Strasse, heading for Alexanderplatz. There were five of them in their brown uniforms, drunk and dishevelled, four of them helping the fifth climb a lamp post to tear down a poster. Hannelore led me across the street away from them but they had heard the clip-clop of our heels and turned to see us, eager for diversion. They shouted something at us – something lewd that I couldn't understand. I glanced back and saw the climber slither heavily to the ground, swearing at us, as if his fall was our fault.

'Don't look at them,' Hannelore said as more catcalls came our way. I heard their hobnails crunching on the cobbles as they followed us, shouting angrily at us, calling on us to stop. A stone skipped across the road in front of us and clattered into a parked van.

'We have to pretend, all right?'

'What? Yes, whatever you say.'

She put her arm round my shoulders and bumped me into a shop doorway. She rounded angrily on the men following us and shouted at them, lowering and harshening her voice. Great bellows of laughter ensued and I saw them stop and talk amongst each other.

'What did you say?'

'I said I'd spent the whole night trying to get you into bed and I wasn't going to let them prevent me.' She glanced back. 'Or something like that. Pretend to kiss. They're still looking.'

So we kissed, mouths slightly askew, and I was transported back to Amberfield and my practice sessions with Millicent. I heard vulpine whoops and yelps from the young men. We set off, Hannelore looking back and making an obscene gesture at them before we turned the corner and broke into a panicky run.

We reached my shabby little hotel, the Silesia Hospiz, in five minutes and rang the bell for the night clerk, both out of breath.

'My God,' Hannelore said. 'A real Berlin night – Ingeborg Hammer, Nazis and you even get a kiss from me.'

The night clerk opened the door and we stepped into the lobby.

'Well,' I said. 'Lucky you were dressed like a man.'

'I dress like this all the time.'

'Oh . . . Still lucky, though.'

I picked up my key and turned to find Hannelore looking round the dark lobby.

'Is it expensive, here?'

'They gave me a good price for one month. Forty marks a week.'

'If you give me half of that you can have a room in my apartment.' She smiled. 'And you can use my darkroom.'

★

THE BARRANDALE JOURNAL 1977

Think of their names. Hannelore Hahn, Marianne Breslauer, Dora Kallmuss, Jutta Gottschalk, Friedl Dicker – not forgetting Edith Suchitsky, Edeltraud Hartman and Annie Schulz and many more I've forgotten. If, in London, I had thought I was something of a rare beast as a woman photographer, I had to think again as my stay with Hannelore progressed and I came to learn that I was joining a sorority of women photographers, all working and making a living in Berlin, Hamburg, Vienna and Paris. It was empowering, not disappointing – like becoming a member of a secret society. We were everywhere, the women, cameras in hand.

When we conceived our Berlin plan, Greville lent me £50 – and it was a loan, he insisted, not a gift, and he expected to be paid back – he wasn't funding a pleasant holiday in Berlin for me. He also gave me the contact with Rainer, assuring me that Rainer knew 'all the best places'. I had the feeling, though, that Rainer was treating me rather as a tourist. Ingeborg Hammer had been photographed thousands of times for magazines all over Europe – there was a ready market for them, Hannelore said, which was why she was at the Klosett-Club. She showed me half a dozen magazine articles. Photographers made a reliable living from Ingeborg – as did Benno – but it was clear to me I had to descend deeper into Berlin's dark underbelly.

In the event I took up Hannelore's offer – the money-saving and the offer of a darkroom were too hard to resist – and I checked out of the Hospiz and moved into her surprisingly roomy flat on Jäger-Strasse near Gendarmenmarkt. There were two bedrooms, a sitting room, a kitchen and a third bedroom converted into a darkroom. The lavatory was on the landing below and if we wanted to bathe we went to the Admirals-Bad baths near the Friedrichs-Strasse station, just a few blocks away. Hannelore, however, didn't give up her pursuit. My first night in the apartment she came into my room and slipped naked into my bed. I recognised the ploy and gently pushed her away when she tried to kiss me. She was unperturbed and resigned and we lay in bed for an hour together chatting about sex and smoking. I remember she asked me if I'd ever been with a man. I confessed I had. 'Damn,' she said. 'Was it good?' It was, actually, I said, thinking of Lockwood, fondly. 'How many times?' she pressed on, hopefully. I'd lost count, I said. 'Too bad,' she said, 'you don't know what you're missing.' I asked her when she'd known she was a lesbian. 'I'm not a lesbian,' she said with manifest pride, 'I'm a pansexualist.'

Just as it had with Greville, the abortive pass made us closer, oddly, and she seemed to relax now she knew I was unlikely to succumb. I told her about my plans for Berlin – Greville's idea about what I had to do to secure my future as a photographer – and she offered to help. We worked together in her darkroom and she showed me how to master the techniques of 'dodging' and 'burning', how to overexpose and underexpose parts of the photograph when you were printing – shining more light on some areas or filtering light into shadow with a variety of implements. Hannelore had her own technique of dodging that employed a very fine-meshed flat sieve. I liked the effects and felt my competence expand. Greville retouched his photographs – everyone did – but he was only interested in removing blemishes and wrinkles from his subjects' faces to make them look better. The manipulation of light and shade when you dodged or burned was something he'd never tried as far as I was aware – perhaps he felt he didn't need it, or didn't even know about it. I began to feel I'd already moved on by coming to Berlin – the 'Amory Clay Society Photographer' era was over. I was changing.

3. EIN WENIG ORGIE

HANNELORE CAME OVER TO the table with a bottle of schnapps and three glasses. We were in a danse-cabaret club called the Monokel. There were a lot of lesbians dressed in sailor suits and a good number of strange-looking men who seemed to be acting out a fantasy as Spanish hidalgos in wide-brimmed hats with long sideburns – and obvious prostitutes here and there waiting to be asked to step on to the small dance floor. Hannelore was dressed like a working-class boy in a collarless shirt, drill trousers and a leather jacket. She had a flat tweed cap on her short hair. She sat down, poured two drinks and we lit cigarettes.

'I feel a bit odd in here,' I said.

'They'll think you're my friend,' she said, giving the last word lascivious emphasis.

'Why this place?'

She explained. 'There's a girl I know who comes in here. She works in a brothel. If you pay her money – and the madame, of course – she might invite you there.'

'How would I take photographs?' I felt a shiver of excitement. A Berlin brothel – that might cause a bit of a fuss . . .

Hannelore looked at her watch.

'If she's coming she'll be here any minute – *et voilà!*'

Hannelore stood and weaved her way through the throng to the bar, returning, moments later, hand in hand with a short tubby girl with her hair dyed a carroty orange. Hannelore introduced her.

'This is Trudi.'

She sat down opposite me. She had a pretty round face beneath her lurid hair and a tired baggy-eyed look that was strangely endearing. She had a woollen shawl knotted round her shoulders covering her décolletage and happily accepted the glass of schnapps that Hannelore poured for her. She sipped at it, looking at me curiously over the rim.

'You just want photo?' she said in faltering English. 'Or you want ficky?'

'Just photo.'

She spoke quickly to Hannelore and Hannelore translated for me. There was a big club-room in this particular house that operated, semi-covertly, as a brothel. But it was a room where everyone gathered, like a bar, and where the girls met their clients. The bedrooms were on the floor above. When it was busy, at the weekend, people came just to watch – couples, husbands and wives, tourists – so it would be easy to explain my presence there, but the camera would have to be hidden, somehow. If Trudi was caught she'd be thrown out and maybe punished in other ways – so she would need a lot of money to be persuaded to help.

'How much?'

She turned to Hannelore who whispered something in her ear.

'Five hundred marks,' Trudi said.

I stayed calm. About £25. Maybe a month's earnings for a working girl like Trudi if she were busy – and just about all I had left from Greville's loan, more to the point. I pretended to waver – frowning, thinking – but I knew this was the best chance I'd have. Maybe if I'd been a man it would have been easier and I tried not to think what kind of risks a single woman in a brothel might run. But there was another risk – what if there was nothing shocking or depraved to photograph? A 'big bar room' didn't sound very debauched. But the chance was worth it, I thought to myself – it would be authentic, real, if nothing else – feeling the flush of excitement spread. I searched my handbag for my purse.

'Half now,' Hannelore intervened, 'half on the night.'

Trudi accepted, with a show of reluctance, but I could see how pleased she was to have the money in her hands.

'When do we go?' I asked.

Saturday night was always best, she said – it was always busy, sometimes fifty people in the room. And sometimes it became like a party, Trudi said, with a laugh. '*Ein wenig Orgie.*' Hannelore translated: a little orgy.

'Sounds good to me,' I said, pouring us all another glass of schnapps. We clinked glasses to the success of our enterprise.

I was running low on funds so Hannelore offered to waive the next month's rent that I owed her. 'I will invest in your talent, my dear,' she said. However, I spent the equivalent of about £2 on a solid patent-leather clutch bag with a flower-shaped diamanté clasp. I removed the facetted stone at the centre of the paste flower, cut a small hole in the leather beneath and stitched in two thin canvas straps in the bag's interior that would firmly hold my little Zeiss Contax, the lens positioned securely and invisibly at the centre of the diamanté flower. I attached a remote release cable that I rigged up, with some glittery ribbon wrapped around it, as a small handle. There was a faintly audible click when I pressed the button but I assumed that in a busy bar no one would notice. Trial photographs that I took at a café came out very well: the key aspect was the positioning of the bag, a matter of estimating with your eyes. Sometimes the framing was askew – but you could always crop, Hannelore reminded me, and maybe it's even better if it looks like it's from a concealed camera. I could sense her own excitement building as Saturday approached.

Hannelore suggested I dress like a *garçonne* – one of the many subtypes of Berlin lesbian – reasoning that I didn't want to be bothered by the clients. If I looked like a *garçonne* then, moreover, any confusion about my role in the brothel would be more easily comprehended – just another strange Berlin night-animal on the prowl. Trudi said the madame should be kept ignorant. Pay your entrance fee, she said, buy a couple of bottles of champagne and she'll let you sit all night.

I allowed Hanna – as I was now calling her – to organise my 'look'. First, I had my hair cut in an Eton crop, then she found me a pair of clear-lensed round-frame tortoiseshell spectacles. I wore a long olive-green worsted jacket, a shirt and tie and tucked my trousers into soft knee-length boots.

'You look good,' Hanna said, inspecting me. 'Masculine-feminine. A pretty *garçonne* with a *Bubikopf*. Keep your spectacles on. Attractive but a little frightening.'

We met Trudi in the smoking room of a confectioner's in Tauentzien-Strasse. She asked for more money – I thought that was a bad sign – but Hanna said I should give her another hundred marks; the rest when I'd checked how the photos came out. I might need to go back a few times, after all. I handed over the money, said goodbye to Hanna, who kissed my cheek and wished me luck, and I followed Trudi into the street and then down an alleyway into a courtyard. We went through an arched gateway into another courtyard. She pressed a bell set into a brass plate that had 'Xanadu-Club' stamped on it. I thought suddenly of Xan, my moody little brother, and took the name of the club as a good omen. I was a bit nervous in my *garçonne* persona but also excited. Amory Clay, photographer, was about to be reborn.

The door of the Xanadu-Club was opened by a weedy-looking man in a commissionaire's greatcoat and he had a few words with Trudi.

'You pay him twenty marks,' she said.

'Of course.'

I paid and we went upstairs to the club-rooms.

The Xanadu-Club, like everything in Berlin it seemed to me, was a strange mixture, both humdrum and exotic. This floor of the house – the social club – was a random collection of rooms. There was a bar in two of them, and a piano on a low stage in another. The furniture was an assortment of sofas, armchairs and standard restaurant tables and chairs grouped here and there. The lighting was low and, while we waited for the band, jazz music was played through loudspeakers. It was already busy and filled with men and women of all ages and sizes. I thought I could have been in the waiting room at a railway station but a second glance picked out the anomalies. Stout middle-aged men in grey business suits chatted to boys in striped sailor jerseys. Eight thin women dressed as men sat round a table. A man in a Pierrot costume danced with a girl in a satin negligee. Trudi led me to a table in the corner on the other side of the small dance floor and I ordered a bottle of *Sekt* from a boy dressed only in white linen shorts. Trudi went in search of the *Kupplerin*, the house madame.

I sipped my glass of warm *Sekt* and took in the room in more detail. Clearly, there were people here who came only to watch – like curious visitors at a human zoo – and there were others who intended to participate. Once again I felt the pulse of excitement at my audacity, pleased with my disguise. Two other *garçonnes* took to the dance floor as if to reassure me I was part of the weird crowd. Nobody was staring at me; I was left alone with my champagne and my clutch bag, carefully positioned on the table in front of me. I turned it slightly, aiming at two men in shiny suits and short wide ties who were eyeing up the girls in their satin shifts and clicked the remote release button. Got you. They approached two girls, conferred briefly and then disappeared through a leather-curtained exit at the side of the bar. I assumed that led upstairs to where the sexual shenanigans took place. I wondered if there was any way Trudi could contrive to let me visit backstage.

'Amory?'

Trudi stood there beside a smiling middle-aged woman with an enormous shelf of bosom. She was introduced as Frau Amoureux and we shook hands.

'I wait here for Trudi,' I said in my rudimentary German.

'*Oui, oui, ma chérie, je vous en prie.*'

Trudi whispered in her ear and turned back to me.

'I think you should offer Frau Amoureux a bottle of *Sekt*.'

I handed over the money.

I left the Xanadu-Club at two in the morning thinking that I'd never get rid of the taste of cheap *Sekt* in my mouth, no matter how many cigarettes I smoked. As the night had worn on the mood in the club had slowly changed. The gawping couples left and the brothel-atmosphere steadily enhanced itself. Clients and girls – or clients and boys – came down from the upstairs rooms and lingered around the bars, drinking and flirting, chatting and playing cards. Clothes were shed and more visits upstairs took place. The place was very crowded on either side of midnight but as the small hours advanced the spirit calmed and the carnality seemed to disappear from the banter and the laughter and the mood in the club became almost domestic. The weedy commissionaire came up from below and had a beer with Frau Amoureux. Men in vests played cards with semi-naked girls who had finished work for the night. The girls chatted and gossiped, smoking and drinking. Trudi joined me at the end of her shift and I ordered yet more *Sekt*.

'How much do you cost?' I asked, *Sekt*-emboldened.

'For ficky I am ten marks.' She glanced balefully at Frau Amoureux. 'But I am giving half to her.'

I could see how earning 500 marks for bringing me here was the most enormous windfall and, as if she were reading my mind, Trudi took my hand and said thank you with obvious sincerity. She chatted on in a low voice but at a speed I couldn't really understand. She was grateful, that much I gathered, and it seemed that if I stayed late even more things could happen in this room. Then, as she drank more, she started telling me about her life and how the Xanadu-Club was much better than being a common Kontroll-girl in the Tiergarten, which was what she used to do, outside in all weathers with all manner of perverts asking you to do unpleasant things. She even, at one stage, leant over and kissed me on the cheek. Then she spotted one of her regulars and sashayed off to greet him. I turned my bag. Click.

The next day Hanna and I developed the negative and printed out and examined the contact sheet. It hadn't worked – somehow the camera had moved slightly in the bag, slipping in its canvas straps, and one half of the images were a blur, like a finger held over the lens.

'You'll just have to go again,' Hanna said. 'It's a shame – some of these would have been really good.'

★

THE BARRANDALE JOURNAL 1977

Hugo Torrance called round today. I heard a car come to a halt outside the cottage – a most unusual event, unannounced, as I have signs on the single-track road leading down to the house saying 'No turning point', 'No vehicular access', precisely to deter the curious tourist to the island, thinking they can rove where they will. I ran quickly to a front window and saw that it was Hugo and I watched him swing his stiff leg out of his old Jaguar, stamp on it to restore circulation and limp towards the front door. I had it open before he could knock.

'My, my,' I said. 'What an honour.'

He kissed me on the cheek and I smelt his aftershave – Old Spice.

'I'm having a party tomorrow,' he said. 'Spontaneous. My daughter and her husband are flying up from London.'

'Alas, I'm too old for parties,' I said.

'Not as old as me. If I can have one you should do the honourable thing and show up – if only for half an hour.'

'Actually, I'm rather busy—'

'It's my birthday, Amory. The big seven-o.'

'Ah.'

He gave me that fierce look of his – an audible inhalation of breath, eyes narrowing, eyebrows buckling.

'See you at the hotel tomorrow evening,' he said, bluntly. 'Eight o'clock. Lots to drink.'

'I'll be there. Can't wait.'

'I'm just off to Greer and Calder's now. You'll be amongst friends.'

I watched him reverse, turn and drive away. Interesting that he's delivering the invitations in person, I thought, instead of just telephoning. Harder to say no, that way – so he must want a good quorum of friends. Hugo Torrance is tall, slim and bald, his white hair, what remains of it, is startlingly set off by ink-black eyebrows. A handsome septuagenarian and an ex-soldier who had his left leg shattered by machine-gun bullets at Monte Cassino in 1944. He owns and runs the Glenlarig Hotel in Achnalorn, Barrandale's solitary licensed premises, so he's an important man and it's hard not to see him on a regular basis, if you fancy a drink in the bar from time to time or a meal in the dining room. I have been avoiding him, however, as I know he has designs on me. Last Hogmanay at the hotel he kissed me as I was about to leave, the bells an hour past. Kissed me seriously as we stood alone in an alcove where the coats are hung and I nearly gave in to him. I kissed him back for a second or two and broke away. 'Stay the night, Lady Amory,' he said, his voice husky with drink. He touched my face then swayed back. 'Don't ever call me that,' I said in shock. How did he know? And now he's asked me to his seventieth birthday party. Not asked, but effectively demanded I be there. Well, I can handle Hugo Torrance – I know his type, these old soldiers, all too well.

★

Berlin. Just as I'd gained exclusive access to the Xanadu-Club, Trudi went missing. We telephoned the number she had given us – no reply. Hanna managed to find out where she was living but there was nobody there. Then a messenger boy came one day with a note saying that she was ill and needed the 150 marks I still owed her. 'She'll be back,' Hanna said. 'You just have to wait.' So I waited. It was summer in Berlin – there were worst places to be and I knew that one way or another the Xanadu-Club contained everything I needed. What do I remember of that summer as we waited for Trudi to reappear? I was happy living in Hanna's apartment on Jäger-Strasse. I had a roof over my head but my money was running out fast.

BERLIN SNAPSHOTS 1930–1

I remember going to Lehrter station to the telegraph office there, open twenty-four hours, and sending a telegram to Greville. I asked him if I could borrow another £20 – a further loan, I stressed – and added 'SCANDAL FORTHCOMING'. I remember I felt a curious exhilaration on leaving, excited by my own prediction and, instead of boarding the tram back to Hanna's flat, I hired a Cyklonette cab (three wheels, cheaper) and had it take me to the Mercedes-Palast on Unter den Linden where I drank a dry martini in the bar and toasted my future.

I remember that for two weeks I taught English to a photographer friend of Hanna called Arno Hartmann. He was in his forties, married with two children, and nurtured this fantasy of going to America to make his name as a landscape photographer. 'Every landscape in Europe is old, tired, overfamiliar,' he used to say. 'I need a new land.' I charged him five marks an hour, about five shillings, slave labour but that was the going rate in Berlin. An hour with Arno was what Trudi made for a single 'ficky', I realised, that probably lasted a few minutes. After two weeks there had been no improvement in Arno's faltering English so I did him a favour and resigned. Greville's £20 had come through and I was rich again.

I remember sitting in a grubby *Nachtlokal* with Hanna one evening just off the Kurfürstendamm – that stretch at the end where it rises towards the Halensee. We were talking about the slump of '29, for some reason, and how, even in Berlin, there were signs of life becoming better and more stable. I lit her cigarette for her and she exhaled a jet of smoke strongly out of the side of her mouth – in that *garçonne*-ish way she had – while she looked at me, fixedly, tossing her lock of hair off her brow with a flick of her head.

'Amory. Look at me.'

'I am looking at you.'

'Are you sure you're not in love with me?'

'I'm sure. I'm not.'

'Not even a little? A tiny bit?'

'I'm very fond of you, Hanna. You're a true friend.'

'*Fond.* How I hate that word.'

I remember a hot afternoon at Lake Motzen. Hanna worked for various magazines whose claim to celebrate an innocent naturism and good, healthy living barely concealed the real motive of their publication, namely that their pages contained many photographs of naked young men and boys – *Das Freibad, Nur Natur, Extra Post des Eigenen*, for example. These naked men and boys often preferred a woman photographer, so she was told, and she was regularly in demand during the summer months while people could sunbathe glorying in the *Licht, Luft* and *Leben* that the lakes and open spaces in and around Berlin offered. We travelled out to Lake Motzen to attend a meeting of the 'League of Air Bathing', Hanna having arranged for me to be paid as her assistant, something she happily did whenever she thought the magazine could afford it.

It was a day of clear unobstructed sunshine and what struck me most during these excursions was not the casual nudity, so much, as the extraordinary depth and hue of the suntans that these fair-haired Berliners sported. Their skins were so burned by the sun they looked Asiatic, basted and burnished with oil to help fry their bodies better. Hanna took her pictures as the men posed naked with discus or javelin, or dived into the lake, and the boys did callisthenic exercises. Meanwhile I reloaded Hanna's cameras, marvelling at the unreal texture of these men's coppery hides, as if they were some alien species or lost Amazonian tribe. There wasn't the least frisson of eroticism, as far as I was concerned, contemplating these naked male bodies cavorting about the lakeside. It was the Berlin effect — it became ever harder to be shocked or affronted. However, I've never really enjoyed sunbathing since, I have to say.

I remember meeting Hanna's mother and father. They came to the apartment for tea and cakes, a concerned, wealthy, bourgeois, faultlessly polite couple in their soft expensive clothes. Hanna was provocatively at her most *garçonne*-like, wearing co-respondent lace-up brogues, Oxford bags, a white short-sleeved shirt with a cerise bow tie, her hair oiled back from her forehead. When she strode out of the living room to make tea I saw her parents' anguished, uncomprehending glance at each other. What had happened to little Hanna?

I remember going to Trudi's flat, a bedsit in an old apartment block near Alexanderplatz. There had been a big street fight outside the synagogue on Kaiser-Strasse and workmen were wearily sweeping up the debris — placards, sticks, lumps of paving, broken glass. On Trudi's door was her name, a handwritten scrap of paper pinned above the knocker: G. Fenstermacher. 'Windowmaker'. Hanna found this very funny. Shamefully, I'd never thought of Trudi as having a surname — she was always a simple 'Trudi' to me. Hanna and I sat on her bed while Trudi took the only chair the room had to offer. She was much thinner and she confirmed she'd been away to have an abortion and there had been complications and a spell in hospital. Her mother was already caring for two of her children and had categorically refused to take on a third. 'What choice did she give me?' Trudi said, sulkily, resentfully. I handed over the 150 marks I had promised her and arranged to meet the following Saturday night at the Xanadu-Club for another session. She asked me for an extra hundred, saying she could take me to a very private place, very secret. I had Greville's money by then so I paid up, very curious.

4. A Very Private Place, Very Secret

I SAT IN MY corner of the Xanadu-Club drinking *Sekt* and smoking, feeling very happy as I covertly clicked away with my handbag camera. It was late and some of the girls – who had also been drinking all night – did an impromptu striptease for the regulars who had lingered on. The men and the women – it had gone very heterosexual by this stage – chatted, kissed and fondled each other like lovers rather than prostitutes and paying customers, as if pleased to see each other and relishing this moment, snug and separated from the sexual commerce of the place for a few minutes, in a warm and friendly atmosphere. I was happy because I had nudity. I had half-naked Berlin prostitutes talking to each other, with their clients sitting alongside, looking on. All was well.

Trudi appeared in her hat and coat and signed off with Frau Amoureux.

'We get a taxi,' Trudi said.

We headed east, towards Lichtenberg, into long dark streets of old apartment buildings. I spotted a theatre and a sign that said Blumen-Strasse and then we turned down a narrow shadowy lane. I saw three other taxis ahead of us dropping off their passengers. We followed them through the usual damp, ill-lit courtyard and found a small queue of men filing in the door of an apartment, their hats pulled down, collars up. Trudi led me round to another door to the side where she rang a bell and a man looked out suspiciously. He had a pouchy, flushed face and a wide moustache. Trudi whispered a few words to him then turned to me.

'You must give him fifty marks.'

'But I just gave you a hundred.'

'And I bring you to this place.'

I paid the man with the big moustache and we climbed a back stairway up one floor to a kitchen. There was a blackened tin range, a cold-water stone sink and a few shelves with pots and pans on them. There was another man standing there, reading a newspaper, naked apart from a towel tied around his waist. He looked up as we came in and I saw that he had a harelip, badly joined. He hugged and kissed Trudi and she introduced him.

'This is Volker, my brother.'

We shook hands.

'If you could give him some money that would be nice.'

I duly gave Volker fifty marks. Thank you, Greville.

'What's happening here?' I asked.

Trudi led me cautiously to another door off the kitchen, opening it an inch or two. Peering through I could see a larger room, a sitting room, perhaps, transformed into a kind of crude theatre. Almost twenty men were already there, scattered about on the rows of chairs. Other men were arriving – prosperous men, so they looked to me as they removed their hats and coats and the place filled up. I saw silver hip flasks being passed around, cigarettes were lit, conversations were low and terse. The audience was facing a simple wooden bed with a headboard, made up with a pillow and sheets, lit by a standard lamp at each end. I began to understand why Trudi had called this a very private place, very secret.

I turned as I heard steps coming up the kitchen stairway. A young woman came in, bespectacled, wearing a tan camel coat and a velour hat with a bow on one side. She had a bony, angled face, her tiredness visible, and she looked as if she was returning from a day's work at an office somewhere. She kissed Volker with familiarity and fished in her handbag, handing him what looked like a tube of toothpaste.

We were introduced – this was Franziska – and I gave her the obligatory fifty marks. I thought I recognised her as one of the girls from the Xanadu-Club. A whispered exchange with Trudi confirmed that this was true. So far I had spent 250 marks on this evening but I didn't begrudge it – I had a feeling that whatever I was about to witness was going to be worthwhile. What I was more worried about was how much film remained in my camera – I had taken many photographs in the Xanadu-Club.

Big Moustache stuck his head round the door and asked if everyone was ready.

'We're ready,' Franziska said and she slipped past me into the sitting room. There was no applause – just the sound of two dozen men shifting in their seats.

Trudi tapped me on the shoulder.

'I go now. Volker will find you a taxi.'

'See you next Saturday.'

She left and I turned back to see what Franziska was up to in the room. She had taken off her hat and coat and was beginning to undress in a matter-of-fact way, exactly as if she was in her own bedroom, humming to herself, sighing with exasperation at a stubborn button. Soon she was down to her underclothes. She took off her spectacles and tucked them under the pillow.

I looked back at Volker. He was naked now – his body was very white with well-defined musculature, only his forearms tanned brown. He had a thin line of dark hair on his chest running down to his navel. He was squeezing toothpaste into his palm, then he rubbed his hands vigorously together to make a softer paste – then he began to massage this cream on to his penis.

'What're you doing?' I said spontaneously, raising my bag. Click.

He was wholly unselfconscious as he pulled and tugged at himself with both hands, easing the toothpaste into his skin.

'Ow. It's burning,' he said. 'The toothpaste makes me hot. *Stechend.*' Stinging. His harelip made him lisp strangely. 'And when it's hot like this it makes me bigger, you see.'

He took his hands away. I could see it was working. No erection but very impressive size, nonetheless.

'Goodness!' I raised my bag and coughed as I pressed the remote release button.

'It's just a trick,' he said, and shrugged, almost apologetically.

I turned to peer through the crack in the door again. Franziska was now naked and she walked round the bed, folding and tidying away her discarded clothes, before climbing in between the sheets. Volker loomed up beside me. All I could smell was toothpaste.

'Ten seconds,' he said.

Franziska was feigning sleep, making deep breathing sounds, tossing and turning as if she was dreaming.

Then Volker walked in – the dream made flesh – and the toothpaste trick provoked a gasp of envy-admiration from the male audience.

And then Volker and Franziska duly made love. Orthodox straightforward sex, the sheet thrown back, lit by the two standard lamps. When it was over Volker strode back into the kitchen. I could hear him getting dressed behind me but my eyes were on Franziska as she awoke from her dream, looked around, saw no naked man, smiled to herself, stretched luxuriously, then stepped out of bed and began to put on her clothes, ending with her spectacles, retrieved from under the pillow, then her coat and velour hat and, the working girl fully attired ready for the day ahead, she left the room without a glance.

Now there was applause – a brief clapping of hands – and I heard a surge of low-voiced conversation as Big Moustache made his way through the crowd collecting money.

Franziska stood beside me watching, expressionless. She had a sharp pointed face, almost pretty, but her lips were thin and turned down at the corner as if she were permanently disapproving or bitter.

'You see him put the money in his pocket?' she asked.

'Yes.'

'These are tips for us – me and Volker – but he keeps them. The men have already paid to get in.' She gave a thin smile. 'But tonight you pay me,' adding in English, 'thank you very much, Miss.'

'Who had the idea for this show?' I asked. 'Him?' I pointed through the door at Big Moustache. The room was emptying fast. 'Or Volker?'

'No. It's my idea. Have you a cigarette?'

I offered her a cigarette and took one myself. We both lit up. Volker had gone to the lavatory on the landing outside the kitchen.

'It's a very clever idea, your show,' I said, marvelling at its potent and absolute simplicity. Franziska's dream. All these men were paying to enjoy Franziska's fantasy, not theirs. 'Bravo.'

Trudi (on top) and Franziska outside the Xanadu-Club, before work. Berlin, 1931.

I returned to the club a few more times and managed to arrange some further photographic sessions with the girls – they had come to know me by now and were actually quite pleased to have their pictures taken. When I left Berlin some two weeks later I decided to fly back to London. It was extravagant, almost £10, and it took up the remains of Greville's second loan, but I'd never been in an airliner before and I felt that a symbolic act of some sort was required at the end of my Berlin adventure.

Hanna came with me to the aerodrome at Staaken. We said our sad goodbyes – we had become real friends, I considered – and yet she managed to snatch a full kiss on my lips, hugging me to her and promising to come and see my show of Berlin photographs when it opened in London.

I was flying Deutsche Luft Hansa and as I walked across the concrete apron with the other twenty or so passengers towards the vast aeroplane – four engines, a kind of enormous flying wing – I turned to wave back at the departure building but I couldn't see Hanna. I wondered if she'd gone.

I had a seat in the actual wing itself – you could stand upright in it easily – with a view forward through a square window, just like the pilots who were sitting in their cockpit a few feet to my right. The doors were closed, the engines started, and we trundled down the runway and, in no time, it seemed, the aeroplane heaved itself into the air, climbing very slowly, heading for Amsterdam, our refuelling stop before Croydon airport. I felt an extraordinary exhilaration, as if I might swoon, to be lifted above the earth in this way, the drumming of the engines in my ears, to be floating and yet feel so secure with a metal floor and carpet beneath my feet.

It was a cloudy day and as soon as the earth below was lost to view I wandered back through the fuselage – the airliner was perfectly steady – to the smoking parlour and had a cigarette and a gin and vermouth, served by a steward in a white jacket.

I asked the steward what kind of airliner I was in – I always liked to be specific, to retain this knowledge for the future.

'It's a Junkers, Fräulein,' he said. 'A Junkers G-38.'

I ordered another gin, enjoying this unique sensation, flying across Europe in a Junkers G-38 with a drink and a cigarette in my hand. I was experiencing my usual simultaneously contrasting Berlin moods – sadness at leaving and excited anticipation at what the future might hold. I had printed no photographs – just contact sheets of what I'd taken at the Xanadu-Club and Franziska's show – all that was to come, with a bit of judicious dodging and burning. Greville would be pleased, I thought – I'd cabled him: 'MISSION ACCOMPLISHED'. And I had the premonition, with a little justified self-satisfaction, also, I admit, that my pictures would cause something of a stir.

5. SCANDAL!

I TURNED TO CONFRONT Greville and held up a rusty tin of mulligatawny soup that I'd found behind a pile of old brown paper bags.

'It's a greengrocer's,' I said. '*Was* a greengrocer's.'

'Then we'll call it the Green and Grocer Gallery.'

Greville paced about, thinking. He was wearing a fawn light tweed suit, cream shirt and a mustard-coloured silk tie – everything toning perfectly. I rummaged in another cupboard and found a damp box of nut rissoles and five tins of baking powder. Suddenly I had an idea. I tore a bit of peeling wallpaper off the wall, searched my handbag for my pen and, when I'd found it, I wrote the words down and showed them to Greville.

'Yes. I like it,' he said, 'somehow managing to be both exotic and sensible at the same time.'

'Grösze and Greene.'

'I like the umlaut and the "e" at the end of Greene.' He tested it out loud several times: the Grösze and Greene Gallery. Then he kissed me on the cheek. 'Clever girl. What're you going to call the show?'

'*Berlin bei Nacht.*'

'Yes, keep it German. More decadent.' Greville looked around and kicked vaguely at a mousetrap – sprung, no cheese. 'Now all we have to do is give the place a lick of paint.'

I'm proud to say that, over the next few weeks, I single-handedly painted ninety-nine per cent of the Grösze and Greene Gallery (I had a little help from Bruno Desjardins). Meanwhile,

Greville occupied himself with securing the lease, which wasn't very expensive – Soho rents were cheap – but I was insistent that the lease was in my name, not his, and this necessitated several trips to a solicitor and even obliged my mother to step in as a guarantor.

I took her to lunch after she'd signed the necessary affidavits. We went to Primavera in Old Compton Street where we ate tough veal escalopes with tinned peas. Pushing her unfinished plate aside, my mother leant back in her chair, staring at me curiously, and simultaneously inserted a cigarette into her holder. I lit her cigarette for her.

'Why do you want to open your own gallery?' she asked, sceptically. 'Surely if your photographs are any good a genuine gallery will show them.'

'My photographs are a bit . . . shocking,' I said, pouring myself a glass of Chianti from the bottle on our table.

'Well, I certainly won't be coming to see them.'

'Well, I certainly won't be sending you an invitation.'

She leant forward and I saw my face twice reflected in the lenses of her tortoiseshell spectacles.

'What's your game, Amory?'

'It's no "game", Mother. I'm just trying to establish myself. Make my way in the world.'

'When you say "shocking", do you mean—' She stopped herself. 'No, no. I don't want any more information.' She sighed, dramatically, flipping her hand as if a fly were buzzing around, bothering her. 'I don't know what's become of my children. Xan has just bought a motor bicycle – he's obsessed with it.'

'What type of motor bicycle?'

'How would I know? Why do you always want to know the precise name of everything, Amory? It's most peculiar.'

I shrugged and said, 'So – no more guinea pigs.'

'He set them all free. Into the countryside – hundreds of them. There'll be a plague of guinea pigs all over Sussex.' She looked at me intently again, puffing smoke as if to create a kind of screen between us, to make me blurry and more obscure.

'Your father asks for you all the time.'

'I sent him a photograph.'

'Made it worse. I think he still feels guilty. Why don't you go and see him again? It does cheer him up.'

'I will,' I said, as sincerely as I could manage. 'As soon as my show is done.'

The lease issues, annoyingly, took some time to sort out but, finally, eventually, I was granted temporary possession – for six months – of number 42a Brewer Street and a painted sign went up signifying the place's new incarnation: the Grösze and Greene Gallery. The exhibition was announced for the middle of January 1932 – a quiet month, we reasoned, therefore we might attract more of the press's attention.

I occupied myself with the printing of some forty of my Berlin photographs, keeping the size uniform – ten inches by six – so I could order the frames and the mounts separately: I didn't want to provide any framer with a privileged early view of my work. *Berlin bei Nacht* had to arrive in its gallery unseen and unannounced, like the explosion of a landmine, I declared.

'Or a damp squib,' Greville corrected. 'Nothing's guaranteed, darling. You never know if we'll be noticed – even in January London's full of exhibitions.'

'You can invite your society friends,' I said. 'Think of all the magazines you've worked for.'

'Good point,' Greville said. 'I'll see what riff-raff I can round up.'

It took me two hard-working weeks to print and frame all my photographs. To my eye they had a professional, artistic air with their unvarnished pale oak frames and a big expanse of cream cardboard mount – a 'museum mount' I was told such a style was called, where the mount is significantly larger than the picture being mounted. As I wrote the titles and signed my name under the photographs, it struck me, not for the first time in my life, that proper presentation was half the battle if you wanted to be taken seriously.

We had ordered plain canvas blinds for the big window that faced Brewer Street so we could be completely shut off from prying eyes. One cold evening early in the year Greville and I hung the photographs, spacing them out evenly on the stark white walls. We had torn up the old oil-cloth floor covering and had painted the floorboards with a dark wood stain. The Grösze and Greene Gallery looked remarkably authentic, we had to admit. More proper presentation.

Greville wandered along the row of photographs before we covered them all with brown paper, pausing at my picture of Volker, naked, apart from the towel hanging from his hand, covering his groin area.

'"Artist's Model",' he said, reading my title. 'My, he looks like a big fellow.'

★

THE BARRANDALE JOURNAL 1977

I let Hugo Torrance kiss me at his party in the Glenlarig Hotel. I'd been enjoying myself, chatting to Greer and Calder, reminiscing with Hugo's daughter, Sandra, about the bits of London we both knew, and I'd drunk just a little bit too much whisky.

I'd gone to the ladies' room and on emerging had found Hugo waiting for me in the half-dark of the landing on the first floor. He blocked my passage down the stairs, put his arms round me and kissed me on the lips.

'Stay the night, Amory,' he suggested and, just for a second, I was tempted – but said 'No,' quietly but firmly.

'I'll keep trying,' he said as he let me pass.

'I should hope so.'

I drove home carefully, knowing I was tipsy, and poured myself another whisky and stirred up the fire, thinking. I wondered if Hugo Torrance was the last man I would ever kiss. The thought made me sad.

★

On the evening of the opening of *Berlin bei Nacht* I decided to wear something demure, suddenly thinking that I didn't want to be noticed or to be identified as the 'photographer', the 'artist'.

'Very discreet,' Greville said, as I arrived. 'You look like you should be taking their coats.'

I was wearing a navy crepe-knit frock with a high silk cross-over collar and a swathed cap.

'I don't want to draw any attention,' I said, feeling nervous, all of a sudden. 'I just want to observe, be in the background.'

'One advantage of being called Amory, I suppose,' Greville said. 'They'll all be looking for a man.' He indicated the cardboard sign propped in the window on a small easel advertising the show and my name. *BERLIN BEI NACHT* – Photographs by Amory Clay.

'Ah.' He raised one finger. 'But what if someone wants to interview you?'

'We'll cross that bridge when we come to it.'

Greville had hired a catering company to serve glasses of hock in green-stemmed glasses – ideally Teutonic, he thought – and various canapés: cheese straws, sausage rolls, vol-au-vents. At the door there was a small stack of my thin catalogue with the prices of the photographs listed. On the invitation we'd sent out it was clear that the exhibition was being 'hosted' by Greville Reade-Hill so he made it his business to greet everyone as they arrived while I stayed at the back of the gallery pretending to look at my own photographs as if I were seeing them for the first time.

There was a good crowd, as it turned out, sixty or seventy people, we calculated, and there was a constant supply of hock so the noise-level in the gallery steadily increased, the atmosphere becoming more like that of a cocktail party than a serious *vernissage*. When everyone seemed to have arrived, Greville and I stood in one corner scrutinising our guests.

'Well they seem quite rich and bourgeois,' I said. 'The right sort of person, I suppose. Are there any journalists?'

'No one was prepared to admit to it.'

'But we need the publicity, don't we?'

'Word of mouth, darling. There's nothing better. Good God, look at that.'

I turned slightly to see a young balding man in a grey coat with a musquash collar.

'Look at the spats,' Greville said, trying not to laugh, then added, 'Insecure, wealthy, ugly, vain.'

I responded. 'Talentless, self-conscious, myopic, stupid.'

Greville had this theory that it only took four adjectives to describe absolutely anyone, anyone in the entire world. The notion had evolved into a private parlour-game that we would play at parties to while away the hours of boredom as we waited for people to come and be photographed.

'There's a good one,' I said, pointing with my chin at a stout older man peering at a picture of half-naked Berlin prostitutes. 'Overweight, rich, lecherous, hypocritical.'

'Sex-starved, boring, pompous, frightened.'

'Let's go for a wander,' I said, beginning to relax and enjoy myself. I picked up another glass of hock from a passing waiter as we strolled around the gallery trying to establish who might be a member of the press. Greville was constantly stopped by people he knew but pointedly didn't introduce me.

'People will assume you're my secretary,' he said, in an aside, as we moved on.

'Perfect. Now, look at him, I think I've seen him before . . .'

We contemplated a lanky young man with a hooked nose and long hair over the back of his collar. He was wearing a well-cut charcoal-grey suit with dull scarlet shoes and an oriental silk scarf draped loosely round his neck.

'Ah. Sir Max Gartside. I think he writes for a newspaper – sometimes.'

'Narcissistic, elegant, moneyed, pretentious,' I said.

'Shall I sound him out?'

Greville sauntered over and I watched the two of them chat for a while, laughing at some joke as Gartside pointed at one of my photographs and I thought: I hope they're not making fun of me. Greville returned, making a moue of disappointment.

'He loves them. And he does write for the *Gazette*, but he's not been assigned.'

'Loves them? Damn.'

'He wants to buy Volker but I told him Volker was mine – not for sale.'

'Isn't he even a little bit shocked?' I asked, hopefully.

'Nothing shocks our Max, I'm afraid.' He looked around. 'Now, here's an interesting candidate.'

I turned to see a smart-looking slim man coming into the gallery and picking up a catalogue. He was wearing a tawny cashmere coat that was almost the colour of his hair. Wet sand, I thought, or sandstone – not blond, not brown. His hair was thick and was swept back from his forehead. I could see the fine grooves set in its oiled density from the teeth of his comb. A big nose, very straight, light blue eyes, I saw as he passed near us. I felt that shiver go through me, that split-second weakening of the spinal column.

'Bland, rich, bored, arrogant,' Greville said out of the side of his mouth.

'Handsome, assured, clever, foreign.'

'Listen to you, Miss Smitten. He's a journalist, I bet you. I have a sixth sense.'

I watched the man – he was in his thirties, I guessed – move carefully along the line of photographs, peering at them, then checking the reference in the catalogue. He looked more like a dealer or a collector, I thought, as I saw him really studying some of the photographs, stepping back and moving in again. At one stage he put on a pair of spectacles, rimless, and moved very close to a photo as if looking for signs of retouching or verifying the grain of the paper. French, I thought, or Middle European: a Hungarian aristocrat, an Esterházy or a Cseszneky – certainly not English.

Greville tapped me on the shoulder. 'I think that might be the *Daily Express*.'

Another thin man, middle-aged, was moving quickly round the room, bald, with a prominent Adam's apple held in the cleft of his wing collar like a bud between two sepals.

'Humourless, religiose, hate-filled, necrophiliac.'

'Sexless, ulcerated, embittered, dying.'

We helped ourselves to two more glasses of hock and toasted each other.

'I suppose I should be careful about what I'm wishing for,' I said, 'But I wouldn't mind just a little furore.'

'We just want your name mentioned in the newspapers. Perhaps even a photograph or two in some magazine. That's not much to ask.' Greville looked round the room again. 'I thought your German girlfriend was coming.'

'She is, but she couldn't make the opening night.'

'Longing to meet her.'

He wandered off and I went into the back room to chase up the final trays of canapés, feeling a sudden exhaustion overcome me and with it a new apprehension about our great schemes for notoriety. I sat down on a wooden chair and gulped at my hock. It was my work, after all, I was the only begetter and I would be in the line of fire, not Greville. I smoked a cigarette trying not to think further and heard the chatter of conversation diminish as the guests drifted off into the Soho night. I told myself to buck up, stood, stubbed out my cigarette, smoothed the skirt of my sensible frock and headed back into the gallery. There were about half a dozen people left, still chatting to each other, enjoying the occasion. Greville and Bruno Desjardins were saying goodbye to departing invitees. Someone cleared his throat close behind me and I turned. It was my Hungarian aristocrat.

'Congratulations,' he said. 'These are very interesting photographs.'

American, I realised, a little disappointed, for some reason.

'How do you know I'm the photographer?'

'I have my ways and means, Miss Clay. I needed to find out, so I did.' He smiled, one of those strange broad smiles where the teeth don't show. He was holding his hand out to shake mine. His grip was light, just a formality, a clench of fingers.

'I'm Cleveland Finzi.'

'Well, you know who I am.'

'I'd like to buy you a drink, if I may.'

'I'm terribly busy—'

'Oh, not now. I'm in London for a couple of weeks. Do you have a telephone?'

'What? Yes.'

'May I call you?'

I went off in a state of silly confusion to find my handbag where I'd left it in the back room. I searched – no cards. Idiot! I scribbled my number down on a sheet of paper torn from my unfilled appointments diary of 1931 and brought it back to him. Very impressive. He tucked the scrap of paper away in an inside pocket and handed me his card. I glanced at it: CLEVELAND FINZI. *GLOBAL-PHOTO-WATCH.*

'Oh. You're a journalist.'

'Was. I'm an editor, now.' He smiled politely. 'It's a magazine in America. You may have heard of it.'

I hadn't, but said, as one does, 'Yes, now you come to mention it. Definitely.'

'I'll call you in a couple of days,' he said. 'I'll look forward to talking to you.'

'I'll look forward to talking to you,' I repeated like a simpleton.

I manned the admissions desk at the Grösze and Greene Gallery for the next three days. It was never busy, I'm sorry to say. Greville had decided, prudently, to impose an admission charge of one shilling, a sum that made you a member of the Grösze and Greene Photographic Club for twenty-four hours. It was a pre-emptive attempt to evade any prosecution for obscenity – he'd become worried about the graphic nature of some of the photographs – as the exhibition would open only to 'club members' not the general public. I happily went along with the ploy, having no idea of whether it would work or not. Its manifest disadvantage was that it put off passers-by from dropping in out of curiosity or on the off-chance. During the three days I was there our takings only broke £1 once. One day we took in a meagre five shillings.

I sat there surrounded by my Berlin photographs feeling I was in a kind of limbo. I should have been exhilarated – this was my first exhibition as an independent photographer and in London's West End, no less – but I found my mind turning again and again to the enigmatic Cleveland Finzi of *Global-Photo-Watch* and his invitation. Was he being sincere or simply polite?

On the third day I was sitting at the desk in my squirrel coat – the weather had turned freezing – and the gallery had been empty for a good hour, when I heard the telephone ring in what had been the back storeroom. I ran for it, knowing somehow that it was Cleveland Finzi at last.

'Oh. Hello, Greville,' I said, unable to keep the disappointment out of my voice.

'You've a very good review in the *Scotsman*.'

'Have I?'

He quoted. 'Listen: "Miss Clay has a horror of 'cliché' and so has searched Berlin for examples of real lives. She has eschewed the commonplace and sees things entirely for herself with great clarity and honesty." Isn't that wonderful?'

'I suppose I should be pleased,' I said. 'My first review.'

'We might get a few more newspapers, now,' he said. 'I'll see if I can circulate this.'

I put the phone down and it rang again immediately.

'What is it, Greville?'

'Miss Clay? This is Cleveland Finzi.'

'Yes.'

'Hello? Are you there?'

'Yes, it's me. Miss Clay.'

'I tried your apartment but there was no reply. Luckily I thought I might find you at the gallery.'

'Luckily, yes.'

'I'd like to invite you for a cocktail. I'm staying at the Earlham, on the Strand. How does six o'clock suit you this evening?'

'Yes, yes. It suits.' I seemed to have lost the ability to speak sophisticated English.

'I'll see you in the Palm Court at six.'

I managed to persuade Bruno to stand in for me after lunch and went to a hairdresser's in Charing Cross Road to have my hair washed and set. I decided that I didn't have time to go back to Fulham and change but I could at least look entirely different from the anonymous creature Finzi had encountered at the *vernissage*. Out of my swathed cap, with my hair down and shiny and some slightly extravagant make-up, plus my squirrel coat . . . If I kept my coat on I might pass for reasonably glamorous, I thought.

I was walking down Charing Cross Road towards Trafalgar Square, feeling good, a silk scarf protecting my new hair-do, when I passed the entrance to the Bardmont Concert Hall. I don't know why I stopped, perhaps because I was early for my six o'clock appointment, but I did and idly scanned the poster for that evening's concert. I read: 'The New London Symphony Orchestra. Soloist Miss Dido Clay.'

Dido Clay?

I looked again at the programme: Chopin, Debussy and a symphonic tone poem, 'Aeneas in Carthage', by Peregrine Moxon. Dido Clay had to be my sister, Peggy.

The new name worked. I'm here to meet my sister Miss
Dido Clay, I said, and I was led by a uniformed porter through
the passageways to the rehearsal rooms at the rear, hearing, as I
approached, piano music in an atonal modern style that I didn't
recognise.

The door was held open for me and there was Peggy at the piano,
head down, pounding out some crescendo, eyes closed, a cigarette
dangling from her lips. Bash! A final dissonant chord. She slowly
lifted her hands from the keys, leaning back, cigarette vertical.

'Peggy?'

She turned abruptly, saw me, gave a little squeal of pleasure,
removed her cigarette from her lips and raced over to me. She
kissed me.

'Never, ever, call me Peggy again,' she whispered sharply.

'Sorry. Dido.'

'I'm Dido, now. Forever.'

'Dido, Dido, Dido.'

Her hair was pulled back from her face in a tight bun making
her look stern, worldly. I felt that strange sensation again that she
was older than me, though she was just seventeen, I realised. Then
she hugged me tightly again, my little sister.

'Darling Amory! You look ravishing. What're you doing? Off to
some party?'

'I'm going to meet a man. An American.'

'Too exciting! Is he rich?'

'Possibly. But I'm late, I must dash. I saw your name on the
poster outside and had to check it was you.' I smiled. 'Dido,
dearest.'

'I'll tell you everything. It was Peregrine's idea. I'll telephone
you – I've a concert and two recitals this week.' She smiled
mischievously and I saw the old Peggy for a second or two. 'I can't
wait to hear all about your American lover.'

We kissed goodbye and I walked back out to the street feeling
the beginnings of a headache. I pushed all thoughts of Peggy/Dido

to one side and turned up the Strand, heading for the Earlham Hotel. At reception I told the clerk I was meeting Mr Finzi in the Palm Court and was led along a corridor towards the sound of a harp and piano and on into the wide over-furnished room, filled with tight groupings of chairs and sofas, its famous huge chandelier glowing brightly. My throat was a little dry and I suspected my pulse was beating faster than normal but I told myself, resolutely, to anticipate nothing.

Finzi saw me enter and stood and waved. He was wearing a dark charcoal suit, very well cut, and his Americanness was advertised only by a strange silver device that shaped his collar round the knot of his tie. And he also wore a tiepin.

'I assume you're not interested in a cup of tea,' he said.

'I'll have a brandy and soda, thank you.'

He ordered our drinks from a waiter – he had a Scotch and water – and we began to talk at once about the exhibition. He was full of praise and as he talked I rather marvelled at the astonishing calm self-assurance he exhibited. In fact he was so self-assured I began to wonder if it was an act. I've known certain people where the most adamantine confidence is just a mask for terrified insecurity but I quickly realised there was nothing bogus about Cleveland Finzi. I thought that perhaps it was his American accent that contributed to the overall *savoir faire*, so—

'You're not listening to me, Miss Clay,' he said, reasonably.

'Yes, I am.'

'I just asked you a question.'

'And I answered it.'

'No, you didn't.'

I sipped at my brandy, playing for time.

'I'm so sorry if I seem distracted but I've just had a perplexing meeting with my sister. She's changed her name.'

'I can see how that might throw you.'

'She's always been Peggy but now she insists on being called Dido.'

He thought about this. 'Dido . . . I prefer it to Peggy. Nice name, Dido.'

'Talking of names,' I said, 'is your family Italian?'

'I'm sorry?'

'Finzi.'

'Oh. Finzi is a Jewish name,' he said.

'Is it?'

'Sephardi Jewish name. I think we were from Italy, originally. Then originally from Spain, of course.'

'Of course, yes . . . How interesting.'

He carried on asking me precise questions about my photographs – how had I managed to gain access to these places in Berlin? Had I been obliged to pay money to take the photographs? Were they posed or candid? – and so on. He was very impressed with my secret handbag-camera when I explained it to him and when he asked me about printing I was glad to be able to throw in a few authoritative remarks about dodging and burning.

We ordered a second round of drinks and smoked a cigarette. I think I managed to stay relatively composed as we talked and tried not to stare at him too intently. However, had Cleveland Finzi invited me up to his room to dance naked round his bed I would have said yes in a second.

He walked me back through to the lobby, apologising for cutting our conversation short as he had another appointment. We shook hands at the main entrance. He wasn't a tall man – taller than me, of course – but there was something spry and limber about him, as if the body beneath the smart tailoring was muscled, fit.

'What happens next, Miss Clay?'

'What? Sorry, what do you mean?'

'Your work. Your photographs.'

'Oh. I'm not thinking beyond the exhibition,' I said, then lied. 'I've already had some intriguing job offers.'

'I'm not surprised,' he said, smiling. 'Your photographs are very . . . intriguing. You have a real eye for capturing people. Please do let me know if you ever come to New York. I can promise you an excellent dinner.'

Out on the Strand the night had turned wet and squally with sharp bursts of rain stinging like hail. The street lamps shone with a watery nimbus as I made my way to the Underground in something of a brandy-and-soda daze.

6. The Wages of Sin

THE TELEPHONE RINGING IN my sitting room woke me at seven. I stumbled through in my nightdress and snatched it up.

'It's happened,' Greville said. 'The *Daily Express*. I think we might be in a spot of trouble.'

I quickly pulled on some clothes, grabbed my coat, jammed a hat on my head and ran to the newsagent at Walham Green Tube station and bought a copy of the *Daily Express*. There was a tea room near the entrance of the Underground so I went in, ordered a pot of tea and a currant bun (lightly toasted) and, slowly collecting myself, sipping and munching, began to leaf carefully through the newspaper. I found the article on page 11. The headline ran: 'A Vile and Obscene Display of Photographs'. The secondary headline below it was: 'Outrageous exhibitionism masquerading as art'. I read on in a curious numbed way as if I were reading about a war in a distant country. 'Miss Clay dips her camera in the most putrid and decadent slime she could find ... Leering men consort with barely clothed women ... It is hard to imagine visions of a more bestial and degrading nature.' My numbness deepened. However, it became clear to me as I read of my utter viciousness that what had really offended this man – the man with the prominent Adam's apple – or, more to the point, excited him, were the photos of half-naked women unconcerned to be in the presence of other half-naked women. He went on and on about it and yet there were only three photographs in the entire exhibition that showed this juxtaposition. Not a word of

Volker and his candid nudity or the girls fooling around in bed or sunbathing on the balcony in their underwear. There was a shrillness in his condemnation that in its near-hysteria was too revealing – as if, having mounted this exhibition, I should be stoned to death or taken to the ducking stool and be tried as a witch. 'This repulsive display of photographs in the heart of our great city, in the heart of our great empire, is an affront to every God-loving, decent-thinking British citizen.'

I sipped at my cooling tea, coming out of my daze, feeling a corresponding new chill beginning to overwhelm me, as I realised what trouble I might be in. I had my notoriety now, all right.

Back in my flat I telephoned Greville – no reply. I telephoned the gallery. He answered with a discernible tremor in his voice, keeping it low as if he might be overheard.

'The police are here. The photographs have all been seized. They're being taken away in a van—'

'Seized? Taken away?'

'And there are three hundred people queuing to get in.'

'Should I come?'

'You might as well. But there's nothing we can do.'

He sounded frightened – and that wasn't like the Greville I knew. I took a taxi to Brewer Street and when I arrived I found the queue of photography-lovers had dispersed and there was a solitary, smiling police constable standing on guard outside the gallery. Greville opened the door to me and, as I stepped in, I experienced a visceral shock – seeing the walls now rudely bare.

'Where have they been taken to?' I asked, beginning to understand Greville's untypical fear. The 'authorities', the guardians of public decency, the state, having been affronted, had acted, and had had their decree fulfilled.

'Savile Row police station.'

'What next?'

'The unpleasant-looking but perfectly civil police inspector informed me that the gallery is going to be prosecuted for obscenity.'

'The gallery? You mean me.'

'Well, you are the leaseholder, darling.'

In a new and more unpleasant form of daze I wandered back into the rear room and made us both a cup of strong tea. When you've got a problem to solve always do something practical, my mother used to say. Suddenly I was seeing the sense in the bland adage. We sipped our tea and discussed our predicament.

'I thought that because we were a club we were more or less safe,' I said.

'So did I,' Greville said. 'Or so I'd been advised.' He lit a cigarette. 'The problem was, it seems, that the photos were for sale. If they hadn't been for sale we might have been fine. Possibly. But now they can prosecute you for exhibiting obscene pictures for "sale or gain". That's the issue.'

I felt my fear mounting – and I wasn't being helped by the evident funk that Greville was in. I'd never seen him so abjectly insecure and jittery.

'What do I do now?' I asked, feebly.

'I think you should find yourself a lawyer.'

The lawyer I found – a solicitor – was the brother of my best friend at school, Millicent Lowther. Millicent's eldest brother, Arthur – in his early thirties, I calculated – was more than happy to take up my case, so he said when we met at his offices in Chancery Lane. He was a gaunt, solemn young man, almost bald. I thought he might have been quite attractive if only he'd allow himself to smile, now and then. Although he was very thin his features were even and his eyes were kind. But he had armoured himself in this persona, all serious intent and rigid efficiency.

'Yes, they're sticking with the obscenity charge, I'm afraid,' he said. 'As the leaseholder of the gallery, you're to appear at Bow Street Magistrates' Court on Tuesday week.'

'What do you advise?' I asked, weakly. Following the assault by the *Daily Express* there had been other pieces written by journalists quick to condemn me even though they had never seen the exhibition, so swiftly had the pictures been confiscated. It didn't matter — the epithets mounted: depraved, sordid, shameful, mentally unbalanced, scandalous, degenerate, vile, disgusting, and so on, were the words whirling around my name. Easy defamations produced by total strangers — it was a perfect vilification.

Arthur Lowther asked if I minded if he smoked his pipe. I had no objection, I said, and lit a cigarette to keep him company. A good two minutes later he managed to produce a thin curl of smoke from his small briar. It made him look foolish rather than grown-up but I knew he was doing it for my benefit, to add weight to his deliberations.

'I suggest you plead guilty,' he said.

'No! Categorically, no!'

He closed his eyes. Waited. Opened them again. They were a nice shade of greyish-brown.

'In that case, we could try and present a defence showing that the photographs were works of art.'

'Yes, good idea.'

'But we would need eminent people to vouch for them. In that light.' He took out a penknife device from his waistcoat pocket and tamped the glowing tobacco in the bowl of his pipe. It seemed to go out at this point. He put it down, irritated. He looked back at me.

'Do you know any famous artists? Politicians, people of standing in society?'

'Ah . . . No.'

'Then plead guilty, Miss Clay. Pay the fine. Promise never to exhibit these photographs again in England.'

'What'll happen to my photographs?'

'They'll be destroyed.'

'But that's so unfair, Mr Lowther!'

'Do call me Arthur. Millicent talked about you all the time. I feel I've known you for years.'

'It's so unfair, Arthur...These are photographs of...of documentary evidence.This is how people live – in Berlin. All I've done is show the world the truth about people's lives.'

'I believe you, Amory – if I may,' he said with manifest sincerity. 'But you managed to cause mighty offence to the *Daily Express*, which is why we're in this stew.You'll save much time and money – not to mention stress and strain – if you do what I suggest.' He went on to outline the case he'd make to the magistrate: my youth, my zeal, the fact that the gallery was a club – all this would help when it came to the fine – that would be somewhere between £20 and £50, he estimated.

I sat there thinking about the options ahead of me and realised that there was nothing I could do, realistically. The Grösze and Greene adventure was over.

On Tuesday week I sat behind Arthur Lowther in the Bow Street Magistrates' Court as he informed the magistrate, Sir Pellman Dulverton, that his client, Miss Amory Clay, wished to plead guilty to the charge of obscenity and apologised unreservedly to the court. I was fined £30 and ordered never to show my 'disgusting images' to the British public ever again. Sir Pellman Dulverton – a pale, impassive, bespectacled man with a small bristling moustache – called me a foolish and misguided young woman and he hoped I had learned a valuable lesson. I kept my head down and nodded – demure, chastened.

Arthur Lowther and I stood outside the court on Bow Street and each smoked a cigarette – no pipe, I was glad to see.

'It seems like an awful defeat, I know,' Arthur said, 'but in a week you'll have practically forgotten about it and in a month it'll have vanished from your life entirely.You don't want something like this dragging on forever, casting a cloud over every waking moment of your existence.'

'You're absolutely right,' I said. 'I just have to think of it that way, I suppose. Try not to be bitter.' I was looking around for Greville, who had promised to come and lend moral support, but there was no sign of him.

'Might I ask you to dinner one evening, Amory?' Arthur Lowther asked, a blush rougeing his sunken cheeks. 'We can commiserate and celebrate. And I'd like to get to know you better. Not have to talk about "obscenity" all the time.' He managed one of his rare transforming smiles.

I said, yes, by all means, not having a ready excuse available, and gave him my card. I was grateful to him, after all, and his fee had been surprisingly modest. I was going to have to borrow more money from Greville to pay my fine. Arthur hailed a passing cab.

'Heading back to the office. Can I drop you anywhere?'

I said no thanks, I had an appointment, so we shook hands and I strode off to the Underground. I had suddenly realised, now my photographs had been destroyed by the court, that I had to make sure my negatives were safe.

I found Greville in the Falkland Court mews darkroom with Bruno, both wearing white coats over their suits as they were about to start developing. Greville apologised for missing the court case – some earl's daughter had announced her engagement and wanted her photograph taken immediately.

'Doesn't matter,' I said. 'You didn't miss anything – it was all over in minutes. I just want to pick up my negatives.'

'What negatives?'

'Of my Berlin photographs.'

'Bruno, dear, could you just pop back to the flat and fetch my briefcase?'

When Bruno left on his errand, Greville turned to me and I could see instantly that his fretful, twitchy mood had returned in full force.

'Darling,' he said. 'The negatives were seized. I told you.'

'Seized? No you didn't tell me anything about that.'

'I'm sure I did. That evening after the gallery was closed. I'm convinced I told you. That same police inspector who raided the gallery called round and demanded them.'

I felt a kind of draining inside me, as if my blood was being sucked out of my body.

'But, Greville, why did you tell him you had them? You could have – I don't know – made up any old story. You could have said I had them.'

'Very easy for you to say, Amory, dear one. But you weren't standing facing an inspector and two ghastly enormous police constables in your own drawing room.' He took off his white coat and threw it in a corner. 'They said they were going to search everywhere. Most aggressive.'

I looked at Greville as he fished in his pockets for a cigarette and felt a sudden heaviness of heart. The old expression was absolutely correct – I felt as if my heart suddenly hung heavier in its cavity in my chest, and I knew that something had ended between the two of us and I suspected that we were both instantly aware of the fact. Nothing would be the same ever again. I exhaled.

'So, they took the negatives as well,' I said, soberly, upset.

'What could I do? I had to give them something. They'd have turned the place upside down.' He closed his eyes and smoothed his smooth hair down and said, still with his eyes closed, 'There's only so much scandal a career can take, Amory. I'm associated with you. I can't let it go on. People will—'

'It's all right,' I interrupted, flatly. 'I understand.'

'I did keep the contact sheets. At least there's a record of sorts.'

He felt guilty, I knew, as he looked them out and handed them to me in a stiff-backed brown envelope. Then he wrote me out a cheque for the fine – he insisted. I was still in his debt, however angry and frustrated I was.

'Well, it sort of worked,' he said with an apologetic half-smile. 'At least everyone knows your name, now.'

'Oh, yes. The vile, depraved, immoral Amory Clay . . . It was your idea, Greville, not mine,' I added, a little petulantly, I admit.

'Well, the best-laid schemes o' mice an' men gang aft agley, as the poet said. Could have worked a treat.'

Then Bruno returned with Greville's briefcase and so I made my farewells. We kissed at the door and Greville mentioned that there was some grand ball coming up in Yorkshire that he'd need extra help for, if I were interested. He'd telephone with the details – might be amusing. Lively crowd. It was a gesture, a pretence that life would continue as it had before, but we both knew, I think, that the old feeling, the old camaraderie, had gone. I made the mistake, as I walked away down the mews, of turning and waving goodbye with the envelope containing my contact sheets – the only extant record of *Berlin bei Nacht* in the world. I'm sure he thought it was my parting shot.

Three nights later at a dull restaurant in Kensington (the Huntsman's Halt), over brandies and coffee, Arthur Lowther took my hand and asked me, a catch in his voice, to become his wife. After I had succeeded in masking my total shock I said no, as politely as I was able to manage: no I'm afraid it wouldn't be possible, I'm terribly sorry, no, and left as swiftly as I could.

Back in my flat in Fulham I sat staring at the three contact sheets of my Berlin photographs, my mind veering erratically between the first proposal of marriage I'd received and the technical problems arising from the use of a rostrum camera with sufficient magnification to take a good photograph of a tiny ungraded photograph, when the telephone rang. I had an awful feeling it would be Arthur encouraging me to take my time, not to rush to a decision. Bracing myself, I picked up the receiver.

'Oh. Hello, Mr Finzi.'

'I read about your trial in *The Times*. Commiserations.'

'Thank you. But it was hardly a trial. I pleaded guilty.'

'That was the right thing to do. But, you know, I think you should look on it as a sign.'

'A sign of what?' I reached for a box of cigarettes, opened it, selected one of the two cigarettes remaining and lit it. I was enjoying hearing Cleveland Finzi's calm American accent – he sounded even more sure of himself, if such a thing were possible.

'A sign of my stupidity?' I asked, exhaling.

'It's a sign that you had done something significant. Your photographs shocked people. They had an effect. How often can any photographer say that in today's modern world?'

'I'll try to console myself with that thought.'

'What're you going to do now, Miss Clay?'

'You mean before I commit suicide?'

'There's no hurry. You can do that any time. Ever been to New York?'

'No.'

'Would you like to go?'

'One day, perhaps. Yes.'

'Before you commit suicide.'

'Obviously. Ha-ha.'

There was a silence, then he said: 'What if I offer you a job? Would that lure you over?'

I felt that heart-lurch, throat-closure. I drew deep on my cigarette.

'Well . . . Maybe,' I said, carefully, sensing implications, expectations – a future – suddenly crowding round me.

'Two hundred a month. What do you say?'

'Two hundred what?'

'Dollars.'

Images from Berlin bei Nacht (now lost). Girls from the Xanadu-Club, Berlin, 1931.

THE BARRANDALE JOURNAL 1977

Today is Xan's birthday. He would have been sixty-one. Poor Xan.
I searched for his book of poems and found it and read the poem
he'd dedicated to me. It made me cry and I hate crying, now.

The Anti-cliché (for Amory)

We were
tropical
opposites,
Capricorn and
Cancer,
diametrically aligned.
But
life is a
vertiginous
elevated railroad.
Timor mortis
has us both
in its
pincer-like
grip.
We cling on
for dear
existence,
fearful of the
undignified isolation
of death,
the long
hello.

BOOK THREE: 1932–1934

1. AMERICANA

I JANUARY 1934. I woke very early, for some reason, as if I wanted to kick-start the beginning of this particular year, set it off and running with due energy as soon as possible. I slipped out of bed and dressed. The morning light was dull and tarnished – that hint of jaundice in the air that presages snow. I pulled on my heavy tweed coat and stepped out. My apartment – ground floor at the rear – was on Washington Square South in Greenwich Village. Consisting of a long corridor that linked sitting room, kitchen, bathroom and bedroom, the place was dark, apart from the bedroom that overlooked a small yard containing a tall slim ailanthus tree – all for $15 a month.

I headed over to '365' on West 8th Street to buy cigarettes. '365' was not the number of the store's address but a signal that it opened every day, even on New Year's Day. When I arrived there, Achilles, the owner, was sliding back the concertina grille on the street door. Across the road a Chinese boy was sweeping the steps of a chop-suey house. The Village was stirring, the year was under way.

Achilles was a stocky, bow-legged man with a permanent white corpse-stubble on his chin and jaw.

'A happy new year, Miss Amory,' he said, leading me into the store, effectively a wide long corridor off the street, shelved on both sides with a counter at the end. Flypaper spiralled from the moulded tin ceiling. There was a sign above the counter that said 'We sell everything apart from liquor'.

I asked for a pack of Pall Malls for me – a little gesture to London in New York – and a pack of Camels for Cleveland.

As I was Achilles' first customer of 1934 I decided to be a good augury and bought some more items at random: a box of Rinso, some Wheat Krumbles and a bag of cinnamon buns.

'And I'll take some Alka-Seltzer,' I said.

'Partying last night?'

'No, no. Early to bed. I've got a friend coming round for some lunch.'

'A friend who smokes Camels, I'm guessing. A true hostess. I know you likes the Pall Malls, Miss Amory.'

We chatted on. I took strange pleasure in being known in my neighbourhood, as if I was settled here for a while, as if it gave my life a semblance of normality – that being here in this city was something I had planned, not simply something that had happened to me.

'Let's hope '34 is better than '33,' Achilles said, as he bagged my groceries.

'At least you can have a drink without getting arrested,' I said. We laughed. In the last three weeks six liquor stores had opened within a two-block radius of Washington Square. America's drinking was out in the open again.

'Yeah, ain't that something new,' Achilles said, nodding, 'though I have to say I kinda miss the speakeasies.'

I wandered home with my groceries and sat in my apartment with the wireless on, listening to jazz, reading a book – *God's Little Acre* by Erskine Caldwell – while I waited. I had painted the walls in the sitting room a pale ivory to maximise the light that came in through the small solitary window. I had hung some of my photographs here and there and had smartened up the rented sofa and two armchairs with quilted throws I'd bought in a junk shop on Bleeker. The tiled corridor led on past the tiny kitchen and bathroom to the back bedroom that gave on to the yard with its stark spindly tree. The room had a big, twelve-paned sash window and at midday in the summer when the sun shone directly down it was so blazingly luminous you felt you were in the tropics, not Manhattan.

Cleve was running late, clearly, so at 1.30 I made myself a gin and Italian and toasted in the new year, recognising as I did so that I'd been in New York for nearly eighteen months, now – though I still felt a transient, passing through, and that this apartment, this address, my job and my salary were very temporary aspects of my autobiography and whatever significance this sojourn would have in any retrospective view was impossible to discern. Why was I thinking in this mean-spirited, uncharitable way, I asked myself? I was so much better off here than in London, in every sense: solvent, housed, gainfully employed, my notoriety unheard-of. But I was unsettled in some way, I knew, and I knew it was all to do with the love affair—

On cue Cleveland Finzi pressed the buzzer at the main door and I let him in.

We kissed, gently, held each other and wished ourselves a happy 1934.

'Do you want to eat?' I asked. 'Or . . . ?'

'I'd like some "or", please.'

I smiled, turned and walked through to the bedroom, unbuttoning my blouse, hearing the metalled half-moons on the heels of Cleve's loafers clicking sharply, confidently, on the terracotta tiles of the corridor behind me.

★

THE BARRANDALE JOURNAL 1977

I drove to Glasgow yesterday to see my doctor, Jock Edie. I was up early as my Hillman Imp took a good three hours to make the journey south. Dr Edie's consulting rooms are on the ground floor of his vast grimy sandstone house on Great Western Road, a renaissance-style villa that would please a pontiff with its own campanile and two-acre garden.

Jock Edie is a large, portly man in his sixties who won three international rugby caps for Scotland when he was a medical student before a spinal injury ended his playing career. Something in the scrum, I'm told – I know nothing more: I loathe rugby. He has magnificent dense untrimmed eyebrows, like greying mini-moustaches lowering above his moist brown eyes. I'm very fond of him and I know he's fond of me – but we both take special care not to demonstrate this by adopting an amiable but clipped no-nonsense manner with each other.

'How're you keeping, lassie?'

'Very good. Very fit.'

'Nothing new to worry us?'

'Absolutely not.'

He opened a drawer in his desk with a key and took out a paper bag with multicoloured balloons printed on it and handed it over.

'These are for you. They're not sweeties.'

'Thank you, Jock. Much obliged.'

'Keep them in an airtight jar or tin, just to be on the safe side. Or in the refrigerator, even better.'

'Aye aye, sir.'

He picked up a book from a side table and I saw that it was called *Marching on Germany* by one Brigadier Muir McCarty.

'There's a fair bit about Sholto in here,' he said, flicking through the pages.

'I don't want to read about Sholto.' Jock and Sholto had known each other as schoolboys.

'All very complimentary,' he said.

'People were always complimentary about Sholto.'

He walked me through the wide hall towards a door glowing with painted glass – St Michael slaying a writhing dragon. Jock hung his good paintings in the hall and there was a small immaculate Cadell by the mirrored coat and hatstand that I always paused by. A meal-white Hebridean beach in sunshine, blue-silvered islands beyond.

'Maybe I'll drive out to Barrandale and see you,' he said, adjusting the painting's hang by a micro-inch. 'I miss the islands.'

'*Mi casa es su casa.*'

'*Gracias, señora.* Heading back?'

'I've a lunch appointment in town.'

'Are you still smoking?' Jock asked. 'By the by.'

'Yes. Are you?'

'I am. Probably the only doctor in the West of Scotland who does.'

'Should I stop? Try to stop?'

'Perhaps. No. Stop when I stop.'

'That's not fair.'

'True.'

We kissed goodbye. I left the car in his wide driveway and caught a bus into the city. I stepped off it at Queen Street and walked past a strange-looking pub called the Muscular Arms as I headed for Rogano's on Royal Exchange Square.

The bar was busy. I eased through noisy young men in dark suits swigging gin and tonics – Glasgow lawyers and businessmen – and turned right into the restaurant, into its pale-walled art-deco splendour, an area altogether more hushed, with a soothing susurrus of muttered conversations and the chime of silverware on crockery.

'Good afternoon, I'm meeting Madame Pontecorvo,' I said to the maître d'.

Dido was sitting at a corner in the back reading a newspaper and smoking a cigarette. She was growing plump, much plumper than when I'd last seen her. Her mass of ink-black hair was swept back from her forehead and coiffed into a great smooth shellacked wave, like some dark calabash settled above her brow. Her dress was silk, a shining tea-rose pink, and she had three ropes of pearls round her soft creased neck. She was giving a recital that evening at the City Halls, still making lots of money.

We kissed and she ordered champagne.

'I like your hair short like that,' she said. 'Very modern.'

'Thank you, darling.' I opened the menu.

'Mind you, you do look a bit like a lesbian, though. And you should wear more make-up.'

135

'It's convenient. Practical,' I said. 'And anyway I don't really care how I look to other people, these days.'

'No! I won't hear that. That's fatal. Don't neglect yourself, Amory – it's a slippery slope.' She drew on her cigarette, studying me, checking out my clothes, my fingernails.

'Talking of lesbians . . .' she said, her old wicked smile flashing.

'Yes?'

'Have you ever been with one?'

'I've been kissed by one but that's as far as I went.'

'No! Really?' She was interested, now. 'She must have thought you'd respond. Sensed something in you, you know, a fellow sister, as it were. When did this happen?'

'Berlin, before the war.'

'I remember. All your filthy pictures.'

'Maybe we've all got a bit of lesbian in us.'

'Not me, darling.' She sipped at her champagne. 'I'm a hundred and ten per cent hetero.' She tilted her head, thinking, and lowered her voice, leaning forward. 'Now we're talking about sex – the other night, when I couldn't sleep, I started counting all the men I'd known.'

'Known?'

'In the biblical sense, I mean. All the men I'd had a fling with, including husbands. Do you know how many I came up with? What the total was? Guess.'

'A couple of dozen?'

'Fifty-three.'

I looked at my little sister. There was no answer to that.

'I'll start with the whitebait,' I said. 'Then the turbot.'

That evening, back at the cottage, I took Flam down to the small bay and sat on a rock, smoking a cigarette as he ran around the beach sniffing at stranded jellyfish and chasing gulls, and I looked out at the scatter of rocky islets in the bay and the Atlantic beyond. Fifty-three men, I thought to myself. My God. I counted up the men I had 'known', in the biblical sense. One, two, three, four, five. The fingers of one hand. Dido would have been very underwhelmed.

Flam ran up to me and I grabbed his muzzle and gave his head a shake, setting his tail beating.

'Silly old dog,' I said out loud and stood and stretched. I felt well, as I always did after a visit to Jock Edie. Surely there was nothing wrong with me – just age, time passing, the body winding down, creaking and groaning a bit . . . I watched the evening sunlight drain into silty orange out on the horizon to the west as the night gathered. Next stop America, I thought. New day dawning there.

I wandered homewards thinking back to Cleveland Finzi and how excited I'd been by his job offer, completely unexpected. New York City; $200 a month; $2,400 a year – almost £500. I'd said yes, virtually instantly, without further thought. However, it took me much longer to sort out the necessary documentation and settle my affairs as I wound down my London life. But in the early autumn of 1932 I booked passage on the SS *Arandora Star* leaving Liverpool, bound for Halifax, Nova Scotia, and New York.

Initially, I stayed in a 'Women Only' hotel on 3rd Avenue and 66th Street until I'd settled into my job and come to terms with this extraordinary new city I found myself in. I was a rookie staff photographer of *Global-Photo-Watch* and I took photographs of anything that the picture editor, Phil Adler, told me to. *Global-Photo-Watch* was one of those heavily illustrated monthly magazines that began to proliferate then: *Life, Click, Look, Pic, Photoplay* and many more. *GPW*, as everyone called it, accentuated its internationalism. 'Our Watch on the World!' was its stentorious slogan.

From time to time, in the course of working in the East 44th Street offices, I'd bump into Cleveland Finzi – or Cleve, as he was familiarly known – and we'd exchange a few words. He was pleased to see me, had I found a place to stay? Was the work interesting enough? We would chat and separate and I would wonder how long it would take him, when and how.

One evening three months after I'd arrived he was waiting in the marbled lobby as I left a meeting. He had promised me a dinner when I came to New York, hadn't he? Was I free tonight, by any chance?

★

Cleve stood naked at the window looking out at the yard through a thin gap in the muslin curtains.

'What kind of tree is that?' he asked without looking round. 'I see them everywhere in the Village.'

'It's an ailanthus. Commonly called "tree of heaven".' I liked this rear view of Cleve: the V of his torso, the deep cleft in his small buttocks, his long thighs. 'If you stand there much longer, however, Mrs Cisneros will have a heart attack.' Mrs Cisneros lived across the yard, a widow. I sat up in bed, letting the sheet fall from my breasts and reached for my pack of Pall Malls on the bedside table.

Cleve turned and I saw that his penis was thickening, springy. His penis was smaller than Lockwood's, though thicker and more heavy-headed; the glans seemed distinctly bigger (no foreskin, of course) – clearly shaped. It was like a medieval soldier's helmet, called a sallet – I once told him, to his surprise – worn most commonly by archers. He was always puzzled by my pieces of arcane knowledge, my need to know the exact names of things. It seemed vaguely to annoy him, in the same way as it had my mother. He leant back against the window frame, and crossed his arms.

'How do you know about that? About the goddam tree?'

'I told you, I like to know the names of things. I don't just want it to be some anonymous "tree" in my backyard. I want to know what it's called. Someone took the trouble to differentiate, name and classify that tree. A "tree" doesn't do it justice.' I lit my cigarette. Cleve was enjoying standing there, looking at me, listening to me, candidly displaying his potency. I crossed my legs under the sheet

138

and rested my elbows on my knees, inclining my back so that my breasts hung forward, free. Lockwood liked me to do that – it always stirred him. Cleve's eyes moved here and there.

'The ailanthus is from China, originally,' I said, goading him with more arcana. 'It thrives in poor soil with little care. Like me.'

'Ah. Hard-done-by girl.' He came over to the bed. I gripped him.

'Hungry?' he asked.

'I told you; I thrive in poor soil.'

Cleve left at six, saying he had to be sure he was back in Connecticut for dinner, home with his family, I knew, his wife, Frances, and his two young sons, Harry and Link. After he'd gone I made another gin cocktail and picked up my book. However, I felt my new-year melancholia returning. Stop it, I told myself, buck up: I was having a passionate affair with a fascinating man and I was earning my living, making more money than I'd done in my life, as a professional photographer in New York City – what was so depressing about that? But I was Cleveland Finzi's mistress, the other, sour voice in my head told me; I was only with him when it was safe and secret. And it was true – when he was with me everything was grand; when he wasn't, life returned to the duller, demeaning business of waiting until the coast was clear and no one would suspect.

I had related as much to him – the plaint of every secret lover since adultery began – and he said he understood, but, for various reasons, he had to be very careful, very careful indeed. What could I say? I had entered the 'deal' knowingly. But sometimes two weeks or more would go by before he could snatch a night or an afternoon with me. I had been in New York for well over a year now; Cleve and I had been lovers for slightly less. I was happier than I had ever been and at the same time more discontented. My world was awry – maybe you just weren't cut out to be a mistress, my sour voice whispered at me.

'Happy 1934,' Phil Adler hailed me as I came into his office. He was a lean young man in his early thirties with rimless spectacles and short wiry hair. We argued a lot, good-naturedly, principally about photography.

'You're from Europe,' he said, waving me into a chair opposite him.

'So I'm told,' I said, sitting down.

'Ever heard of a French writer called . . .' He looked at his notes in front of him. 'Jean-Baptiste Charbonneau?'

'No.'

'Well you're going to take his photograph this afternoon.'

Charbonneau was a mid-ranking diplomat at the French consulate – Phil told me, reading from his notes – who also wrote novels. His third novel, *Le trac*, had just been published in the US as *Stage Fright* (Steiner & Lamm) and had been very well received with excellent reviews in *The Times*, the *Post*, the *New Masses*, *Esquire*, the *Atlantic Monthly* – its little splash had attracted *GPW*'s attention.

'Et cetera, et cetera. Culture can be news too,' Phil said feigning a yawn. 'You know: foreign literary star, strong light and shade, cigarette poised near face, backlit smoke, Gallic charm.'

'I think I can manage it.'

This Charbonneau lived in a serviced apartment off Columbus Circle. He was a solid chunky mess of a man with rumpled clothes – there were food stains on his tie – and a tousled mass of curly dark hair. He had a very heavy beard, his jaws and chin dark with incipient stubble, and a big nose and full lips. There was really nothing attractive about him at all but, mystifyingly, he gave off an aura of facetious charm as if everything he saw around him – including the people he encountered – amused him in some secret way. He spoke good English with a strong French accent.

He looked at me in surprise when he opened the door. 'Who are you?' he said.

I held up my camera. 'The photographer.'

He smiled. 'I was expecting a man. A mister photographer.'

'Well, I am not Mister Photographer.'

'But you are meant to come tomorrow.'

'But I am here today.'

He let me in and hurried off to put on a clean tie, at my suggestion. His sitting room had no bookshelves but was full of books stacked in random piles like bulky stalagmites growing towards the ceiling. I pulled down the blind, rigged my spotlight at his work table and took the standard portrait shot in strong chiaroscuro but with no smoking cigarette – rookie or not, even I had my standards – but with chin propped in palm, index finger extended to cheekbone. It was all over in half an hour. We chatted about Berlin, where he had recently been posted.

'What do you think about the new chancellor?' I asked.

'Crazy, no? *Un fou.*'

I said I hadn't paid much attention but had seen enough Nazis in the few weeks I was in Berlin to last me a lifetime.

As we nattered on, Charbonneau offered me one of his yellow French cigarettes. I declined and he lit my Pall Mall. We stood and smoked for a moment or two, then he said, 'Now I suppose you expect me to ask you for dinner.'

I showed him my engagement ring. It was Cleve's idea for me to wear it – bought in a dime-store. The story was that I was engaged to a young man in England; it pre-empted many problems at work with my unmarried male colleagues and explained my absences at parties and after-work get-togethers. It worked – Charbonneau held up his hands in mock apology.

'I never saw it. I yield to my rival.'

'On second thoughts – thank you very much. I accept.'

'Second thoughts – don't you find they're often the best ones?'

What made me accept Charbonneau's invitation? I think it was a product of my lurking discontent. Why should I go home to Washington Square South for another lonely night with my gin, my radio and my book? I found Charbonneau amusing and suspected he'd be good company – I owed it to myself.

Enthused, Charbonneau suggested the Savoy-Plaza Hotel at seven o'clock. I caught a cab up to Central Park South and met him in the lobby. He took pernickety care over the choice of wine and ordered a steak so rare it was effectively raw, to my eyes. He asked me lots of questions about myself – where was I born, who were my parents – and, enjoying this gentle interrogation, and the second bottle of wine, I found myself opening up to him, telling him the story of the Grösze and Greene fiasco and, indirectly (I wasn't wearing my engagement ring), that I was having something of an affair here in New York.

'And what about your poor fiancé in England?'

'Well, he's more of a friend than a fiancé. It's a useful ruse.'

We were at the end of the meal. Charbonneau was on his second brandy and second coffee. I was sipping at a glass of port.

'Enough about me,' I said, fishing in my bag for my cigarettes. 'Tell me about your novel.'

He shrugged. 'It's just a little thing. A hundred and thirty pages. I wrote it seven, no, eight years ago but now they've published it in English so I have to remember what I wrote . . . It's about a man who has stage fright – *le trac*, we call it – but stage fright whenever he has to make love.'

'He's impotent.'

'No, no. Have you ever had stage fright? It's a terrible, physical sensation. You can still go on stage, you can still perform but, I assure you, *le trac véritable* . . .' He gestured with his cigarette, making a tightening spiral. 'It seizes your entire being.'

'Is it an autobiographical novel, then?'

He laughed, loudly enough for nearby diners to turn and stare.

'I think you are a very bad young woman, Miss Clay. *Méchante*. No, I've had stage fright but only in the theatre. When I was very young.'

'That's a relief,' I said.

He stared at me and I saw ash fall carelessly from his cigarette on to his sleeve. He didn't bother to brush it away.

'Actually, I'm taking a bit of a holiday from sex,' he said. 'Personally speaking.'

'Really?'

'Yes. I'm a bit bored with the whole *brouhaha*, what do you say? The surrounding nonsense.'

'I see.'

'Yes. These days I'd rather have a conversation with an interesting and beautiful young woman' – he leant forward and whispered – 'than fuck her.'

It was a test, of course – but Charbonneau could have had no idea that I'd worked with the foul-mouthed Greville Reade-Hill and so I listened unmoved and unperturbed.

'It's not an either-or, you know,' I said, then leant forward and whispered to him myself. 'You can still have a conversation with the people you fuck.'

He sat back in his chair, an uncertain smile on his face. I think that, for a very rare moment in his life, Jean-Baptiste Charbonneau found himself at a loss for words. He said nothing, just pointed his finger at me and wagged it in amused admonishment.

★

THE BARRANDALE JOURNAL 1977

And so my New York, American life progressed in its alternating, vaguely satisfying, vaguely unsatisfying, way. I saw Cleve whenever he could free himself from his wife and family and, as compensation when he wasn't free, I began to have a regular dinner date with Jean-Baptiste Charbonneau – once a week or so.

I remember a trip Cleve and I made to California for the opening of the Santa Rosa Bridge in Sonoma – one of the first big New

Deal projects to be completed – and we managed to spend a whole four days together, the longest consecutive time we'd ever passed in each other's company. We took a Boeing Air Transport 247 across country, my second flight in an aeroplane, and then my third flight back home to New York. Perhaps because I was with Cleve, sitting beside me, and those four days were bracketed by long cross-country flights with many take-offs and landings, I found I loved flying – despite the rocking turbulence we encountered. I was never alarmed or fearful though I suppose I might have had cause to be so: instead I was intoxicated by the improbability of being in these shiny metal machines powering themselves into the air, looking down on the land we soared over, slicing through clouds into the luminous blue above.

I remember the first night Cleve and I made love. I knew it was bound to happen – it was why I had come to America, after all, though I have to admit that the money was an extra inducement. He drove us north-east out of Manhattan to Westchester County to a roadhouse on Highway 9 called the Demarest Motor Lodge. We ate an indifferent meal but we hadn't come all this way for the food. There were eight double rooms with attached bathrooms on the floor above.

Cleve said: 'I could drive you home but I took the precaution of booking a couple of rooms here, just in case we were too tired.'

I said: 'Now you mention it I am feeling a bit too tired to go back to Manhattan. What a good idea.'

And so we went upstairs to our rooms. Five minutes later Cleve knocked softly on my door.

I remember we made love twice that night, and then once again in the morning. Cleve was adamant that he should wear a contraceptive: he had come prepared. And I remember, on the drive back to Manhattan, the almost drug-like mood of happiness I was in. I hunched over on the bench seat and leant up against Cleve as he drove, feeling his warmth, my hand on his thigh. I looked through the windscreen at the commuter traffic heading back into Manhattan idly noting details: the colours of the cars – mushroom, mouse-grey, glossy black, dull crimson – and the sky with great rafters or bars of cloud set against the blue, almost as if measured and deliberately spaced. I looked with unknowing, innocent eyes, it seemed to me and, as I touched my throat, I felt my skin was hypersensitive, tingling, frictively alive, because, I assumed, of the feeling of bliss inside me: it was almost as if I were coming down with flu.

I remember Phil Adler asking me if I was all right when I came into the office. Why do you ask? You just seem different, as if you're not quite here, he said. You take about three seconds to answer my questions. Oh. Then I said I wondered if maybe I was coming down with flu. He sent me to photograph the Brooklyn Bridge for the third time. There were a lot of repairs going on and I strayed from my brief. It was one of my first 'abstract', compositional photographs. Maybe I was inspired. Phil said it was unusable.

2. THE HOTEL LAFAYETTE

MY DINNERS WITH CHARBONNEAU took on a pattern. Missing Paris, he always tried to seek out a French restaurant and, however well we dined there, he always claimed to be vehemently disappointed; that what had been presented was a travesty of French cooking, an American fiasco. I often contradicted him just to set his indignation raging – to my British palate everything seemed delicious. He was very analytical about the food he ate – even the bread rolls and the salt claimed his gourmet's focussed attention. Almost without trying I began to learn a lot about what one could demand from the necessities of eating: the meat, the fish, the vegetables that we masticated and swallowed to allow us to live. But Charbonneau gave the process so much forensic thought it seemed almost unhealthy to me.

In search of the perfect French cuisine in New York we ate our way through the French restaurants that the Village had to offer: Le Champignon, Charles, Montparnasse – and numerous others. *Pas brillant*, was his mildest judgement.

One night we were in the Waldorf Cafeteria on 6th Avenue, where Charbonneau claimed to have tracked down an 'acceptable' Bordeaux, a 1924 Château Pavie. He was in a strange unruly mood and had already criticised me for my choice of lipstick – 'It doesn't suit you, it makes your mouth look thin' – but I paid no attention. I was in an odd state of mind myself as I hadn't seen Cleve for over three weeks – he was off on a *GPW* trip to Japan and China – and I wasn't at my most tractable.

'Don't you live near here?' Charbonneau asked, abruptly.

'Washington Square. A few blocks away.'

'Would you show me your apartment?'

'Why do you want to see it?'

'I'd just like to see where you live, Amory. To fill out the picture, you know.'

So we wandered home and I showed him in. He prowled around and looked at my photographs for a while and then stuck his nose in my bedroom. I was pouring him a Scotch and water when he came up behind me, cupped my breasts and nuzzled my neck.

'What the hell are you doing, Charbonneau?' I said, angrily, wheeling round and pushing him away.

'I think it's time we got to know each other better.'

'So, your sexual vacation is over?'

'Yes. It seems to be. Back to work.'

He tried to grab me again but I snatched up the ice pick from the drinks table and thrust it out at him.

'French novelist stabbed to death by English photographer,' I said. 'Stop this now!'

'But I want you, Amory. And I think you want me.'

'Why are you trying to spoil a beautiful friendship like this?'

He sagged. 'I don't want a "beautiful friendship",' he said, pleadingly. 'I want something much more complicated and interesting than that. More dangerous. Now, if we can just go to your bedroom—'

'No, Charbonneau! *Non, merci*. I'm in love with somebody else.'

'Love. What does that have to do with anything?' He picked up his Scotch and sat down, muttering irritatedly to himself. Then he apologised. He was tired, out of sorts, I was a pretty girl, his libido was alive and kicking once more.

'Don't be angry with me, Amory.'

'I'm not angry. Just don't do this again.'

'I promise, I promise.'

The now familiar paradoxical aspect about the Charbonneau 'pass' and its conspicuous failure was that we became firmer friends as a result. Something had come out into the open and had been pointedly shooed away – but the fact that it had appeared changed our future encounters for the better. We now talked with a frankness and abandon as if we had actually been lovers. The air had been cleared in every way.

Cleve came back from his trip to the Orient. 'I just don't understand that world,' he said, in a strange, baffled voice. 'I can see what's happening in front of my eyes in Shanghai or Tokyo but can't analyse it. I might as well be on Mars or Neptune.'

He paused and looked at me. 'Are you all right?' he asked.

'Much the better for seeing you, after all these years.'

We'd spent the afternoon making love in my apartment; now we were in the café of the Hotel Lafayette on University Place. I was drinking gin and orange, Cleve had an Americano. On the table next to us two old men were playing chequers. I lit a Pall Mall.

'Did anything happen while I was away?' he asked, aware of my mood – prickly, almost resentful.

'Lots of things happened. The world didn't stop turning, Cleve.'

'You seem different, somehow.'

'People can change in a couple of months. You haven't seen me for a long while. Likewise.'

I looked down at the small lozenge-shaped tiles on the café floor: pale cream with a dirty magenta flower effect dotted regularly across the room. Cleve said something, softly.

'What did you say? I didn't catch it.'

'I said, I love you, Amory. I want you to know that. That's what being away from you has brought home to me.'

I looked at him and felt a huge weakness sweep through me as I stared at him across the table, this handsome, super-competent, confident man with his thin straight nose and thick wet-sand-coloured hair. I think I was a bit shocked because I never thought he would say it to me first. I was always certain, in my predictive fantasies about our life together, about this moment, that I would be the one to make the declaration and that he would respond. But no – he said it first.

'Thank you,' I said. 'You know I feel the same about you.'

He reached across the table and took my hand.

'When I saw you that night – at your exhibition in that strange gallery – I knew something had happened to me.'

I felt emboldened. 'And here we are,' I said, 'over two years later. Something happened to you, then – but something has to happen to *us*, now, Cleve, don't you see?' I said with deliberate emphasis.

'I know,' he said, frowning suddenly. 'I know. I've not been fair.' He signalled for another drink. 'I want you to come to the house. I want you to meet Frances.'

'Are you completely out of your—'

'It's her birthday next week. We're having a big party. There'll be a hundred people there. You just need to see for yourself. Meet her.'

'Why do I feel a horrible sense of foreboding?'

'If you come – everything will be a thousand times better. You'll see.' He smiled his wide smile, not showing his teeth. 'We're going to be together, Amory. Always. I can't let you go.'

Who can tell about human instincts? Something fanciful in me wondered if Charbonneau's sexual interest in me had subtly changed my comportment in the way I reacted to Cleve. It was rutting season and there was another bull-male wandering around the neighbourhood. I do believe that our Stone Age natures still function strongly in certain situations – particularly to do with sex and mutual attraction – and are felt at gut level, deep beneath the skin, far from the brain. Anyway, however I had played it, I felt stupidly happy remembering his last words: we're going to be together, Amory. Always. I can't let you go.

Charbonneau was being at his most provocative the next time we dined – at a very bad Midtown restaurant called P'tit Paris. As we consulted the menu he spent ten minutes denigrating the apostrophe.

'Moody, petulant, selfish, spoilt,' I said.

'What's that?'

'You. I wish I had my camera,' I said, trying to make him stop moaning. 'I'd take a great photograph: "Angry Frenchman".'

He wasn't amused.

'I've seen your photographs,' he said.

'And what's that supposed to mean?'

'You think you're an artist. I read your titles: "The boy with the ping-pong bat", "The boy, running".'

'Wrong,' I said. 'I think I'm a photographer, not an artist. I give my pictures titles so I can remember them – not to make them seem pretentious. But there are great artists who are photographers.' I began to name them. 'Stieglitz, Adams, Kertész, August Sander—'

'It's not an *art*,' he said, interrupting me, aggressively. 'You point your machine. Click. It's a mechanism.' He took his fountain pen from his jacket pocket and proffered it to me. 'Here's my pen.' He turned the menu over. 'Here's a piece of blank paper. Draw an "Angry Frenchman" and then we'll discuss if it's art or not.'

I wasn't going to enter this argument on his terms.

'But you have to admit there are great photographs,' I said.

'All right ... There are memorable photographs. Remarkable photographs.'

'So, what makes them memorable or remarkable? What criteria do you use to judge them? To make that decision?'

'I don't think about it. I just know. Instinct.'

'Then maybe you should think about it. You judge a great photo in the same way you judge a great painting or a film or a play or a novel or a statue. It's art, *mon ami*.'

'Shall we get out of this shithole P'tit Paris and have a proper drink somewhere?'

'I've got to have an early night,' I said. 'I'm going to a birthday party in Connecticut.'

Charbonneau looked at me shrewdly. I had told him too much in the past.

'Ah. The American lover. Going to meet the wife and kids?'

'Going to change my life.'

3. The Watershed

I WAS GIVEN A lift up to New Hastings, Connecticut, by Phil Adler and his wife, Irene. They picked me up outside Grand Central Station in their Studebaker station wagon – with its wooden side panels it was like a travelling garden shed, it seemed to me – but we whizzed on up to Connecticut in fast time. Quite a few of the *GPW* staff had been invited, they told me. It was cool drizzly weather, not at all like late spring, and I was sitting wrapped up in the back of their car in my camel coat, and glad of it.

'Have you been to their house before?' I asked.

'I have,' Phil said. 'Sometimes Cleve has a big Labor Day party.'

'I haven't,' Irene chipped in. 'Usually it's no wives.'

'So what's different about today?' I said.

'I believe it's her fortieth,' Phil said.

'Frances?'

'The same.'

'So, she's older than Cleve.'

'You're on fire today, Amory,' Phil said.

'No, I mean ... I hadn't thought, realised ...' My brain was suddenly busy. 'What's she like, Frances?'

'Beautiful, sophisticated ...'

'Rich?'

'Oh, yeah,' Irene said with feeling.

'Clever?'

'Bryn Mawr.'

'So,' I said, 'beautiful, sophisticated, rich, clever.' Somehow I felt Greville would have done better. I had no clear picture in my head about Frances Finzi so I told Phil and Irene about Greville's Game – how anyone could be summed up in four well-chosen adjectives.

'That's very English,' Irene said. 'Very.'

'Have you met Frances?' I asked her.

'Once. Years ago.'

'Fine. So give me Frances Finzi in four adjectives.'

She thought. 'Cold, patronising, elegant, plutocratic.'

'That's not fair,' Phil said. 'She can't help inheriting money. I'd say "lucky".' He thought a second. 'Maybe that's not appropriate.'

'Her father is Albert Moss,' Irene explained. 'Moss, Walter & Co. The investment bank? It's part of the picture. I'm sorry. She's very plutocratic in her particular way. Wait till you see the house.'

I was beginning to warm to Irene, a small sharp-faced woman with intelligent, knowing eyes.

'I think the "plutocratic" adjective is inappropriate,' Phil said. 'I don't see it.'

'Phil said, loyally,' Irene added. 'Precisely.'

The Finzi house in New Hastings was a suitably impressive red-brick Colonial Revival mansion set in abundant gardens. It had a shallow-hipped roof with a wide overhang. There was a centred gable with an odd rounded porch with pillars and all the ground-floor windows had broken pediments. Ever so slightly over-decorated, I judged – the rounded porch looked like a bad afterthought, spoiling the clean lines.

We were directed by men in red slickers to park on a terraced lower lawn in front of the house and then more of these men, with umbrellas aloft (it was drizzling, now) walked us up brick pathways to the house itself and along its side to a vast rear lawn where the party was taking place.

On this main garden lawn behind the house was a bedecked marquee. A jazz band played at one end and toqued chefs dispensed hot food from chafing dishes at the other. Waiters and waitresses patrolled with jugs of fruit cocktail, alcoholic or non-.

For all the manifest expense on display the mood was informal. Men were in sports clothes, some without ties. Children ran around pursued by nurses and nannies. Effortless, moneyed ease was the subtext but the main message was clear: enjoy yourselves, eat and drink, wander around the capacious grounds – above all, have fun.

I felt overdressed in a black sequinned day-frock with a cape collar and co-respondent black and white shoes with a low heel, and so decided to keep my coat on. Anyway, it was freezing. But it wasn't the weather that was making me edgy and jumpy – it was the anticipation. I lost Phil and Irene as soon as I decently could and went in search of Cleve.

I found him on the back terrace – a long platform porch with a balustrade – in the company of four other men. Cleve was smoking a cigar and was wearing a pale blue seersucker suit, a mauve tie and cream canvas shoes. I walked past this group twice so he could see me and then found a corner at the far end of the terrace and snapped him with my little Voigtländer that I was carrying in my pocket. I had been seized with the perverse desire to take a photograph of the legendary Frances and so had brought the camera along with me, on the off-chance. Not a good idea, I now thought, a little daunted by the scale and panache of the Finzi home. I waited.

Cleve was with me two minutes later. We shook hands. His eyes, it seemed to me, were full of feeling, almost tearful.

'Thank you for coming,' he said. 'I was convinced you wouldn't.'

'I couldn't not come—'

'It means a lot to me, Amory.'

'I hope . . .' I began and then couldn't recall what I was hoping for.

'Come and meet Frances.'

I put my Voigtländer down with my bag on a wrought-iron table and followed Cleve into the house, trying, and failing, to drive all apprehension from my mind.

Inside it was airy and tasteful, if a little over-furnished. Not an empty corner to be seen – occasional tables and grouped chairs, planters with ferns and palms. It was painted in pastel colours throughout and the vast arrangements of flowers on all available surfaces created a slightly oppressive sense of crowded elegance.

As we crossed the chequerboard marble hall – beige and brown – two little boys ran up to him shouting 'Papa! Papa!' They were made to stand still and face me.

'This is Harry and this is Lincoln,' Cleve said, introducing his sons to me (six and four, I guessed, or seven and five – I wasn't good with children's ages).

I shook their proffered hands.

'Hello, I'm Amory.' They also said hello, politely, dutifully, absolutely incurious. One dark, one fair: plain little boys with short identical hairstyles and round faces – in neither of them could I see a trace of Cleve.

'You boys run along, now,' Cleve said. 'Amory's going to see Mumsie.'

The boys ran off through the hall and Cleve led me to a spacious long drawing room with four bay windows overlooking the rear lawn. There was a baby grand piano, half a dozen soft sofas and a stacked drinks table. Over the fireplace was an eight-foot swagger portrait of a woman from the last century in a silk ballgown draped with marmoset skins.

Cleve raised his voice. 'Frances? Are you there?' He turned to me. 'Will you have a drink?'

'I certainly will, my darling. Brandy and soda. A big one.' I had to remind myself that this man was my lover, that we had been naked in bed with each other, days previously. The fact that I was about to meet 'Mumsie' didn't change those facts one iota.

Cleve busied himself at the drinks table and I turned to see a woman in an apricot-coloured silk organza tea gown steer herself through double doors at the far end of the room in a wheelchair. She rolled silently towards me across the parquet.

Cleve handed me my brandy and soda, smiling.

'Amory Clay, let me introduce you to Frances Moss Finzi.'

We shook hands, smiling furiously. I noticed she was wearing the finest grey suede gloves. I thought I was touching skin. Despite my smile my mind was a disaster area: props falling, the roof collapsing, fires flaring, men screaming, waves of water breaking.

'Hello,' Frances Moss Finzi said in a deep smoky voice. 'How charming to meet you.'

'Amory's our new star photographer from England.'

'Congratulations. I'd like a cigarette, Cleve.'

A figured brass box was found, proffered, cigarette selected, lit. I said no thank you, gulping at my potent brandy. She had an unusual, arresting face, Frances. Pale hooded blue eyes, a high forehead, a mannish face – her looks compromised by a poor buckled perm of her auburn hair, crimped over her ears. She could have afforded better, in my opinion.

'Happy birthday,' I said, raising my glass.

'A watershed,' she smiled away the compliment. 'Nobody's going to be spared. That's one consolation.'

Was that for my benefit, I wondered? In the event we talked away, politely. How was I finding New York after London? Had I a decent apartment? How she adored the Village. Photography was the democratic art form of our age. She loved taking photographs, herself. Snap, snap, snap.

'Why don't you wheel me out into the world, Cleve. And fetch me a shawl. I'll brave the elements.'

I followed them out on to the terrace and then darted away, making my temporary farewells, and raced for the marquee where I gulped down a glass of the alcoholic fruit punch and smoked a cigarette.

Phil and Irene ambled by.

'Hey, there's Amory. Thought we'd lost you. Having fun?'

'Why didn't you tell me, Phil?'

'Tell you what?'

'That Frances was in a fu—. In a flipping wheelchair.'

'I thought you knew. Everyone knows.'

'I didn't.'

'It's like Roosevelt has callipers. Our esteemed president is a cripple. Everyone knows, nobody bothers to mention it.'

'Well, it was a bit of a shock. What happened to her?'

'Car smash,' Irene said. 'Just after the little one was born.'

'Lincoln,' Phil said. 'No. Harry. Lincoln? What's the youngest called?'

'Lincoln. There was a crash,' Irene continued. 'Awful. And she's been in a wheelchair ever since. With the two little boys . . . Very sad.'

I was calculating. If Lincoln was four or five she'd been in a wheelchair for many years, now. I looked round, distractedly, and saw Cleve signalling to me from an opening at the end of the marquee.

'I'll be right back,' I said and headed off.

Cleve and I wandered out into the garden and down a wide flight of steps towards an ornamental lake fringed with bullrushes and teazles. A dozen geese cruised about on the water. There was a boathouse encrusted with gingerbread moulding with a jetty and an extravagantly prowed giant canoe moored to it.

'You somehow forgot to tell me your wife was confined to a wheelchair,' I said, managing to keep my voice calm.

'I don't even think about it. It's been years now.'

'Well, it was a bit of a shock to me. To put it very mildly.'

He looked at me. 'You know how I feel about you, Amory. It doesn't change anything.'

'I'm sorry, but I think it does.'

'I needed you to see for yourself.'

'Why?'

'Because I can't leave her, obviously.'

'Obviously.'

'I was driving the car when we had the accident. We'd both been drinking but it wasn't my fault. Some kid in his dad's Buick swiped us and we rolled down an embankment. I had a bruised elbow. Frances broke her spine – became paraplegic.'

'My God. How awful.'

We stood silent by the lake looking at its choppy, slatey waters. I hugged myself. I had an overwhelming urge to leave.

'That's why I wanted you to meet her,' he said in his entirely reasonable way, 'so you could understand.'

'Understand what?'

'What we will have. You and me.'

'You've lost me. What're you talking about? What *do* we have? You and me.'

'Everything. Everything – short of marriage. But, all the same, a marriage of two people, of two minds, in everything but its judicial formalities.' He faced me. 'I want to kiss you. To hold you. These are just words. I want you to feel the love I have for you. I love you, Amory. I need you to be part of my life.'

'I need to think . . .' I thought I might faint, then, and topple into the cold lake. I stepped back. 'Think about it all. Take it in.'

I turned and walked away without looking round. I was remembering something my father used to say. 'Inertia is a very underrated state of mind,' he once told me. 'If you feel you have to make a decision then decide not to make a decision. Let time pass. Do nothing.' Which was what I decided to do. I returned to the terrace, picked up my bag and my camera and set off in search of Phil Adler.

Phil said he and Irene weren't ready to leave but he would drive me to the station at New Hastings where I could catch a train back to the city. He wandered off to find his car while I mooched about the hall and the big drawing room, trying to keep my brain inert and ignore the clamouring contradictions that were queuing up to be heard. As I prowled around, distracting myself, I saw a small, framed photograph amongst a clutch of others on a side table. It was an impromptu photo of Cleve and Frances, not looking at the camera, in near profile, both of them in casual clothes and taken early in their marriage, I imagined, long before the accident. I picked up the frame – tortoiseshell – and swung the little brass clips free on the back. I pocketed the photo and slid the frame into a bureau drawer. I had no idea why I'd done this or what had prompted me – it was a strange kind of trophy, I supposed, something that I had stolen and could keep and that would remind me of this cold afternoon in Connecticut: a symbol of something that had ended or was about to end.

I strolled back into the hall and saw Frances saying goodbye to a couple. I froze but she turned at that moment and saw me. She wheeled her chair round and propelled herself towards me, smiling her empty hostess smile.

'You're not leaving already, are you?'

'I'm going back to England tomorrow,' I lied, easily. 'Still a lot of packing to do.'

She looked up at me from her chair – a fine ebony seat and bleached woven strand-cane, as elegant a wheelchair as money could buy, I thought – though she might as well have been looking down from some elevated throne, such was the regal hauteur and condescension in her manner.

'Cleve is sleeping with you, isn't he?'

'Don't be absurd! Really, what a—'

'Of course he is. I can always tell which ones are his girls.'

'I refuse to dignify your disgraceful accusation by any kind of—'

'You're not the first since my accident, Miss Clay. You may be the fourth or fifth – I don't keep a precise count. One thing I'm sure of, though: you won't be the last.'

She wheeled herself away but not before delivering a little pitying smile at me. I watched her leave the hall. Smug, frightened, powerful, threatened. Phil Adler ducked his head round the front door. Ready to go?

Cleveland and Frances Finzi, about 1929, before the accident.
The photo that I stole.

4. SOUTH OF THE BORDER

I COULDN'T SEE CLEVE after the Connecticut Incident, as I referred to it. I told the office I'd been diagnosed with a bad case of pleurisy and would be confined to bed for at least a week.

Of course, Cleve telephoned and I didn't answer. And then he came down to Washington Square, buzzed the buzzer, somehow gained admittance, beat on the door and, when I didn't respond, slipped a note under it saying 'I've been phoning. We have to speak. Everything is fine. I love you, C.'

I wondered what world he was living in where 'everything is fine'? I didn't blame or hate Cleve – just marvelled at his complacency.

One strange thing: I had the roll of film from my Voigtländer developed – I was keen to see the covert shot I'd taken of Cleve from the end of the terrace. It wasn't very good but I found an image on the roll that I'd had nothing to do with. It was a long shot of me and Cleve standing by the lake, talking. Who had taken it? Someone had picked up my Voigtländer and had snapped that moment and preserved it. And, I thought, that someone had also wanted me to see it, or at least had known I'd see it one day . . . Phil Adler? Irene? A stranger? No – I suspected the suede-gloved hand of Frances Moss Finzi. It unsettled me.

And then, in the perverse, unscripted way that life works, an upheaval arrived in the shape of a telegram from Hannelore Hahn, announcing that she and her travelling companion, Constanze

Auger, were in New York for a few days before moving on south to Mexico. We had to see each other.

We met in the Brevoort Hotel on 5th Avenue. Hanna had changed: her hair was long, shoulder-length; she was wearing a cream crêpe de Chine dress with a red velvet collar. It was Constanze Auger who looked like the beautiful boy, the *Bubi*. Short blonde hair with the thick forelock hanging over one eye, face tanned, a shoulder-padded navy bolero jacket over apple-green Oxford bags, flat brogue shoes – but all this masculinity undercut by a pair of dangling jet earrings. She was very stern and tense as a person – even within a minute of meeting her I was aware of this: she didn't have Hanna's ease or sardonic sense of humour. For Constanze, it was as if her life was a serious mission of some sort, with an import only she could appreciate or understand and where 'fun' really had no part to play. She was striking-looking, slim, tall – heads turned in the Brevoort. She was a journalist, she said: she and Hanna were going to Mexico to write a book – text by Constanze, photographs by Hanna.

As I sat there listening to their plans I found myself envying them. This was a potent whiff of Berlin and its sense of everything being possible passing through Greenwich Village and rather showing the place and its denizens up. We ate, we drank, we smoked, we laughed – even Constanze, eventually. I could have been back in the Klosett-Club. The Brevoort, where I'd deliberately taken them, the Village's beating intellectual heart, seemed sclerotic, timid, impoverished, provincial.

But maybe it was my own sour, damaged mood making me think like this. As I became more drunk, repeatedly ordering rounds of bourbon and ginger ale, my latest favourite tipple, I opened up to them and told them both about my affair with Cleve and the fiasco of the New Hastings weekend.

'I tell you, Amory,' Constanze said, lighting a hand-rolled cigarette, 'he did it deliberately. He's setting out – how do you say it? – marking the ground linings and the goalposts in a different configuration.'

'The playing field. On his terms, you mean. Yes . . .'

'How could he take you to meet his crippled wife?' Hanna said, seeming genuinely upset. 'It's disgusting.'

'He just sees the world differently,' I said, feeling I had to defend Cleve, somewhat. 'Something that appears difficult, or a problem, to me, or to anyone, doesn't seem like that to him. Everything has a way of being solved.'

'It's called arrogance, that attitude,' Constanze said. 'Or *Solipsismus*, yes? I live alone in my world. I have no problems. Who are you? What do you want?'

'I don't think he has any idea how I see him,' I said, becoming confused, my mind blurry with drink, all coherence going. 'I think he'd be outraged if I called him arrogant. Shocked.'

Hanna took my hand. 'But you can't stay here – in this situation. It's impossible, *Liebchen*. Why don't you come with us?'

'To Mexico?'

'Yes,' Constanze added. 'Bring your camera. Two photographers and a writer. We will make a wonderful book.'

In my mood of pleasant self-pitying inebriation, fuzzy and heroic with drink, in the company of these vibrant confident women, it seemed the perfect solution. I had money in the bank, it would be an adventure and, more significantly, it would show Cleve that I wasn't prepared to fit in with his skewed, solipsistic vision of our future.

The next day I made an appointment to see him. We met in his office at the end of the afternoon. He was very calm.

'How are you feeling, Amory?'

'Much better, thank you. I needed the rest.'

'Of course.'

He was sitting behind his wide desk, his jacket off, braided wire garters on his shirtsleeves, keeping his cuffs trim. I wished, not for the first time, that I had my camera, to capture Cleve like this, his eyes full of messages despite his compromised position as my boss – all his contradictions gathered in one room: casual, formal;

editor-in-chief, adulterer; handsome man, inadequate husband; a power-broker who was about to find himself powerless in this instance.

'I'm quitting,' I said, deliberately using the American term.

'No, you're not. I won't accept it.'

'It's not up to you. I'm going back to London.'

I think he was genuinely shocked – he hadn't remotely expected this.

'Don't do anything rash,' he said.

'This is the opposite of rash. How I was living before was rash.'

'Take a vacation. I'll think of something. Don't worry.'

'I don't need you to think of anything, Cleve, for once in your life,' I said, feeling myself sag inside and my love for him well up, unbidden, unwanted. The man who could think of something. Who could think of anything. No.

I stood up and offered my hand, not confident of being able to speak without my voice breaking – and there was a secretary just outside the door. He took my hand in both of his and squeezed.

'Amory . . . I'll work something out. This isn't finished. Call me when you get back home. I'll come over to London and see you.' He mouthed, silently: I love you. I love you.

'Goodbye, Cleve.' I dropped my voice to a whisper to cover up the emotion. 'I really did love you as well, for a while.'

★

THE BARRANDALE JOURNAL 1977

I lied to my sister, Dido. I did sleep with a woman, once. It was Constanze Auger in Guadalajara, Mexico, in 1934, though I'm convinced now that the whole thing was set up by Hanna. We had arrived in Guadalajara and had found a small, clean hotel – with running, drinkable water, electric light – when all of a sudden Hanna had to go to the German consulate in Mexico City to sort out a problem with a residency permit, or some such bureaucratic muddle, and she'd be away for a couple of days.

So Constanze and I were left on our own in the hotel – the misnamed Emporia Paradiso – waiting for Hanna to return, thrust together. We were perfectly at ease in each other's company – the roles we occupied on our adventure south of the border were clearly defined. However, as the first day wore on it seemed to me that I was just a listening post – Constanze talked constantly, passionately, about this book she and Hanna were going to create (with a little help from me, perhaps). It was a bit manic but I couldn't recognise true mania, then.

The first night she knocked on my door and I thought, oh God, not more monologuing, but before I could switch on the light, she shucked off her cotton pyjamas and slipped into my bed. We kissed – her tongue touched mine. There is always an animal instinct of arousal that flares up instantly when two human beings, of whatever sex, find themselves naked and pressed up against each other in the confines of a bed in the darkness of a room. Whatever you may be thinking – no, not for me, thanks – the close proximity of a warm unclothed body activates different triggers. It may not last long, this surge of atavistic lust, but it makes itself known very quickly. Constanze and I kept on kissing. She nuzzled at my breasts, I ran my hands down her back and squeezed her buttocks. She was incredibly flat-chested, like an adolescent girl, little mounds with nipples, and to me it felt like being in bed with a tall lithe boy (one key component missing) and I felt that sex-urge. Perhaps something might have happened but suddenly she asked for the light to be switched on, pinched one of my American cigarettes and lay beside me, smoking, and began talking about her book and her new doubts that Hanna was the right photographer to fulfil the ambitions she had for it, as if the last few minutes had never taken place at all. As I lay there, bemused, all excitement draining from me – I had lit a cigarette myself – I wondered if I was being offered the job as attendant photographer to the Constanze caravan. *Nein danke*, Constanze . . .

Then she said she felt incredibly tired, kissed me goodnight, put on her pyjamas and left. Hanna, returning the next day, asked me, as soon as we found ourselves alone, if Constanze and I had slept together. I said yes, sort of.

'She's very aggressive in that way, Constanze,' Hanna said, thoughtfully, unperturbed. 'Because we – you and me – have known each other in Berlin she wanted you – for herself.'

'Well, she didn't get me.'

Hanna then began to outline her plans. Mexico City was no longer on our route, it transpired – we were going to head down to Costa Rica instead and find somewhere to stay in San José. I let her chat on, half listening. Then Constanze joined us, kissing me affectionately, almost possessively, on the forehead – as an aunt would kiss a favourite niece – something she'd never done before. And I knew – at once – that I had to leave these two to their complex, unfathomable relationship and go back to London. There was nothing for me here any more – I was an adjunct, a toy, a spur for emotional skirmishes I had no desire to participate in. New York was over and the Hanna/Constanze voyage through Latin America was destined to end in some fraught crisis – I felt absolutely certain. It was time to discreetly make an exit; time to reposition my life on its old trajectory again.

BOOK FOUR: 1934–1943

1. BLACKSHIRTS

I WOKE VERY EARLY those summer mornings in London – the dawn light seemed to arrive around 5 a.m. and, once more, for the hundredth time, sleep despatched, I resolved to replace my filmy flower-print curtains with something more opaque and tenebrous. I used to toss about under the sheet, punch the pillows, and try to go back to sleep but never with any success. So – it was tumble out of bed, haul on dressing gown, plod into kitchen, set kettle on stove, light gas ring beneath it and let the day begin.

I was living in Chelsea now, on the King's Road, in a small flat on the top floor of a building halfway between the town hall and Paultons Square. Beneath me was a maisonette rented by the writer Wellbeck Faraday and his American wife, May, a sculptress, and beneath them was a shop, an ironmonger's. The Faradays went to bed very late, always well after midnight, and loudly so. When I woke early I was careful to pad about in slippers or bare feet – not to wake them – because I liked the Faradays. They liked me too, I think, as they were always inviting me to dinner to meet their friends but I kept my distance to a certain extent, pleading pressure of work. They led a complicated life (who doesn't?). May Faraday had a studio in Fulham and while she was out all day Wellbeck would receive visitors – mainly female. May used to ask me, when we were alone, if anyone came while she was out but I always pleaded ignorance. They had sublet the top-floor flat to me so were effectively my landlords and I wanted them to cherish me as the ideal tenant.

I sat quietly in my small kitchen and made myself a pot of tea and watched the sun begin to irradiate the tops of the plane trees on Dovehouse Green. I ate a slightly stale Bath bun that I found in the bread bin and returned to my bedroom to choose my outfit for the day. The *Global-Photo-Watch* office was in Shoe Lane off Fleet Street where the staff consisted solely of me and my secretary, Faith Postings, but, as I was deemed and titled the 'manager', I felt – for some perverse reason – that I should dress for the role and always tried to look smart. As my mother would say – you never know whom you might meet; always best to step off on the front foot – and many other homilies. This morning I selected a two-piece beige jumper suit in a ripple knit with a plain chocolate-coloured blouse with a bow at the neck. Cleve had insisted I had expenses for my clothing and so I'd taken him at his word. My cupboard was bulging but I felt a bit of a fraud: this wasn't truly me, this 'manager'.

I was still thinking that as I walked the ten minutes down the King's Road towards Sloane Square Underground and took the train to Blackfriars. It was another ten-minute walk from there to the office. I was in before Faith and brewed up. She arrived promptly at 8.30, feigning shock to see me already at my desk, cup of tea on the go.

Faith Postings was a large ungainly girl from Bermondsey in her early twenties and a tireless and diligent worker. I think she rather worshipped me – nothing I could do would pre-empt her occasional outbursts of compliments. I'm sure it was my former life in New York that impressed her – given that I wasn't much older than her, anyway – and that I had a career as a photographer. Or it may even have been the new stylish clothes I wore. In any event, she was steadily eroding her South London accent to make it conform more with mine but I liked her for her dedication to me, and by extension to *GPW*. I was only six years older than her, yet I felt I occupied not so much a sisterly as a near-maternal role in her life, much to my vague disquiet. She would do anything Aunt Amory asked of her, I knew.

Faith made herself a cup of tea and sat down at her desk, by the door across the room from mine, and flicked through her jotting pad.

'Oh yes. After you left last night, Mr Mosley's office called: they'll accept an interview on Thursday week.'

This was most intriguing news. 'Where do they suggest? Black House? It's not far from me.' Oswald Mosley's headquarters were in Chelsea, in a former teacher training college.

'To be confirmed. They said a hotel would be more suitable, perhaps.'

'Send a teleprint to New York.'

The pride and joy of the *GPW* office – our Delphic Oracle, as I called it – was the Creed Teleprinter Mark II that stood on its own table in a corner. From time to time it would click into life and spew out a thin tape of paper with, miraculously, alphanumeric lettering on it. I had no idea who actually sent the instructions written on the tape – surely not Cleve himself – as they were never signed, but the Creed Teleprinter's messages organised the business of our daily round. 'Photo reqd of Dk and Dchess of Yrk'; 'Arrange intrvw with Irene Ravenal'; 'Supply team selections of FA Cup finalists'. And so on.

Yesterday the injunction had come: 'Intrvw with Oswald Mosley soonest.' Faith duly made the telephone call to the British Union of Fascists. While our petition was being considered – we were an American magazine, it always impressed – another quirkier message arrived: 'BUF to march through East End. Investigate. Need photogs rgnt.'

What march? I made a few telephone calls to some of the journalists we employed but none of them had heard of any proposed fascist march. No marches or rallies were planned at all, as far as I could discover. I wasn't surprised as Mosley's BUF had suffered humiliating public defeats over the disruption of their rallies at Leicester, Hull and Newcastle in the previous year. Membership was dropping; they hadn't stood in last year's general election, so somebody in New York seemed to know more than we did in London. Therefore, clearly we needed better intelligence. I looked across the room at Faith Postings, Bermondsey girl, as she lit a cigarette.

'What is it, Miss Clay?'

'Grab your hat and coat. You're going to join the British Union of Fascists.'

At lunchtime, feeling hungry, Faith having been gone a couple of hours, I walked down Shoe Lane to Fleet Street looking for a pie shop or a chop house. In the end I went to a Sandy's Sandwich Bar and bought a chicken and ham croquette and a glass of milk and sat at a counter in the window watching the bustle of Fleet Street and wondering what news Faith would bring back with her.

I drained my glass of milk and was rummaging in my bag for my cigarette case when I heard a voice say, 'Amory? Amory Clay?'

I turned in my seat to see God standing there. Miss Ashe, immaculate in black silk and velvet with a fur collar and a buckled sailor hat set cockily to one side.

'I can't believe it,' she said, seemingly genuinely pleased to see me. 'I was thinking of you just last night. How uncanny.' She pointed at the scrap of veil folded up on her hat's brim. 'I'm off to a funeral at St Bride's. Always gives me a terrible hunger, a funeral – I've just had two pork pies and a bottle of ginger beer.'

I walked out with her on to Fleet Street, telling myself that she was simply an elegant elderly woman and one, moreover, who wielded no power over me any more. Relax – I was allowed to smoke a cigarette if I wanted to – and I paused and pointedly lit up.

'What're you up to these days?' she asked, as I put my lighter and cigarette case away. 'Married? Children?'

'No to both,' I said.

'Don't leave it too late,' she said.

'Like you?' I saw the old cold gaze come into her eyes for a moment and I said, quickly, 'Actually, I'm almost engaged.'

'Almost congratulations, then. Are you in town shopping?'

'I'm running an office here.' I pointed to Shoe Lane. 'Just up there. *Global-Photo-Watch*. It's an American magazine. I'm the London manager.'

'Really?' Miss Ashe paused and looked at me anew.

'I'm a professional photographer,' I said with some pride, letting the information sink in.

'Goodness me.'

'I make five hundred pounds a year,' I lied.

'You must come down and talk to the school. But don't tell them how much money you make or they'll all want to be photographers.' She smiled her thin smile. 'And that would never do.'

I felt a fool, now, having blurted out a sum of money like that, but I wanted her to know that she had been wrong, that she was fallible, that she didn't know her girls as well as she thought she did.

'I'd love to come,' I said.

'Have you a card?'

I searched my bag and found one and handed it over. She studied it intently, as if it might be forged.

'Well, well, Amory Clay,' she said. '*Global-Photo-Watch*. I'll write with a formal invitation. How is your dear father?'

'Not much improved, I'm afraid.'

'I'm so sorry. Casualties of war . . .' She turned and pointed to a middle-aged man selling matches in a doorway. 'Some brave soldier, no doubt, reduced to that.' She looked moved, for a second, then briskly said, 'Goodbye, Amory, my dear, I'm very proud of you.'

With that she touched my cheek with her gloved hand and darted away across Fleet Street towards St Bride's.

I stood there for a while feeling oddly shaken by the encounter and irritated with myself. God still had the power to destabilise me, I was annoyed to realise. I walked slowly back to the office wondering how I could have handled the meeting better but coming up with no good or coherent ideas.

173

Faith was back and showed me her membership card of the British Union of Fascists.

'Well done,' I said. 'Any news?'

'Turns out there's lots of marches planned,' she said, pleased with herself. 'Big ones – to celebrate the fourth anniversary.'

'Fourth anniversary of what?'

'The founding of the party. October '32.'

'Right. Of course. But the teleprinter said something soon.'

Faith consulted her notebook.

'There's a small march next week. Wednesday, 11 a.m. Sort of testing the water – a trial run for the big ones in October.'

'Where?'

'Tower of London to St Dunstan's Church Hall in Maroon Street. William Joyce is speaking. Not Mosley, unfortunately. There'll be one hundred blackshirts, they say.'

'Where's Maroon Street?'

'Stepney.'

I almost said, where's Stepney? – but stopped myself. I looked fixedly at her.

'I'd like you to be on that march, Faith. But only if you want to.'

'If you want me there, I'll be there, Miss Clay,' she said, loyally. 'But I don't think it'll be much of a show.'

'Doesn't matter. No one else will be covering it. This might just be our scoop. Blackshirts marching into the East End ...' I felt excitement building. 'You'll be marching, I'll be taking photographs – and then we've got our Mosley interview. Send a teleprint to New York.'

I bought a gazetteer of London with detailed fold-out maps. As I studied them I realised that the East End might easily have been in Siam or Tanganyika or Siberia as far as I was concerned. It seemed that London stopped at Aldgate and the City and all those streets of low houses and docks and wharves and the meandering river

174

were part of a terra incognita that only its denizens penetrated. In the gazetteer, I read:

'To the east of the City lies Whitechapel, a district largely inhabited by Jews (tailors, dressmakers, furriers, bootmakers, cigar-makers, etc.). Their presence here, and in Mile End and Stepney, is chiefly due to the Russian persecutions of the nineteenth century.'

I unfolded my delicate beautiful map and saw the districts east of the City, traversed by the great thoroughfares heading towards the Thames Estuary – Whitechapel Road, Commercial Road, Cable Street – carving their way through Stepney, Limehouse, Bromley, Poplar, Bow and Stratford . . . I felt that strange frisson of anticipation that an explorer in Africa must experience, about to set off into the unknown. Except in this case the map wasn't blank – every little street, lane and alleyway had its appointed name. This land was densely populated – it had its churches and schools, its police stations, hospitals, post offices and civic buildings. I would be entering Olde England and the names I read were redolent of the country's long and complex history: Shadwell, Robin Hood Lane, Regent's Canal, Lochnagar Street, Ropemaker's Field, Wapping Wall . . . But nobody I knew ever went there.

★

THE BARRANDALE JOURNAL 1977

In anyone's house at any given time there will, I suppose, be half a dozen appliances or components not functioning properly. A light fused, a door-handle loose, a floorboard creaking, an electric iron inexplicably giving no heat. In the cottage's case, for example, there is a permanently dripping cold tap in my bathroom, a drawer in the kitchen that will not fully shut, and an armchair that has mysteriously lost one castor. Also, the Hillman Imp seems to be leaking oil from somewhere, judging from the dark stains on the gravel, and my wireless reception will switch off completely for ten minutes or so, offering up muffled voices obscured by crackling gunfire, before it bizarrely resumes normal service.

As with your house, so with your body. I've a bruise on my shin, the remains of a splinter in my palm that seems to be turning septic, an ingrowing big toenail and my left knee cartilage twinges with a spasm of pain when I rise from a seat. We make do – favour the right leg, use the left hand, slip a paperback under the armchair where the castor should be. It amazes me what compromises we happily live with. We limp along, patching up, improvising.

Talking of compromises in my life, I see now that Cleve Finzi was my knight in slightly tarnished armour. The fact that he was handsome and successful, selfish and self-absorbed – not to say a little vapid, from time to time – doesn't reflect badly on me, I believe. At certain periods of our lives we – men and women – need exactly this type of person. Their easiness on the eye is all you require – handsome men, beautiful women, it's a pleasure just to be close to them. Then growing maturity tells you that this type of person simply will not do any more and we sense instinctively that we need someone, something, altogether more intriguing.

So I ran away from Cleve and New York and his terrifying wife and took off, heading south with Hanna and Constanze. A mistake, another mistake.

I remember Cleve calling the office that week before the march. The teleprinter informed us of the time of the call; the phone rang; the operator connected us and we spoke across, or rather, under the Atlantic. There was a lot of hissing and interference on the line but I could hear his voice distinctly. I waved Faith out of the office, stuck a fingertip in my free ear and listened to my one-time lover's voice crossing the thousands of miles between us.

'Everything's ready,' I said, all brisk professionalism. 'We've the whole march covered. And I'm going to hire another photographer. I'll be taking pictures as well. Between the two of us we should get something good.'

'It's wonderful to hear your voice, Amory.'

'I know the other photographer. He's very competent.'

'I miss you.'

Why do the simplest most timeworn declarations affect us so?

'I miss you too,' I said, clearing my throat, glad he wasn't in the room with me. 'But it's much better this way.'

'Send me everything you have as soon as possible. You choose and crop the photos. We're going to do this big piece on fascism in England. Italy, Germany, now England . . .' He paused. 'When's the march, again?'

'Wednesday.'

'Perfect. We're going to beat everyone on this. They sound as unpleasant as the Nazis, your blackshirts.'

Well, we shall see on Wednesday, I said, and in close-up. We talked a little more about the practicalities of sending the photographs to the USA and he told me to spare no expense. Motorcycle courier to Southampton, the fastest liner available, and so forth. I assured him I would make every expensive effort and he hung up with a breezy 'Good luck. Don't let me down, sweetheart.'

I remember at the weekend going to Sussex, to Beckburrow and finding that Xan was there and, to my surprise, my father. He looked well, though slimmer, and he wore a beret. It was clear that beneath it his head was shaved. Before lunch we went for a stroll around the garden.

'I'm better now,' he said, with a wide smile. 'Cured. I'm home for good.'

'What happened?' I said. I still felt odd with him, couldn't judge his mood and consequently was a little tense. Was this cheery humour genuine or feigned?

'It's a wonderful new operation.'

He took off his beret and I saw two round pink scars, like small coins, set just above both his temples, his hair short stubble growing back.

'They just bore into the skull, you see, from both sides and then cut the fibres, you see, the connections, to the frontal lobes of your brain. It's amazing. I've stopped worrying about everything. Everything. I'm back.'

He opened his arms to me and I stepped into his embrace. He held me tight.

'Have you forgiven me, my darling?' he whispered in my ear.

'Of course, Papa. Of course.'

I remember meeting Lockwood in a pub on Fleet Street, the Dreadnaught. We shook hands, formally, smiling nervously at each other. He had grown a small moustache – it didn't suit him – and he told me almost instantly that he was engaged to be married. I congratulated him, showing real pleasure, I hoped, and he began to relax.

He said he was working part-time for the *Daily Sketch* but was hoping for full employment there, soon. I asked him if he'd do some freelance work for *Global-Photo-Watch* and he said yes, immediately.

'I love that magazine,' he said. 'Better than *Time*. Better than the *Illustrated*.'

'Wednesday morning, eleven o'clock, Tower of London.'

'What is it?'

I explained – and added I'd be working as well.

'But we won't be seen together,' I said. 'And be discreet, keep the camera hidden as much as possible. I've heard that the blackshirts don't like photographers.'

Lockwood thought for a few seconds, smoothing his small moustache with his fingertips.

'What're you paying?'

'Five pounds for the day. Plus ten shillings for every photo we use.'

'Sounds good to me.'

I went on to tell him the kind of photograph that *GPW* liked to run but I could see he wasn't really listening and stopped.

'I think about you a lot, Amory,' he said, a little awkwardly. 'Can't get you out of my mind, sometimes. Wondering where you are, what you're up to ...'

'I've been away for a good while,' I said. 'After Berlin I went to New York and was even in Mexico.'

'Ah. The glamorous life.'

'It wasn't that glamorous, to be honest.'

He went to the bar to buy another round of drinks and I looked at him standing there – slim, tall, broad-shouldered – and I thought about the times we'd had in his small garret above Greville's darkroom. And I didn't feel anything. It's strange how strong emotions can be so easily diminished as your life continues; how deepest intimacies become commonplace half-recalled memories – such as an exotic holiday you once went on, or a cocktail party where you drank far too much, or winning a race at the school sports day. Nothing stirs any more. My affair with Lockwood had happened and had ended and had become part of the texture and detail of my personal history. I was fond of Lockwood and I knew he was a good photographer – that was what mattered, now.

I remember a letter arriving from Hanna, from Berlin, on the day before the march. She was back from her travels, she said, but she was really writing to me to convey the sad news that Constanze had taken her own life some two months earlier in São Paulo. I was initially shocked and then the shock became surprise and then a kind of understanding. I didn't know Constanze well but I could see how febrile and overwrought she was and how she clashed with the world. It turned out that the two had quarrelled – 'it was very bitter', Hanna wrote – and had split up after almost a year living in Costa Rica. Hanna went east and roved the Caribbean

Hannelore Hahn, Guadalajara, Mexico, 1934.

while Constanze headed south for Brazil. The letter accompanied a copy of the book they had somehow managed to compile together before the eruption: *Winter in Mexico und Costa Rica: Tagebuch einer Reise*. It contained three of my photographs, uncredited. It was my first appearance between hard covers.

2. The Maroon Street Riot

ON THE WEDNESDAY MORNING I met Lockwood at Fenchurch Street station, as pre-arranged, at ten o'clock. He showed me the small camera he was using, a Foth Derby. I had my Zeiss Contax that fitted neatly into my handbag. It had rained in the night and the streets were still damp, giving the morning air a raw grey light. I was glad I was wearing my mackintosh and a green felt bowler.

We found a coffee stall and each had a mug of tea.

'You hungry?' he said. 'I fancy one of them cream buns.'

'Help yourself, Lockwood, please. You're on unlimited expenses.'

'Looking forward to this,' he said, munching away.

'I think we just have to be extra careful,' I said. 'This march hasn't been announced. The police know, but the details have only been circulated to BUF members. They don't want any press attention otherwise there'd be posters everywhere.'

'Why so secretive?'

'They've got bigger marches in October. This is a trial run. If someone spots you taking photos just pocket the camera and move on.'

'You're the boss, Amory.'

We made arrangements to keep as separate from each other as possible so as not to reproduce the same photographs and to meet back at the office at the end of the day. We'd then go straight to a darkroom, develop, print and select the images we liked and send them straight off to America.

We wandered down to Trinity Square, opposite the Tower, where we could see a crowd had gathered – about 200 marchers, I calculated and, also, some thirty blackshirts, young burly men in their pseudo-uniforms, peaked caps and jackboots, giving off an air of pre-emptive menace and self-importance as they organised the marchers (BUF members, I assumed) into a column. I spotted Faith amongst them, wearing no hat, just a violet scarf tied over her hair.

At eleven o'clock a large banner was unfurled that read 'BRITISH UNION OF FASCISTS AND NATIONAL SOCIALISTS' and four mounted policemen appeared on their magnificent chargers.

There was a series of blasts on a whistle and the march moved off sedately, led by the blackshirts, heading north up Minories then turning right into Whitechapel High Street, and then everyone was diverted once more on to Commercial Road. Traffic was stopped by the police on their horses and passers-by looked on in mildly amused curiosity, it seemed to me. There was no sense of a fascist threat overwhelming the nation's capital.

I walked briskly ahead and overtook the front of the march and then, hiding in doorways and lurking behind parked cars and vans, started taking photographs. I looked around but could see no sign of Lockwood.

As the march moved on in orderly fashion down Commercial Road I became aware of small groups of young men standing watching on street corners, but watching in a nervy, fidgety way, chatting amongst themselves in lowered voices. Then the odd unlocatable shout could be heard – 'Fascists!' and 'Fascists go home!' These shouts were answered in turn by the blackshirts, raising their hands in a Roman 'hail' salute and shouting back in unison, 'Aliens! Aliens! Aliens!' As soon as any of the blackshirt stewards approached the groups of spectators, the young men split up and drifted away. However, it was evident that the mood had intensified. The march was evidently no surprise; intelligence had been leaked. The marchers closed ranks and the blackshirt stewards spread out to cover the column's flanks.

I felt a premonition that this was going to turn nasty and I noticed that, mysteriously, the number of blackshirt stewards was increasing as more young, uniformed men joined the march, inconspicuously. I managed to take a photograph of twenty or so blackshirts coming out of Stepney station in a kind of phalanx as the whole march now veered left up White Horse Street, heading for the meeting hall at St Dunstan's.

And here I saw the absolute proof that the secret march had never been secret. At the junction of Matlock Street a lorry had been turned over on its side and rudimentary barricades flanked it – barrows, packing cases, bits of old furniture. The police horses stopped, more whistles were blown and the march slowed and halted. The groups of young men standing in the alleys and side streets were much larger, now, and I saw there were women with them, also. Stepney wasn't prepared to let this march happen. They began to chant: 'You shall not pass! You shall not pass!'

I took a photograph of a young woman holding a frying pan behind her back – as a potential weapon, I supposed. Then across the street I saw Lockwood hovering around a gaggle of police officers, one of them an inspector holding a megaphone.

The inspector stepped forward and shouted through the megaphone, apparently addressing the upended lorry itself, as if it were intentionally responsible for the obstruction it posed.

'I order you to remove these barricades!' his amplified voice boomed out. 'This is a legal procession. You have no right to stop it!'

The reply came in the form of a roar of abuse and a hail of stones and vegetables, mainly potatoes. The marchers recoiled instinctively and backed away a few yards down White Horse Street.

I heard the sound of running feet and turned to see more blackshirts streaming out of an alleyway. There were many more policemen as well – clearly everyone had been expecting trouble – and they began to back the march further away from the Matlock Street barricade and then turned left up Salmon Lane. I looked at my map, torn from my gazetteer. The aim was to outflank the barricade and march everyone down Maroon Street to St Dunstan's Hall. So Maroon Street was the place to be, I thought, and decided to make my own roundabout way there so I could see the march approach down it. I ran into Belgrave Street to find people – men and women – streaming out of the houses carrying rudimentary clubs – chair legs and pickaxe handles, spindles from banisters – all racing for Maroon Street to stop the marchers before they could progress down it. I snapped a photograph of a young man in a singlet with a slingshot and a bag of marbles – no one spotted me – and ran on to St Dunstan's.

Astonishingly, Maroon Street was already blocked by a requisitioned tram and kerbstones were being dug up and hammered to pieces to provide potential missiles. Furniture was being hurled from the upper windows of the terraced houses as impromptu barricades were built. However, it was clear that the anti-fascist Stepneyites were now going to have to fight the police, not the blackshirt stewards. Huge reinforcements had appeared from somewhere – and there were now dozens and dozens of police constables, a thick dark-blue line of them, at the head of the march. The BUF banner had disappeared and I hoped that Faith had made herself scarce.

The march began to move forward steadily down Maroon Street and the police constables in the front line linked arms. In the row behind them truncheons were ostentatiously raised. Heads were going to be broken. The strange thing was, I realised, as I took my photos of the police line, that all the blackshirt stewards had suddenly disappeared.

I assumed there was going to be another flanking movement. The blackshirts were going to secure and surround the meeting hall before the march arrived, I reasoned. I ran up Ocean Street to Ben Jonson Road, paused at the junction and peered round the corner.

About fifty blackshirts carrying leather whips and clubs were being spoken to urgently by a man in a pale grey suit. He was issuing instructions, pointing up streets, gesticulating.

I eased myself round the corner, raised my camera and took, in quick succession, five photographs. Then one of the blackshirts saw me – shouted and pointed.

'Get her!' the man in the pale grey suit yelled hoarsely, furious. 'Get her, now!'

I didn't stop to see how many came after me, I turned and fled away round the back of St Dunstan's and into a little quadrangle of sooty streets called Spring Garden Square.

That was my mistake. Or rather: that was my bad luck.

I think I would have escaped but, in Spring Garden Square, about thirty blackshirts were standing around waiting for orders. I ran right into them, camera still in my hand, and stopped. They all turned as one to stare at me. I slipped my camera into my bag.

'She's Red press!' somebody shouted from behind.

'No, I'm not!' I shouted back as the blackshirts quickly surrounded me, hemming me in as the first pursuers from Ben Jonson Road now arrived. My gaze flicked here and there – I saw the man in the pale grey suit for an instant – and I had a horrid moment of recall, thinking back to Berlin, of that night when Hanna and I ran into that group of drunken Brownshirts. Brownshirts and now blackshirts. But I had no Hanna with me today.

Again I saw the man in the pale grey suit and I shouted over to him.

'Hey! Listen! I work for an American magazine!'

I realised almost as soon as I'd spoken that, as far as these men were concerned, I might as well have said, 'I work for a Jewish magazine.'

'Get the fucking camera!' the man in the pale grey suit ordered.

One of the young blackshirts grabbed my arm. He had a snub nose and flushed pink cheeks, excited, angry.

'Gimme the camera, Jewish bitch!'

'No!' I shouted back. 'Let me go!'

I flung a glance behind me, looking for the man in the pale grey suit as if he were some potential source of reason amongst all this unreasoning anger, but he seemed to have disappeared. From beyond St Dunstan's I could hear the baying of voices on Maroon Street as the march advanced.

Then three of the blackshirts seized me. My bag was snatched, my camera found, opened, the film ripped out and exposed.

Snub-Nose slapped my face, hard, enough to make my hat fall off, snapping my head round, and I cried out in pain.

'Jewish Red whore!' he shouted at me and I felt his spittle fleck my cheeks.

I was thrown to the ground. I saw boots stamping on my camera, crushing it to pieces. I could hear police whistles, now, loud and shrill above the clamorous low baying of the mob in Maroon Street, and, ringed as I was by these young men standing above me, looking down on me, I could sense their uncertainty, their anxiety. Police were drawing near, they didn't control the streets yet, these blackshirts, unlike the Nazis in Berlin – law and order still prevailed in London in a fragile way. I sensed their urge to turn and run, saw them look this way and that, uneasily.

'Teach her a lesson, lads!' Snub-Nose shouted as the crowd around me began to thin and drift away, seeking safety. He spat at me. Then one of his friends, almost as an afterthought, kicked me in the arm. That first kick unleashed something in the others and half a dozen or so began to hit at me with their fists as I lay on the ground, thwacking me with their clubs. I rolled into a protective ball, folding my arms around my head – don't kick me in the head was the chant keening in my brain, don't kick my head – but I left my back exposed, curved and defenceless and a blow to the kidney made me unfold reflexively, arching in pain and, just at that moment – vulnerable, supine – Snub-Nose kicked me in the stomach, low and very hard, and I felt something crack and give in me. I couldn't 'roll with the punch' as I was worried about the spearing pain in my back and when the toe of his jackboot connected with my lower abdomen I felt it sink in deep and do its damage.

I was now semi-conscious and blood was beginning to flow across my face from a cut above my eye. I clutched at my belly with both hands – my wounded belly – and screamed an atavistic howl of agony. It made them recoil and back away as if I had the plague.

'You done it now, Lenny,' I heard someone dimly say as the world went dark and blurry. Then there were police whistles, like shrill violent birdsong, until, all of a sudden, I was aware of Lockwood's voice in my ear saying, 'You're safe, Amory, you're safe. Don't worry, we're going to take you to hospital.' And that was that.

★

THE BARRANDALE JOURNAL 1977

The Maroon Street Riot – or Skirmish, or Affray, as it was variously referred to – was overshadowed two months later by the famous 'Battle of Cable Street' in October when thousands of Eastenders blocked and then repelled a huge march by Mosley's blackshirts and some thousands of BUF supporters. Six thousand police were in attendance that day and fought the anti-fascist crowd. The blackshirts, thwarted, turned away from the East End of London and were ruefully dismissed by Mosley at Charing Cross Bridge and that rebuff, that defeat, it can be argued, saw the end of any real continental-style fascist movement in Britain. However virulent the message that continued to be delivered by Mosley and his acolytes, the fact was that the British Union of Fascists never won control of the streets in London and perhaps that's what sapped their morale and saved us.

It has to be said that I was completely unaware of anything else taking place for the rest of 1936 – such as the course of the Spanish Civil War or the abdication crisis, Roosevelt winning a second term, or the beginning of the Rome–Berlin Axis pact – as I lay in a ward in the London Hospital in Whitechapel. It was felt to be 'too dangerous' to move me, the doctors advised, and who was I or anyone else to disagree, given the severity of my condition after the beating I had received?

However, *Global-Photo-Watch* had its pictures, all taken by Lockwood, and so, capitalising on this exclusive, they duly ran a special issue of the magazine. The world was alerted to the sinister potential of the British Union of Fascists and something of a stir ensued, I learned later. Lockwood made a name for himself and was swiftly employed as a senior photographer by the *Daily Sketch* but, as I say, all this passed me by at the time.

My medical problem was clear enough: I was suffering from near-constant, stop-start bleeding from my vagina as a result of that final kick delivered by Snub-Nose Lenny. I'd lie in bed for two days without any problems, thinking everything had calmed and then wake in the morning with my sheets drenched in vivid red.

I had three blood transfusions before the year ended but they seemed to make no difference at all. I wore a form of padded nappy-cum-elasticated-rubber-knickers device that managed to contain the bouts of bleeding and save any gross embarrassment

Images from the Maroon Street Riot, 1936 (photographs by Lockwood Mower).

but, as the months passed, I became steadily weaker. The doctors who stood deliberating around my bedside had no solutions for me. Diet and rest were all they could prescribe. I ate nothing but bland foods – junket, blancmange, rice and suet puddings, potato cakes and milk dumplings – as if anything tasteless and vaguely pale could stem the ceaseless sanguine flow.

Nevertheless, in the spring of 1937 I was estimated to be well enough to be moved to a cottage hospital near Lewes called Persimmon Hall, closer to home. And, once there, I did seem to begin to recover my health slowly, sitting on a bench in the garden on sunny days (wearing my heavily padded rubber nappy) where I could receive visits from friends and family. I was still very underweight, despite my milky, creamy diet, anaemic and continually tired but, I told myself, I was finally on the mend. Lockwood came and recounted the full story of my rescue – and thanked me profusely for the proper job with the *Sketch* that had ensued after his photographs were published. Faith Postings came and told me of the motorcycle dash to Southampton with Lockwood's photographs and negatives. My mother and Xan were my most regular visitors and even my father came by from time to time, though I sensed the quiet trembling of unease in him, despite his constant smile, unconsciously unhappy at finding himself in a hospital environment again. Dido sent a vast bouquet of flowers once a week. Greville came and made me laugh. Then Faith Postings popped in one day and told me the *GPW* office was being closed down.

And then Cleve Finzi came.

3. PERSIMMON HALL

'COTTAGE' HOSPITAL SEEMED THE wrong appellation. 'Rural hotel' hospital was more apt. Set in its own capacious grounds off the Lewes–Uckfield road, Persimmon Hall resembled a small country-house hotel with annexes. There was the central building, a medium-sized Georgian mansion in pale sandstone, and connected to it were two long low modern wings overlooking the terraced lawns and gardens. There were a couple of wards but most patients had their own private rooms where they were well catered for by uniformed staff (cleaners, porters, serving girls) as well as nurses.

Through the French windows of my room in the east wing I could see the front terrace with its York stone pathways, herbaceous borders and well-placed teak benches in front of a low retaining wall. Steps led down to a couple of lawns and a lily pond. Cedars, rhododendrons and monkey-puzzle trees marked the boundary. It was all very bourgeois and calming.

I found that the process of recovering from a long illness simplified life unimaginably. All you – the patient – had to do was endure the malady and try to become well. All further concerns – bathing, eating, communicating with the outside world – were dealt with by others offstage, as it were. I lay in bed feeling weak and tired, was fed and medicated, taken for strolls, had my padding changed when it was blood-soaked and lost consciousness punctually each night after my sleeping draught.

And the world turned and history was made – the incendiary destruction of the *Hindenburg* airship, the Sino-Japanese War, the release of *Snow White and the Seven Dwarfs* – and also the *GPW* office in Shoe Lane was closed and Faith Postings paid off. My mother and Xan emptied my King's Road flat and put my bits and pieces, my sticks of furniture, into store and wound up the lease as I lay in my bed, lethargic and uncaring. There is, it should be said, something addictive about being so useless, so dependent. One regresses. An agreeable, creeping sensation of total irresponsibility found me asking myself – sitting on a bench outside my room, on a sunny, warm day, a cup of tea in my hand – why life couldn't always be like this. It was near ideal. I was succumbing to the potent allure of semi-invalidism.

Months past. I lost more weight, but more slowly, despite the amount of pale pabulum I ingested. I still felt tired and every few days my body would ritually expunge a half-pint or so of blood.

It was my mother who alerted me about Cleve. We were sitting on my bench outside my room, wrapped up because it was chilly.

'I meant to say,' she broke off from whatever anecdote she was recounting. 'I've had a peculiar telephone call from an American. A Mr Finzi. He claims to know you.'

'He was my employer in New York, Mother.'

'Well, he wants to come and see you – here. Can you imagine?'

I experienced the first sensation of genuine excitement in ages. I felt, for a moment, that I was fully alive again.

'Fine with me,' I said, trying to keep the smile off my face. 'Be a distraction.'

Cleve came to Persimmon Hall. It was a Wednesday morning in June and I was in my tartan dressing gown, sitting on my bench, looking out over the lily pond and the South Downs beyond, when I saw him being led by a nurse along the pathway from the main building.

I sensed that old heart-lurch, the weakening spine-shudder – and then rallied.

He was wearing a three-piece navy blue suit with a brilliant red tie – with the usual tiepin securing it to his shirt. His thick hair was oiled flat and he looked very tanned, as if he'd been sailing for weeks on some sunlit ocean. Absurdly handsome, I thought. Too handsome, really – it was something of a joke.

He kissed my cheek and sat on the bench beside me, staring at me, taking me in.

'May I take your hand?'

'There would be terrible gossip. All right, go on, let's risk it.'

He took my hand in both of his.

'You look well, Amory. If a little too thin, I must say.'

'Right. Not true, but compliment duly paid. You, however, look disgustingly well.'

We talked a little more about my state of health, of the general air of bafflement surrounding my condition. I explained that I had seen a dozen doctors, I had had X-rays taken, that I was now on a regime of concentrated iron pills but something profound had happened during that attack, that last kick administered by Snub-Nose Lenny, that had deeply injured me, and my body still hadn't recovered.

At this he looked pained and unhappy. He stood up, thrust his hands in his trouser pockets and paced about.

'I have to say this, Amory. I feel it's all my fault, somehow.'

'Don't be ridiculous.'

'I pressed you to go on that march. I insisted. Look what's happened in the world since. It wasn't important. Why was I so obsessed with it?'

'You weren't to know that,' I said. 'It was just rotten bad luck. What if I'd been hit by a bus? Would you blame yourself?'

'It was because you were carrying a camera.'

'If I'd turned up another street it wouldn't have happened. It was just bad luck.'

He sat down and took my hand again.

'Bless you for saying that. But I can't help feeling that my . . .' He searched for a word. 'My eagerness. That my urging had—'

'Nothing to do with it.'

He sagged. Smiled. Kissed my forehead.

'Am I allowed to smoke a cigarette out here?'

'As long as I can have a puff.'

He smoked a cigarette – I shared it – and he said he wanted to send a specialist down from London, an eminent gynaecologist. Cleve was worried that a diet of white food and iron pills wasn't good enough, wasn't modern medicine.

'Well, of course,' I said. 'That's very kind of you.'

When he left, he said, 'As soon as you're well, we'll reopen the office. Get you back to work. Get you taking photographs again.'

Sir Victor Purslane had overseen the delivery of some dozens of babies to minor members of the royal family and major aristocrats and charged twenty guineas per half-hour for a consultation in his Wigmore Street rooms. He was very tall and thin, with the slight stoop that very tall men affect. He was bald and his grey side-hair was swept back in two oiled wings above his ears. An elegant, expensively suited, faultlessly polite man, if not handsome – he had small watery baggy eyes.

He was escorted to my room by a guard of honour of two nurses and Dr Wellfleet, the director of Persimmon Hall. The great man had deigned to visit the provinces; the obeisance was almost grotesque.

He examined me thoroughly, internally and externally, he looked at my X-rays, he consulted the records from the London Hospital, Whitechapel, and the daily reports from Persimmon Hall. However sizeable the reimbursement Sir Victor was receiving from Cleve, I still sensed in him an urge to be gone as soon as decently possible, gamely resisting the temptation to look at his pocket watch, hanging from its gold chain and tucked in his waistcoat. Persimmon Hall was not his natural habitat.

Eventually Sir Victor did look at his watch and exhaled.

'You're going to be disappointed, Miss Clay,' he said.

'Disappoint me, Sir Victor.'

'I don't know what's wrong with you. Why you're bleeding like this.'

'Oh.'

'The trauma you suffered was the cause – but you know that as well as I do. Better.' He seemed uncomfortable, for a moment. 'Modern medicine . . . Its triumphs . . . We think we understand all about the human body, have solved its mysteries. But actually I think we know very little.' He reached into his pocket for a small battered silver case and selected one of the five cigarettes it contained and lit it.

'Last week,' he went on, 'I was present at the delivery of a perfectly healthy, bouncing baby boy. Eight pounds. He died yesterday. I haven't a clue why.'

'There are more things in heaven and earth, Horatio—'

'Than are dreamt of in your philosophy. Exactly.'

He stood up and placed his palm on my forehead and smoothed my hair back. It was a spontaneous, unreflecting gesture, perhaps prompted by his recollection of that baby's unaccountable death – and here he was confronted by another mystery. As soon as he realised what he was doing he took his hand away, quickly.

'Time, Miss Clay. Time. You will be well but your own body will have to do all the work. We doctors and our medications can't help you. I've no idea how long it'll take but, in some months, I surmise, you'll start to feel truly better. You'll know it yourself. You're a young woman in her prime. Nature will effect her cure.'

'Thank you.'

'Don't thank me. That's the good news. Now for the bad.'

'Bad?' I felt a spasm of alarm.

'In my judgement, as a result of the severe internal injuries you received in the attack, I believe you will never be able to bear children.'

I looked at him in astonishment. I'd never considered this, not for one moment.

'Really? Are you sure?' I said vaguely, feeling hot, all of a sudden.

'The continual bleeding. The clotting that was observed in the blood in the initial weeks. Everything points at permanent infertility.'

'Right.' Now I felt tears prickle at the corners of my eyes. 'I'll have to think about that. Take it on board.'

'Yes, of course. And now I really must go for my train.'

He shook my hand formally and left.

★

THE BARRANDALE JOURNAL 1977

Today was one of those weird Mediterranean moments you are sometimes blessed with on the west coast of Scotland. A sky of unobstructed azure, no breeze, a constant, steadily warming sun, razor-edged shadows. If only we had cicadas . . . Flam and I walked down from the cottage to the little bay and I had a picnic lunch there – a cheese sandwich, an apple, a square of chocolate and iced gin and tonic from a Thermos flask.

When I think back to my encounter with Sir Victor Purslane and his pronouncement I can still remember the sense of shock I felt, but the strangest consequence of his visit was that the bleeding stopped, almost immediately. Two days, four days, six days went by – no blood. He was correct in another matter: I sensed the change in myself – something had happened, some corner had been turned, I knew, and I began to feel better, slowly and surely. I felt less tired, felt my natural energy returning, I wanted to eat food that had colours in it. My weight loss arrested itself and my pale face began to recover its usual healthy mien.

Dido made one of her rare visits bearing her weekly bouquet herself.

'My God,' she said. 'What's happened? Health – picture of. You've got to leave this ghastly place.'

And so I returned home, to Beckburrow, and reclaimed my old bedroom. A nurse was hired to look after me but she left before two weeks were up as she had nothing to do. I began to eat food that the family ate – steak pies, roast chicken, broccoli, raspberry crumble – and I went for walks, progressively longer, with my genial, ever-beaming father.

My parents had been informed, by handwritten letter from Sir Victor, of my now infertile state. There was little emotion expressed. In fact my mother – mother of three – said quietly to me one day when we were alone, 'You may find it's a blessing in disguise, my dear.'

Xan was at the house a great deal as I convalesced, I remember. He was an undergraduate at Balliol College, Oxford, of all astonishing eventualities. After years of dullard mediocrity, he had experienced a sudden spurt of intellectual energy, as if a dam had been broken. His Higher School Certificate results were excellent. When he went for his interview at Balliol he wore a canary-yellow suit and a matching bow tie. Asked his ambitions, he said he wanted to be a poet. He was awarded a £100 exhibition.

I started to become interested in the world again and what was going on in it. I listened to the wireless, I read newspapers and learned that Germany had annexed Austria, that a 500-ton meteorite had landed near Pittsburgh, Pennsylvania, that something called 'instant' coffee had been invented and that Orson Welles had broadcast *The War of the Worlds* and caused widespread panic.

My father, however, lived in the immediate, proximate here and now. His lobotomy – that was the operation he had undergone – seemed to have left him pretty much unchanged, on casual examination. His mood was uniformly good but he had lost all interest in his old profession, the world of letters: he didn't write a word, he didn't read a word. His entire intellectual life, it seemed, was concentrated around the business of two-move chess problems – composing, plotting, testing and then sending them in to newspapers and chess magazines. And he was extravagantly unpunctual, showing up for lunch at 5.30 in the afternoon, or going to a dentist's appointment in Brighton three days late. I once waited for him at Lewes station for two hours (he had arranged to pick me up in the car). I telephoned the house and was told that he'd set out to collect me just after breakfast. We had no idea what he'd been doing or where he'd been when he returned home shortly before midnight. He smilingly said he'd gone to pick me up but I wasn't there. He gardened diligently and went for long walks on the Downs, a small travelling chessboard bulking out his jacket pocket. His world had become very circumscribed but he was entirely happy within it.

Towards the end of the year Cleve sent me a lengthy apologetic letter (I had written telling him of the transformation in my health, but not Sir Victor's diagnosis). The London office would not be reopening, he said, offering up the usual excuses – money, the world crisis, the state of US publishing, retrenchment in the magazine business, other areas of expansion taking precedence – but he wanted me to meet a friend, a certain Priscilla Lucerne, who was coming to London early in the new year. He would set everything up – he thought it would be worth my while.

In February 1939 Priscilla Lucerne's letter arrived. She would be in London for a week, staying at Claridge's before moving on to Paris. She would love to invite me for tea. So I went up to London to meet her in the Palm Court. She was a petite, slim, elegantly dressed woman in her forties with her hair dyed Bible-black with a short fringe to mid-forehead. Her lips were painted the deepest scarlet. She smoked cigarettes from a ten-inch holder. She failed to hide her disappointment when it became apparent that I had never heard of her, apart from her connection with Cleve. She wasted no time in enlightening me: she was the editor of *American Mode* – and she wanted to offer me a job as a staff photographer.

I saw the hand of Cleve Finzi everywhere – Cleve's sense of guilt in action, trying to make life good for me again after the disaster of *Global-Photo-Watch*.

'But I'm not a fashion photographer,' I said to Priscilla.

'Cleve Finzi says you're an excellent photographer and that's all I'm interested in,' she said, fixing another cigarette into its holder. She looked at me, openly. 'Let's be honest, dear Amory, taking a photograph of a fashion model is well within your capabilities. You know how to light an interior shot, I assume.'

'Yes, of course.'

'We choose the model, the outfit, the location – even, sometimes, the pose. I'm sure you'll cope admirably.'

I wondered what she owed Cleve Finzi, what debt to him had been cancelled by her offering me this opportunity. She didn't seem particularly enthused; she didn't even ask to see my portfolio. I requested some time to think about it. I explained I was convalescing after a long illness.

'Take all the time you wish, my dear,' she said with a wide but empty smile. She had done her duty.

I did think about it, for some weeks, as my strength returned and I began to feel like my old self again. Cleve wrote, prompting me further. Nothing else appealing was on the horizon and I had to earn a living so, eventually, I replied to Priscilla Lucerne saying I would like to accept her kind offer. Formalities ensued; there were the inevitable bureaucratic delays, but in the summer of 1939 I embarked once again for the United States of America, leaving Europe on the brink of war.

4. LE CAPITAINE

WE HAD SPENT THE morning in Central Park, west side, up in the 80s, shooting outdoors as if we were in the country, and now, in the afternoon, had moved back to a rented studio on 7th Avenue in the Garment District. I was taking photographs for a section of *American Mode* entitled 'As You Were Leaving'. On the final two or three pages of the magazine there would be a spread of fashion shots of 'affordable' clothes by unnamed American designers, tacked on as an afterthought for readers who couldn't afford French couture – not that there was much of that available now the war was well under way. This was my daily bread; I didn't enjoy it particularly and I wasn't very good at it, to be honest, but it paid my wages and my name was never credited.

Similarly, the models we employed on 'As You Were Leaving' were not the best known, perhaps a little past their prime, happy to accept a reduction in their usual fee just to be in work. The model I had been photographing in Central Park was Kitty Angrec, in her thirties, like me, and, like me, relatively content to be a back-page girl.

I took her photograph, setting her against a wide paper magenta roll lit with a 500-watt spotlight and a photo-flood number one with silver reflector. I knew it would look fine but my heart wasn't in it and neither was hers – we were both growing tired; it had been a long day. I had an assistant, Todd – they were always changing, some kid or other – and I left him to remove the film from the camera, label it and send it round to the *Mode* labs and followed Kitty into the changing rooms for a drink and a cigarette.

Kitty was a rangy girl who just missed out on being a true beauty. That strange geometry that a face has – eye versus nose versus lips – had managed only to make her ordinarily good-looking. Her top lip was a little too long, the brow-lash connection slightly skewed . . . I had tried to analyse it but couldn't quite understand what was so slightly out of kilter. We both lit cigarettes and I took out a quart of rum and poured a couple of shots into paper cups. Kitty began to undress.

'You want to meet up tonight, Amory? I've got a sitter.'

Kitty had a three-year-old son whose father was in the US Navy.

'Not a bad idea. What'll we do?'

We ran through the options as she removed her clothes. She slipped off her skirt to reveal fishnet stockings and high heels, and as she shimmied out of her slip she dropped her cigarette and stooped to pick it up.

'Don't move,' I said and scampered off to find my camera. I snatched it from Todd – it was a Rolleiflex.

'You haven't unloaded.'

'Not yet, Miss Clay.'

I ran back into the dressing room and switched on all the lights.

'Just do what you did before,' I said to Kitty. 'Stoop down as if you're picking up your cigarette.'

She stooped, bending her knees reaching for an imaginary cigarette. Click.

The resulting image was my best ever fashion shot, in my opinion, of all the hundreds I took for *American Mode*. I shot it in ten seconds with the lighting available in the room. I had it printed up and took it to Priscilla the next day.

'Nice,' she said. 'But I can't run this in *Mode*.'

'Why not?'

'We're not *Bazaar*, we're not *Vogue*. We're *American Mode*. It's a big difference.' She handed the print back to me. 'Nice try, Amory. But it's too . . . provocative. It would have been fine in your scandalous show but not in my magazine. Sorry.'

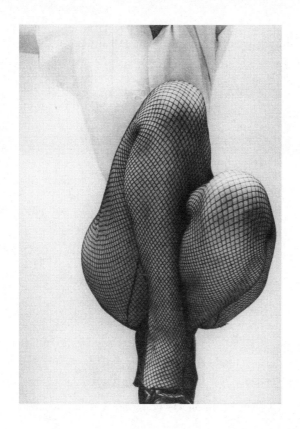

I thought about this as I slipped the print back into its buff envelope.

'How do you know about my show? It was years and years ago.'

'Cleve Finzi told me.'

The Cleve connection, once again.

'Well,' I said. 'It was worth a try.'

'Just keep up the good work, Amory,' Priscilla said, beginning to rummage through papers on her desk. 'We're all very pleased with you.'

It didn't take long to make me realise that I was no fashion photographer – time and again I looked at my photographs for *American Mode* and I saw only stiffness, fakery, self-consciousness – mediocrity. The few snapshots that I managed to take of the

The American Mode *years. The best and the worst.*

models as they changed or grabbed a cup of coffee or chatted at the end of a session seemed a thousand times more full of life. However, nobody wanted those images.

But I dutifully fulfilled my assignments when I was called upon and I lived the good life that the USA effortlessly provided. I was earning $300 a month and was living on the Upper East Side (I didn't want to go back to the Village). I was well, weight regained, hair glossy. No bleeding at all, apart from the odd smear or speckle on my knickers, and my menses had never restarted – stopped altogether, just as Sir Victor had predicted. Some months I would get the familiar cramps, the sensations, the scratchiness, the mood change – but nothing happened. Snub-Nose Lenny's boot had done its damage.

As time went by I sometimes asked myself why I had come back to New York. The main reason, so I rationalised, was that it was a symbol of my return to health. My old life had resumed, Amory Clay was taking photographs again and being paid to do so even if it was strange to be in America as the war in Europe unfolded. I read about it in newspapers, heard bulletins on the radio; I had letters from home; I started sending parcels of food to Beckburrow – it was undeniably there, undeniably taking place, but somehow far in the background.

In the morning I would leave my apartment on 3rd Avenue and 65th and walk to the subway, picking up a newspaper in which I read about the Blitz, that Japan had invaded Singapore, that the Afrika Korps had retaken Tobruk, that the US Navy had triumphed in the Battle of the Coral Sea, but it was as if I were studying something in a dusty historical tome. Here in Manhattan all the lights were turned on, America's profligacy was on tap and there was fun to be had.

Of course, the real reason I came back was Cleveland Finzi. Our affair restarted within two weeks of my landfall, though it was not like the old carefree days. I was worried, also, that first time we made love – it was the first time since my accident, however, to my relief, all seemed well – no pain, just pleasure. My libido was working as normal.

I may have felt the same but Cleve was different – so watchful he seemed almost terrified. We had to meet under conditions of secrecy that an expert spy would have been proud of.

'Frances doesn't even know you're in the country,' he explained to me when I moaned about the preposterous lengths we went to in order our tracks should be covered. 'If she did, it would finish her.'

'That would be a start,' I said. 'Sorry, not funny.'

We were lying in my bed drinking Scotch and soda. We had made love. It was lunchtime.

'She can never know you're in the city,' he said. 'You can't imagine the consequences.'

'All right,' I said, reaching for a cigarette. 'Got the message.' I didn't want to talk about Frances Moss Finzi.

Cleve found a lighter and lit my cigarette and then lit his own.

'We just have to be very careful, Amory. Very.'

'Of course. I don't want to jeopardise your happy marriage.'

He seemed to relax when I said this, as if I were being serious.

'But you're here and you're well and we're together, that's the main thing.'

He held me and kissed me and I felt the familiar lung-inflation, the headspin. He had that effect on me, Cleve. He still moved and disturbed me, whatever guilt he was experiencing, or trying to assuage, or fooling himself, or however irritated or dissatisfied I was at his self-regarding complacency. I could see him for what he was but couldn't resist him. Or at least I couldn't be bothered resisting him, to be more precise. I didn't care: I was in that one-day-at-a-time mode. I owed it to myself, I thought, as recompense for all I'd suffered since that awful day at the Maroon Street Riot. If I wasn't entirely happy, I was at least not entirely unhappy, and that state of affairs wasn't to be disparaged.

The Pearl Harbor cataclysm had altered everything, instantly, like a vast weather system sweeping across the country. Pressure changed, social barometers went crazily awry. In New York I felt it was as if we were suddenly instructed to become serious and responsible; the long endless vacation was over, duty was calling, the conflicted world had come knocking at our door. It was as if the nation collectively grew up and assumed adulthood overnight.

I had exultant letters from my mother and Dido. At last, at last! What took you so long? From my point of view – however happy I was at the change in the military balance of power – the major effect of Japan's surprise attack on the American fleet in Hawaii was that it brought Jean-Baptiste Charbonneau back into my life.

I was in my apartment, one Saturday afternoon in January 1942, when the telephone rang.

'Amory Clay?'

'Yes, speaking.'

'I don't believe it! *Putain!*'

'Who is this?'

'Who do you think? Charbonneau!'

In honour of our first dinner together we agreed to meet again at the Savoy-Plaza the following evening. I was deliberately early and sat in the lobby waiting for him, in a good mood, anticipating. Perhaps Charbonneau was what I really needed, now – a true friend.

A tall thin man with a moustache and an unusual military uniform came in through the revolving doors and looked around. Was it? Yes! Charbonneau, a soldier – impossible. He saw me and strode over, arms wide. We embraced then he took my hand and ducked his head over it, not kissing it, in that formal, symbolic French manner. Then he embraced me again and I felt him press himself against me in an overfamiliar way.

I pushed him off.

'Steady on!'

'You look beautiful.'

'You look bizarre.'

'I'm a captain in the Free French forces. You should salute me.' He stepped back and assessed me, up and down, like a farmer inspecting livestock.

'Yes. Your hair is shorter,' he said. 'And you've lost weight.'

'So have you.' I shrugged. 'I've been ill – for quite a long time. But now I'm better.'

'And I've been running away from Nazis.'

We walked into the dining room. Charbonneau didn't like the table we had been given so we tried another two until he was finally happy. He then ordered a bottle of champagne and a bottle of Château Duhart-Milon 1934 to be decanted, ready for the main course.

He raised his goblet of champagne to me and smiled.

'I feel I'm alive again, Amory. As if nothing has happened since the last time we were sitting here.'

We both savoured the irony. The century was galloping away without us.

Then he told me about the fall of France, the flight from Paris to Bordeaux where the interim government had established its temporary capital for a couple of weeks. After the Armistice, he had thought about staying on in France but had decided it was better to trust his luck abroad, so he headed for Spain and then Portugal.

'It's an interesting city, Lisbon,' he said, musingly. 'I'll take you there one day.'

In early 1941 he had made his way to London – by seaplane – to join de Gaulle's government in exile, the Forces Françaises Libres.

'Yes, and when I was in London I came looking for you,' he said. 'I went to your little flat. All closed. No Amory.'

'I was already over here, in New York.'

He leant back. 'And here we both are in New York. Now. Isn't life very strange?'

'Your uniform doesn't fit you very well.'

'We are a very poor army, the Free French. But they think that if I wear a uniform I will be taken more seriously. I borrowed this uniform. Even these medals are borrowed.' He pointed at the row of medal ribbons over his left breast-pocket. Then he looked rueful and downed his champagne in one gulp. 'They don't like us Frenchies in Washington. Roosevelt hates de Gaulle. Churchill hates de Gaulle. My compatriots don't understand it. Aren't we allies? But no.' He poured more champagne. 'This American civil servant in the State Department said to me: de Gaulle is just a brigadier in the French army, why should we give him all this money, all this support?' He frowned. 'It's a real problem, I tell you, Amory, *ma puce.*'

Our meal arrived, another repeat: rare steaks with a tomato salad. Charbonneau poured the Duhart-Milon.

'American meat, French wine, beautiful English girl. The world is at war but life is good.'

We clinked glasses and drank a mouthful. Then he took my hand. I knew what was coming next.

'I feel it is our fate, our destiny,' he said, lowering his voice and looking me in the eyes, 'to meet like this. I want to spend the rest of the night with you. I don't want to tell you stupid romantic things, talking for hours in this kind of rubbish talk. I respect you too much, I tell you straight, Amory, *en toute franchise*.'

'No.'

'Why not?' He seemed genuinely annoyed. 'What's wrong with me?'

'Nothing. But I'm in love with somebody else.'

He muttered to himself in French, then sighed and looked at me.

'I will get you one day, Amory. You wait and see.'

I had to laugh.

'Eat your steak, *mon capitaine*,' I said. 'It's getting cold.'

I remember exactly when I heard the news about Pearl Harbor. I was in a small deli on 6th Avenue having a late lunch, eating a meat-loaf sandwich with a Dr Pepper to wash it down. I was acquiring American tastes. It was Sunday morning in Hawaii and the first baffled news reports were coming in over the radio to the East Coast. The whole delicatessen fell silent and we looked at the radio on the counter as if it were some demonic instrument of propaganda.

'John Jack Anthony!' somebody shouted at the back of the room – an oath I'd never heard uttered before or since. 'What the heck's gonna happen now?'

I remember Dido coming to New York towards the end of 1941 to play in a recital at Carnegie Hall – part of a big pro-British, join-our-war push. There was a programme of English music: Elgar, Delius, Moxon, Vaughan Williams.

Dido and I went to the 21 Club after her recital. The room stood and applauded as she entered – twenty-seven years old, my little sister, plucky, pale, beautiful, radiating self-assurance as she blew kisses and bowed gently as the acclaim washed over her. A new Britannia. I took a few steps back from the limelight.

We ate eggs Benedict and drank cold Chablis.

'I feel I'm in another world, another universe,' she said. 'The voyage over was completely terrifying. And you should see London. Blackout, impenetrable darkness. Then as the sun rises, smoking ruins everywhere. People frightened, miserable. Try to buy a box of matches – impossible. People saying to you, "Better dead than defeated." It's appalling.' She looked around the bright, raucous room. 'We're losing, Amory. We're not going to win on our own, not even with the Russians – and they'll be done for any day now. That's what's terrifying us.' She lowered her voice. 'Why won't the Yanks join in? What's stopping them? Can't they see the awful danger?'

'It's very complicated,' I said. 'When you've been here, even a day or two, you'll begin to understand. What's going on in Europe seems a million miles away. Nothing to do with us.'

'I'm going to order another eggs Benedict,' she said. 'Is that too, too greedy? Eggs, eggs, eggs. What wonderful things.'

I summoned a waiter over and ordered another round of eggs Benedict and another bottle of Chablis.

Dido lit a cigarette. 'By the way,' she said. 'hold on to your hat. Xan has joined the Royal Air Force.'

I remember being sent out by *Mode* on a fashion shoot to Taos, New Mexico, in January 1942, just before I met Charbonneau again. This wasn't for 'As You Were Leaving', this shoot was to be used as backdrop for the summer fashion issue and we needed sunshine. I assumed Priscilla couldn't find a photographer of any repute so she had decided to entrust me with the assignment. It rained the entire week we were there and all my photographs were rejected. I offered my resignation. It was accepted and then promptly rescinded twenty-four hours later. Cleveland Finzi running my life again.

What the incident showed me was that I had to stop taking photographs of pretty girls in expensive frocks and I began to search through my small archive trying to assemble a collection of my own work, work that I was proud of. It was not substantial. So I began to take new photographs – a sequence that I called 'Absences'. Clean plates on a kitchen table. Empty chairs on the gravelled path of a garden square. A hat and a scarf hanging on a coat stand. The human presence was absent but its traces remained. I told myself that the impetus for these pictures arose because I was lonely in America, far from home, but a little further thought made me realise that these photographs of empty or recently vacated places might have had something to do with my infertility. The absence looming in my life.

I remember going into Saks Fifth Avenue and buying a grey suit with green check for $35. I wore it out of the store and went straight to the Algonquin Hotel to meet Cleve. We drank cocktails then went upstairs to the room he had booked to make love. That evening we saw a movie called *Dark November* and ate at Sardi's before returning to the Algonquin. As we walked back the streets were full of soldiers and sailors – America at war! – and I recall feeling particularly happy, as if I had won a prize. But as I acknowledged that happiness the thought came that life couldn't continue like this. Change was in the air for everyone; the world was changing, me included.

I remember the moment when I knew it was over. Cleve and I were staying at a small hotel – the Sawtucket Inn – on Cape Cod Bay. I hadn't seen him in over a month but somehow he'd managed to secure this two-night break for us. Frances suspected nothing. Cleve had told her he was at a colleague's funeral and would be away for a couple of days.

We were lying in bed in the morning in that fuzzy self-indulgent mood of bliss you experience when you've made love on waking and know you don't have to get up and go to work, or anywhere, if you don't feel like it, and are vaguely contemplating the possibilities of one more fuck before a big breakfast. Shall we? When will we be together like this again? I don't know if I can. Oh, you'll be fine, leave it to me . . .

Somehow the idle conversation turned to a movie. Cleve leant over me and brushed the hair from my brow. I felt his cock thickening against my thigh. He kissed my throat.

'It's just like that moment,' he said, 'you know, in the movie we saw – when Haden Frost looks at – what's her name? – Lucille Villars. What was it called? And you just know. You know they're going to jump into bed.'

I frowned, thinking. 'What movie?'

Cleve ran his hands over my breasts. Kissed my nipples, kissed my right ear.

'Come on. You said it yourself. The sexiest look between actors in the cinema. Ever.'

'I said that?'

'The sexiest look *ever*.'

'Haden Frost wasn't in *Dark November*.'

'I know. It was *I Want Tomorrow*.'

'I haven't seen that film.'

He wasn't really listening, that was his mistake.

'We talked about it for half an hour, honey. Remember? How in movies these looks – if they work – can do more than ten pages of dialogue. That's the acting skill . . .' He stopped, realising suddenly.

I sat up slowly, my brain working fast. He rolled back off me, reached for his cigarettes.

'I haven't seen that movie,' I repeated. 'We never had that conversation.'

He was good, Cleve, didn't give anything away. He took his time lighting his cigarette and smiled at me, shrugged.

'Sorry. Must have been talking to Frances about it, then.'

'Probably.'

I snuggled back down next to him, not wanting him to see my face and the shock registering on it. That's when I knew he was seeing somebody else. Frances never went to the movies because of her wheelchair. There was another woman in Cleve Finzi's life. Now we were three.

★

THE BARRANDALE JOURNAL 1977

Lunch today at the Glenlarig Hotel with Alisdair McLennan, Greer and Calder's son. He was up on a visit with his two children, parking them with his parents as much as he could. He wanted to meet me, he said, wanted to talk about Vietnam, hence the lunch. He was in his thirties, with fine reddish-blond hair, and a blunt ordinary-looking face – pale-lashed, pale blue eyes – but he was attractive in a vital, super-intelligent way that was all to do with his brain. He had one of those restless, opinionated minds, always seizing on something to say or comment on; some sharp observation was made whether it was about the daily amount of seaweed washed up on a beach, or trade-union manipulation of the Labour Party, or ferry monopolies in the Western Isles, or that Anthony Eden was the best prime minister we'd ever had – but never realised. Everything was potential grist to his brain power.

Within about two minutes I knew I didn't like him – not because of his manifest intelligence but because he was one of those men who cannot conceal their sexual interest – their sexual curiosity – about any and every woman they encounter.

I was aware of him eyeing me up, looking at my breasts, my face, my hair, my clothes – stripping me naked, mentally – as we sat drinking our gin and tonics in the hotel bar. Here I was, sixty-nine years old, chatting away, as this young man's querying lust, his snouty evaluation, first assessed and then casually rejected me. Maybe all men do this – instinctively consider the sexual potential of every woman they meet. I can't say – but all the men I've known have taken care to conceal it from you, if you're a woman, unless that encounter is taking place expressly with some sexual end in mind, of course.

I saw Alisdair's sexual radar switch from me to Isla, the young waitress who brought us our menus. Isla was a big plain girl with strange caramel-brown eyes and I sensed Alisdair McLennan's idle carnal interest now play over her as she stood there, taking our orders, like an invisible torch beam, probing, considering, and then being switched off. Nothing doing.

As a consequence, I became a bit dry with him, a bit clipped and cynical, as if to say: I've got your number, my friend – and it doesn't appeal. But I don't think he picked up the nuances – these kind of men don't. It's a variant version of pure ego – they're never aware how others are judging them.

In any event, we did talk about Vietnam, vaguely. I said it had been so long since I was there that I didn't think any observations I might make would be valid any more.

'You got into a bit of trouble when you were out there, didn't you?' he said, casually, pouring us both another glass of wine.

'How do you know that?' I said, at my driest.

'You know, that whole SAS thing.'

'You haven't answered my question: how do you know that?'

'I read your file.'

'What file?'

'Everyone has a file somewhere – especially if they've led a life as interesting as yours.' He smiled, and couldn't keep his patronising manner concealed. 'I'm in the diplomatic service, I get to see files.'

I took my time, drank a mouthful of the Bordeaux, and put my glass down, turning it on the tablecloth for a moment. Then I looked at him squarely.

'It was a very difficult time, back in the late Sixties. Everybody was lying. Everything was falling apart.'

'Well – all ancient history.' And he smiled again and changed the subject.

I knew then at once that although he may ostensibly have been going to Saigon as a diplomat he was in fact working for the security services — a spy, or a handler of spies. That was why he wanted to meet me.

'Do you still keep in touch with anyone out there, by the way?' he asked, later, pouring the rest of the wine.

'No,' I said. 'They're all dead, now.'

5. Operation Torch

THE STRANGE ASPECT ABOUT the affair I embarked on with Charbonneau was that it seemed almost immediately normal – as if we'd been lovers for years – the question in my mind being why had it taken us so long?

We had dined together two or three times, whenever Charbonneau could slip away from Washington and come to New York. I remember towards the end of the year he called me in a foul mood, saying he had to escape from the hell of DC and his '*foutue mission*'. What about dinner? Choose a new French restaurant – it had to be French – let's test it, as we used to. I need some fun, he said. Come to the apartment and have a drink, first, I said. I'll find somewhere interesting.

My new place was on 65th Street between 3rd Avenue and Park. I had the top floor of an old crumbling brownstone with my own entrance at the side. An ancient lady and her maid lived in the rest of the building but I rarely saw them. Once a whole two months went by without a glimpse.

Charbonneau arrived, took off his ill-fitting captain's jacket and explored my rooms as I mixed two manhattans. I heard him opening cupboards and drawers, running taps in the bathroom as if he were a prospective tenant.

He wandered back into the sitting room and I handed him his drink.

'Are you all right?' I asked. 'You seem a bit depressed.'

'We are invading French Africa tomorrow,' he said. 'Morocco. Or rather you are. Americans and British fighting the French. *C'est bien déprimant.*'

'Fighting the bad French – you're good French.'

'It's very complicated.'

'Everything's very complicated, Charbonneau. Life is complicated. It's what you always tell me.'

'It's top secret. Don't tell anyone.'

I raised my glass. '*Bon courage aux alliés.*'

'Your accent is terrible but the sentiments I approve.' He paused, thinking. 'Approve of.' He smiled ruefully. 'At least we have twelve million Russians soldiers on our side. How can we lose, in the long run?' He seemed uncomfortable, all of a sudden. 'What is it, Amory? Why are you looking at me like this?'

'I'm just looking at you. A cat may look at a king.'

'Have you found us a restaurant?'

'No.'

His exasperation was obvious.

'All right. So we don't eat. We call for a Chinese meal.'

'Afterwards.'

He looked at me, understanding now what was going on. He closed his eyes and did a little shimmy on the spot, shuffling his feet, rolling his shoulders. He looked at me.

'So?'

'The answer is yes.'

I lay in the dark of my bedroom beside Charbonneau – who was sleeping the sleep of a satiated man – thinking about Cleve. Had I done this because of what I'd discovered about the other woman, whoever she was? Perhaps. Then I thought: maybe it's more complicated, like everything, as Charbonneau said; maybe it was a way of showing myself that I was free.

In the morning I brought Charbonneau a cup of coffee as he lay in bed.

'Is this "light" coffee or "dark" coffee?' he asked.

'I think it's light. Lots of hot milk.'

'Only in America.'

I sat down beside him.

'I want you to know something,' I said. 'I told you I'd been very ill. One of the consequences is that I can't have any children.'

He shrugged, put his coffee down and took my hand.

'Well, you know, it could be worse. I have a child. I never see her.'

'You have a daughter?'

'From my first marriage. She's called Séverine. She's ten years old.'

'I don't know very much about you,' I said.

'And I don't know very much about you,' he countered and flipped back the sheet. 'Shall we get to know each other better?'

★

THE BARRANDALE JOURNAL 1977

I suppose I should add, in the spirit of fair comparison with the other men whom I have made love with, that Charbonneau's penis was quite small and stubby, though he had a surprisingly and disproportionately large and heavy scrotum. What shook me first, though, when he was naked, was his hairiness. He had a great pelt of black hair over his chest and belly and loins. Out of this thicket his small, darkly pigmented penis protruded. He had hair on his back also and of course on his arms and legs. I was initially in a state of some alarm – I'd never seen such a shaggy monster of a man – but as soon as he embraced me I realised that the hairs on his body were soft and yielding, like a fine expensive fur, and after a while I found his hirsute presence quite stimulating.

Today, I took out my old Leica and went down to the end of the bay where the rock pools are. It was sunny, with just a few speeding clouds going by and I wanted to take pictures of the rock pools with the sun bright and glaring overhead – spangling, dazzling. I intended, in other words, to take pictures of light in such a way that you would never know it was light reflected in rock pools. This was my new plan, my new obsession. Snapshots of light-effects were what I wanted to capture – luminescent starburst abstract moments that no painter could reproduce. Windows reflecting street lamps; close-ups of chrome bodywork in full sunshine; shallow puddles clustering dappled sunspots. Light stopped – light static. Only the automatic eye could do this. I had a new book in mind.

★

It seemed to me that, after my intermittent affair with Charbonneau had been going on for a few weeks, Cleve was beginning to sense something. He sensed a change in me – but it would be wrong to say that he was suspicious.

About two days after Charbonneau's latest visit from Washington and his '*projet inutile*' I received a telephone call from Cleve late at night. I was alarmed as he never called the apartment.

'What's happened?'

'I want us to meet. But at the office. A proper meeting.'

'What if Frances hears about it?'

'It doesn't matter any more.'

'What's changed?'

'Come and see me. I'll explain.'

We met the following day at *GPW*'s offices in Midtown. I passed Phil Adler in the corridor on the way to Cleve's office. He had a wax paper cup of water in his hand and he stopped so abruptly on seeing me that it slopped over the rim and splattered on to the floor.

'Amory! You're back. My God! Call me, we have to get together.' He kissed me on the cheek. 'This is great.'

'Back after a fashion,' I said. 'But I'll call you.'

Cleve sat me down across from his desk and we both lit cigarettes. I was still in Charbonneau mood and found that I could look at

Cleve objectively with no miasma of emotion blurring the view. He was wearing mauve braces – suspenders – over his pale blue shirt and his cerise tie was loosened at the neck. He looked every square inch the handsome magazine editor in his corner office but I wasn't quite so beguiled by it in the way I used to be. It struck me that this was what pleased and satisfied Cleve about his life and it explained why he would never leave Frances. It would be too inconvenient, too hard and awkward to maintain the image, otherwise. And of course I was part of that perfect big glossy picture, also. Thank you, Jean-Baptiste. I was seeing Cleveland Finzi plain.

'What's going on, Cleve?'

'We're reopening the London office.'

'Really?'

'And of course I want you to run it again.'

'Why?'

'There are hundreds of thousands of American servicemen in England. Pouring in. Soldiers, sailors, airmen. We're missing out – *Collier's*, *Life*, *Saturday Evening Post* – everyone is running over there. I put it to the board – they agreed we should reopen. You've done the job before; you have all the contacts. We can steal a march.'

I sat there in silence for a few seconds then tapped the ash off my cigarette. I knew at once I was going to say yes but I wanted him to earn it.

'I like it here,' I said. 'And I'll miss you.'

'I'll be coming over all the time. And when I'm over it'll be different – better. No ducking and diving, none of this secret-agent stuff.'

'But my apartment, *American Mode*—'

'I'll take care of everything. Seventy-five pounds a month, plus expenses.'

I thought to myself: Diana Vreeland is on $500 a month and she's the fashion editor of *Bazaar*.

'Can I think about it?'

'No. Absolutely no. It has to be you. I can't send anybody else.'

'When would I have to leave?'

'Yesterday.'

Charbonneau poured himself another glass of wine, and then emptied the bottle at my invitation.

'Let's have another,' he said. 'I leave *chiant* DC and I come here to New York to see you – and life has some meaning, at last. It makes me want to get drunk. Like a fish.'

'As drunk as a fish – I like that. But don't get too drunk. We want to enjoy our last night together.'

He actually spluttered, then dabbed at his chin with his napkin and set his glass down carefully.

'What are you saying to me, Amory?'

'I'm going back to London. I've got a new job. Sorry to bring you the bad news on our lovely evening.'

'Well, not so bad.' He smiled, his big, tigerish, pleased-with-himself smile. 'One reason I'm drinking so much is that I didn't know how to tell you my own news.'

'Which is?'

'I'm going back to London, also.'

BOOK FIVE: 1943–1947

I. Typhoon

'FLIGHT LIEUTENANT CLAY, PLEASE,' I said.

'Ah, yes . . . Yes, Miss, we're expecting you. And the name of the organisation again? If you don't mind?'

'*Global-Photo-Watch*. It's an American magazine.'

I was in the adjutant's office of RAF Cawston in Norfolk. A flight sergeant was checking the appointment diary and collating the entry with my identity papers and letters of introduction. All seemed well.

'I'll drive you out there, Miss,' he said. 'Can I give you a hand with the cameras?'

'No, no. I'm fine thanks.'

We stepped outside and he showed me into an olive-green staff car and we sped off through the base, past low hangars, with grass growing on their roofs, and anti-aircraft gun emplacements dotted here and there, towards distant aeroplanes parked by a long thin runway.

'Thought you'd be more interested in the Yanks next door,' the flight sergeant said.

'I'm going there tomorrow.'

'You'll eat well, that's for sure. Oh, yes sirree.' He went on in the same envious culinary vein comparing what was available in the sergeants' mess in RAF Cawston with the gourmet feast of 'amazing grub' served up at USAF Gressenhall. 'It's a different world, Miss, I tell you.'

I let him chat on, not telling him of my familiarity with American 'grub', preoccupied with the prospect of seeing Xan after all this time. I felt I'd missed a whole chapter of his life. Two chapters. The diffident schoolboy and guinea-pig breeder I knew best had gone to Oxford, published a book of poetry and was now a fighter pilot. How did these drastic changes happen in life? Then a moment's thought told me that it happens all the time. Time is a racehorse, eating up the furlongs as it gallops towards the finish line. Look away for a moment, be preoccupied for a moment, and then imagine what has passed you by.

We pulled up at a parked Typhoon fighter plane, surrounded by a thick six-foot semicircular glacis of sandbags. The Typhoon was big and bulky for a single-seater aircraft, canted steeply back on its solid-looking undercarriage, and it had a gaping intake – like a mouth – under the three-bladed propeller. Xan stood beside it, one hand in a pocket, watching us arrive, smoking a cigarette. He was wearing his sheepskin jacket and his flying suit, as requested. He seemed taller and thinner since the last time we'd seen each other at Beckburrow. We embraced. I stepped back and looked him up and down.

'Well, well, Marjorie – who would've thought.'

He laughed and just for a second I saw the little boy in him again.

'Oh, yes,' he said, wagging his finger at me. 'When I saw the request, "Miss A. Clay of *Global-Photo-something-or-other*" wanting to take my photograph, I did smell a rat.'

'I just wanted to see you,' I said. 'I've got to take pictures of all these American airmen and their bombers tomorrow so I thought I'd sneak in a visit to my little brother.'

I made him stand by his Typhoon, leaning on the wing by his open cockpit, as if he were about to climb into it and take off on a mission, and pretended to take photos of him – there was no film in my camera – for the benefit of the flight sergeant from the adjutant's office who was standing looking on, approvingly.

I wandered round the aeroplane. A big solid machine – like a tank with wings, it had remarkable heft, not like the other fighters, the Spitfires or the Hurricanes. This was a beast.

'What kind of plane is this?' I asked.

'A Typhoon.'

'I know that, silly. What kind of Typhoon?'

'A Hawker Typhoon Mark Ib. It can fire rockets.'

'Why is it painted with these black and white stripes?'

'I'm not allowed to tell.'

'Something to do with the invasion?'

'Shall we go to the mess? I've got a present for you.'

We were driven to the officers' mess, an old rectory outside the base perimeter. The drawing room looked on to a wild garden with an unmown tennis court. Outside I could hear a cuckoo calling in the woods beyond the pink-brick boundary wall.

Xan brought me a gin and orange and he had a half-pint of beer. We lit our cigarettes and talked dutifully about the family: Father's health (good, stable), Mother, Dido's fame, cousins, aunts and uncles. Then he handed me a slim book in a brown paper bag.

I took the book out and stared at it in some wonder. A purple cover with dull gold lettering. *Vertical Poems* by Xan Clay, V. L. Lindon and Herbert Percy. I felt tears of absurd pride brim at my eyelids. I hastily flipped through a few pages to distract myself from my emotion. I understood the title immediately – all the poems were thin like ladders, one or two words per line.

'Why like this, vertically?'

'Read the afterword – not now, obviously, but when you have a moment.' He smiled, leaning back, searching for an ashtray. 'It's a little poetic movement we've started – me and two friends from Oxford – trying to do something different with poetry, out of the ordinary, shake things up a bit, if we can. Maybe you could write about us in your *Global-Photo-Thingamajig*.'

'You have to sign it for me.'

'Oh, but I have.'

I looked at the title page: 'For Amory with love from Marjorie Clay.'

I blew my nose, had a small coughing fit, all to cover up the tears that had now begun to flow.

'You're meant to be happy, not tearful,' Xan said.

'These are tears of happiness, Marjorie,' I said. 'You've no idea how proud I am of you.'

I grabbed his head with both hands, pulled him towards me and covered him with kisses. He had to beat me off.

Half an hour later he had the mess steward telephone for a taxi to take me to my hotel in Fakenham. As we stood waiting under the rectory's porch he introduced me to his fellow pilots, fellow officers, as they came and went. They all looked as if they were playing truant from school. This was the curious effect my siblings had on me. I felt like Xan's great-aunt – decades older than him – while Dido made me feel like a child.

He kissed me on the cheek and opened the door of the taxi for me.

'It's absolutely appalling,' he said. 'I haven't asked you a single question about yourself. It's all been me, me, me.'

'That's precisely why I came to see you,' I said. 'Now I'm completely *au courant*.'

'Are you happy, Amory? You seem happy.'

'Happy to see *you*, darling,' I said, ducking the question.

We drove off down the lane to Fakenham and I looked back through the rear window and saw him wave at me. Then someone asked him for a light and he turned, fishing in his pocket for his lighter.

I wiped away residual tears. Why was he making me so lachrymose? The transformation in him, I suspected – while I wasn't looking he had become someone entirely different. A competent Xan, a young man who could take his strapping plane, armed with its rockets, power it into the air and go into battle. It shook you up, that kind of realisation.

'So, Miss,' the taxi driver said, over his shoulder, 'what's your bet for the invasion? July or August?'

The Vertical Poets, Oxford, 1942. Left to right, Herbert Percy,
V. L. Lindon and Xan Clay.

'Premonitions' by Xan Clay

Stars
foretell
the fall
of
czars.
Strummed
guitars
lead to
hidden
bars.
Huzzahs
greet
news
of life
on
Mars.
Time
stands
still
in
Shangri-las.

2. HIGH HOLBORN

THE NEW *GPW* (London) offices were at the west end of High Holborn. We had three rooms on the top floor of a building with an oblique view of the dirt-mantled roofs of the British Museum. There was my office, Faith's annexe and a kind of waiting room where journalists and photographers would gather and that swiftly came to be an informal club. We had a cupboard with a decent supply of liquor (gin, whisky, bourbon, sherry) and cigarettes – courtesy of our New York parent office – a couple of shabby, soft sofas and walls covered with framed photographs and past issues of *Global-Photo-Watch*. In the time between the pubs closing after lunch and reopening in the evening it was an even more popular venue to gather and while away the dead hours of the afternoon. Free booze, free cigarettes and kindred spirits.

We had opened the offices in the early summer of '43 and had become something of a holding pen for various American newspapers, magazines and the smaller wire services. Apparently our ability to supply swift accreditation via ETOUSA (European Theatre of Operations US Army) had become well known. It was nothing to do with me – Faith Postings did all the liaising and paperwork and she was clearly very good at it. So, as it turned out, we were also acting as proxies – and charging a fee – for around a dozen other American publications and press agencies, including *Mademoiselle* and the *Louisiana Post-Dispatch*. Once the journalist or the photographer had the accreditation from ETOUSA they would be assigned to a particular unit in the services – the air force was the most popular – where they would be handled and supervised by that unit's press officer and department.

By this stage of the war the process was running fairly smoothly. The journalists – including several women – once accredited, were issued with uniforms and granted the honorary rank of captain. There was always a considerable amount of paperwork involved but, once assigned, the working atmosphere depended on each unit's particular disposition towards the press – ranging from lax and friendly to hostile and authoritarian – an attitude usually determined by the personality and character of the commanding officer.

One day at the end of May '44, Faith popped her head around my door and screwed up her face apologetically.

'There's a strange gentleman here asking for you. Insisting. Says he knows you.'

'What's his name?'

'Mr Reade-Hill, he says.'

Greville was standing in our club-room peering at the photographs on the walls through spectacles so cloudy they seemed opaque.

'Greville?'

He turned, snatching off his glasses, and strode across the room to embrace me, kissing me on the cheek. I smelled the odour of poverty coming off him, that sour reek of the unbathed, of unwashed clothes. He looked pale and considerably older and his moustache was untrimmed and grey. His suit was shiny with wear and the obvious repairs had been crudely stitched – by Greville himself, no doubt.

We went for a stroll, had a cup of tea and a sandwich in a café and ended up sitting in the watery May sunshine on a bench in Bloomsbury Square. The talk had been banal – all about family matters and a lot of disingenuous quizzing of me about my job at *GPW*. I was waiting for the real reason for our encounter to arrive.

At the Great Russell Street end of the square, a silver, deflating, three-finned barrage balloon was being winched down on to its lorry. About half a dozen young WAAFs were fussing around and their excited girls' voices carried across the grass to us.

'The thing is, darling, I'm pretty much broke, these days,' Greville said, looking across the square at the barrage balloon, not wanting to meet my eye. 'I'm afraid young Bruno rather cost me a fortune, one way and another.' I sensed Greville's old pride and confidence had turned to bitterness. I remembered the handsome, dashing figure he used to cut in his dinner suit, hobnobbing with royalty, aristocrats and millionaires.

By now the balloon had been pulled down on to the grass and the WAAFs were fussing about its rear end, looking for the leak, I supposed. The balloon was huge, fifty feet long, and as it was half deflated it pulsed and billowed as if it were alive, somehow, gasping for breath, a fantastical sea monster washed up in this small square in central London.

'I was talking to your mother,' Greville said, his voice heavy with shamefaced apology, 'and she mentioned, just in passing, that – ah – you were hiring half the photographers in London.'

'Not true. We tend to deal only with Americans. We're an American magazine.'

'Yes. Of course – silly of me. Thought she'd got it wrong. Anyway, it was a chance to catch up, at least.' Now he turned to me. 'I always regret our . . . Our little falling-out over your lost photographs. Your Berlin ones.'

'We didn't fall out, Greville. The whole thing was a nightmare.'

'I wish I'd been a bit braver, though. I think it was having all those policemen in the drawing room. And then the word "obscene" being mentioned all the time. Very disturbing word, "obscene", especially when it's repeated every five seconds, very destabilising. I wasn't thinking straight.'

'It was all a long, long time ago,' I said, consolingly, and unreflectingly put my hand on his knee, feeling it bony and fleshless, like a thin log beneath the worn worsted of his trousers. I took my hand away.

'And then this bloody war finished me off,' he said with some vehemence, and went on to relate that since 1939 his work as a society photographer had virtually ceased.

'And I'm someone who took a portrait photograph of the Prince of Wales,' he said. 'And do you know what my last job was? Three months ago. Some fucking woman wanted me to take a picture of her cockatoo.'

'Ah. Pet photography.'

'Exactly. The graveyard.'

I thought a bit. I couldn't bear to think of Greville Reade-Hill photographing people's pets.

'There is one job I might be able to swing your way,' I said. 'But it would mean going abroad. Italy.'

'I love Italy.'

'Greville, the war's on there, also. It's not a holiday.' I had remembered that one of our *GPW* photographers had been invalided home, injured by shrapnel.

'Yes, of course. You're not sending me to Monte Cassino, I hope. That doesn't sound much fun at all.'

'No. But I could get you accredited as one of the photographers we have with the Second Army Corps.'

'British Army?'

'American.'

'I love Americans.'

'On one condition – that you don't go near the front line.'

'No fucking fear!'

We stood up and I suggested he return to the office with me and give all his details to Faith, and we wandered slowly back to High Holborn. I sensed Greville's confidence returning: an almost physical change seemed to be taking place; he stood taller, his stride lengthened, as if he'd had some sort of mystical transfusion.

'Where do you live these days?' I asked.

He looked a little embarrassed. 'Actually, I'm living in a sort of hotel in Sandgate, on the south coast. Your mother's very kindly helping me out. What does this job pay, out of curiosity?'

'A hundred dollars a week.'

'What's that in real money?'

'About twenty pounds.'

'Marvellous. Bloody hell. Saved my life, Amory, darling.' He nodded, squared his shoulders and turned to me again. Smiled at me. 'Darling Amory – resourceful, helpful, sympathetic, lovely – you couldn't give me a small advance on my salary, could you?'

★

THE BARRANDALE JOURNAL 1977

This morning I brought Flam back from his overnight stay at the vet's in Oban and carried him into the cottage and laid him in his basket by the fire. He seemed a little livelier, trying to lick my face, patently glad to be home. I set him down and then placed a bowl of 'high protein' dog food in front of him. He sniffed at it but otherwise wasn't interested.

Yesterday morning I had come downstairs and he was standing awkwardly by his basket, neck and head held low, coughing every five seconds or so. I looked at his face and saw there was a little mucous discharge from his nostrils. He rallied a bit when he saw me but he was moving sluggishly. So I picked him up, dumped him in the front seat of the Imp and drove in to see the new vet in Oban. The vet, oddly enough, was a young Dutchwoman (married to a Scot) called Famke Vogels. 'Big made', as my mother used to euphemistically say, but I liked Famke because she didn't bother much with niceties, just made her point. She told me to leave Flam in overnight and come back tomorrow for the diagnosis.

'Just a bacterial pneumonia,' she said when I returned. 'Nothing to worry about.'

She had given him an antimicrobial vaccination and supplied me with a course of antibiotic pills to be administered twice a day.

'Do you know how to do this?' she asked.

'Yes. He's not my first dog.'

My first dog, also a black Labrador, was called Flim. He was run over by a farm tractor and his spine was broken. When the anguished farm labourer brought me to him – he was lying in the verge, all twisted, whining – I knew there was nothing I could do. Or rather, there was only one thing to be done.

The vet in Oban, Famke's predecessor, a Mr McTurk, took one look and said to me, 'There's no option, you know that, don't you?' I agreed, and Flim was taken away, after I'd given him a farewell kiss, and he was put out of his significant misery, poor dog. I buried him – weeping uncontrollably – at the edge of the beach looking over the bay. I was thinking: poor dog – lucky dog, that his pain ended and his departure from this world was achieved so speedily and with no further suffering than that he'd already endured. You lucky dog – we should be so lucky, as lucky as sick dogs.

As Flam made himself comfortable I went and fetched the pill bottle and crouched down by him.

'Time to take your medicine, laddie,' I said.

I try not to talk to my dog as if he's a sentient human being but it's impossible, as any dog-owner will tell you.

I opened Flam's mouth and placed the pill at the back of his tongue to the side. Then I held his jaws closed with one hand, holding them upwards – he was perfectly compliant – and waited a second or two. He didn't seem to have swallowed so I blew on his nose and massaged his throat, gently. I felt the reflex in his gorge and let him go. He licked his teeth; the pill had gone down.

I gave him a kiss on his forehead and scratched behind his ears and saw his tail give a beat or two of pleasure.

'What would you do without me, eh, Flam?' I said.

He was trying to climb up me to lick my face but I pushed him back, the unwelcome thought entering my head: who will feed me my pill when the time comes?

★

I remember, now, that Charbonneau had been far too overconfident about his destination. I travelled back to London from New York in early 1943 – on the *Queen Mary*, no less – while Charbonneau was sent to North Africa in the aftermath of the Operation Torch invasions and was plunged into the internecine mayhem of who was to take control of the Free French. I assume that the Free French governmental authorities, whoever they were, thought that his American experience and know-how would serve them well with Eisenhower and his staff.

I remember walking into the wide lobby of the Savoy to meet Cleve on his first visit over and seeing him standing there, waiting for me, in his dark suit and brilliant white shirt, and feeling I was taking part in some absurd dream or fantasy. We ate in the downstairs Grill and then went up to his suite and made love. Everything about his demeanour had changed in London; it was like the old days in the Village. He was perfectly relaxed, his usual enthusiastic, funny, dry self and we wandered about London without him glancing once over his shoulder.

Cleve had been right, to that extent – the move away from New York and its attendant paranoias reinvigorated our encounters as they newly occurred, every six weeks or so. But I had changed in the interim – there was the Charbonneau quotient to consider now, unbeknownst to Cleve. I had one short, frustrated letter from Charbonneau – from Algiers, sent to me at the office. The line I recall was 'I thought Washington was bad. I would cut off my right hand to be back there, now.' Poor Charbonneau.

I remember accompanying Greville to Victoria station to see him off to Italy. He was going to join a convoy sailing from Portsmouth. He looked smart and raffish, wearing his dark war-correspondent's uniform with its designated shoulder patches, and he had a fore-and-aft forage cap set on his head at a suitably rakish angle. He carried a musette bag slung over his shoulder with his camera equipment and other essentials in it. I was touched to see that his moustache was trimmed and dyed a hazelnut brown. He looked almost like his old self and I complimented him.

'Actually, I had the uniform altered at my tailor's,' he said. 'It was very ill-fitting.'

'Well, you look very pukkah, Captain Reade-Hill, very much the dashing war correspondent. Just don't do anything dashing.'

'Cowardice is my middle name,' he said, kissed me and whispered, 'Bless you, darling.'

I remember that the most irritating consequence of my precipitate departure from New York was that I had to miss the publication of my first book, *Absences* (Frankel & Silverman, 1943). It appeared, to deafening press silence, two months after I returned to London. My publisher, Lewis Silverman, said he was sending me six copies. They never arrived, victim, I suppose, of erratic wartime postal services or of some U-boat attack. I asked Cleve to bring me over some copies on his trips to England but he always – typically – forgot. I finally managed to see a copy of *Absences* after the war, in 1946, three years late, by which time it was already long out of print. I wonder if this experience is unique in the history of publishing. It was a collector's item, very rare, booksellers told me when I tried to track one down.

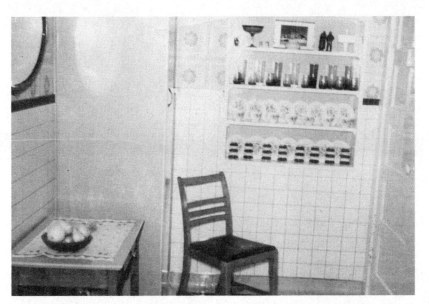

Images from Absences *by Amory Clay (Frankel & Silverman, 1943).*

3. D-DAY

CLEVE CAME OVER AT the end of May for a week. We spent two nights together at the Savoy in his suite with its splendid view of the brown, ever-changing river. On the morning of 4 June, after our second night together, we stayed in bed until noon, calling up room service to order toast and jam and a pot of tea that we spiked with bourbon. We made love again before we sauntered downstairs to the Grill for lunch.

The Grill was full of senior military and naval types along with a smattering of old regulars. If it hadn't been for the uniforms – and the somewhat reduced menu – you would never have believed we were in our fifth year of the war. We amused ourselves listening to the conversation of two elderly, heavily made-up ladies of a certain age who were sitting behind us and whose patrician voices were ideally clear and carrying.

One said, 'I'm going to live in Ireland after this war.'

The other, 'I worry that Ireland will become over-smart.'

'It'll never be Kenya-type smart.'

'I suppose not . . . There are some nice houses.'

'Nice houses and cheap and plentiful staff.'

'Always an advantage. Why won't you stay in London?'

'London will be drab and dreary. I need change. I need heavenly dullness.'

Cleve leant over and whispered.

'And these are the people our boys are dying for?'

'Well, they're not really representative of—'

Then I saw Charbonneau come into the Grill and stopped talking in mid-sentence. He was in his khaki uniform and was wearing his round gendarme-style hat that he swiftly removed. He was led to a table some distance away against the far wall. My mouth was dry and I felt suddenly faint. Cleve signalled to a waiter for more coffee.

'Let's just pay our bill, shall we?' I said.

'No, no,' Cleve said. 'I don't want to miss the next chapter. Not for the world.'

On cue, the first old lady said, 'Do you know, I think Gloria lacks feminine charm.'

Her companion said, 'She doesn't have a developed social instinct, that's the problem.'

I heard no more because at that moment Charbonneau spotted me and our eyes met. For an awful moment I thought I was going to vomit as I saw him rise to his feet and cross the dining room towards us.

'Hello,' I managed to say, hoping there was sufficient surprise in my voice. 'How are you?'

Cleve had switched his attention now. So I made the introduction.

'Cleveland Finzi, this is – I'm so sorry, I've forgotten your name.'

'Jean-Baptiste Charbonneau.' He shook my hand, giving it a surreptitious squeeze, then Cleve's.

'I met Miss Clay in New York, she took my photograph.'

'That's right,' Cleve said. 'We ran a story on you, I remember. You wrote a novel, a bestseller.'

'For a week or so,' Charbonneau said, with appealing but untypical modesty. I could see he was enjoying himself, now.

'What a coincidence,' I said, more faintly than I meant. 'And here we all are in the Savoy Grill.'

'Very good to see you again,' he said, giving me a little bow. 'Nice to meet you, Mr Finzi,' he said to Cleve and strolled back to his table.

'Are you all right?' Cleve asked.

'Actually, I feel a bit sick,' I said. 'I think I'd better get back to the room.'

Back in the suite I kept up the charade. I went into the bathroom and retched and spat, ran water. It must have been something I ate, I said, better get home, see you tomorrow.

Cleve wanted to call a doctor – I said no, I'd be fine, I insisted. He made me sit down and drink a glass of fizzing Bromo-Seltzer that he had in his bag and I composed myself.

'Is this good for nausea?' I asked.

'It's good for anything.'

Half an hour later I walked out of Savoy Court on to the Strand to find Charbonneau waiting for me in a shop doorway, smoking a cigarette.

Back in Chelsea – in my new flat on the corner of Oakley Street and the King's Road – I poured each of us a whisky and water while Charbonneau did his usual prospective-tenant act, opening drawers at random, peering into my small bedroom, flushing the WC.

'That was him, wasn't it?' he said as I handed him his whisky.

'What do you mean?'

'Your American boyfriend. He's the one.'

'Boyfriend is the wrong word. He's the man I'm in love with, yes.'

'You don't love him, it's obvious.'

'Wrong, Charbonneau, I do.'

'I thought you loved me.'

'Ha-ha. I'm very attached to you. I love Cleve.'

'Nonsense. Deep down, *au fond*, you really love me.'

I closed my eyes. I wasn't going to continue this conversation.

I had never thought of myself as promiscuous, or a 'loose woman', as my mother would have put it. I was thirty-six years old and had only made love with three men. It was hardly evidence of nymphomania, but, as I lay awake in bed beside the gently snoring Charbonneau, I found it hard to come to terms with the fact that I had slept with both my lovers in the last twenty-four hours – well under twenty-four hours, in fact. It didn't feel like me, somehow – and yet it incontrovertibly was the case. What was happening? It hadn't been planned, so that was some reassurance.

I slipped out of bed and padded through to the kitchen. It was five past five in the morning according to the clock on the shelf by the cooker and a faint citrus light – grapefruit and orange – was beginning to seep into the sky above Chelsea and I could see it was a cloudy blustery day if the darkly tossing crowns of the plane trees in Carlyle Square were any indicator. Where was summer? – it was June, for heaven's sake. I put the kettle on the gas hob and fetched out the teapot. I'd let Charbonneau sleep on and see if my mind cleared a bit. I had never expected him to re-enter my life with such embarrassing surprise.

He emerged looking for coffee at around nine o'clock, wearing his khaki trousers and my too-small dressing gown, his hairy wrists protruding from the tartan sleeves. I was dressed by this time and had been going over *GPW* paperwork. I had telephoned into the office saying I still felt ill – I was due to meet Cleve for lunch – impossible with Charbonneau around. He took me in his arms and kissed my neck.

'You're the best thing for me, Amory. When I'm not with you, I find I'm thinking about you – not all the time, but enough.' He smiled. 'It's not normal for me.'

'What is normal for you?'

He ignored me. 'Have you some coffee? I can't drink your English tea.'

'What made you go to the Savoy?' I asked. 'It was an incredible coincidence that you should just walk in like that.'

'No, no. I knew that you were there. I went to your office and your charming secretary said you were in a meeting at the Savoy. So I go to the Savoy, I ask for you at the front desk. No – no Miss

243

Clay. Then I see you – with this man – going into the Grill. I went away, I had a drink in a pub and I thought – no, I must see my Amory, I don't care who she's with.' He spread his hands. 'And here we are. Aren't you pleased?'

'I have some coffee essence.'

'No, don't worry. I smoke a cigarette.'

He went to the window and lit up and stood there looking down on the King's Road. I heard a sudden patter of rain on the glass.

'No invasion today,' he said. 'For sure.'

'What're you talking about?'

'The invasion of France. It will probably be tomorrow.'

Faith knocked on the office door, her double rap that meant it was important. I was interviewing a photographer. Five more were waiting in the club-room – we needed people in Normandy, urgently. *GPW* had nobody with the invasion fleet and I couldn't understand why we'd been so remiss or how we'd been overlooked. Cleve had no idea so I had to work fast.

'It's your mother,' Faith said. 'Says it's a matter of some urgency.'

I took the telephone at Faith's desk.

'Mother, what is it? I'm incredibly busy.'

'Prepare yourself for sad news, my dear.'

'What? What sad news?'

'Your father has died.'

It was 6 June 1944. Le Débarquement. And the day my father died. D-Day. Dead Dad Day.

My father had been sitting in his favourite sheltered spot – a small open wooden gazebo that he'd had constructed at the foot of the garden at Beckburrow, working on one of his two-move checkmate chess problems when my mother had summoned him in for lunch. After lunch he said he was feeling tired and was going to take a nap. She called up to him in his bedroom when supper was ready and when he didn't appear she went to look for him and found him still asleep, so she thought, and shook him by the shoulder – but he was dead. From a heart attack, seemed to be the likely explanation.

The funeral was on 10 June, remarkably speedy, given the momentous times we were living through, and was in Claverleigh's parish church, St John the Less. It was a short service, one hymn, one reading – I read one of Xan's poems from his collection, called 'A Monk, Watching' – and an address given by Eric Maude, the playwright who had adapted my father's story 'The Belladonna Benefaction' – the one bona fide success in his life. Maude was an elderly, flushed man with a dandelion mane of white filmy hair and whose memory was not sure. He kept referring to my father as 'Brotherton', for some reason, not Beverley. 'Brotherton was the most generous of collaborators.' I could see my mother growing increasingly irritated.

Other mourners included some colleagues from *Strand* magazine and the publishing houses that my father read for. His own publisher was not present. Dido was there, of course, and she played a loud and complex toccata by Buxtehude as we all filed out into the graveyard, our ears ringing. Xan was flying combat missions over northern France in his Typhoon and Greville was away in Italy with the 2nd US Army Corps.

As the coffin was lowered into the ground the air was loud for a few minutes with the passage of dozens of high-flying bombers heading across the Channel and we all looked up. As the final blessing was spoken the noise of the planes diminished and I glanced round the small churchyard, dry-eyed, glad that my father's death had been so sudden and just sorry that the two and a half decades since his awful experience in the First World War had been so devastating and undermining. I was pleased that his last years had been calmer and that his troubles were now over. 'Rest in peace,' the vicar said, barely disguising his boredom – he might have been saying 'Pass the salt' – but I had to agree.

The day was cool but sunny here in East Sussex, at least, and as the drone of the planes vanished it was replaced by the sound of a wood pigeon calling in the beech trees that lined the graveyard behind its waist-high ashlar wall. Every time I hear wood pigeons I will think of my father, I said to myself, and found the mnemonic consoling.

We decided to walk back to Beckburrow where sherry and biscuits were waiting to be served as a modest wake. Dido and I accompanied Eric Maude, who wielded a stick, but strode briskly, all the same, saying he was more than happy to stroll back, remembering – entirely falsely – the many walks he and Brotherton had taken around Claverleigh. We soon caught up with my mother who was at the head of the party, keen to be first at the house. She was in something of a state, frowning and upset.

'Don't worry, Mother,' I said, taking her arm. 'It was a lovely service.'

'There's been no obituary. It's a disgrace!'

Her mood didn't improve and she took to her bed in the afternoon when the guests had departed.

Dido and I went down to the gazebo with a bottle of sherry and a box of cigarettes. My father's chessboard was still set up with six pieces laid out on it: a rook, a pawn, two knights and two kings. The last two-move composition he had been working on.

'Make any sense to you, these problems he posed?' Dido asked, pointing at the chessboard.

'No, not a clue. Mate in two moves. Baffling.'

'He couldn't remember the time of day but he could solve fiendish chess problems . . . Funny old thing, the human brain. You were Papa's favourite,' she said, suddenly, topping up our sherry glasses. 'Strange fellow, our father. He only tolerated me and Xan.'

'He tried to kill me, Dido.'

'Oh yes, of course. Forgot about that.' She lit a cigarette.

I thought about what Dido had said and wondered if that were true. Had I been my father's favourite? If I had, then that made his descent into madness all the more poignant, and the inevitable rift that occurred between us all the more sad and remorseful. Everything had changed after that day at the lake and as I sat here looking at his impossible chess problem the regrets began to accumulate within me almost unbearably. Just what had I lost, in fact? What had that war done to my father – and what part of him had been taken away from me forever?

Dido was saying something – I was glad of the distraction.

'Sorry. I was just thinking of Papa,' I said.

'I've got something to tell you. I'm leaving Peregrine.'

I thought for a moment. Yes, this was significant: leaving Peregrine Moxon, the composer, the mentor, the man who had created Dido Clay from humble Peggy, the child prodigy.

'Are you just leaving him? Or leaving him for someone else?'

'For someone else.'

'Do I know him?'

'Reggie Southover.'

Blank. 'Should I have heard of him?'

'For heaven's sake, Amory! Reginald Southover, the playwright.'

'At least it's not Eric Maude.'

'That's not in the least bit funny. You must have heard of him. He had two shows running in the West End in the summer before the war.'

'I was in New York.'

'Well, we're madly in love.'

'How old is he?'

'Fifty-five. No, fifty-seven.'

'Dido, you're twenty-nine.'

'I'm old for my age.'

'That's true. Is he rich?'

'That's got nothing to do with it.' Pause. 'He's well off, I admit.'

'What about Peregrine?'

'He says he'll kill himself.'

'Poor thing.'

'Good luck to him, I say.'

I closed my eyes as Dido rambled on about Peregrine's failings – his enormous selfishness, his profound weakness as a man, his persistent jealous attempts to control her career – and tried to conjure up an image of my father before he was ill and I saw him, in my mind's eye, standing on his hands, mocking and pitying us poor deluded inhabitants of our topsy-turvy world.

Peggy (Dido), my father and me around 1918.

I remember the month of June 1944. I stayed on at Beckburrow to keep my mother company, commuting to London by train, but it wasn't really necessary as she seemed to pick up her old life without fuss. I suppose my father's inconspicuous presence these past years had barely registered as she went about her business. He kept himself to himself, working on his chess problems; there was a cook and a housemaid to provide for and supervise him and they both met only at the evening meal – or sometimes not. Now he was gone so were the small traces he left at Beckburrow.

The sky above East Sussex in those weeks of June was full of aircraft flying to France and back again. Then in mid-June came the flying bombs – the doodlebugs – announced by the annoying sputtering roar of their engines. 'Bugs' was the wrong name – they were big, like small single-seater aeroplanes. I remember standing on the roof of the Holborn offices and seeing three of them at once and then the motor cut out on one of them and it arced down, like a thrown stone, somewhere in the region of St Paul's. There was a percussive boom and a cloud of smoke and brick dust blossomed up prettily from the impact. In Chelsea I would lie in bed and hear them coming over – like a small motorcycle in the sky or an aerial lawnmower. There was something almost comic about the noise. But I lay there rigid – the noise was what you wanted; when it suddenly stopped, the fear kicked in as you imagined it hurtling down out of the night sky.

I remember I saw Cleve just once, briefly, after my night with Charbonneau. He seemed to suspect nothing; all was well and he said he'd be back in August. But I told Charbonneau he couldn't stay on in my flat – to his sulky irritation. I found it impossible being the meat in a Charbonneau–Finzi sandwich. I didn't like them both being in the city, paradoxically – I found it different from the situation in New York. How can I explain this? Perhaps because Cleve was back to his old self and I felt guilty betraying him. Life is complicated enough and I think I felt that, now my father had died, I didn't need any more complications.

In the event, Charbonneau didn't stay long in London. He left the week after Cleve, posted to Corsica to prepare for Operation Dragoon, the invasion of southern France that took place two months later. He was liaising between General Lattre de Tassigny's French Army B and the US 7th Army. He sent me a regular supply of postcards detailing how fed up he was – and how well fed he was.

I remember going on a three-day holiday to Woolacombe in Devon towards the end of June. An English *GPW* photographer – Gerry Mallow – had a cottage there and a ketch, named *Palinurus*, moored in Ilfracombe harbour. We would take the ketch out with a picnic and many bottles of beer and cider and sail out to Lundy Island.

It was an odd experience being on a holiday like that with people I didn't really know very well. I went for walks and read books, happy to leave the running of the office to Faith. In an unconscious way I was also coming to terms with my father's death, I now realise. I wasn't feeling grief; I was assessing the end of a relationship. My natural father–daughter relationship with B.V. Clay had ended that afternoon when, in his madness, he had tried to kill us both. Every encounter I had with him subsequently had been shadowed by that event and despite the civil, dutiful signs of affection between us, I was always wary of him, watchful. The bonds had been broken and all that was left was the official designation – a father, a daughter.

I took a camera with me to Woolacombe, of course, but barely used it. One day when we were out sailing on the *Palinurus* I left it by the wheelhouse and somebody took a photograph of me. I discovered it two weeks later when I had the film developed.

★

Me on the Palinurus, *1944.*

I don't have many photographs of myself – a trait common to most professional photographers, I believe – but I've always been fond of this one, for some reason. It's probably my second favourite photograph of myself, after the one taken on my wedding day.

Flam has made a speedy recovery. The familiar dog in him is back. We walked over to the McLennans' today and it tired him out rather – I mustn't forget he's as old as me in dog years.

★

I remember the doorbell ringing in my Chelsea flat very early in the morning on 1 July. It was 6.30, I saw by the kitchen clock. It rang and rang. I hauled on my dressing gown and hurried downstairs to the street entrance. It was my mother, but my mother as I'd never seen her – hair wild, eyes red-raw from weeping. I rushed her upstairs, she was wordless, sobbing, and sat her down. She sat there shaking, staring at her hands.

'What is it mother, what's happened?'

'It's Xan. I've had a telegram.'

I felt my lungs empty and my spine arch. I sat down slowly.

'Xan's missing. Missing in action, they say.'

4. PARIS

I LOOKED AT THE map again.

'Take the next right,' I said to Pearson Sorel, the driver of my jeep.

We bumped along a track, a sunken lane between high hedges of beech and hazel in the depths of the Normandy *bocage*, and turned right, pulling into the front yard of a farm called Le Moulin à Vent. A tethered collie gave a harsh peal of angry barks and then lay down again.

'Wait here,' I said to Pearson, stepped out of the jeep and approached the front door of a low stone building with a shallow-pitched tile roof. To one side of the courtyard there was an open wooden barn and a small stable with two loose boxes. I was wearing olive-green fatigues and a tin helmet, wanting to look as martial as I could. I had my camera in my knapsack and a box of 200 Lucky Strike cigarettes for use as a potential present, if required. I knocked on the door and said '*Bonjour*' to the stooped ancient woman wrapped in a shawl who opened it. She looked me up and down and shouted 'Arnaud! Arnaud!' – and Arnaud duly appeared, a toothless smiley man with rosy cheeks and an immense soup-strainer moustache, like Nietzsche's. Son or spouse? It wasn't clear. I showed him the document I had – in French – my French wasn't good enough to explain what I wanted. He searched for and found a pair of spectacles and read it carefully.

'*Ah, finalement,*' he said. '*Suivez-moi, mademoiselle.*'

We walked across the farmyard and through a gap between the barn and the stables. The land sloped down to a large apple orchard, an acre or so in extent. It was now September and the leaves were turning yellow and the ground between the trees was lumpy with windfalls. We made our way down through the orchard towards its end. Halfway through our progress I began to see the smashed trees, some snapped cleanly in half, and there, like some sort of bizarre tilted metallic ruin, was Xan's Typhoon. The great boss of the propeller was buried deep in the turf, the blades shattered, the plane's back broken. The Perspex canopy had been pushed open and the seat and the instrument panel already looked mossy and mouldy and I saw a spider's web strung from the joystick to the cockpit faring. One wing was fifty yards away, ripped off by the impact; the other wing was lifted crazily, near-vertical, showing the empty rail mountings where the rockets had been slung.

Strangely, the Typhoon, smashed and broken up like this, seemed even bigger and heftier in the orchard than it had when parked by the runway at RAF Cawston. Maybe it was the size of the apple trees, mature yet stunted and broad as apple trees are, that caused this delusion of scale, making the crashed plane seem even more surreally out of place in this orchard than it already was.

Arnaud was complaining and I understood enough to know that he was asking why this wreck that had been in his orchard for over two months now had not been cleared away.

'*Bientôt*,' I said, confidently. '*Très bientôt*,' as if I had some power to effect its removal. I walked around the Typhoon, taking photographs, thinking about Xan's last flight. I had used my journalistic connections with the air ministry, and then his squadron, to piece together as much information as was available.

Xan had flown a sortie at the end of June, the target a chateau in the Argentan area that was believed to be an army-group headquarters. He and the three other Typhoons in the flight had released their rockets in the face of only light anti-aircraft fire and had substantially damaged the chateau. It was therefore bad luck that Xan's plane was hit, I was told, as it was observed peeling away after the first pass and trailing smoke and was then seen to crash in an apple orchard a few miles away. Apparently Xan had survived the crash and was standing waiting by his plane when he was shot dead by the first panicked German troops that arrived. A week later when Canadian forces overran the sector they were led by the local priest to Xan's body, lying in a crypt in the church.

These were the few facts I had and as I walked around the plane I tried not to let my mind fill in the gaps and failed. Xan's relief at surviving the crash, climbing stiffly out of the cockpit – maybe he lit a cigarette ... Then hearing shouts, seeing the German soldiers running through the trees towards him, resigning himself to becoming a prisoner, raising his hands in surrender. Then the shots ...

I turned to Arnaud.

'*Le pilote. Il était là?*' I pointed to the ground beside the plane. '*Ou plus loin?*'

Arnaud shrugged. He didn't know. There were a lot of German troops hiding in the village from the air attacks. They had seen the plane crash and had come running. He stayed back.

'*Il a été abattu, le pilote. Vous savez?*'

'Yes. He was my brother,' I said without thinking, then, seeing his uncomprehending face, translated it into French. '*Il était mon frère.*' It sounded so different in French, so final, somehow, and it proved too much for me. I began to cry and the old man took my hand and led me carefully out of the orchard.

★

THE BARRANDALE JOURNAL 1977

I still think about Xan, all these years later, thirty or so years on, and still curse myself for not having had any film in my camera that day at RAF Cawston. Why does it bother me? I've plenty of photographs of Xan – as a boy, as a young man – he's stopped in time forever. But somehow I feel it would have been good to have snapped him by his plane, his Typhoon that became his coffin. Stupid mistake. Another mistake.

I was thinking about the mistakes we all make – or rather the concept of a 'mistake'. It's something that can only be realised in hindsight – big mistake or a small one. It was a mistake to marry him. It was a mistake to go to Brighton on a bank holiday. It was a mistake to write that letter in red ink. It was a mistake to have left home without an umbrella. We don't sense mistakes coming, there's this crucial unforeseen factor to them. So I found myself asking the question: what is the opposite of a mistake? And I realised there wasn't a word, in fact, precisely because a mistake always arises from best intentions that go awry. You can't set out to make a mistake. Mistakes happen – there's nothing we can do about them.

I walked along the beach on my little bay thinking of Xan. He was only twenty-seven. Almost 100,000 RAF airmen died during the Second World War, I read somewhere. The fact that Xan was one unit in that huge number makes it all the more terrible. One butcher's bill for one family amongst the myriad served up by that conflict.

★

But it was Xan's death that sent me to Paris. I felt I had to leave London, do something, and after the liberation of Paris in August I sent a teleprint to Cleve saying that we should set up a *GPW* office in Paris. '*New York Times* and *Chicago Tribune* have reopened their Paris offices,' I wrote. 'We will be left trailing behind.' A week later the go-ahead came with one caveat: I was to be joined as co-bureau chief by one R. J. Fielding, a seasoned journalist and foreign correspondent who had just been let go by the *Washington Post*, for some obscure reason, and promptly hired by Cleve. I didn't mind – I didn't care – I only had this overwhelming desire to go to France and find out where Xan had died.

R. J. Fielding – 'Jay' – was a lean, tall fifty-year-old who had covered the Spanish Civil War and the Sino-Japanese War in the 1930s. He had his grey hair shaved in a severe crew cut and wore rimless spectacles that made him look like a sporty professor. He was a widower and had a wry, unperturbed view of the human predicament. I became very fond of him and I'm sure, following on the death of my father, I saw him as a handy paternal substitute.

Paris in 1944 was a beautiful illusion. If you kept your eyes half open the city seemed unchanged and as perfect as ever, even after four years of war. If you opened your eyes wider the changes forced on it became apparent. Little things: the clatter of wooden-soled shoes, not leather; a very erratic electricity supply; no hot water; a main course of tinned peas and nothing else served without apology at a fancy restaurant. But the mood, despite these privations, was buoyant and intoxicating – liberation was liberating – somehow these minor inconveniences were not going to be allowed to undermine Paris's spirit of place.

The new *GPW* office was in the *deuxiéme* arrondissement – a top-floor flat in an apartment block in the rue Louis-le-Grand, just a couple of blocks away from the Hotel Scribe, the journalistic headquarters for all newspapers, radio stations and press agencies covering the Allies' push towards the German border. In rue Louis-le-Grand we had converted the sitting room into our office (we had no telephones) with desks for Jay Fielding and myself. One bedroom was for our rather grand secretary, Corisande de Villerville, a pale moon-faced young woman, almost terminally polite, who spoke perfect English and was happy to work all hours for our limited wages. I had a room in the Scribe but I often slept in the apartment's spare bedroom – something about the crazed bustle of the Scribe put me off – rather too many people playing at being war correspondents, intoxicated and self-important at being in liberated Paris. All communications were at the Scribe and the military censors, also, vetting copy and photographs, and so I was obliged to spend much of the day there. It was a relief to leave and go back to the calm and solitude of the apartment. Jay Fielding had a room at the Lancaster – I suspected he was independently wealthy – and of course I had Charbonneau.

Charbonneau's small apartment was on boulevard Saint-Germain though he was rarely in it. He gave me a set of keys but I spent only one night there alone as I found the Charbonneau atmosphere – his possessions, his clutter, his smells, his personal spoor, as it were – too unsettling, *sans* Charbonneau, himself. He was busy travelling through liberated France on Forces Françaises de l'Intérieur business, seeming permanently exhausted, always complaining – but he was glad, nonetheless, to have me in his city and was very keen on me in uniform.

'You know, American uniforms are so much better than British or French,' he would say, looking me up and down. 'More chic. More rugged. Even the shape of the American tin helmet is better. *Soigné.*'

'Yes, yes, yes.' He was driving me mad with this analysis. Like many French intellectuals of the time Charbonneau had a sophisticated contempt for the USA – crass, vulgar, philistine, no cuisine, money-obsessed, and so on – but was simultaneously passionately Americanophile when it came to cultural matters – films, jazz, literature.

One of his favourite authors, Brandon Ritt, was in Paris working for *Time* magazine and Charbonneau had contrived to meet him and they had struck up a sort of friendship and he often asked him to dine with us. I'd vaguely heard of Ritt during my New York years. He had written one hugely successful, 600-page novel, *The Beautiful Lie*, that had been an enormous pre-war bestseller and was made into a movie (that flopped), and he had been living off its success now for nearly a decade while working on its long-awaited, much-heralded sequel, *The Ugly Truth*. He was in his mid-forties and good-looking in a ravaged, dissipated way – he was the heaviest drinker I'd ever met, up until then – and was a strange mixture of occasionally disarming and funny self-deprecation at war with an off-putting, overweening egotism. 'I may be a shit writer,' I remember him saying once, 'but I'm richer than any of the good ones.' Charbonneau was oblivious to this polarity, always ready to exalt Ritt as a genius – something Ritt was happy to hear as often as Charbonneau cared to mention it.

After my trip to Normandy to find Xan's crash site I tried to concentrate on my work. We were busy, Jay and I: Allied armies were in Italy, and advancing up from the Mediterranean and racing on through France and Belgium on a front that now stretched from the Channel to Switzerland, all readying themselves for the final push into Germany. Apart from *GPW* business we were still accrediting journalists and photographers from other magazines and newspapers so our days were filled.

I went one day to the Scribe to introduce a young woman journalist, who'd just flown in from the States, to the chief press relations officer of SHAEF (Supreme Headquarters Allied Expeditionary Force – that had superseded ETOUSA). She was called Lily Perette and was twelve years younger than me. As we sat in the lobby waiting for our appointment she began speculating about what unit she'd be assigned to – 'Anything in Patton's Third Army,' she said – and I found myself envying her. Lily Perette was duly assigned to the 3rd Army and was absurdly grateful to me – as if I had been responsible, somehow. I realised, as we had a drink in the Scribe's bar to celebrate her posting, that I was still restless, still troubled by Xan's death, and I wanted to be up and doing things not buried under bureaucratic documentation in Paris. I was a photographer, I reminded myself, not an administrator – so why shouldn't I be assigned to a unit as well, just like Lily Perette?

I cabled Cleve seeking permission and he refused. I threatened to resign and he reluctantly conceded. I sped myself through the accreditation procedure – I would still be working for *GPW* – and waited to see where I would be assigned. It turned out to be longer than I thought as there were so many journalists heading for the European front, now that the war seemed to be entering its final phase, that units in the field didn't want any more – they were becoming a burden. I looked about me at the Scribe and saw dozens of men and women hanging around waiting for their posting. I asked Jay Fielding to use his old war-correspondent experience and pull some strings.

I remember Charbonneau telling me he had a week's leave and that we were going on a trip. He had a car, he had a laissez-passer and, more importantly, he had six jerry cans of petrol. I told him that if I was assigned I'd have to leave and return immediately but, in all honesty, it didn't seem likely, so I was keen to go.

We drove south down the *routes nationales* to Provence, to a village called Sainte-Innocence about ten miles east of Saint-Rémy. It took us two days to reach there, travelling through a provincial France that showed few signs of the occupation. We might have been driving south in the 1930s, I thought, in Charbonneau's big black Citroën, staying at small hotels, eating surprisingly well, setting off in the morning sunshine with the windows open, the plane trees at the side of the road swishing monotonously by.

We arrived at Sainte-Innocence at dusk and Charbonneau picked up the keys to a house from the local butcher. We drove out of the village and turned up a dirt road that climbed to a small wood of umbrella pines on a bluff that was a stepping stone, a threshold, to a bigger, rockier mountain behind.

He swung open iron gates and we drove into an overgrown garden – there was just enough light to see – of oleanders, rosemary bushes and a great stand of cypresses planted as a barrier to the mistral. The house itself was a classic pink *crépis* Provençal *mas*. Two storeys, long and thin, one room deep with a terrace running along the facade and an old stone barn set opposite so that a sort of courtyard was formed.

'It's called the Mas d'Epines,' Charbonneau said, stepping out of the car and looking about him. 'It was all thorn bushes here before they cleared it.'

'It's very beautiful,' I said. 'Wonderful. Whose is it?'

'It belongs to me,' Charbonneau said with a proprietorial smile. 'I bought it with the royalties from my fourth novel – *Cacapipitalisme*. A little present to myself. I haven't been here since 1939.'

'Goodness,' I said. 'Lucky you.' Somehow Charbonneau always managed to surprise me.

The house was filthy, full of blown leaves and years of accumulating dust. Birds had been roosting in some rooms. Spiders and their webs were everywhere and I didn't want to think about the rodent population. We lit an oil lamp, swept out a bedroom, and on a horsehair mattress we laid fresh sheets that we had brought with us. Charbonneau had bought several bottles of local red wine and a large *saucisson sec* in Sainte-Innocence and we sat on the terrace wall as the night came on eating slices of *saucisson* and drinking as much wine as we reasonably could. At a nice pitch of inebriation we went to bed, chasing a bat out of the room before we settled down.

'I love this house,' I said, lying in his arms, stroking his soft pelt. 'I don't know why but I just love it.'

'We could be happy here, I think,' Charbonneau said. 'Don't you?'

'Is that a proposition?' I asked.

'Let's say it's an invitation.'

'But I have to get back to Paris. I'm going to be assigned.'

'This war will be ending soon,' Charbonneau said, rolling on top of me and looking down at my face. 'Sooner than you think. What will you do then, Amory Clay?'

I remember one day, when we had come back from our week in Provence and I was still waiting for my assignment to arrive, Jay Fielding and I were hanging round the lobby of the Hotel Scribe wondering where we could go and eat when I saw Brandon Ritt step out of the lift. He sauntered over to us – he seemed a little unsteady.

'Jay, Amory. Wanna go to a party at the Ritz?' he said. 'Lots to drink.'

'Sure,' Jay said. 'And maybe I could take a shower.' The Ritz was famously the only hotel in Paris with constant hot water in 1944. 'Coming, Amory?' he asked.

'Why not?' I said, and so we strolled the short distance from the Scribe to the place Vendôme. I had never been in the Ritz, and walking across the wide square with its tall monument towards the hotel entrance – Ritt involved in some harsh denunciation of an American writer I had never heard of – and then stepping into the huge lobby was another of those Paris '44 time-travelling moments. I was in my uniform – dark brown khaki jacket, pearl-grey skirt, my forage cap in my handbag – but, as we rode up in the elevator to the suite of rooms on the third floor where the party was taking place – I could hear the volume of noise in the elevator by the second floor – I had the sensation of being some ingénue in a 1920s film, a young girl going to a decadent party where bad behaviour would occur.

Ritt led us down the corridor – a dozen people had already spilled out of the rooms as the party spread inexorably. We pushed our way in; the roar of noise was tremendous, as if everybody was shouting instead of talking. The windows on to the place Vendôme had been flung open to try and dispel the fug of cigarette and cigar smoke, most of it rising from two poker tables with eight-man games under way. On a large dresser under an ornate cut-glass mirror with crystal sconces were ranked bottles of bourbon, gin and rum, and ice buckets filled with bottles of champagne.

I lit a cigarette quickly – it's curious how smoking in a smoky room clears the sting from your eyes. Ritt brought me a glass of champagne – Jay had disappeared, maybe in search of an unoccupied bathroom with a shower.

'You're a very attractive woman, Amory,' he leered. 'Tell me about you and Charbonneau. What exactly is the situation?'

'We're getting engaged,' I lied.

'That's great. Congratulations. So maybe we could have some fun before you're actually *fiancés* ...'

'I don't think Jean–Baptiste would be very happy about that.'

Ritt put his arms around me.

'Jean–Baptiste would let me fuck his—'

He never finished because from behind came a great bellow.

'Get your dirty hands off that young woman, you talentless cunt!'

I turned to see a thickset man with a full beard. He embraced Ritt and then they shadow-boxed each other. Ritt introduced us, out of breath.

'Amory Clay, the most beautiful photographer in the European theatre. Meet Waldo Fartface.'

More raucous laughter. I said hello, pleased to meet you.

'Are you English?' the man asked, looking me up and down. 'But in an American uniform. I like that.' He looked at my sleeve badge. 'Ah, war correspondent, like me. Welcome to the club.'

'I am indeed English.'

'Well, listen, my English beauty, if you're a photographer there's one man here you have to meet.' He started shouting in Spanish. '*Dónde está Montsicard?*'

A shout in reply came from one of the poker tables and 'Waldo' led me over to the table – he was reeling drunk, it was clear by now – where a thin young man in a cheap suit stood up. He had very olive skin and the white of his open-necked shirt seemed to glow against it.

'Felip Montsicard, meet a beautiful English photographer.' We shook hands and Waldo turned to me. 'Felip was the best fucking photographer in the Spanish war.'

Waldo lurched off leaving me with Felip Montsicard himself. I felt I was in some sort of weird parlour game. Who would I meet next? Marlene Dietrich? Maurice Chevalier? Oscar Wilde?

Montsicard offered to refill my glass and off he went leaving me alone again. I lit another cigarette and moved to the window, feeling the density and weight of the heavy gold brocade curtains hanging there, held back in a swag by plaited black velvet bands.

Across the room, surrounded by cheering onlookers, Brandon Ritt was breaking up a chair, stamping it to tinder, as if it had attacked him in some way.

Montsicard returned with my champagne.

'You are photographer? With who?'

'*Global-Photo.*'

'Is good.' He had a thick Spanish accent. 'I am with *Life.*'

'I know.'

'So you know who I am. Montsicard, the photographer.'

'Yes, it's a pleasure to meet you.'

'You know Capa? He's here also.' He pointed at a poker table, at a small-dark haired man studying his hand.

'No I don't know him.'

'That's Capa.'

Ritt was now throwing the remains of the chair out of the window on to the place Vendôme.

'He means well,' Montsicard said, diplomatically. 'But Ritt is very unhappy. In love matters, you know.'

I saw Jay Fielding pushing his way across the room towards me, his cropped hair gleaming with water droplets.

'Where've you been?' I asked.

'Taking a shower, I told you.'

I looked round and saw Capa sliding out of his seat at the poker table, heading for the drinks. Jay scanned the room.

'They're all here tonight. Look, there's Irwin Shaw. George Stevens, John Steinbeck ...' he smiled at me. 'All we need now is Marlene Dietrich.'

And then Marlene Dietrich walked in.

Charbonneau was actually very annoyed when I told him where I'd been. Extremely annoyed.

'Brandon took you there? To the Ritz?'

'He just said come to a party. How was I to know?'

'Why didn't you tell me? Why no telephone call?'

'I thought you were in Bordeaux. Ritt asked and I said you were out of town.'

His exasperation made his voice uncharacteristically shrill. He was growing even more annoyed.

'But I was here – here in my apartment, doing nothing.'

'How was I to know?'

'Irwin Shaw was there?'

'Everyone was there, yes, and Irwin Shaw. Everyone. Even Marlene Dietrich.'

'*Putain!*'

He paced about his little sitting room, sulking, cross. Just as in his New York apartment the walls were lined with ascending columns of books, heading for the ceiling.

'I saw Robert Capa and met Felip Montsicard.'

'Who are they?'

'Photographers. Famous photographers.'

'I don't give one shit for photographers.'

'Thank you very much.'

'Did you speak to Shaw?'

'Yes, for quite a long time.'

'What about?'

'I can't remember. I was shockingly drunk by then.'

'*Ce n'est pas vrai. Ce. N'est. Pas. Vrai.*'

He calmed down after a while and we went to the Café de Flore across the street and had a plate of carrots and a bottle of very bad Burgundy.

'I have news,' I said, as nonchalantly as I could manage, as we finished the wine.

'You're going to marry Ernest Hemingway.'

'I've been assigned. Finally. I'm going to the US Seventh Army in the Vosges mountains.'

5. THE SUPER-TANK

ALL OF US, the four journalists and two photographers, sat in our folding canvas chairs waiting for Colonel Richard 'Dick' Bovelander to arrive. We were sitting in the chilly entrance hall of the small chateau near Villeforte in the foothills of the Vosges mountains, west of Strasbourg, some miles behind the notional front line that the US 7th Army was holding, now in November 1944.

Our mood ranged from very disgruntled to indifferent. Colonel Bovelander, commanding officer of the 631st Parachute Infantry Regiment, to which we were all assigned, did not like the press. He had kept us well away from all combat, far in the rear, corralled in a series of houses – an abbey, *maisons de maître*, and now a chateau – as the 7th Army advanced remorselessly on the Rhine. We had been taken to see the mayors of liberated villages present bouquets to various American units. We had visited base hospitals and rear-echelon supply dumps. We had witnessed hundred-lorry convoys passing by; had photographed tank transporters debouching their tanks; we had watched squadrons of P-51 Mustang fighters take off from airbases on ground-support missions. And so on. In short, we had witnessed everything that a modern army did in the field, except fight.

We had lodged a unanimous protest on behalf of our newspapers and magazines, hence this face-to-face encounter with Colonel Bovelander. Of the six of us, there were two women – me and a veteran reporter for *McCall's* named Mary Poundstone (who, I strongly suspected, didn't much like me. Mary preferred to be the only woman in the team). The four men, three journalists and a photographer from Associated Press, weren't too unhappy with this boring but easy life. It was Mary and I who had allied to provide the consensus, this united front of free expression, and we were not going to be cowed by Bovelander's bluster.

He strode in, accompanied by his public relations officer. Bovelander was thirty-two years old, one of the youngest regimental commanders in the US Army, fair, tall and handsome, and was wearing his trademark, a red bandana tied loosely at the throat. 'Farm boy,' Poundstone had sneered when she'd first seen it. 'Oh, yeah. Nice touch.'

'Ladies and gentlemen,' Bovelander began without any formalities, 'your protest has been noted – and rejected. I resent this waste of my time. Anyone who does not follow the precise instructions of Captain Enright here,' he indicated the PRO beside him, 'will be arrested and charged.'

'Charged with what, pray?' Mary Poundstone called out.

'Insubordination. Good morning.'

He smiled and walked out.

'Well, at least we protested,' I said.

'I've got to get reassigned,' Poundstone said and went to speak to Enright.

I wandered out on to the rear terrace that overlooked a long untended garden. The lawns had been churned up by vehicle tracks and at the far end by an ornamental stable block was an advanced dressing station that had a big tarpaulin with a red cross draped over the stable's tiled roof. I lit a cigarette and wandered over. I knew a few of the medics – they were as far behind the front as we were and seemed to travel with us as we advanced. I saw a young private I knew – Ephraim Abrams – stacking packs into the back of a jeep that had its engine running. I had taken Abrams' photograph standing by an abandoned 88 mm field gun and developed the print so he could send it back to his parents in New Jersey.

'Where're you off to?' I asked.

'Heading up to Villeforte. We cleared it out yesterday.'

'Can I hitch a ride?'

'Sure.'

'I'll be two seconds.'

I ran into my room and grabbed my helmet, cameras and film, and raced back out to the stables. I jumped in the rear of the jeep, pulled my helmet down low and wrapped a scarf around my face as Abrams gunned the motor and we drove out of the yard up a muddy lane towards Villeforte. As usual the traffic was heavy, and going both ways – trucks, jeeps, half-tracks and a long column of German prisoners tramping sullenly back towards captivity – and it took us almost an hour to travel the two miles to the small town. Villeforte showed few signs of fighting. There was a large hole in the roof of the *mairie* and some of the bigger farms on the outskirts that had been used as strongpoints were pretty much levelled – shattered walls and piles of rubble – but there were no fires burning and the clock in the church tower was telling the correct time.

Abrams pulled into a supply dump and I hopped off, but not before I had covertly snaffled a red-cross armband that I found on the jeep's floor.

'When are you heading back?' I asked.

'In an hour. Give or take.'

'Don't leave without me.'

I wandered off, up the road to the town, slipping on my armband, feeling a sudden surge of excitement in me as if I were playing truant. I was certainly disobeying Bovelander; categorically ignoring his explicit order. Fuck Bovelander, I thought and then paused, as I saw a small unit of military police up ahead directing traffic. I turned right down a farm track and as soon as I was out of sight cut across a meadow heading for another road that would lead me to the town centre, aiming for the spire of the church. I climbed over a wooden fence. And stopped.

The body of a German soldier lay there, his head a battered turnip of blood, bone and hair. He was supine on flattened meadow-grass a few yards from a tall blackthorn hedge. I looked around, feeling a little dizzy. How had he been missed by the corpsmen? I took out my camera and snapped him lying there. My excitement had disappeared, replaced by a hyper-alert apprehension. It was my first picture as a war photographer. I moved on.

Dead German soldier, Villeforte, November 1944.

I wandered cautiously into the narrow lanes of Villeforte, all the houses shuttered and locked. Here and there on the streets were groups of soldiers, sitting, lounging, eating, smoking. None of them paid me any attention – my red-cross armband the perfect passport.

However, I was stopped by a sentry as I tried to enter the main square.

'Sorry,' the soldier said. 'We got brass checking out the tank.'

I backed off and circled round. The tank? From another side street I managed to gain an oblique view of the square and I could see an enormous German tank – the size of a house, it seemed – painted a matt sandy-grey and apparently undamaged, with American soldiers clambering over it. I could hear excited chatter and the odd whoop of elation. I crept forward to a doorway and fired off a few shots. I'd never seen a tank this large – some sort of captured secret weapon? Was that another reason the press were being kept out of Villeforte?

German mystery-tank, Villeforte, November 1944.

I looked at my watch. Time to return to Abrams at the supply dump. I headed off down a sloping paved lane – I could see fields at its end. I felt elated, pleased with my initiative at going AWOL like this. I intended to do the same as Poundstone and apply to be reassigned to a different unit with a more accommodating CO. Bovelander wasn't worth bothering about, he—

The air was suddenly filled with a curious combination of noise: shrill tin whistles and the ripping of stiff canvas. Then, from somewhere on the edge of town a volley of percussive explosions. I felt the blast sweep through the streets to tug at my clothes. I crouched down. Shouts. Then more shrill whistling and explosions. Within seconds there was a crazed reaction of firing, as if every weapon in Villeforte was being loosed off.

I ran down the lane to its foot and hugged the wall of the last house before the countryside began. I could see a wide ploughed field and beyond it straggling copses of leafless trees. Peering round the corner I saw a squad of GIs sheltering in a patch of garden behind a waist-high wall. Every now and then one of them would poke his head up and fire off a few shots at some target across the field towards a distant wood. I peered – I could hear some vehicles revving in the scrub by the trees and I thought I saw small figures in green-grey uniforms scurrying about.

I shouted at the soldiers and ran over, ducking down behind the wall.

'What's happening?'

'Fuckin' counter-attack. You a medic?'

'What? Yeah.'

Artillery shells – ours, I assumed – began to explode in the wood across the field. Great towering billows of chocolate-brown smoke, then the shock wave rocking us. I watched a tree slowly fall – creaking, the tear of timber splitting – then the crash and blustering cloud of twigs and branches. The air was full of the fat-popping noise of small arms. Then bits of tile began to fly up in the air on the roof of the house behind us and shards fell tinkling on and around us. We all ducked down. I'm under fire, I thought, so this is what it's like.

The man I spoke to had a stubbly beard and a circular patch on his arm with a star in it.

'OK, fellas,' he shouted. 'We're getting outta here.'

He pointed at the entry to a narrow sunken lane. 'Let's get our asses in there. I'll check it out.' And he scurried off towards the lane, running in a crouch. Nobody fired at him and he arrived at the entry to the lane, squatting down between its thick banks.

'OK, come on!' he shouted. 'One at a time.'

More roof tiles behind us were hit. The shards fell with a fragile, near-melodic sound like a wind chime. Nobody moved. One of the men was looking at me strangely.

'You a nurse?'

'Sort of,' I said.

'For fuck's sake, come on, guys!' the man in the sunken lane shouted. I rummaged in my kitbag and took out my other camera and fitted a 50 mm lens to it and wound the film on. The photographer in me was thinking: don't miss this. A counter-attack. Under fire. Don't miss this.

The man in the lane shouted again but no one seemed very keen to follow the intrepid soldier and run the few exposed yards along the ploughed field, even to the evident security of the lane with its high banks. He waved and shouted once more and then suddenly, there was a boom of an explosion behind him and a great puff of smoke seemed to rush down the lane to envelop him. He fell down and his carbine went spiralling high up in the air to land twenty feet away. He stood up, apparently unhurt, and began to run back towards us, not bothering about his weapon, his pack banging against his hip as he raced for the cover of the garden wall. I peered over the top and took some shots of the wood. I could still hear the firecracker pops of rifles and machine guns but could see nothing stirring any more amongst the trees.

'Get the fuck down!' the running man screamed at me as he raced towards us. I swung round as he shouted and saw him hit, just a jolt that shortened his stride, and, entirely reflexively, my finger pressed the release button. He fell to the ground and others raced out to drag him back behind the wall. He was completely limp. They pulled him into the cover of the street that led down from the town square, and laid him against a wall, the men huddled round him, fumbling with his jacket and webbing. Click, I took another photo. Just at that moment I saw a half-track lurch into view at the top of the sloping street and I sprinted up towards it, having the presence of mind to thrust my camera back in its bag.

'We've got a casualty down here!' I yelled, and men began to spill out of the half-track and run towards me.

Colonel Richard 'Dick' Bovelander sat behind his desk and looked me over. It was a disdainful stare.

'You know that you have the rank of captain in the US Army,' he said.

'Yes, I do.'

'So, as you're attached to my regiment, I am your commanding officer.'

'In theory.'

'In theory I can have my military police arrest you and lock you up pending a court martial.'

'Listen, Colonel, we all know that—'

'No. You listen, Miss Clay. Within minutes of me giving that order you disobeyed it. You could easily have gotten yourself killed.'

'I was just curious.'

'This is a war zone. Not an opportunity for someone like you – some photographer – to take photographs.'

I closed my eyes for a second. Bovelander was going to exact his pound of flesh whatever I said. However, I had the feeling that at another time, in another place, we might actually have liked each other.

'I want the film from your camera,' he said, holding his hand out.

'No. Out of the question.'

'Provost Marshal!'

'All right. All right.'

I had been expecting this. I took my two cameras from my knapsack, rewound the film, opened the rear flaps and handed over the rolls. They were brand new: the two rolls that I had used were snug beneath my armpits, tucked in my brassiere.

'Colonel,' I began, 'we, the journalists and the photographers, are not a subversive presence, trying to make your job harder. Your soldiers – sons, fathers, nephews, grandsons – have another army, the hundreds of thousands of their family members back in the US, who care about them and want to know about the lives they're leading. Your orders are preventing us doing our job. It's wrong.'

'You're English, aren't you, Miss Clay.'

'I am.'

'Maybe they do things differently in the British Army but while you're under my command you take orders as an American soldier.' He looked at me in that disdainful way again. I crossed my legs and took out a cigarette. I wanted to rile him.

'Have you a light, by the way, Colonel? Please?'

'Sergeant McNeal will take you to the railhead. If you're still here in ten minutes you'll be in jail.'

I stood. 'I wish you luck, Colonel,' I said, and left his headquarters without a backward glance.

★

THE BARRANDALE JOURNAL 1977

Colonel Bovelander was killed in a friendly-fire incident a few months later in March 1945 when Allied artillery shells dropped devastatingly short during Operation Varsity and he and two of his staff were killed in their observation post. He was posthumously promoted to lieutenant general. I would like to record it as an instance of the Curse of Clay but I was sorry to hear the news. I bore him no ill will even though he was a self-important man, albeit a good-looking one – all the same, someone like Bovelander deserved a more heroic demise than a tragic accident.

My smuggled photograph of the mysterious German tank – some kind of vast self-propelled gun, I learned later – made the cover of *Global-Photo-Watch* in December 1944, as did my shot of the dead German soldier I'd discovered in the field outside Villeforte. The headline of my issue – as I like to think of it – was 'Exclusive: First Glimpse of Nazi Super-Tank'. I achieved a certain notoriety in the purlieus of the Hotel Scribe. Cleve was delighted at my scoop and urged me to return to the front line. Easier urged than achieved, as Bovelander had left a scathing and damning report about me and my unreliability, and I found it very difficult to be reassigned. I continued to apply to other units while running the *GPW* offices with the indefatigable help of Corisande – the French equivalent of Faith Postings – as Cleve had sent Jay Fielding to Guam to cover the Pacific theatre.

I never published my photo of Private First Class Anthony G. Sasso – until now – whose snapshot I took at the very moment of his death. I learned his name later – he was the only fatality of the futile and quickly aborted counter-attack on Villeforte – and as luck, good or bad, would have it, I was there to preserve the instant of his passing for posterity.

'Falling Soldier'. PFC Anthony G. Sasso at the moment of his death. Villeforte, 15 November 1944.

When I developed the image and printed it I immediately called it 'Falling Soldier' after Robert Capa's famous photograph from the Spanish Civil War of a Republican soldier. The soldier, rifle falling from his hand, is flung backwards, arms dramatically spread, against a background of rolling scrubby hills. It is one of the most famous war photographs ever taken and it made Capa's name. Of course, there has been a mass of controversy surrounding the image. Was it faked? A photo opportunity carefully staged? Other questions arrive: do people really die in such a histrionic way when a fatal bullet hits them? Does a rifle or machine-gun bullet fling you backwards like this? I think that's the problem. Capa's soldier, falling back, arms akimbo, would not have looked out of place in a Hollywood B-movie western. This soldier seems to be dying 'on stage', as it were.

By contrast, my photo of the death of Anthony Sasso is mundane in the extreme. He has just been hit in the body by a bullet and his face, for a split second, instinctively registers the shock and the realisation. The jolt of the bullet's impact has brought him slightly

GIs tend to the fallen body of Anthony Sasso. Villeforte, 15 November 1944.

more erect and his helmet strap is flung forward by the momentary arrest in his run. I discovered later that the bullet entered under his right armpit and tore through his chest cavity. He was dead by the time he hit the ground, half a second later. And I was there. My follow-up photo of his comrades gathered round his body is overexposed and blurry (I was in shock) but it is authentic. Capa's follow-up shot just adds more queries. The body has been moved. The background is slightly different. Too many anomalies.

The key fact that I remember about Sasso's death is that he just fell forward, crumpled forward. He didn't cry or scream or throw his arms out wide, he just went down. I remember asking a veteran of the First World War – an old comrade of my father – who had seen dozens of men shot alongside him during attacks on the German line what happened at the moment of bullet impact and death. 'They just fall forward,' he said. 'Don't make a sound. Thump. They just go down like a sack of potatoes.' That's what happened with Anthony Sasso. Thump. Dead.

★

I spent the Christmas and New Year of 1944–5 with Charbonneau at the Mas d'Epines where we had made some rudimentary improvements. Rooms had been painted; there was a functioning outdoor lavatory. We had installed a wood-burning stove and range in the kitchen that also heated water so baths could be had (with some effort). There was still no electricity and it was a cold winter of iron frosts, that year, even in Provence. We built great log fires in the main room that we kept going all day, burning vast amounts of wood, until we went – usually drunkenly – to bed.

It turned out to be the longest sustained period that Charbonneau and I had spent together, as a couple living under the same roof, and the time passed agreeably smoothly. The house and its setting helped – even in winter the place was beautiful – but the key factor in our mutual pleasure was that we enjoyed each other's company, which, banal though it may seem, is the fundamental explanation of any successful and enduring union. Charbonneau was an interesting, amusing and provocative man and I like to think he brought out the best in me, also. Even two minutes in his company provided some comment or observation that would make me laugh or make me violently disagree with him and so those two minutes of my day were well spent as a consequence.

I remember he said he was going to write a memoir of his time in the glittering literary circles in Paris before the war and call it *Lettres et le néon*. He found this extremely funny and chuckled away to himself. I didn't understand at all until he said it would make Jean-Paul Sartre very angry – then I got the pun. I asked him if he'd ever read *L'Être et le néant* and he said he'd tried. What did you think of it, I asked? '*Ça ne vaut pas tripette,*' he said. What's '*tripette*', I asked? 'It's tripe,' he said. 'It's not worth little bits of tripe.' Oh, yes, I replied – in English when something's really bad we call it tripe, as well. Well, he said, *L'Être et le néant* is tripe. Then he smiled. 'Tripe *à la mode de con,*' he said – and found this even funnier, laughing out loud at his sally. He chortled away for days. I had no idea what he was talking about.

I made the mistake once of telling him how clever and funny I found him (we were in bed and I was feeling indulgent) and he replied, with annoying self-satisfaction, 'Now you understand why beautiful women enjoy the company of clever ugly men. *On s'amuse.*' Then he corrected himself. 'Clever ugly *poor* men. We all know why beautiful women like ugly rich men.' Then he smiled at me. 'And if we're not amused by life we might as well take our cyanide pill now – no?'

My new assignment arrived in February 1945. It was to General Bill Simpson's 9th US Army, poised in the Rhineland waiting to cross the great symbolic fluvial barrier that would lead the Allied armies into the heart of Germany and bring about its cardiac arrest.

I made my way to join the 9th, and was flown up to Geldern, about five miles west of the river.

We journalists and photographers, the radio reporters and the newsreel cameramen attached to the 9th Army – there were a dozen of us – were billeted in a semi-ruined town hall in a village north of Rheinberg. There were three PROs looking after us – a measure of how the army and the mass media were now coexisting and being mutually supportive. Everybody was learning fast.

Bill Simpson's Army Corps was at the southern end of the massive British and Canadian thrust across the Rhine, Operation Plunder. We heard the artillery barrage begin on 23 March and waited until our time came to be ferried up to the front to see what had happened. To be honest, I was beginning to tire of being herded and controlled by the PROs. At some briefing I met Mary Poundstone again and asked her what unit she was attached to. 'I'm

My crossing of the Rhine in the aftermath of Operation Plunder, March 1945.

not attached to a unit, my dear, I'm attached to a general. It makes all the difference.' She was having an affair with Lieutenant General Edson Carnegie. If she needed a plane to return to Paris a plane was provided. If she wanted to rove the Allied front unchecked she did so. If she found herself in trouble she simply called Carnegie so she could be extricated without fuss or demanded transport back to his headquarters. It wasn't an option open to me.

Thirty-six hours after Plunder had begun we were driven up to the Rhine. It was at least 500 yards wide where we crossed on a Bailey bridge – already constructed – and we were duly impressed.

Once over, the mood was jubilant amongst the troops we encountered. The war, it seemed, was nearly at an end. Thousands of German prisoners were being shepherded back to holding pens

German POWs, March 1945.

and it was both striking and disturbing to see how young they were – teenagers in the main, wispy adolescent fuzz on their chins and cheeks, all in uniforms that seemed far too large for them, borrowed from men.

We were shown to our billets in an intact farmhouse a mile or so from the town of Wesel. Wesel had been bombed flat on the night of 23 March before it was taken and secured by the British 1st Commando Brigade. Our PRO told us that we were on no account to go near the town as it was still being searched for snipers and crazed last-stand defenders. It sounded exactly the sort of place I should visit.

I bribed a motorcycle courier (sixty cigarettes) to take me to Wesel as his pillion passenger. He dropped me off at a lorry park and I hitched another ride in a four-ton, six-wheeled flat-nosed truck delivering various types of ammunition to the forces in the town. I jumped out when we stopped in the centre and slipped on my 'PRESS' armband. The air was full of the choking smell of masonry dust and only Wesel's cathedral seemed to have partially survived the carpet-bombing – insofar as it could still just be recognised as a church of some sort. Every other building was a shell, a few walls standing, teetering, roofless, girdled with banks of broken bricks and shattered stonework.

There were soldiers everywhere, clean, recently arrived soldiers, curious, poking about the ruins, evidently there to occupy rather than fight. I took some photographs around the cathedral and wandered down a bomb-cratered road to what must have been a park with a boating pond. All the trees were splintered stumps and the shallow pond was filled with floating objects, some of them once human beings, I thought. I wondered if I might find better images in the park – the world had seen too many ghost cities, grey lunar ruins – tortured nature might deliver something more striking. I walked round the boating pond, keeping my distance, not wanting to look too closely at what was floating there and then came upon a group of men, a hundred or so, sitting around the twisted remains of a bandstand.

They were soldiers, British soldiers – I recognised the shape of the tin helmet – though they might have been troglodytes or some race of miners allowed up from underground, after weeks of toil, so filthy were they, almost black with dirt and sweat and mud. They were sitting quietly, smoking, eating rations, swigging from canteens, but their conversations, such as they were, were muttered, hushed, almost inaudible. I moved closer, carefully. They looked as if they had suffered some collective trauma, survivors of an earthquake or some other natural catastrophe. Their blackened faces were drawn and gaunt from awful shared experience, it seemed to me.

A tall man rose to his feet and intercepted me as I drew near. He was wearing an old darned V-neck sweater, moss green, a civilian sweater, over his battledress shirt. His trousers were tucked into heavy, caramel-coloured brogue ankle boots of the sort you go deer-stalking in, and he had a revolver in a canvas holster hanging from his right hip. He was bareheaded and a lock of his greasy black hair hung over one eye. He had deep creases in his cheeks and had a lit cigarette in his hand.

'What do you want?' he said. His voice was ragged and patrician. I might have been a housemaid who'd barged in on a bridge game.

'I'd like to take some photographs,' I said, pointing to my armband. 'If I may.'

'Go away, young lady,' he said. 'You're not welcome here.'

Now I was close to him I could see the lean contours of his face and the colour of his eyes, a pale grey-blue, stark against the grime of his skin. There was a muscle twitching on his cheek and matted blood on his hairline.

'What unit are you?' I asked. 'I work for an American magazine,' I added, vaguely hoping the old magic formula would work, and I held up my camera. 'People at home would really like to—'

'If you try to take any photographs of these men I'll kill you, here and now,' he said, entirely reasonably, but not smiling.

'All right, I'm going,' I said, suddenly frightened of this tall thin man with his pale eyes. I turned and walked briskly out of the park not looking round, feeling his gaze on my back, and unsettled by the absolute seriousness of his calmly delivered threat.

I made my way back to the farmhouse – my absence unnoticed by anyone – and asked the PRO on duty to provide me with a movement order back to Paris. I'd suddenly had enough of war-reporting and I wanted my old life to be returned to me. Seeing those exhausted, filthy British soldiers sitting resting by the bandstand in the smashed and obliterated park had been disturbing in some profound way. Or was it the tall thin man? Their commanding officer, perhaps, who had so mildly and casually threatened to kill me. What had these men done or undergone in Wesel, I wondered? What death and destruction had they witnessed or effected in the ruined town that had left them so debilitated and quiet? What terrifying bleak tales would they have to tell their children, if they dared? I wanted to be back in Paris – back in Paris with Charbonneau.

My movement order took two days to arrive – the headlong breakout from the Rhine crossings was in full urgent flow and requests such as mine were the lowest priority. The other journalists were shipped forward to Frankfurt while I went in the other direction. A jeep deposited me at a surprisingly undamaged station in Holland in a small town called Nettwaard. I had a piece of paper authorising me to take my place on a troop train heading for Brussels. Once there I had to make my own way home to Paris.

There was a train standing in the station and it had a number painted on it that corresponded with my docket, but it was locked and so hundreds of soldiers, American and English, waited patiently with their kitbags and knapsacks for someone to come and unlock it and give us all permission to board. I wandered up to the furthest end of the platform, away from the soldiers, and found a bench, lit by watery sunshine, settled myself down and smoked a cigarette. It was a cold frosty March day with an intermittent sun piercing the hazy cloud cover. I was glad I was wearing my mackinaw overcoat and turned the collar up.

'Hello again.'

I turned. It was the tall thin man from the park at Wesel. He looked much better – clean, shaved, his uniform pressed and unmuddied. He was even smiling.

'Hello,' I said. 'I assume you've not followed me here to execute me.'

He winced, as if my remark had caused him pain.

'No, no. Just waiting for a train, like you. May I?'

He lowered himself on to the bench beside me with undue care, as if he might break into a thousand pieces.

'It seems I've fractured half a dozen ribs,' he explained. 'I'm all strapped up but if I cough, or laugh . . .' He looked at me. 'Please don't make me laugh.'

He was wearing a baggy green beret and a camouflaged smock beneath a leather jerkin. His shoulder ribbon read '15 Commando'. He was obviously an officer but I couldn't see his rank because his jerkin covered his epaulettes. However, as I looked more closely I could see that his jerkin was lined with sheepskin and his smock was closed with horn toggle-buttons. It was a uniform, yes, but a uniform run through the hands of an expert tailor.

'I want to apologise for the other day,' he said. 'It's been bothering me – my rudeness, my threat – and then I couldn't believe it when I saw you sitting up here at this end of the platform.' He took his beret off and ran his hand through his very black hair. 'We weren't in the best of shape when you found us in that park.'

'Don't bother to apologise,' I said. 'I'm sure it was very tough in Wesel, whatever went on.'

He cocked his head and screwed up his eyes as if trying to remember.

'It was very . . . Yes. Severe.' He smiled, vaguely. 'You were just doing your job. I had no right to be so offensive. So – apologies.' He offered his hand. 'Sholto Farr.'

'Amory Clay.'

We shook hands.

I was hugely, instantly attracted to this man – drawn to him in a way that alarmed me. I had noted this effect before – with Cleve, with Charbonneau, with any number of men I'd fleetingly encountered. It just arrives, this cognisance – though that word gives it too much logical weight. It's uncalled-upon. Your body notes it first, as a pure instinct, then transmits the information to your brain where it's acted upon with more reason, with a bit of luck. I was sitting waiting for a train at a railway station, a bit cold, a bit bored, and then this man appeared and sat beside me and everything changed.

'You're English,' he said. 'But you told me you worked for an American magazine, if I recall.'

'It's a long story,' I said and then quickly ran through the basic details of my strange professional journey: London to Berlin to New York to Paris.

'And now I run the office in Paris,' I said. '*Global-Photo-Watch.* It's a big magazine, lots of work, but I decided I wanted to get out from behind my desk.' I paused. 'So I did that and now I want to get back behind my desk again.'

He was staring at me intently as I spoke as if I were saying something of profound importance instead of chit-chat. I suddenly found myself incapable of coming up with a coherent sentence so spread my hands and lapsed into silence. He was meant to speak now, so I thought, but he said nothing, and the silence between us built until it became unignorable. Finally, he broke it.

'Paris,' he said. 'Yes.'

He reached into his smock and pulled out a burnished silver hip flask and offered it to me.

'Would you like a drink? Malt whisky. The best.'

'Yes, please.'

I unscrewed the top and had a swig, savouring the peaty burn of the malt as it went down, my nostrils and sinuses warming with the finish.

He took a large gulp himself when I handed the flask back.
'Medicinal,' he said.

'Of course.'

Then we were distracted by the arrival of another train chuffing into the platform opposite, halting with the usual tortured scream of metal on metal. A soldier appeared and saluted Sholto Farr.

'This in fact is our train, sir,' he said, pointing at the new arrival.

'Are you coming with us?' he asked me.

'No,' I said. 'I'm on this one.'

'Too bad.'

'Trains that pass in the night,' I said, smiling. And he laughed and clutched his ribs.

'I specially asked you not to do that,' he said, rising carefully to his feet, one hand on his injured side, the other replacing the beret on his head.

'I hope we meet again one day.'

15 Commando, Western Desert, Tunisia, 1943. Sholto Farr on the right.
Aldous King-Marley on the left; David Farquhar in the middle.

'Yes, so do I,' I said, sincerely, knowing full well that would never happen, that this was one of those encounters to be celebrated in song or story by someone else, in due course. What might have been. He gave a small wave of his hand, turned and walked away with his soldier to join the shuffling files of men crossing the tracks to board the troop train. I had a camera in my kitbag, I realised, why hadn't I thought of taking a photograph of Sholto Farr?

★

THE BARRANDALE JOURNAL 1977

I had the McLennans for lunch yesterday. I'm not a good cook, I know that. I can cook – I can place hot food on the table – but not very well. I started off with macaroni and tomatoes and added a pinch of curry powder as the recipe suggested. Then I served up *poulet au paprika* but I think I stirred too much flour into the gravy and my braised rice was also on the dry side. The key factor when you're not a particularly accomplished cook is to compensate by overdoing the wine. I poured and poured the Valpolicella – two bottles – and I think that by the end of the meal I could have served up banana sandwiches and Greer and Calder wouldn't have complained. I was happy enough myself as I presented my orange pudding with orange sauce – infallible – and relinquished my role as chef. Coffee, whisky and cigarettes saw us through to the late afternoon.

The McLennans were planning a trip to Paris and I found myself, in my brief euphoria, giving them all kinds of detailed advice about where to go and what to do.

Greer looked at me questioningly.

'Anyone would think you were a Parisienne,' she said.

'Well, I did live there for a good while.' I regretted saying that as soon as I had spoken.

'Oh, yes? When?' Calder said. He was quite tipsy by now. 'You lived in Paris? I never knew.'

'A while ago,' I said. 'You know. End of the war. And 1946.'

Greer sat back and looked at me squarely.

'Any more secrets, Amory?'

★

We continued to run the *GPW* office – Corisande and I – for some months beyond VE Day, in May 1945 – though, inevitably, we had less and less to report; our newsworthiness, as far as *GPW* was concerned, diminished fairly rapidly. Months went by without a 'Dateline Paris' story. I tried to cut costs by moving us out of rue Louis le Grand and into a single-room apartment (with WC) in the rue Monsieur. I did make savings but, inevitably, the call came. We had a functioning telephone by now and Cleve gently suggested, one afternoon in February 1946, that I return to London and resume my responsibilities in High Holborn once more. I offered my resignation – Cleve refused to accept it and backtracked. Paris could remain open as long as more economies could be made. I realised that Cleve would agree to almost anything I asked – a situation that was both pleasing and troubling. I suggested a fifty per cent cut in my salary – Cleve said that would be helpful and so the Paris office stayed open, for a while. I hadn't seen Cleve for over a year and in the way that certain love affairs just fizzle out or die a quiet, almost unacknowledged peaceful death, so did my relationship with Cleve pass away. Charbonneau was the man in my life now.

Or, occasionally in my life, let's say. Post-war French politics meant that he was away from Paris a great deal, mainly in Algeria and Tunisia and other outposts of the French Empire, doing what he could to support the Quatrième République. I had moved into his Saint-Germain apartment and made it as homely as possible. The climbing columns of books were now in bookshelves; rooms had been repainted in my usual choice of vivid colours (our bedroom was Lincoln green, the kitchen terracotta); the parquet had been sanded and revarnished and I had added some bright cotton rugs. When he came home Charbonneau professed himself pleased once I'd pointed out the changes. We had an insomniac above us who paced the floor all night and a cellist below who practised four hours a day, but, as was the case with most Parisians, your apartment was merely a place where you bathed, changed and slept (sometimes). Real life, the rest of life, was lived outside on the streets. I never complained.

In early February '46 I slipped on a patch of ice on the rue Monsieur and fell heavily to the ground, stunning myself. I fractured my right elbow (and wore a sling for two weeks) but, more worryingly, the fall made my vaginal bleeding start up after years of quiescence, and I was obliged to resume wearing my padded rubber knickers again. I was on the point of going to see a doctor when it suddenly stopped.

I didn't tell Charbonneau any of this, though he kept rebuking me – when he was home – for being boring. I wasn't my usual annoying, animated self, I admit. But when the bleeding stopped and I discarded my nappy I felt my *joie de vivre* return. Except that Charbonneau was away again and couldn't appreciate my rejuvenation.

6. Transformations

IT WAS THE DAY after my thirty-eighth birthday – 8 March. The doorbell rang at the street entrance of 12 bis rue Monsieur, and Corisande went down to see who it was. She returned in some perplexity.

'It's a man, Miss Amory.' She called me 'Miss Amory' even though I begged her repeatedly to drop the 'Miss'.

'Well, show him in.'

'He has flowers.'

'He's delivering flowers from a florist?'

'I don't think so.'

I smiled to myself. Charbonneau was home. Playing one of his tricks, surprising me.

'I'll get it,' I said, and left our little apartment and went down to the lobby by the street door.

Sholto Farr stood there with a posy of primroses in his hand.

How can you describe these physical sensations, these instinctive body-wide manifestations of your mental state, without sounding like some sentimental fool? When I first saw him in that split second – he was wearing a dark pinstriped suit and a camel overcoat – I felt my lungs empty, sucked dry as if by some sort of vacuum pump. I was in a form of shock, I realised. Then I felt heat – all in a further split second – my belly warmed, my ears glowed. Then I lost power over my limbs: my knees seemed unable to support the weight of my body; I felt a tremor pass through my shoulders and run down my arms. And then all these symptoms disappeared in another split second and I became entirely calm. Ice-lady. Calm with absolute certainty.

'Hello, hello,' I said, breezily. 'What a lovely surprise. How did you track me down?'

I remember the four days we spent together as vividly as if they had taken place last week. Sholto handed me his bouquet, we shook hands and he asked me to dinner. I said I'd be delighted. He was staying at a small hotel in the rue de l'Université, the Hotel Printemps, aptly enough – I said I would meet him there at seven o'clock.

I went back home, to Charbonneau's flat, bathed and selected my clothes with some care. I wore a black dull-surfaced silk dress with a stamped motif of acorns and cherries and a sequinned collar – stylish but unflashy. Not too much make-up. I felt like a sixteen-year-old going to her first dance. Despite the many signs of Charbonneau all around me in the apartment I managed to banish all thoughts of him from my mind – tonight I was a single woman, I told myself.

Sholto took me to Voisin in the rue Saint-Honoré. It was expensive, even for post-war Paris, and he insisted we eat as well as we could. We had *foie gras, boeuf en daube*, cheese, and a *soufflé Monte Cristo*. Sholto smoked three cigarettes to my one. He was one of those smokers for whom the act of smoking is as natural as breathing – he lit and smoked cigarettes with the same unconcern as he would scratch his chin or run his hand through his hair.

We told each other something of ourselves. His important news was that he was recently divorced. He had married too young, he said (he was two years older than me), and he had one child, a son, Andrew, aged sixteen, at a boarding school in Scotland. I asked him what his job was, now his soldiering was over, and he said he was a farmer. He had a large farm on the west coast of Scotland, between Oban and Mallaig, if I was familiar with those towns and that part of Scotland. I said I wasn't. I told him about my family – he knew who Dido was, had heard of her – and about Xan and his death in Normandy. I didn't ask him much about his war, about what he and his commandos had got up to before I came across them in the park in Wesel. I don't think he wanted to tell me, in any event: he steered clear of military matters.

This was what we talked about as we dined. Under the surface – and I know he felt the same – was a surging boiling current of mutual attraction. Let's call it lust. But we chatted away and smiled, smoked countless cigarettes and ached for each other.

Sholto had fine hair, almost blue-black, parted at the side, which he tried to hold in place with some potent oil but which, under the lights of the restaurant, lost its grip halfway through the meal, and fell, his forelock hanging over his brow. He would sweep it back – a particular gesture I came to associate with him – and seconds later it would fall again.

Sholto Farr. Alexandria, 1943.

He was something of a dandy, I noticed – like Cleve, unlike Charbonneau. His shirt was tailored – you can always tell by the set of the collar – as bespoke as his suit. His maroon silk tie had a neat hard knot the size of a hazelnut, as if pulled tight by pliers. He had a tiny ruby jewel of a razor nick on his jaw by his left ear. His eyes were a very pale blue-grey (I think I've told you that already). For a Scotsman he had no trace of a Scottish accent.

I remember, when he dropped me back at Charbonneau's, I almost gave in and I nearly said, do you want to come up for a drink? I resisted, somehow. I wanted him but I didn't want him in Charbonneau's bed. He said goodnight, kissed my cheek – just a brush of his lips – said how much he'd enjoyed the evening and was I free for lunch tomorrow. I said that, as it happened, my lunch appointment had been cancelled, luckily, and that I was able to meet him, that would be lovely. Weber at one? Perfect.

I remember we ate ice cream at Weber – it was famous for its ice cream. By now we had pretty much run out of conversation and the subtext to our second Parisian encounter was almost grotesquely obvious. We weren't exactly panting at each other with our tongues hanging out but we might as well have been.

We ordered coffee and brandy. We ordered more coffee and brandy. I couldn't think of anything to say and, clearly, neither could he. So we sat there, smoking our cigarettes, drinking coffee and brandy, smiling stupidly at each other.

'What really brought you to Paris?' I said finally, something I hadn't in fact asked him. '"On business" isn't working, I'm afraid.'

'I came to Paris to find you,' he said simply, as if it was self-evident.

'Oh. Right ... Was it difficult?'

'No. Surprisingly easy. I remembered everything you said to me at that station in Holland. Your name, that you were a photographer, that you worked for *Global-Photo-Watch*, that you had an office in

Paris. The receptionist at my hotel looked you up in the phonebook and there you were: Agence *GPW*, 12 bis rue Monsieur, Septième.'

'Well. Good thing I told you what my job was.'

'Very fortunate.'

'Of course I could have moved. Changed jobs.'

'I would have found you, one way or another.'

I felt tears in my eyes at this – possibly the most romantic words that had ever been said to me.

'Good.'

He took my hand and looked at my fingers for a moment. 'My hotel is very small,' he said. 'So, I went to the trouble of booking a room at the Crillon.' Now he glanced up. 'I think a big hotel – lots of coming and going – is better. More discreet. Don't you?'

'What a good idea,' I said. 'Shall we go there now?'

I remember travelling up in the lift to the third floor where our room was. We had no luggage, of course (it was being 'sent on' from the airport at Le Bourget, Sholto improvised, when we checked in). The lift operator was a small, thin, frail old man who kept his head down, looking at his shiny shoes. He had no doubt seen many a luggage-less couple to their room in the Crillon of an afternoon.

I whispered in Sholto's ear. 'There's something you should know,' I said. 'Before.'

'What?'

'I can't have children.'

'Lucky you.'

★

THE BARRANDALE JOURNAL 1977

I had a postcard from Greer McLennan this morning, from Paris – a view of the Jardin des Tuileries. 'I demand to know the full Paris story on return!' she had written.

★

Sholto and I spent four days together that March in Paris, most of the time in our big room at the Crillon that looked out on to the place de la Concorde, wandering out to eat from time to time, then running back to the hotel, unable to restrain ourselves, sexually. But then Sholto had to return to London and, anyway, Charbonneau was due back from Algiers.

'What're we going to do?' Sholto said. 'I know it's more complicated for you.'

'Yes,' I said. 'Don't worry. It may take a little time but I'll work something out.'

'Let me know if you need me and I'll just come over.'

It's funny how, sometimes, one can be so convinced, so utterly certain, about something as entirely fickle as strong emotion. There was an instant, unspoken mutual trust between us, as if we'd known each other for forty years, not four days.

I may have been certain about Sholto but I was in a state of nerves, worried about how I'd feel and act once Charbonneau was back. Obligingly, the day after Sholto left, my body gave me a severe cold so that when Charbonneau returned, I was in bed, coughing and sniffling, my bones aching, my nose rubbed raw, red and running – most unsightly.

'You need a holiday,' Charbonneau said, with untypical sweetness. 'You're working too hard. Leave it to me.'

He took me south, by train to Bordeaux and then on to Biarritz on the Atlantic coast, to the Hotel du Palais, perched on its rocky promontory at the end of the gentle crescent sweep of the *grande plage*. I was apprehensive – and not just because of my own troubled emotional state – Charbonneau seemed to be acting out of character – caring, selfless. What was he up to? Had he some idea about Sholto and the days we'd spent together?

However, Biarritz worked its charms. Charbonneau had said that we needed surf, real ocean – not lapping Mediterranean wavelets – and early spring on the Atlantic coast provided spectacular foaming breakers in endless succession. And the unique aspect of the Palais, as opposed to other grand hotels on seafronts, is that there is no wide promenade between the hotel and the ocean.

We were shown to our suite on the third floor and, flinging open the windows, received the full panorama of the sea, with no interruption of traffic, there in all its surging glory. The creaming white surf rolled in to break on the rocks directly below us. It was loud – the ocean can be very loud – but invigorating.

We settled in to our room but now I was sensing an edginess in Charbonneau – he wasn't quite his usual hedonistic, cocksure self and I began to suspect this new solicitous persona as he kept asking me how I was feeling. Did I need a rest, should he order me some coffee? No, no, I said, I was feeling much better now that I was beside the sea.

He suggested that we eat that evening in the town rather than in the Palais' rather stuffy restaurant and we found a big brasserie on the main square. Biarritz had been bombed in '44 and the repairs to the damaged buildings were still in evidence, almost two years on, roads patched up, gable ends and shopfronts held in place by heavy timber raking-shores. There were concrete gun emplacements on the cliffs – and one realised this was the southern end of Hitler's Atlantic Wall. The carefree resort town hadn't fully expunged its wartime persona.

Charbonneau as usual fussed over the wine list, opting finally for some obscure Basque wine with a rare grape variety. I was, meanwhile, feigning a tranquil, utterly benign mood: everything pleased me, the brasserie was charming, the wine delicious, the freshness of the ocean air, perfection. I knew my serenity was making Charbonneau even more ill at ease.

He waited until the end of the meal.

'You know that I love you, Amory—'

'Oh dear, that sounds ominous.'

'Please don't make everything a joke. It's the worst habit of the English.'

'Wrong, it's our best feature, our saving grace.'

'Please.'

'Continue.'

I lit a cigarette in my most *mondaine* manner and plumed smoke at the ceiling.

'I am going to be married,' he said, solemnly. 'The announcement will be in *Le Figaro* next week.'

This did take me by surprise. I almost dropped my cigarette.

'You're obviously not going to marry me. Do I know the lucky young woman?'

'You have met her, once or twice.'

'And her name?'

'Louise-Elisabeth.'

'Louise-Elisabeth Dupont?'

'No. If you must know – her name is Louise-Elisabeth Croÿ d'Havré de Tourzel de la Billardie.'

'Goodness. No contest with plain old Amory Clay, then. Is she from Paris?'

'From Burgundy.'

'No doubt they have hillsides and hillsides of expensive vineyards.'

'Yes that's true.' He looked at me and smiled. '*Le coeur a ses raisins que les raisins ne connaissent point.*' He laughed at his joke as he always did and then his smile disappeared and he actually looked miserable for a moment, playing with the rind of cheese left on his plate. He gave a kind of rueful chuckle.

'You know, I was wise once,' he said.

'Oh, yes? When was that?'

'When I was born.'

'I know what you mean. It gets difficult from then onwards.'

'I want you to know, Amory, that my relationship with you will be unaffected by this marriage.'

'Wrong. I assure you it will be very affected.'

'Don't be difficult. Let's be sophisticated.'

'No. Let's be sensible. Let's be honest. Why are you marrying this person?'

'Because . . . Because I wish to have a son. I'm forty-five years old. I'm at a certain age when a man—'

'Do excuse me. I need some fresh air.'

I left the brasserie and strolled back towards the hotel, an unstoppable smile growing on my face. I wandered down to the esplanade, past the Casino Municipal, bright and noisy, right on the beach, and walked down some steps on to the sand, slipping off my high-heeled shoes and picking my way towards the foaming surf-edge. The constant roar of the waves was the sonic interference I required – I needed my head filled with noise. Off to the right the irregular sweep of the lighthouse on the clifftop flashed in my eyes. My clear eyes. I was happy for Charbonneau with his young aristocratic, fertile woman from the *gratin*. No doubt along with the vineyards there was a small perfect chateau to add to her allure. More importantly, I was happy for myself. I would give Charbonneau something of a hard time, of course, exacerbate his guilt over this betrayal, but, as I stood on the beach at Biarritz, I felt like dancing and singing; I felt like throwing my shoes in the air and running into the sea I was so happy. I knew where my life was heading, now, after so many years of mistakes and uncertainty and wrong turnings. I was going to marry Sholto Farr.

BOOK SIX: 1947–1966

1. The House of Farr

I CAN RECALL THE exact day when I realised Sholto was seriously ill, seriously damaged by his condition. It was 12 August 1959, the opening of the grouse season and – as we did every year – there was a shooting party for the first day of driven grouse.

I was sitting in the pony and trap with Rory McHarg, the second gamekeeper, as we clopped up the track towards the moor on the westerly slopes of Beinn Lurig, the big mountain that rose up at the end of our glen. We were bringing up lunch for the shooting party and the beaters – sandwiches, sausage rolls, a crate of beer, and Thermos flasks of soup and coffee. It wasn't a grand shoot – no tables set and laid, staff attending – but it was a tradition that Sholto insisted on keeping. There were around a dozen guests – neighbours whose estates marched with ours, and, as usual, army friends of Sholto: David Farquhar, Aldous King-Marley, Frank Dunn (all ex-15 Commando) and our family doctor, Jock Edie.

It was a windy, cool day for August with an intermittent drizzle, but occasionally the clouds were ripped apart and the sun shone down on the mountains and the wide glen beneath, with the river, Crossan Burn, winding through it, making the heart lift at the astonishing splendour and beauty of the view. Up on the moor, on a clear day you could see a silver finger of the Sound of Sleat and, if the day was exceptional, beyond that the purple humps of the Cuillins on Skye.

I could hear a clink of glass coming from a jute sack bundled by Rory's feet.

'What've you got there, Rory? Liquid lunch?'

'Nothing, Lady Farr,' he said, and I saw the blush spread beneath his beard. I reached down for the sack and opened it. Two bottles of Bell's whisky.

'Who's this for?'

'His Lordship asked me to bring them up.'

'Why would he do that?'

'I don't know why, My Lady. I just received the instruction.'

I replaced the sack at his feet and said nothing, though I wasn't surprised. I saw the beaters making their way across the burned-off heather to the stone bothy – the drive was over for the morning. Rory gave the reins a shake and the pony picked its feet up.

We laid out the picnic on a trestle table and I looked up to see the shooters wandering over from the line of butts. I intercepted Sholto and drew him to one side.

'How's it going?'

'Twenty-two brace. Not bad. Birds coming in nice and low and fast. Better than last year.'

'No. I meant how's it going with you?'

He looked at me, puzzled, his eyes unfocussed, glazed. Dead drunk. I was always amazed how he could function – make coherent conversation, shoot a gun, drink more. I had Rory's sack in my hand and gave it to him.

'There's your whisky. Please ask *me* in future if you need it – not the staff.'

'Apologies. Did you bring the wine?'

Then I lost my temper.

'Couldn't you have held off today? Just for one day? The girls are coming home.'

'What girls?'

'Our fucking girls! Our daughters!'

'Oh, yes. Them. Don't worry, darling. They'll never guess.' Then he turned and shouted over to Frank Dunn, 'Save a sandwich for me, you greedy bastard!' and sauntered off to join the others, leaving me standing there, tears filling my eyes.

In 1946, in Paris, when Sholto described himself as a 'farmer' he was telling a sort of truth. It was true that he owned half a dozen farms with tenant farmers, as well as around 20,000 acres of hill, moor and mountain on the west coast of Scotland. He also neglected to tell me during those four days that he'd ended the war a much-decorated lieutenant colonel and that he was, in fact, Sholto, Lord Farr, 12th Baron Farr of Glencrossan.

He admitted to all this when we met again in London after he'd proposed marriage, formally.

'Why did you keep it from me?' I asked, a bit astonished.

'I didn't want to put you off,' he said. 'Not everybody wants to be married to a lord – and be a "lady" all of a sudden. I can understand that.'

I suspect his motives were more shrewd. As a recent divorcé, Lord Farr was probably one of the most eligible new bachelors in Scotland. Better to start a love affair unencumbered by this baggage. It was a test of my sincerity, I suppose, but in a sense I now see he was right: I didn't particularly want to be a 'lady', at all, and as I slowly discovered more of what was involved in being married to Lord Farr, 12th Baron Farr of Glencrossan, I might indeed have thought twice.

Let's start with the house – the House of Farr, as it was known. It stood at the end of a wide glen some six miles long, and about ten miles from the nearest village, Crossan Bridge, and almost twenty miles from Mallaig, the nearest town of any size. There had been a house in Glen Crossan since the early eighteenth century but in the 1850s almost all of it was demolished and a classic Victorian shooting lodge – with castellations and turrets – was built in its place by Sholto's grandfather, the 10th baron. Only the entrance hall with its extravagant programme of plasterwork by Dunsterfield and the Robert Adam staircase remained from the old house.

But the House of Farr was decidedly cold and damp when I came to live in it and needed considerable and continued

The House of Farr, Glencrossan, Lochaber, 1958.

maintenance to make it remotely comfortable and modern. Another surprise was the presence of Sholto's mother, Dilys, the Dowager Lady Farr, who occupied a suite of rooms on the ground floor, next to the billiard room, with her own maid to look after her. Dilys Farr was a small skinny scrap of a woman, still dyeing her hair a curious bluey-black in her seventies, and she greeted my arrival with unconcealed suspicion. The barbed remark was her speciality and she seemed deliberately to take no pleasure in anything the world could offer. 'Just ignore her,' Sholto said to me once when I complained about some unnecessary, cruel comment she'd made. 'She was born miserable and, anyway, she's bound to die soon.'

Another minor irritation was the presence of his ex-wife, Benedicta, Lady Farr, who was living in a large house, a former manse, in Crossan Bridge. Their son, Andrew, the so-called Master of Farr, the heir, aged sixteen, was in the sixth form at Strathblane College, near Perth.

As if a mother-in-law and an ex-wife were not enough, the House of Farr had a sizeable staff. There was a housekeeper, Mrs Dalmire and her husband Peter – a chauffeur-butler-handyman – and two permanent housemaids (more could be summoned if the house was full of guests). On the estate were two gamekeepers and a forester/gardener all living in tied cottages scattered about the glen. There was a factor who appeared Monday to Friday – Mr Kinloss – who ran the estate and supervised the rents from the farms. I learned that there was property, some flats and houses, in Edinburgh and Glasgow, some remote cottages in the neighbourhood of Oban, and a small mews house in South Kensington, not to mention various trust funds and portfolios of stocks and shares managed by the family's bankers, Carntyne Petre & Co., in Edinburgh.

This was, in essence, the new world I entered. Sholto would say to me, as its landscape was progressively revealed, 'I'm not a rich man, Amory. I inherited an estate – and it's a nightmare: to run, to organise, to earn a decent living from. I'm just a rentier with a big house that's slowly falling apart. It may sound glamorous, being a baron and all that, but it's not glamorous at all.'

I remember our wedding, of course, in a small church full of tombs and plaques commemorating dead Farrs called St Modans in Crossan Bridge. Its antiquity was rather spoilt by a rash of new council houses built too close that had been put up just after the war. I didn't care – I was marrying Sholto Farr, the man I loved, and the meanest registry office would have suited me fine. We were married in June 1946, two months after our encounter in Paris. I hated all the official wedding photographs – Dilys Farr glowering by my side – but Donalda McCrae, one of the two housemaids, snapped me as I stepped out of the car (about to take the arm of Aldous King-Marley who was giving me away). It was a bit out of focus and a 'bad crop' as we say in the photography trade, but it is my favourite photograph of myself. I had no idea it was being taken – it's candid, in the best sense – and it was a day during which I was supremely, unequivocally, continually happy. Time stopped by Donalda. And whenever I look at it I can recall all the emotions I was feeling at that moment she inadvertently pressed the button. Life seemed almost insupportably good.

I remember writing a long letter to Charbonneau telling him I was going to be married and explaining why I'd left Paris so suddenly. I wrote to Cleve, also. Charbonneau's reply was sweet and rueful. 'Marrying? So fast?' I think he suspected I'd been disloyal – but then so had he. Cleve was gracious, thanking me formally for everything I'd done for *GPW*, making a point of saying how personally (underlined) grateful he was and how he'd enjoyed our close (underlined) collaboration over the years. If I ever wanted his help, just call, etc., etc. It wasn't intimate – I think he felt someone else might read it – all fondness was implicit, between the lines, in the underlines.

I had the odd pang, quitting my job, saying goodbye to Corisande – and the office was closed a week after I left. I realised that a significant portion of my life – my life as a professional photographer – was over. No doubt Miss Ashe would have approved of my change in status.

I remember that Dido and my mother came to the wedding. My mother couldn't hide her astonishment and relief that her thirty-eight-year-old daughter was finally marrying, and to a handsome Scottish aristocrat, no less. I think she thought it all some kind of charade or pantomime – the pipers outside the church, the House of Farr lit by hundreds of candles, the kilts and the sporrans, the reeling and dancing in the cleared billiard room – and that she would find herself back in East Sussex, waking from her dream, still with two unmarried daughters on her hands.

Greville was living in Italy with a young man called Gianluca and felt the journey was too long to make at his time of life. He sent me a magnum of Brunello di Montalcino.

Dido – my solitary bridesmaid – hadn't yet married Reggie Southover, and she didn't bring him to the wedding. For the first time in my life I thought she was jealous of me.

'My, my, Lady Farr,' she said, checking the hang of my wedding dress. 'Do I have to curtsey?'

'Only on my birthday. And you can always call me Amory when we're alone.'

'Fuck off!'

I remember in August, at the end of my first summer in Glencrossan, falling strangely ill. I began to suffer odd pains in my abdomen suffering from what is called 'timpanism' or 'meteorism', a painful bloating of the stomach. I thought I had some kind of bowel obstruction or an internal hernia. When I wasn't in pain I was immensely fatigued.

Sholto drove me down to Glasgow to see Jock Edie. I liked Jock – he and Sholto had been at school together – and he was self-confessedly one of those doctors for whom medicine is simply the means by which they lead a sophisticated, pleasure-filled life. I had made the mistake of looking up my symptoms in an old medical dictionary I found in the library and had become convinced I had 'ascites'. I was tapping my bloated stomach with a wooden spoon imagining hearing sounds of 'shifting dullness' or 'fluid thrill', ghastly symptoms that were listed in the dictionary under 'ascites'. I was worried I had some kind of chronic liver dysfunction, also, as I kept having to urinate, or some horrid abdominal cancer.

So I was in something of an ill-concealed state as Jock Edie examined me, palpating my stomach and then listening with his stethoscope. He stepped back from the examination couch – as I rearranged my clothes – first smiling, then frowning, tapping his chin with a finger.

'Do you know, we'll have to get it confirmed, but I would lay short odds on you being pregnant, Amory.'

'That's impossible. I can't have children. I was badly beaten up, years ago. A specialist told me I was infertile – Sir Victor Purslane.'

'Well, I'm afraid to say I think Sir Victor has made a serious mistake.'

The pregnancy was confirmed. More than confirmed – I was going to have twins. It was a strange time for me as I retrospectively had to reconfigure almost every certainty I had had about my life and person. I was pleased and I was worried. I was confused as I had resigned myself to childlessness, and was perfectly contented, and now, heading for my thirty-ninth birthday, I was about to have two children, simultaneously. Sholto professed himself delighted at this total surprise but it wasn't hard to imagine his own consternation. He had thought he and I were going to live as a couple, having had one failed marriage behind him and a child already, but all of a sudden he was about to become the middle-aged father of two babies.

When I think back, now, I realise what a bomb it was that erupted in our lives and blew them apart. All pleasant expectations, all happy assumptions gone – to be replaced by new ones, equally happy, one assumed, but entirely different and unprepared-for. And I was baffled as to how it had happened. Jock Edie said I shouldn't blame Sir Victor Purslane. Any doctor at that time would have made the same prognosis.

'But I didn't have any periods,' I pointed out.

'Maybe you had very mild ones or very intermittent ones,' Jock said. 'Because you thought you never had them you never noticed them when you did.'

'No, that's impossible.'

Then I thought back to my fall on the ice in the rue Monsieur and how the bleeding had restarted and then stopped. Had something been loosened or unlocked in me then? It hadn't been that long before Sholto had arrived in Paris looking for me ... How could I explain it? How could anyone? I recalled Sir Victor's words: we think we understand all about the human body but actually we know very little.

'When did that attack happen, by the way?' Jock asked.

'In 1936. It was when Mosley's fascists were marching in the East End of London.'

'My God ... It seems like another century ... So, ten years ago.'

'But why didn't I get pregnant before this?'

'Who knows? Did you have an active sex life? Forgive me for asking.'

'Well, yes ...' I thought about Cleve and Charbonneau. 'Pretty active.'

'Maybe you were just lucky. The timing was always right, if you know what I mean.'

'And now I'm having bloody twins.'

'Think of it as a blessing.'

'Yes. Yes, I will, Jock. Exactly. We're lucky. We're blessed.'

The twins duly arrived very early in January 1947. Conceived, as I'd always thought, during those four days in Paris in March with Sholto. Because of my age we took no risks and went to the Western Infirmary in Glasgow instead of the cottage hospital in Oban – and it was just as well because my parturition was complicated. One twin was born after twelve hours of excruciating labour. I understood why that word had been chosen to describe the process of giving birth. The first twin was a girl, whom we called Andra – an old Farr family name. The second twin, also a girl, was born by Caesarean section as I was deemed too weak to go through more hard labour. In fact I didn't see or hold my new babies for forty-eight hours, such was the practice in the hospital in those days. Eventually I had them in my arms and felt decidedly strange. Sholto was there, with a bunch of carnations, and I began to sob – from joy, I suppose, but also timorous confusion, suddenly confronted with this dual responsibility and a sense that my life was irrevocably turned upside down. No route ahead clear – a topsy-turvy world, as my father would have described it. I looked at my baby girls, Andra and Blythe – as twin number two had been named – and I could see, even that early, that they weren't identical. That made me pleased, for some reason.

After a week in hospital we all went back to the House of Farr, our surprising new family of four, to find a nanny waiting, a capable girl from the village called Sonia Haldane, who took instant control and suddenly all was well: Sonia could cope with anything, it seemed – two babes in arms were a mere nothing. Life regained a form of stability, a normality began to impose itself.

And we were happy – I mustn't forget that, as I look back. I was happy with Sholto and we were happy with our growing little children, Annie – as we called Andra – and Blythe. We had four – no, five – entirely happy years. Then Sholto's mother died. It wasn't anything to do with her passing away but I date the beginning of the change from the moment of her death. Life was still good but beneath the surface demons were stirring.

2. THE CELLAR

DILYS, LADY FARR, was buried in the small graveyard of the church where Sholto and I were married in Crossan Bridge – St Monad's. There was a good turnout of tenant farmers and neighbours and both Andrew, the Master of Farr, and his mother, Benedicta, were there as well, Benedicta impressively moved and teary. By then I knew Andrew a little better. He was now at Heriot-Watt College in Edinburgh, studying estate management. He was a tall, ungainly, dull young man with the same sharp-faced look of his mother. The only feature that I could see he'd inherited from his father was his fine straight hair – except Andrew's wasn't black, it was mousey-brown. He had a slight cast in one eye that gave him a sly, watchful aspect. When you talked to him you had to resist the urge to turn and look over your shoulder.

Benedicta was a bustling little dynamo of energy, blonde, chatty and knowing. She didn't like me at all, even though I had had nothing to do with her divorce from Sholto. But because I was the new, slightly younger wife she decided to blame me for the collapse of her marriage – illogically, perversely. What could I do about that? I didn't care and as I didn't warm to her I tried to keep out of her way as best I could.

After the funeral everyone returned to the house for drinks and canapés and she cornered me there, all affable concern.

'This is going to hit Sholto hard,' she said, dolefully.

'I don't think it will,' I said. 'He and Dilys weren't that close.'

'Just make sure the door to the cellar is locked.'

'I don't know what you're talking about,' I said.

'How are you coping, generally?'

'With the children?'

'With Sholto?'

'We're very happy. Very, very, very happy. Thank you for asking, Benedicta. Very happy indeed.'

But Sholto, as if to confirm Benedicta's snide malice, became very drunk that night – as drunk as I'd ever seen him. After everyone had gone I found him sitting staring at the fire in the small drawing room, a tumbler full of whisky in his hand – half a pint of whisky. I took it from him but he was already incoherent, slurring his words. He lurched to his feet and tried to kiss me and I pushed him off, angry.

'Look at yourself,' I hissed. 'Disgusting!' And stalked away, hating myself almost instantly because I knew I had sounded and behaved exactly as loathsome Benedicta would.

I remember how we used to drink in those days. Never gave it a passing thought. Gin at lunch – two or maybe three glasses with soda and Angostura bitters. A few whiskies before dinner and then wine. Sholto didn't sleep well so he'd take a slug of chloral before he went to bed that knocked him out until morning. And we smoked from breakfast onwards. We didn't care, we were happy, the little girls running around, and Sholto, it seemed to me, took great joy in his surprising new family. We went fishing in lochans up on Beinn Lurig; we took a boat out to Skye and the Hebrides; we spent several weekends a year at the London mews house; we all went on a holiday to Rome in '55 before the girls went off to boarding school. Of course there were problems, mainly financial, that meant one of the farms had to be sold, and the two flats in Edinburgh, but the House of Farr – crumbling, damp, cold in the winter – was a real home, a place of good cheer, especially now that bitter Dowager Dilys had gone for good. I started repainting her suite of rooms, buying new rugs and curtains. Yes, we were happy, then.

I remember that the one aspect of my new life that I vaguely resented was that I stopped being a photographer. I took photographs, of course – family snapshots – but it wasn't the same: it was as if some part of my being had been sloughed off, now I was married, a wife and a mother, running the big house. The old Amory Clay had disappeared, drifted away.

I kept my cameras in a locked cupboard, wrapped in chamois leather and sealed in plastic bags. I would take them out from time to time, like an old gunslinger nostalgic for the feel of his weapons, wanting to savour the weight and contours of his six-guns, make sure they were in working order.

Amongst the few pictures I did take some were in colour – Kodachrome slides, expensive but becoming the norm. However, even as I could see my pictures reflected the world as it was I somehow wanted the world as it wasn't – in monochrome. That was my medium, I knew, and in fact I came to feel it so strongly I wondered if, as the world turned to colour photography, something vital was being lost. The black and white image was, in some essential way, photography's defining feature – that was where its power lay and colour diminished its artfulness: paradoxically, monochrome – because it was so evidently unnatural – was what made a photograph work best.

I would carefully rewrap my cameras – my Leica, my Rollei, my Voigtländer – and place them back on their shelf in the cupboard and, as I locked the door on them, I wondered if I'd ever be a proper photographer again.

I remember Hanna came to stay. Elegant, mannish again, her short hair dyed a white-blonde. How she turned heads in Mallaig! However, the strange and troubling aspect of her visit was the antipathy that sprang up between her and Blythe. The twins were six years old at the time and I remember Blythe came to me one day and said, 'Mummy, I want Hanna to go away.'

'Why, darling? Hanna's my friend.'

313

'I don't like her, I want her to go.'

'I want – gets nothing. Don't be silly. Run along.'

A day later Hanna confided in me.

'Is everything all right with Blythe?'

'Of course. What's happened?'

'I was walking yesterday down by the river and someone threw stones at me. It was Blythe. When I went up to her she shouted, "Go away!"'

'She's just a little girl – she gets these silly ideas. I'll talk to her.'

Hanna shrugged. 'See how she looks at me. Look at lunchtime today. She hates me.'

I did look and I saw Blythe staring down the table at Hanna with a ferocity that I found alarming. I took her aside after lunch and asked her if she'd thrown stones at Hanna. She denied it, vehemently, so I sent her to her room with no supper.

But I was troubled. As your children grow up and become small, thinking people you would be a fool to deny that, like the rest of the human race, they begin to develop their distinct personalities – and there's very little at all you can do about it. Little Johnny can be shy or stupid, or funny or odd, or carefree or cruel, or duplicitous or guileless. I could see from quite early on in their lives how Annie and Blythe were becoming entirely different people. Annie was sweet, helpful – life was fun, to be enjoyed to the full. Blythe was cleverer, quicker on the uptake, but had dark destructive moods and had a stubborn streak that was almost pathological. When Hanna finally left after her ten days it was as if Blythe had triumphed, somehow. It sounds odd to say this about a six-year-old but for a couple of days her mood was elated, arrogant, and she swaggered about the house, almost insufferable.

I mentioned this behaviour to Sholto but he said he hadn't noticed anything out of the ordinary.

Something Benedicta said stayed with me: 'Just make sure the door to the cellar is locked.' We had a large cellar at Farr where we

The twins, Blythe and Annie, 1953.

stored wine and other alcohol and all manner of detritus from the house's past. It was Sholto's domain – he kept the house's drink supply stocked; he did all the ordering from Naismith & McFee Ltd, the big general grocer in Oban. Their olive-green vans were a regular sight in the House of Farr's driveway – we bought almost all our provisions from them. Mrs Dalmire would phone in the order and the next day a van would appear.

I went down to the cellar and found the door locked. I asked Peter Dalmire for the key and he told me it was kept in His Lordship's gunroom on its own hook. Peter showed me where it was hung and I explored the cellar. We had an enormous supply of booze, it seemed to me, doing a swift inventory – six cases of gin, ten of whisky, both blended and malt, several hundred bottles of wine, not to mention beer, vermouths, sherry and the like. I counted the bottles of gin and whisky and a week later counted them again, calculating that in those seven days the household at Farr had downed two bottles of gin and four bottles of whisky. There had been two visits from friends passing by but that didn't explain the amount. I knew how much I had drunk – the usual lunchtime and pre-dinner glass or three – and realised with something of a shock that all the rest had effectively been consumed by Sholto.

I began to watch him and notice how often he refilled his glass. I searched his study and gunroom when he was absent and found other bottles stashed in cupboards. Yet on the surface all was as it had always been: he was funny, affectionate, enjoying himself, happy to be running his big estate with its many responsibilities. But he was obviously drinking like a desperate man and I found myself at a loss.

*

THE BARRANDALE JOURNAL 1977

I looked through my bookshelves today searching for a Bible, but in vain. I was sure I had an old one with cracked black leather binding and gold embossed letters but there was no sign of it. Then I had an idea – I knew where I could borrow one.

I drove into Achnalorn and parked outside the church at the end of the main street, St Machar's, or the Auld Kirk of Barrandale, as it was known. It was an unpretentious building in its small bumpy churchyard, circled by a slate wall with rowan trees growing amongst the tilted gravestones. It was simple, like a rectangular house, with a steeply pitched roof with stepped gables and an ornate small cupola with a bell in it – never rung – and a pineapple finial on top, gift of some rich and devout parishioner in the early nineteenth century. A simple stone porch had been crudely added on to one side – it looked like the entry to a garden shed or coal store – and there were four large coloured-glass windows in the nave depicting scenes from the life of St Machar. Inside there were two rows of wooden pews on either side of a central aisle and a table altar on a dais with a heavy brass crucifix in the middle.

The Reverend Patrick Tolland himself was putting the finishing touches to the vases of flowers flanking the crucifix – yellow geraniums and bracken – and he looked round as I came quietly in. He was a young vicar – in his thirties, I guessed – with long hair over his ears and collar. He had an African beaded necklace from which his crude pewter cross hung. I'd met him a few times but, as he clearly couldn't remember my name, I introduced myself and said I was hoping to borrow a Bible. An authentic King James, if possible.

He strode off to fetch one and as he handed it to me said, 'I hope we'll see you at the Sunday service, Lady Farr.'

I never introduced myself as Lady Farr – I always said Amory Farr – so he had obviously realised who I was.

'No. I'm afraid not,' I said.

'But the Bible . . . ?'

'I want to look something up. I'll bring it back tomorrow.'

'Oh. Right,' he said, seeming momentarily cast down. Then he walked me solicitously to the door. 'Lovely day,' he said, gesturing at the sunlit sky with its drifting clouds. 'And God saw every thing that he had made and, behold, it was very good.'

I thanked him and set off down the path to the main street and as I did so walked into a fizzing shimmer of midges. I waved my arms about but I could feel the sharp sting of the bites. I turned back to the reverend and shouted.

'Couldn't you get Him to do something about the bloody midges?'

★

We sent the girls off to boarding school when they were ten, in 1957. I never really asked why – I had been sent off myself, of course, and had resented it. I raised a mild protest but Sholto insisted – there was no school for them in Mallaig, he said, and we can't afford private tutors. Of course there was a school – but not for the children of Lord Farr. Selfishly, secretly, I thought it would be good for the two of us to be a couple again – we'd had so little time without the girls. Selfishness is almost always the real, hidden reason why people send their children away to board. I told myself that it was something one did at this level of society and so I drove them to Edinburgh, feeling guilty all the same, and saw them installed in the Maxwell-Milnes School for Girls. They seemed untroubled. Benedicta was an alumna.

I missed the girls but soon saw this change in our family circumstances as something more alarming – the benefits I was expecting never materialised. Perhaps because I suddenly had more time on my hands I began to notice Sholto's decline more clearly. It was his habit to go to London on a fairly regular basis to vote in the House of Lords on matters relating to Scotland, and Scottish landowners. There was a grouping of Scottish peers who had organised themselves into a form of lobby and Sholto took his responsibilities seriously. Sometimes I went with him but most often he travelled on his own, taking the sleeper from Glasgow, staying at the South Kensington mews house, and returning three or four days later, legislative business done.

One Friday afternoon while Sholto was away in London I had a telephone call from a reporter on the William Hickey column at the *Daily Express*.

'How can I help you?' I asked.

'Have you any comment to make about your husband's predicament, Lady Farr?'

'I'm afraid I don't understand.'

'He's been arrested.'

'What for?'

'Drunk and disorderly. He tried to beat up a photographer.'

I hung up and didn't answer when the phone rang again, immediately. I called the mews house but there was no reply. The next day I went into Mallaig and bought the newspaper. There was a picture of Sholto in a dinner suit, his bow tie loosened, his hair plastered with sweat, snarling like an animal, trying to rip the camera from the hands of a photographer. Behind him, pulling at his coat tails was a young woman, screaming out, in a short white fur coat and a dress that revealed much of her breasts. I could see a neon sign behind him that read 'The Golden Wheel Club'. The caption declared: 'WAR HERO SCOTTISH LORD ARRESTED'.

Sholto was released with a caution after twenty-four hours in the Rochester Row police station cells and came home at once. I met him in the morning at Glasgow's Central Station and we drove home in a mood of some tension. He was sheepish and apologetic, explaining that he'd had too much to drink and gone with friends to this club to gamble. Some film star was there, he said, and that explained why press photographers were lurking. He was drunk, he confessed, and had lost his temper.

'Foolish of me, I know, darling,' he said. 'Won't happen again.'

'Who was that girl with you?'

'What? Oh, some Mayfair tart who'd tried to pick me up.'

I wanted to say why was she screaming and pulling you away? Tarts usually run for it.

'Well, you're the talk of the neighbourhood,' I said. 'As you can imagine. Not a copy of the *Express* to be had for miles around.'

'They'll get over it. They know the Farrs are a wild lot. Seen it all before.'

'Yes, in the sixteenth century.'

He didn't want to talk about it any further and I could feel his shame, burning, however light-heartedly he tried to laugh it off.

That evening we were having a drink before dinner, in the small drawing room on the first floor.

'What's happening, Sholto?' I said in a reasonable, unaggressive voice. 'What went on in London? What goes on in London?'

'Nothing. I had too much to drink, I told you.'

'You have too much to drink every night of the week. I meant what's happening with us?'

319

'What're you talking about?'

'You, me, the girls. The family, the estate. The school fees, the House of Farr. The staff. Everything.'

He stood up and arched his back, his hands pressing into his spine as if he had some acute lumbar pain. He swayed over to the drinks table, inevitably, and poured himself a quadruple whisky.

'I drink as much as my father did,' he said, sullenly.

'What kind of justification is that? He died when you were twenty-three. And you haven't answered my question.'

'We are in a bit of trouble,' he said. 'A bit. We might have to sell a couple more of the farms.'

I continued with my gentle interrogation and discovered that Sholto had lost nearly £10,000 at baccarat that night in the Mayfair casino. There had been no celebrity actor present. It was casino practice routinely to alert the press when a big loser was leaving the premises — the unwelcome publicity, the blinded stare faced with popping flashbulbs, had the effect of reminding everyone — particularly the loser — of the loser's fiscal responsibilities.

Worse was to come. My questioning opened the door to Sholto's occasional gambling binges. He tried to confine them to his trips to London, but further enquiries unearthed a bookkeeper in Glasgow who held his notes for his flutters on the horses. Sholto owed him close to £8,000. These were vast sums, by any standard.

My worst suspicions were confirmed when I went into Oban, to Naismith & McFee. I had my chequebook at the ready but never expected a line of credit that had recently crossed the £1,000 mark. 'We would appreciate an early settlement, Lady Farr,' Mr Naismith himself requested in his office, his polite smile and inclined head failing to disguise his anxiety. I wrote him a cheque and the next day went to see our banker in Edinburgh, Mr Fairbairn Dodd, managing director of Carntyne Petre & Co.

Fairbairn Dodd was a plump, smiling, clever man with perfectly white hair, a fact that added to his spurious aura of disinterested benignity. He was extremely polite, ordered me a pot of tea, and outlined the details of Sholto's stewardship of the House of Farr estates since he had inherited them on the death of his father in 1929. There were only two farms left, it turned out, providing an income of £800 a year. The land remaining was still several thousand acres but of a less valuable non-agricultural nature – fen, moor and mountain. There were still the few cottages in the Oban–Mallaig area but they brought in insignificant revenue. The Glasgow and Edinburgh properties had almost all been sold and the mews house in South Kensington now had a second mortgage. The current overdraft with Carntyne Petre was running at £23,000.

'We're effectively bankrupt,' I said.

'No. You have the House of Farr and its contents and several thousand acres of Scottish countryside. These are considerable assets.'

'What should we do, Mr Dodd?'

'First of all, Lord Farr has to stop throwing money away with such promiscuous abandon. Then, perhaps, sell the Raeburn portraits, and the tenth baron's porcelain collection. Sell the house in London.' He smiled. 'We can arrange all this for you, very discreetly. Let the grouse moor to a wealthy sporting Englishman. August and September – it's a fifteen-hundred-brace moor. A real asset.' He thought. 'And surely Lord Farr could be a further asset to the boardrooms of certain companies . . . Defence, whisky, tourism. Let me look into that. Everything's changing, Lady Farr. Your husband has a name and a reputation he can exploit.'

'Get a job, in other words.'

'It's an option. Worth considering.'

I went back to Farr and laid out the facts to Sholto as Fairbairn Dodd had laid them out to me. Sholto seemed chastened as I outlined the brutal details of his massive indebtedness.

'You have to stop drinking, darling.'

'I'll cut down, I promise.'

And then, a month later, he had a heart attack. Again it was in London, in the entrance hall of his club, Brydges. It wasn't serious and he was out of hospital within a week, armed with many bottles of pills to take. I went with him to see Jock Edie and refused to leave the room when Sholto asked me to.

Jock had copies of Sholto's X-rays.

'Well, the bad news is that you have to stop drinking and smoking, now. Forever,' Jock said, amiably. 'And the good news is that if you do as you're told you should see your daughters married and you may even dandle your grandchildren on your knee.'

'That's the good news, is it?' Sholto said, his voice small and monotone. 'I suppose you think I should see a trick-cyclist, as well.'

'Only if you want to. You have to want psychiatric help if it's going to be of any use.'

'We can certainly think about that,' I said, trying to be positive.

★

THE BARRANDALE JOURNAL 1977

End of September on Barrandale equals end of midges. These little blurry clouds of stinging flies are the bane of Scottish summers and, to celebrate their absence, I took Flam out for a walk and wasn't bitten once. We walked round the headland on the western edge of the bay and I was surprised to see a Land Rover parked by the ruined cottage. There was a young man taking photographs and measuring the rooms with a multi-yard tape. He was a surveyor, he said.

'Somebody's interested in buying it,' he confided. 'Wants to put a new roof on, do the whole place up.'

I asked him who it was but he wouldn't tell me.

I walked home, my head full of thoughts, of suppositions. This new person would be my closest neighbour but would be over half a mile away and entirely out of sight. I could hardly complain. But, I thought, I could certainly find out who it was with a bit of judicious asking around. It was hard to keep a secret on Barrandale.

★

Sholto became physically transformed after he left hospital – thin, diminished – and he looked unwell, his face unnaturally flushed, his fine straight hair losing its lustre, becoming dry and brittle. It was if the memento mori he had received – the attack of his heart – had surprised him profoundly. Sholto Farr, the invincible man, baron, war hero, commando, had been brought low.

Sholto followed doctor's orders – but on his terms. He cut down – only two packs of cigarettes a day, not three. He only drank whisky in the evening, contenting himself with a glass of beer at lunch. Or so he said. I kept finding bottles here and there, secreted about the house. I found his hip flask half full of gin in his fishing jacket. He stashed bottles in the walled garden and I would watch him from the sitting room unearthing them and having a few covert swigs and then pretend to inspect the roses.

But we became solvent, after a fashion. We quietly sold the Raeburns to the Scottish National Gallery – double portraits of the 7th Baron Farr and of his wife, Lady Zepherina – and the porcelain collection of Sholto's grandfather. The South Kensington mews went, and a shooting syndicate rented the Beinn Lurig grouse moor for three years. Our overdraft with Carntyne Petre & Co. was reduced to £2,000. Sholto joined the board of Glen Fleshan Distilleries Ltd for a generous annual stipend. A trust fund continued to pay for the girls' school fees and we managed, amazingly, to live approximately in the style we were accustomed to on our remaining rents and the odd dividend from our stocks and shares.

However, slowly but surely, the house began to fall apart. The staff was reduced to the Dalmires. I started doing more housework. We let one gamekeeper and the forester go and rented their cottages to tourists in the summer.

And as the house grew dingier and damper, and other pieces of furniture were sold at auction to pay the bills (we made an astonishing £1,000 from a lacquered Chinese cabinet), so Sholto seemed to decline in tandem. We had screaming rows – or rather

I screamed at him as he sat in his armchair, a cigarette in one hand, a glass of whisky in the other, his head bowed, a prematurely old man being castigated by his harridan wife.

I remember I was hoovering our bedroom when I heard a gunshot – inside the house, down below on the main floor. As I raced downstairs I heard more blasts – a shotgun – coming from Sholto's gunroom. My terrified panic – suicide – turned to irritation: Sholto shooting at rabbits on the lawn from the window. I flung open the door and saw him sitting behind his desk taking aim at something high on the cornice. He fired and I reeled away as a blast of powder erupted on the ceiling.

'Got him!' he shouted.

'What are you doing, you madman!' I yelled at him. Mrs Dalmire had now appeared at the door.

'A fucking fly,' Sholto said. 'Buzzing around, driving me insane.'

He broke the gun and took out the spent cartridges and stood up, one hand on the desk top for support. He was falling-over drunk.

'No need to make so much fuss, ladies,' he said and sank to his knees and vomited all over the parquet.

I remember Annie and Blythe coming to me one evening as I was watching television in the back parlour where we kept the set.

'What's wrong with Papa?' Annie said, looking alarmed.

'Nothing's wrong.'

'If there's nothing wrong why is he lying on the front lawn in his underpants?' Blythe said, dispassionately.

I remember going to Glasgow to see Jock Edie and asking his advice.

'It's very simple,' Jock said. 'And I've told him to his face. If he doesn't stop drinking and smoking he's going to die. Very soon, I'm sorry to say.'

'But why's he doing this – to himself, to us?'

Jock gently touched his fingertips together several times as he thought further.

'I think it was something that happened in the war. At the end, in '45.'

'He never talks about it. He refuses.'

'It was something Frank Dunn said, in passing. I just picked up on it. "Sholto's massacre", is what he said. A throwaway remark. You should ask Frank about it.'

I remember in fact I asked Sholto, myself. It was quite late at night and we were in the television room. He'd had a couple of large whiskies and was like his old sharp observant self commenting on something we'd seen on the news – the Bay of Pigs invasion: war was in the air so it seemed a good moment, the perfect cue. There was a fire going and it was warm, the curtains drawn. I lit a cigarette and gathered myself.

'What happened in the war, darling? To you, I mean?'

The question took him aback. He blinked as he thought how to reply and opted for insouciance.

'Quite a lot. I had rather a busy time of it, from 1942 onwards.'

'Was it something that happened in Wesel? When we met up.'

The name Wesel seemed to jolt him, physically.

'Oh, Wesel. Jesus. Yes, that was ...' He searched for the words. 'A fucking nightmare.'

I remembered coming across him and his men, sitting silently around the shattered bandstand; remembered their faces, filthy, drawn and gaunt.

'Did something happen, then?' I pressed gently. 'In Wesel. March 1945.'

'Oh, God, what happened? ... Oh, yes. That's right. I killed dozens of people. Lots.'

'People?'

'Soldiers. Well, hardly soldiers.' His face began to crumple and his lips trembled. 'Kids.'

Then he wouldn't say any more.

I remember, in the next school holidays, Annie coming downstairs to find me, saying, Mummy come quickly, something's gone wrong with Papa. I sent her away and went upstairs, walking quietly into our bedroom. Sholto was sitting on his bed in his pyjamas, looking out through the big bay window at the view down Glen Crossan, weeping.

'What's wrong, my love?' I said softly, sitting down beside him and putting an arm round his shoulders.

'I want to die,' he whispered. 'Why's it taking so long?'

Sholto had his wish when his second, fatal, heart attack took place in September 1961. Mrs Dalmire found him unconscious on the floor of the gunroom. An ambulance was called and sped him to the hospital in Oban and then, when he couldn't be revived, he was rushed to the Royal Infirmary in Glasgow where, just before midnight, he was pronounced dead. He was fifty-five years old.

3. Consequences

THE MASTER OF FARR, Andrew Farr (unmarried), became the 13th Baron Farr of Glencrossan. And Benedicta, Lady Farr, became his Cardinal Richelieu, Jezebel and the Duchess of Malfi combined. Another mistake – Sholto had died without changing his will. The will that existed was the will he had made when Andrew was born. He'd never added any codicil that referred to me, or Annie and Blythe. And thus my troubles began, anew.

There was immediate consternation about the disarray in the Farr estate finances. Two weeks after Sholto's funeral I was summoned to a meeting at Benedicta's house in Crossan Bridge. Andrew was there and Mr Archibald Strathray, the family solicitor, and Mr Fairbairn Dodd from Carntyne Petre & Co. Tea was offered; I asked for a whisky and soda.

Benedicta wasted no time in apportioning blame. What exactly had occurred in the fifteen years I'd been married to Sholto? How could a once-thriving estate now be so penurious? I suggested that Fairbairn Dodd confirm to Benedicta what he had once told me, namely that Sholto had gambled away tens of thousands of pounds without my knowledge and that he had progressively sold off the estate's assets in an attempt to conceal his addiction.

'Addiction?' Benedicta scoffed. 'That's absurd.'

'Mr Dodd, please.'

'Yes, I was aware of the problem, Lady Farr,' he said to Benedicta. He was uncomfortable but there was nothing he could do. Then Benedicta and Andrew – Andrew meekly nodding and muttering consent as his mother spoke – laid out their plans. I was to vacate the House of Farr: the will was explicit, Andrew was to inherit everything. I sat there and listened resolutely as my new future was blocked out, feeling the ache of the loss of Sholto and also a growing anger at his oversight. Everything could have been so much simpler – another bloody mistake, I thought, as we began to bicker over the scraps that remained. Benedicta was particularly incensed by the sale of the Raeburns – 'Our heritage, gone forever!' – and the South Kensington mews house (her holidays in the capital ruined). At every rebuke I turned to Mr Dodd and he edgily backed me up. 'Lady Farr had no alternative,' he told Lady Farr.

'In point of fact, Mr Dodd,' I said, 'it was on your advice that I sold the Raeburns.'

'I believe it was.'

We broke up with nothing resolved. Archibald Strathray, as we collected our coats in the hall, turned to me and, in a low voice, recommended that I find myself a lawyer, fast. I had allies among the functionaries.

So I asked Jock Edie if he knew someone ferocious and uncompromising and not too expensive and he recommended a patient of his, a young Glasgow solicitor called Joe Dunraven. We duly met. Joe Dunraven was a small, fair, handsome man with a distinct Glasgow accent and a quickly revealed social anger at anyone he regarded as lazy and over-privileged. I think I only escaped his censure because he could see I was broke and being persecuted by the family. After five minutes' conversation I asked him to represent me and, to my surprise, he agreed instantly. He wasn't cheap, in fact, but Dido had offered to pay his fee. I looked forward to his coming encounter with Benedicta, Lady Farr. I told him what I required, as a matter of basic survival – first, a place to live, now I was being turfed out of the House of Farr, my home of fifteen years. It was clear I was unwelcome anywhere on the Glencrossan estate; that my daughters' school fees be paid, and that I receive a basic income until their education was over.

'I think we can do better than that, Amory,' he said with a confident grin. I had invited him to call me Amory after he insisted that I call him Joe. It established our egalitarian standards.

I didn't attend the next meeting at Crossan Bridge, leaving it to my fired-up proxy to make my case. After it was over he came to the house, not quite managing to keep the smile from his lips, and we each drank a large whisky together and smoked a cigarette in celebration as he told me what he had won from the Farrs.

I was to be given the choice of three 'dwellings' owned by the estate, and the one I chose would be mine 'in perpetuity'. The trust fund that was paying the girls' school fees would continue and they would each receive a benefaction of £1,000 on their twenty-first birthdays. I was to be guaranteed a personal income of £500 per annum for the next ten years. The quid pro quo was that I and my family could make no further claim on the estate.

I declared myself well pleased and warmly shook Joe Dunraven's hand – and then spontaneously kissed him on the cheek, such was my relief. Thus encouraged, he asked me out to dinner but I made an excuse: if he didn't mind, I was still grieving, I wasn't fit company. But I was a little taken aback – I think Joe Dunraven had acquired a sudden interest in the Scottish aristocracy, however spurious a member of that clan I was.

I looked at the three properties I was offered and chose the least valuable, a cottage on the island of Barrandale. The other two were a terrace house in Mallaig and a large bungalow in Newton Mearns, Glasgow. It showed me that Sholto hadn't entirely depleted the Farr estate and I wondered what other assets were hidden away. But I didn't care. Once I'd seen the cottage it wasn't a difficult decision. Even though Barrandale was barely an island, it was symbolically separate from the mainland and I liked the idea of living in an isolated house, if somewhat decrepit, with its own small bay and a view of the Atlantic Ocean beyond. The girls agreed, instantly, and were very excited. It was the perfect contrast and antidote to the House of Farr – a place I never returned to again.

★

THE BARRANDALE JOURNAL 1977

I still dream about Sholto, all these years later. His death came as a dreaded and devastating shock even though I knew it wasn't far away; but at the same time I couldn't deny how ardently he had wished for it – and who was I to demand that he prolong the unending torment that his living hours so obviously were? He wanted to go more than anything else and I was glad for him. I was dry-eyed at his funeral, concentrating on this, thinking: you're free, Sholto, all your troubles are over. We will soldier on without you but you are now part of the transcendental history of the universe. Dust to dust, atoms to atoms. I realised, as I heard the eulogies and we sang the hymns, that Sholto had enjoyed very little of his life these last several years – not me, nor his daughters, nor his home, his lands, his heritage had made any difference – and if you feel that way about being alive, if life doesn't offer you the slightest consolation, if you savour nothing, not even the tiniest insignificant feature that the planet and your fellow humans can offer, then you shouldn't hang around, in my opinion. As Charbonneau once said to me – take the cyanide pill, now.

But it was also clear to me that whatever awful event had occurred in Wesel in 1945 had come, slowly but surely, to dominate his conscious being and had started to define the sort of person he thought he was, and that this had made him drink so much, explained why he was so careless, in every sense of the word, explained why he lost his love for everything. He was too much of the brave soldier to blow his brains out or swallow pills so he killed himself with other means to hand – alcohol, tobacco, prescription drugs, self-neglect. I felt an enormous weight of sadness at his death but – and is it shocking to admit this? – a huge relief and a

330

kind of happiness for him now he was free of himself, of the world and its burdens.

I kept all this from Annie and Blythe – who were initially shattered, abject, uncomprehending, and then recovered quickly, as the young will, with their own lives to lead beckoning them onwards. Poor Papa, they both said. Why didn't he take more care? Didn't he realise what he was doing to himself? We talked about it a great deal, the three of us, and I alluded to a dark unhappiness, to something that had happened to him in the war that had made him go a bit mad, and they both said they understood and provided me with more anecdotes of Sholto's bizarre behaviour that they had witnessed but hadn't told me.

We left the House of Farr, with few regrets, once the cottage was ready for us. I bought us a Labrador, Flim, from a kennels in Oban and our new life began.

Flim, Barrandale, 1962.

★

I travelled to England, to Hereford, to meet Frank Dunn. He hadn't been able to come to the funeral but Aldous King-Marley (who gave the address) told me how to make contact with him.

Frank Dunn had been a twenty-year-old second lieutenant during the Commando Brigade's attack on Wesel in 1945. Now, aged thirty-seven, he was still in the army, a major in 22 SAS Regiment. He was married with two young children and he still had that lean, super-fit aspect about him that I remembered from Sholto just after the war. He was no jowly pot-bellied habitué of the officers' mess – Frank Dunn hadn't stopped serious soldiering, that was very plain.

We left his house and went to a pub down the road so we could talk, uninterrupted by his children. We spoke about Sholto, candidly, and Frank admitted that the man he had become at the end of his life was a bleak shadow of his former commanding officer.

'What happened in Wesel?' I said. 'Sholto would never tell me.'

'Well, I wasn't there the whole night,' Frank said. 'A bit of shrapnel hit me in the ankle and I had to be strapped up at a dressing station, so I missed a lot – but heard the story later, of course. In fact everyone knew – but nobody ever really wanted to talk about it.'

Frank told me what had taken place that night – using our glasses, ashtray, cigarette packets to make the geography of the town more intelligible. Sometime after midnight on 23 March, 15 Commando's progress, mopping up and clearing out pockets of resistance that had survived the massive bombardment, had been stopped by heavy fire from one particular building – a former post office – that overlooked a crossroads. This building had a large cellar basement and there were squat, barred, recessed windows with thick mullions set at pavement level in the ground floor's heavy rustication that gave excellent protection and afforded perfect firing positions on the streets converging on the crossroads.

'We were losing men. It was like a bunker, that place. The top had fallen in but the ground floor was solid, thick walls and these embrasures let them fire on us from all angles. Machine guns, *Panzerfausts*, *Panzerschrecks* – like bazookas, you know. Then someone spotted a small back entrance in the next street.'

He said that Sholto took the decision to lead a section round himself and they saw that if they could blast the door off they might have a way into the cellar.

'And that's what they did. Blew the door off,' Frank said. 'Sholto had a kitbag full of grenades and he just slung them in, one after another. Boom-boom-boom. Anyone who tried to scramble out was gunned down. Then one of the grenades must have hit a stock of ammo and the whole place was ripped apart. All went quiet.

'So,' he went on, a little grimly, 'Sholto goes in first, then David Farquhar. Almost everyone's dead, blown to pieces, suffocated, whatever. Thick smoke everywhere. A few wounded, screaming and crying.' He frowned. 'The trouble was, once the air cleared, we saw they were all Hitler Youth – adolescent boys, fourteen or fifteen – younger. A couple of older officers, but basically we'd been fighting kiddies, little lads. And Sholto had single-handedly killed them all. That was the thing that got to him.'

Frank went on to say that when he limped up, some half an hour after the battle around the post office had ended, the bodies had been carried out into the street and laid out in rows. 'About thirty or so of them, all told,' he said. 'It was very upsetting, no getting away from it, seeing these dead boys. It wasn't right, you know, asking these children to fight our lot. They didn't stand a hope in hell.'

I thought back to that morning, to the bandstand in the ruined park and the eerie silence of the commandos, taking in what they'd just seen and done.

'There's a difference between a young soldier and a boy,' Frank said. 'Most soldiers are very young – but those Hitler Youth. I mean, I was only twenty, for God's sake. But I was a man, exceptionally well trained in my job. These boys should have been at school or at home with their mum and dad. And I could see, even then, that Sholto was affected very badly. I think it was because he'd taken it on himself to throw all the grenades in. We all said: how could anyone know? They were shooting at us, killing and wounding us. As far as we were concerned they might have been SS storm troopers. But it shook him up – it shook me up. I think now we shouldn't have brought the bodies up from the cellar, laid them out in the street like that; we should have just left them in the house and moved on. A lot of the guys were very upset when they saw how young they were . . .'

He tailed off and finished his gin and tonic. He was looking a bit grim and upset himself, thinking back in this way.

'I definitely need another large one of these,' he said.

I said I did too.

4. SCOTIA!

'Right everybody. Big smile! Say "cheese"!'

The group stiffened up, checked their positions, put on their unnatural smiles and I took the photograph. Some twenty people were lined up, arranged in two rows, the bride and groom centred, in front of the entrance to the old parish church in Peebles, in the Tweed Valley. I took two more photographs for luck and let the wedding party disperse to the reception at the Tontine Hotel about a hundred yards away.

I packed away my camera and tripod and lugged them back to where I'd parked the Imp. I felt the usual depression settle on my shoulders and ignored it. No, Amory, stop it. I wasn't photographing pets but it was close. Still, I had a job, I was earning money. I had no right to complain or feel aggrieved.

I was working for a monthly illustrated magazine called *Scotia!*. It was a rival to similar magazines such as *Scottish Field*, *Caledonia*, *Scotland Today*, *Bonny Scotland* and the like, whose staple journalistic menu dealt with the seasonal traditions of our small country – shooting, fishing ('Rod, Reel and Line'), stalking, game fairs, agricultural shows ('Country Notes'), robust outdoor fashion, motor cars and – this is where I came in – the social round. Weddings, balls ('How to Wear a Sash'), christenings, Highland gatherings, tournaments, military tattoos, funerals and so on, were covered by *Scotia!* with all the nuance and artistic flair reserved for team photographs of rugby, football, golf and cricket clubs. The subjects formed a line and they were photographed. Couples stood side by side, ditto. These subjects and couples then usually asked for copies of said photographs and thereby provided a significant revenue stream for the magazine. It was not to be taken lightly, so the editor regularly told me.

Scotia! was edited by a client of Joe Dunraven. Joe had secured me the job as a favour once he knew my history as a professional photographer. His client, Hughie Anstruther, was more than happy to take me on, given my experience (and my title), but he very quickly advised me: don't get any fancy ideas, Lady Farr, this is not *American Mode.* I didn't.

Hughie Anstruther was a neat, waspish, vain man who combed his side hair over his bald pate in an elaborate coil, like a table mat or hemp rope, and was oblivious to the tonsorial effect of this on his otherwise respectable appearance. But I came to like him and the job he gave me allowed me to supplement my allowance from the Farr settlement. I wasn't poor but I had to budget carefully. I had a house to live in but it was certainly no palace. It struck me that, entirely inadvertently, I had come full circle. I had started off an impoverished young woman, taking society photographs with Greville in the 1920s to make ends meet, and here I was, decades on, an impecunious middle-aged woman, doing exactly the same.

The world of Scotia!, © *Scotia Media Enterprises Ltd, 1964.*

I was beginning to feel, also, after the turmoil of my recent years with Sholto, that I'd entered a form of quietus. The cottage was entirely comfortable, though a little basic; the girls were on the point of leaving school; I was relatively solvent, relatively comfortably housed, secure enough, employed, after a fashion. I couldn't complain. But was I happy?

I had integrated myself, as far as any newcomer could, into the small but diverse island community of Barrandale. I had found a few new friends and, another bonus, because they were new I could tell them as much or as little about my past as I wanted. I never advertised myself as the widow of Sholto, Lord Farr. I was just Mrs Farr, or Amory, to the people I dealt with or counted as my new acquaintances.

I hadn't sought the *Scotia!* job. Joe Dunraven who, as a matter of course, knew far too much about me, had suggested me to Hughie, and Hughie, thinking my background would open more doors, had eagerly hired me. The job was undemanding: once I'd returned home from whatever wedding or grand ceilidh or memorial service I would develop the film, print contact sheets, annotate them with the names to fill the captions and post them off with the rolls of film to the office in Glasgow. And the next month there would be the evidence of my work on the 'social pages'. I was consoled only by the thought that I had insisted on remaining uncredited and that I was – in a manner of speaking – still a professional photographer.

I remember when she was fourteen Blythe said that she wanted a guitar for her birthday and so I bought her one. She was quite musical, it turned out – Dido was delighted – and also took piano lessons at school. One night in the cottage when she and Annie were home on holiday I asked her to play something. She sang a song she had written, a plangent minor-key version of the folk song 'Bobbie Shafto'. She sang it in a husky but true voice as Annie and I sat opposite her, Annie sitting on the floor by my feet, Blythe perched on a stool in front of the fire, her big guitar balanced across her knee.

Bonny Sholto's gone away,
He'll not be back another day.
Wherever he's gone, he's there to stay,
Bonny Daddy, Sholto.

The song continued – 'Bonny Sholto went to war' – but the three of us were sobbing halfway through the second verse and had to stop and hug each other. It was a moment of real catharsis for us all and I had a full sense of the girls' loss, also. It wasn't just my grief; the difficult, complicated life of Sholto Farr wasn't just my problem; the damage wasn't just limited to me.

I remember that we all went on holiday to Italy to see Greville in his new life. Having sent him out there on assignment in 1944 for *GPW*, I'm not sure we ever received one photograph in return. But somehow, in his leisurely travels as he – at careful distance – followed the 110th Infantry Division as it advanced north up through Italy, he had contrived to engage a young artist as his translator, called Gianluca Furlan. Gianluca had inherited a small but rather lovely house up in the hills behind Viareggio, in northern Tuscany. After the war Greville moved in. He took photographs; Gianluca painted the Tuscan landscape. They seemed entirely happy and Greville swore he owed it all to me.

We spent two weeks with them in 1965. The girls had just done their A levels. We were there in July and every two days or so we'd drive down to the wide beach at Viareggio and spend a day by the sea. Greville took this photograph of the three of us. The three Farr women, he called us.

Me and the twins, Viareggio, 1965.

I remember buying a book, a popular military history about the last months of the Second World War called *Desperate Endgame: British Armies in the Final Year, 1944–1945.* There was a page or two dedicated to the battle for Wesel during Operation Plunder. All it had to say relevant to Sholto was this:

15 Commando, under the command of Lt Col Lord Farr, encountered stiff resistance at a crossroads to the east of the town centre. It took some hours to clear out the strongpoint. At daybreak 15 Commando gathered in a small park where it was discovered that their casualties were six dead, fourteen

wounded. The assault on Wesel was a copybook Commando action: in the ferocious street fighting they had proved their mettle.

No comment.

I remember once we were having a picnic, me and the girls, out at the foot of Beinn Morr on a windy, sunny day, the grass bleached and bending in the tugging breeze, and Blythe, who was sitting beside me, asked if we could play Greville's Game. At that time of her life she was always asking me if we could play the game with her. Annie couldn't be bothered joining in – she thought it was 'stupid'.

'All right,' I said. 'What about that little river?'

'Wet, brown, fast, silky. Too easy, Ma. Let's do people.'

'Mr Kinloss. Remember him?'

'Fat, grey, polite, mysterious.'

'Good. Yes! I never thought of that.' She was fast, Blythe, never taking more than a few seconds to come up with her adjectives.

'Now it's your turn,' she said, brightly. 'Do me. And be honest.'

'That's not fair.'

'No, you do me, then I'll do you.'

I felt a little shadow of worry – this could have consequences, I realised, not necessarily welcome, but there was no avoiding the issue. Annie had wandered off with her bottle of lemonade and was tossing pebbles into the shallow burn that gurgled by our picnic spot – she couldn't hear our conversation, I was sure.

I looked at Blythe.

'Pretty, stubborn, clever, complicated.'

She thought about this, frowning, making a little moue with her lips, weighing up the epithets and seeing if they fitted.

'Now you do me,' I said.

'Pretty, stubborn, clever, complicated,' she said instantly.

I laughed and she joined in but I had received the message – especially as she now glanced over her shoulder to make sure that Annie hadn't overheard. I was beginning to think she'd laid a trap for me – and now there was a private bond between us. She was telling me – so I reasoned – like mother, like daughter. She was probably right.

'Now do Andrew Farr,' I said, wanting to break the mood.

'Dull, shifty, boring, dominated.'

Annie wandered over.

'What are you two laughing at?' she asked, irritated.

I remember receiving the A level results for the twins in the post and undergoing the ritual opening of the envelopes at the breakfast table. Annie had done well; Blythe less so – but she said she didn't care. She was going to be a musician, A levels were of no use. I agreed.

Annie secured a place at one of the new universities, Sussex, to read for a degree entitled 'International Relations', whatever that was.

I took her out to dinner in Oban, to celebrate (Blythe was away, somewhere). I looked at her across the table and allowed my love for serious Annie to brim. She had a long thin face – Blythe's was rounder, prettier – and she was taller than Blythe, also.

'Ma, would you mind if I asked you a favour?' she said.

'Anything.'

'You know that, because of Papa's title, I'm "the Honourable" Andra Farr?'

'Yes.'

'Well, I don't ever want to be called that. I got a letter from the university and it called me "the Honourable". I was so embarrassed.'

'That's all right, darling. I understand.'

'I just don't want that title ever to be used. Ever again. No disrespect to Papa, and all that.'

'Of course. I don't much like being "Lady Farr" either.' I squeezed her hand. 'It's expunged.'

At the university, in her hall of residence, she was less than an hour from Beckburrow and, much to my surprise, went there every other weekend or so to spend time with her grandmother, who was old, and ailing, but still feistily alert. While Annie was there she unearthed a cache of my early photographs, and others of the period. She sent me a small selection: there was a tattered one of me when I was twenty, standing in the pond at Beckburrow, posing; and one of me as a little girl with my father, taken by Greville. It must be in 1913 or 1914, just before he went off to war.

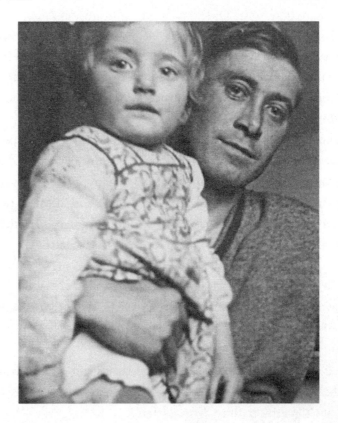

I remember one odd moment. Blythe and I were out for a walk on the beach with Flim – Annie had gone south to check out her new hall of residence.

'I hate that bitch, Benedicta,' Blythe said, all of a sudden.

'Well, so do I,' I admitted. 'Nasty piece of work. Grasping, smug, malicious, insincere.'

'Do you think if someone killed her anyone would mind for one minute? For one second?'

'Don't say that sort of thing, Blythe, not even as a joke.'

'It's not a joke. She kicked us out.'

I took her hand – she was flushed, there was a real rage building.

'It doesn't matter, darling. We wouldn't have been happy there, at the House. It was never really our home.'

It seemed to mollify her. She was leaving as well, the next day, for London, to stay with Dido and Reggie Southover at their rather grand house on Camden Hill. Blythe wanted to audition for folk bands or rock groups – she didn't care, keyboard or guitar, she just wanted to play music. Dido was her inspiration and they became quite close. There was a musical gene in the Clay family, shared by Dido and Blythe – they were different from the rest of us, the *littérateurs*, the photographers.

I remember I had a rare letter from Charbonneau telling me the news of the birth of his second child – a son, Luc. He enclosed a photograph of himself, 'So you won't forget what I look like.'

Jean-Baptiste Charbonneau, 1962.

I saw he'd put on weight and grown a moustache again. He was standing on a terrace on the Italian Riviera, somewhere, and I supposed he vaguely wanted me to feel jealous about the high life he was leading. I couldn't help thinking he didn't look particularly happy.

★

THE BARRANDALE JOURNAL 1977

I liked to quiz Greer about her old subject, cosmology, as there were aspects of it that intrigued me, to her occasional exasperation.

'So the Big Bang happened thirteen billion years ago?' I once asked her, when we were out for a walk.

'Thirteen point eight billion years ago. Give or take a day or two,' she said. 'Oh God, you're going to ask me more questions, aren't you?'

'Because I'm interested,' I said. 'You've stimulated my interest, Greer. You should be pleased.'

We were walking down from the heights of Cnoc Torran, that we'd climbed that morning, heading back for lunch at the cottage. We had a magnificent view of the various islands around Barrandale. I could see Mull as clearly as I'd ever seen it – I could see a red car driving on the road along the north end of Loch Don.

'The Big Bang explains all this,' I said, gesturing freely towards Mull and the ocean beyond. 'Everything started then.'

'Everything. It explains everything. You and me. This grass, the clouds above.' She pointed. 'That insect – and the universe. It all began then.'

'How can you be so sure?' I paused to tie a lace on my walking boot.

'Well, we have something called the "standard model". It explains almost everything.'

'Almost.'

'Yes.'

'And the stuff you can't explain?'

Greer looked at me shrewdly. 'I know I'm going to regret this.'

'That's where your dark matter comes in, doesn't it,' I said. 'Dark matter explains the things that don't add up, in theory.'

'In a manner of speaking.'

'And dark gravity. And dark energy.'

'I know it sounds rather spooky and exciting, but it's complicated. There has to be dark matter to explain the anomalies.'

I snapped my fingers.

'You need all these "dark" things to explain why the "standard model" doesn't supply all the answers.'

'In a manner of speaking.'

'You see that's what I love about cosmology. It's exactly the same for the rest of us.'

'You mustn't do this, Amory. We hate this. Scientists hate this . . . this appropriation. You don't understand.'

'No, I don't,' I said. 'Or yes, I do. Just like you cosmologists, we can't explain everything. Things don't add up. What about "dark" love? Why did I fall in love with that hopeless person? "Dark" love explains it. Why did I get this annoying illness? "Dark" disease. Stuff I can't see is affecting me, the way I act.'

'No, no, no. You're turning hard science into a metaphor.'

'Which I'm entitled to. "Dark" illness. "Dark" weather. "Dark" incompetence. "Dark" politics.'

She had to laugh. We walked on, almost bouncing downhill on the springy grass.

'The "dark" concept explains why you can't explain things,' I said. 'It's wonderfully liberating. Why won't my car start this morning? It started yesterday. "Dark" auto-engineering.'

'Just don't tell anyone you got it from me.'

'You see, the "standard model" of the human condition just doesn't work, either. It's inadequate. Just as the "standard model" of the universe doesn't work for you lot.'

'What're we having for lunch?'

'Dark shepherd's pie.'

I remember we drank a lot at that lunch – we always drank a lot but I think Greer wanted the inhibition-removal that a boozy lunch sometimes provides. She told me about an affair she'd had with a colleague of Calder's. The affair had ended when he had gone to join a think tank in London – distance working as prophylactic – but he'd written to her, recently, asking her to come and see him.

'Have you ever had an affair, Amory?' she asked me.

'Well, not when I was married,' I said. 'But I did have an affair when I was having an affair.' I paused, thinking back. 'Twice, in fact.'

'Only you could make it that complicated,' she said.

'I don't quite know how it happened,' I said. 'Dark love?'

'I'm beginning to see your logic.' She sipped at her wine. 'Should I go to London? What do you think?'

'I think you should do what you want to do. As the poet said: the desires of the heart are as crooked as corkscrews . . .'

She laughed. 'You're no help.'

'Exactly.'

★

For some bizarre reason Dido took a strong liking to Barrandale. She came to stay for a week or so two or three times a year, to 'rest' after her concert tours and recitals. 'I need to recharge every battery, darling,' she would say. 'Peace, silence, nothingness, and a large gin and tonic, that's all I ask.' In 1966, she was at the height of her fame – Béla Bartók had dedicated a horn trio to her; she was a regular at the BBC Proms; Harold Wilson invited her to lunch at 10 Downing Street; she was awarded the CBE. However, her marriage to Reggie Southover was ending. She was having an affair with a clarinettist from the Orquesta Nacional de España – 'Poor as a church mouse,' she said. 'But rather lovely, all the same.

It's the Latin spirit I crave, I should never have anything to do with Anglo-Saxons.'

Dido Clay CBE, 1966.

I teased her once, asking her if she had an affair with one member of every orchestra she played with.

'Not every orchestra,' she said, entirely seriously. 'No, I'm very picky.'

She once said, 'Have you noticed, Herbert von Karajan and Lenny Bernstein have exactly the same hair – same floppy front, same distinguished grey, same style – do you think it's a conductor thing?'

'Have you slept with either of them? Or both?' I asked.

347

'Well, I had a bit of a moment with one of them, I confess – but I won't tell you which.'

Even though she obviously loved coming to Barrandale, she always complained about the cottage and its minor privations. She also began to dig away at me.

'What're you going to do now the girls have gone? You can't take photographs of Scottish weddings for the rest of your life.'

★

THE BARRANDALE JOURNAL 1977

It happened again. I tried to pick up a jam jar this morning with my left hand to put it back in the refrigerator but I couldn't. My hand just wouldn't grip. I sat down, had a minute's rest, and tried again. It worked – but just as I was going to put it on the shelf my grip loosened and the jar fell to the floor and smashed.

This is as bad as it's ever been, my particular, worrying problem. My brain told my hand to grip but it refused. Jock Edie – whom I'd told about this problem, and who told me what he suspected was wrong – said that one day I'd have to go and see a neurologist. Perhaps the time has come.

I had lunch with Hugo Torrance at the hotel – during which my hold on the cutlery seemed secure. We were at our usual corner table tucked in beside the fireplace – where, as it happened, the first fire of the autumn was burning nicely, so Hugo informed me. As if to justify its being lit, it was raining quite heavily outside. We ate rare roast beef and drank red wine. I was feeling ideally mellow but suspicious.

'All this is heading somewhere,' I said. 'I can tell by that look in your eye.'

'It can head anywhere you like.'

'Come on, spit it out.'

'I've sold the hotel.'

This was indeed a surprise. 'Congratulations,' I said. 'Are you pleased?'

'Yes. And – more news – I've bought that ruined cottage round the headland from you. We're going to be neighbours.'

★

After Dido left to go back to London, Hughie Anstruther called and reminded me that I was covering the Northern Meeting in Inverness. It would be an overnight stay and he wondered if I'd need an assistant.

'The world and his wife seem to be going this year,' he said. 'Get your best frock out, sweetheart.'

I was not enthused. This would be my third Northern Meeting. I could just about handle the ball but the prospect of photographing the bagpipe-competition winners filled me with prescient fatigue. Dido was right – I had to make a change, do something entirely different. But what? All I knew was photography.

I went out for a walk, ostensibly to think, and headed unerringly for the bar at the Glenlarig Hotel. I ordered a whisky and water and asked if Mr Torrance was in and was informed that he was upstairs in his flat. I thought he might be exactly the man to ponder my dilemma with and headed off to find him. As I made my way towards his private rear stairway I passed the residents' lounge where the door was open wide and a mute television set was silently broadcasting the evening news to a ring of empty armchairs. A flowering fire and dust-filled explosion filled the screen – oddly beautiful in its expanding terrible energy, like a giant grey chrysanthemum or monochrome dahlia – that caught my attention and I stepped inside for a second.

An unsteady hand-held camera was focussed on a bespectacled woman in a dirty, sweaty uniform crouched in a ditch talking into a microphone. She was wearing a tin helmet with the word 'PRESS' written on the front in white letters. In the background two ragged columns of smoke rose over jungle hills. Despite her grimy face and the unfamiliar spectacles I realised I knew who this woman was and stooped forward to turn up the volume just as she was signing off.

'This is Lily Perette, Dang Tra province, with the US Marine Corps.'

What was it that made me decide I had to go to Vietnam? Initially, it was seeing Lily Perette on the television screen and remembering the last war we'd been involved in together. Suddenly I had this feeling that I wanted urgently to be there with her, to ask her questions: what was it like, was it dangerous, how had she come to be in Vietnam of all places? And then I realised – more analysis kicking in – that the emotion I was actually experiencing was envy. I envied Lily Perette at that moment and I felt that unbidden surge of excitement run through me. Perhaps I could go to this war, just like her. I had the same experience, the same qualifications, the same talent . . . I didn't go up to see Hugo but returned to the bar for another pensive drink.

I sat and considered my options. Could I rejoin *GPW*? No. That road was closed. Was there another way? I couldn't just buy a plane ticket and fly out to the country like a tourist. Or could I . . . ? And then the sensible portion of my mind recalled that I had a secure and steady job, albeit moderately paid, and I should just head on up north to Inverness and the bagpipe competitions and forget all this impulsiveness, this foolishness.

Yet the more the realistic, sensible, solutions lined up and presented themselves the more the idea of somehow trying to go to Vietnam began to consume me. I wanted my old job back – I wanted to be a proper photographer again. The thought of Vietnam and its distant war seemed like the perfect antidote to more Scottish weddings and eightsome reels.

I think now – now that time has passed – that what I really wanted, fundamentally, was to confront warfare again. Not so much to test myself – I had been tested – but to see how the 'me' that existed then would function in a war zone, would experience war differently. War had shaped, directed and distorted my life in so many ways – through my father, Xan, Sholto – that I think that the zeal I was feeling was an unconscious response to this deeper need. After Sholto and my life with him, I wanted to experience something of what he had gone through but with my new knowledge – about him, about me – informing everything. I couldn't rewind time and be wise after the event but I could go forward and seek some answers out for myself. The newer, older, wiser Amory Clay could live through what the former, younger, more innocent Amory hadn't been able to evaluate fully. My education as a person, so I reasoned, would never be complete if I didn't do this, if I didn't see for myself – and then see myself, plain. I needed to learn how I would react and respond, what it would tell me about my life and my being.

Or so I internally argued as the evening wore on in the bar of the hotel. But I was a mother, also, I made the point, with two much-loved, precious daughters. Were my arguments specious or genuine? Was I being true to myself or selfish? Well, I would never know until I actually travelled out there and confronted my demons face to face.

It was as I wandered homeward in the dark that the answer came to me: I realised I knew exactly whom I could call – not Cleveland Finzi, but another former lover who might well be in a position to help me out. More to the point, he owed me a big favour, did Lockwood Mower, from way back.

I travelled down to London and arranged to meet Lockwood – much to his delighted surprise – in his offices at the *Daily Sketch* where he was now the senior picture editor. Lockwood was stouter, greyer and his moustache was wider though startlingly dark, like his eyebrows. The effect was strange, as if he were wearing a rather bad and conspicuous disguise. Once the pleasantries were over, I told him why I needed his help in what I wanted to do. He was aghast.

'Vietnam? Are you out of your mind? You can't go out there, Amory, you're too—' he didn't finish as he could see my expression change.

'You owe me this favour, Lockwood. Look at you – picture editor, big office, national newspaper.' I leant forward. 'Just add me quietly to your team.'

'We don't have a team. You can't go out there on our ticket. Mr French would have a fit.'

'Who's Mr French?'

'The editor.'

'Then where do you get your Vietnam stuff from? You do know there's a war on out there.'

'Very funny, Amory. We buy it in from agencies.'

'What agencies?'

He thought for a second.

'We get most pictures from the Yanks, of course. A lot from this company, Sentinel Press Services. Very reasonable.'

'American. Even better. I worked for an American magazine for years. Tell this Sentinel I worked for *Global-Photo-Watch*, ran their London and Paris offices in the war.'

He rubbed his chin.

'No harm in trying, I suppose.'

'I really want this to happen, Lockwood. Think about it – if I'm out there I can make sure you get all the good stuff.'

He agreed, it made sense. I lit a cigarette, sensing him looking at me in his old intense way, almost as if we were working together back in Greville's studio.

'You're serious about this, aren't you, Amory? It's not some kind of whim, some mad idea?'

'Deadly serious.'

'All right. I'll put a call in to the Sentinel people. See what I can do.'

I stayed on in London while I waited for news from Lockwood. I took Blythe and Annie out for dinner to a Vietnamese restaurant on the Cromwell Road called the Nam Quoc Palace as a rather too obvious pretext for letting them know my plans. When I told them that I wanted to pick up my old career again and go out to Vietnam to be a photojournalist, Annie appeared as excited by the prospect as I was – but Blythe seemed almost shocked.

'It's bloody dangerous, Ma,' she said, frowning darkly at me. 'What're you thinking of?'

'I've done it before,' I said. 'It was my job. I know what I'm doing – and I won't be taking any risks, I can assure you.'

But Blythe kept on at me.

'If you've done it once I don't see why you need to do it again.'

'I have to prove something to myself.'

'What? Prove that you're stupid?'

I let that go because I didn't want to sour the mood of the evening any further. When Annie left to catch her train to Brighton Blythe stayed on and we ordered another coffee and some kind of sweet rice dumpling. Her mood seemed to calm and she took my hand and twiddled my wedding ring.

'It's because of Papa, isn't it?' she said. 'That's why you feel you need to go.'

'Partly, yes,' I said, trying to hide my surprise at her insight. 'And it's partly to do with me. And my life.'

She turned my ring round on my finger, then sighed and let my hand go. She busied herself meticulously rolling a thin cigarette. I lit up to keep her company and the two of us puffed away in silence for a few moments.

'It's so far away,' she said, finally. 'I think that's what's bothering me. You're going to be on the other side of the world.'

'I won't be there forever.'

'For how long, then?' she asked, almost aggressively.

'I'm not sure, yet. I have to get out there first.'

'I may never see you again,' she said, her eyes suddenly large with tears.

'Don't be so silly, darling,' I said, perhaps more testily than I meant. 'You know, I have a life to lead as well as you two. I can't just sit and rot on Barrandale.'

'Of course,' she said, letting her body sag in the chair, closing her eyes and smiling to herself. 'I just like the idea of you being close at hand.'

We hugged goodbye on the pavement and I promised I would call her as often as possible. She seemed more reconciled to the idea of my going away, now we were outside the restaurant, and I wondered if the pointed Vietnam theme had been a bad idea. Too late, anyway. I watched her saunter away towards her bus stop, a tall, thin and limber young woman in her shaggy coat, her long hair halfway down her back, and felt the old love-pang corkscrew through me. My pretty, stubborn, clever, complicated daughter.

When I returned to the hotel there was a message to call Lockwood at the *Sketch*.

'Hello, Lockwood, it's me.'

'You're on. *Bon voyage.*'

BOOK SEVEN: 1966–1968

1. The Vietnam Scrapbook

Lockwood was not entirely accurate: I wasn't wholly 'on' at all. Sentinel Press Services had grudgingly agreed to take me on as a stringer but only for a trial month for which I would be paid $200. I would also have to pay for my own transportation out to Vietnam and my accommodation once I arrived in Saigon. And no expenses. I could only agree. Sentinel did have a small permanent bureau in Saigon, Lockwood said, with a staff of three, including a photographer. 'They did take a bit of persuading, Amory,' he said, knowingly, and I wondered if Lockwood or the Daily Sketch *were underwriting my meagre paycheck. One photographer is never enough, I said, surely. I think Lockwood was trying to make me understand the brutal realities of the situation but I was already excited. I didn't care – I was going to my war. I negotiated one further condition in the light of these restrictions – and the fact that I was hardly being paid at all. I don't know why I insisted but it was one of the smartest moves I ever made in my life, as it turned out. I told him I would license my photos to Sentinel for first-use but I would retain the copyright. That shouldn't be a problem, he said. Just make sure we get all your best stuff, here. I think by then Lockwood was assuming I'd go out there, have my short adventure, then suffer and be miserable, flush the idea out of my system and come home, having proved myself. I think he calculated I'd last a couple of weeks and $200 was a small price to pay for getting me off his back. How wrong he was.*

When I arrived in Saigon I started keeping an intermittent journal, filling it with my impressions and thoughts and sticking in some of the

355

photographs I took. I think I already had the idea that I might make a book out of this experience.

Saigon, Vietnam, 1967. From Vietnam, Mon Amour.

I was sitting in the Saigon press centre yesterday listening to the new IO give us the latest KIA and MIA[1] facts, thinking that he looked a bit like Xan, and simultaneously remarking on the dozens and dozens of empty seats – someone had told me there were 700 journalists in Vietnam; where the hell was everybody? Then Mary Poundstone slipped into the plastic chair beside me. Her face was taut, her lips thinned.

'They won't renew my visa,' she said. 'Bastards. Let's go and get a drink.'

So we went to the rooftop bar at the Caravelle Hotel[2] and ordered two gins and tonic with lots of ice and found a table some distance from everyone else. Mary and I had met up again shortly after I had arrived in February (1967) having last seen each other in the Vosges mountains in 1944. I knew what she'd been up to in the

---

[1] 'Killed in Action' and 'Missing in Action'.

[2] The Caravelle Hotel was the favourite of the Vietnam Press Corps. AP and UPI had suites of offices there and its rooftop bar was the prime hang-out.

interim. She had become even more of a legend since then – books of reportage, two collections of short stories, a cluster of prizes, lionisation by a new generation of writers – but in Saigon the two of us began to spend a lot of time together, seek each other out at the press briefings, so much so that we became known to the press corps as the 'Old Gals'. I was fifty-nine, Mary was sixty-four – by some way the oldest journalists in Vietnam.

Right from the outset she started giving me advice over what to wear: khaki, white or beige masculine clothing – pants and shirts – with one feminine touch. Wear combat fatigues when you go out with the troops but don't look like a soldier or a fashionable woman when you're in town or at the bases. Add a bright scarf, a brooch, bangles, she advised. I decided to go the earring route and chose a pair of small gold hoops, about an inch in diameter, that

Truong, my driver. Without whom . . .

I wore all the time – my trademark – even with a tin helmet. My 'look' was khaki chinos and a white T-shirt under an untucked, multi-pocketed cotton drill shirt, mostly tan, sometimes denim, sometimes linen, with epaulettes. Truong,[1] my driver, found me a tailor on Cong Thanh Street who would run me up half a dozen of these pseudo-military shirts for a pack of 200 Salem cigarettes.

The SPS bureau is in a house on a narrow side street called An Qui Alley, about a block away from *Time*'s offices. The bureau chief is a grumpy, officious man called Lane Burrell. The two assigned journalists, the 'staffers', are Ron Paxton and a young woman with the unlikely name of Renata Alabama, the photographer. Lane Burrell told me that I was only 'attached' to SPS and that if ever asked I should say I was working for the London *Daily Sketch*. He'd do what he could to expedite my accreditation, however. He said, 'What did you ever do to Lockwood Mower? Boy does he love you.' I'm almost certain Lockwood is paying my way out here. Lane seems happy enough with the arrangement but I don't think Ron and Renata are particularly pleased at my arrival and I suspect I won't ever win them over.[2]

Burrell, Paxton and Alabama live in a roomy three-bedroom apartment above the bureau offices. As part of SPS's conditions I have to find my own place to live. I checked out an apartment

---

[1] Truong Ngoc Thong was hired by me on my third day in Saigon. I had rented a scooter that I thought would allow me to whizz about the city. Two near-accidents in half an hour showed me I had made a possibly fatal miscalculation. Truong spoke bad English, better French and, of course, fluent Vietnamese. His car was an old blue Renault Colorale. I would never have survived without him.

[2] Lane Burrell was as good as his word and my accreditation duly arrived. I had my ID: my 'non-combatant' certificate of identity issued by the US Department of Defense. I was described as a 'British Photojournalist'. I was entitled to go to the daily Military Assistance Command Vietnam (MACV) briefing – the 'five o'clock follies', as they were known – draw combat fatigues, C-rations, travel on military transport, and had the right to go into battle.

above a French restaurant on Nguyen Van Thu Street, on the bad side of the Saigon River. The restaurant is called Le Mistral de Provence and that's what made me rent the two-room apartment – memories of Charbonneau. No hot water, no air conditioning, a bed, two plastic chairs and a table and a bathroom with a shower that dripped rather than ran. It cost $50 a month.

When I arrived at Tan Son Nhut airport and stepped off the Pan Am flight from Hong Kong it was the heat that almost drove me back on the plane. I'd never experienced heat like that, furnace hot and wet at the same time. Like being dry in a warm sea. Like being wet in a dry desert. I could never quite describe it properly. Also I'd never seen so many aircraft in one place, hundreds, it appeared, civilian and military, single-seaters, four-engine Boeing jetliners – Pan Am, Cathay Pacific, PAL, Flying Tigers – Phantoms, DC-3s, and on and on – landing, taking off, parked seemingly haphazardly in ragged rows, as if casually abandoned by their pilots who'd walked away looking for a bar.

There is a curious, unspoken class system working here amongst the journalists. 'Staffers' versus 'stringers'. Staffers are serious professional journalists; stringers are wild cards, eccentrics, fools, war-lovers, freaks, potheads, dangerous. There's a celebrated stringer called John Oberkamp (an Australian) who has been here since 1965 and has been wounded in action three times. He and some friends rent a big house on My Loc Street – near Tu Do Street (where all the bars are) – that is known as the 'Non-Com Hotel'. It's like a just-under-control-twenty-four-hour nightclub. Lots of drinking, music, drugs – and, most valuably, information, contacts, rumours.

There's still a strong prevalence of the French colonial days in Saigon, despite the fact that there are hundreds of thousands of Americans in Vietnam. And you can eat very well in the old style if you can afford it, and find it. I remember the other day I went to the café at the Hotel de la Poste and I asked for a whisky.

The waiter said, 'Do you want a *bébé*? Or a *grand bébé*?'
'What's a *bébé*?'
'A small whisky.'

I made contact with Lily Perette at a MACV briefing, and she claimed to remember me from Paris in '44. 'No, no, absolutely. You got me assigned to Patton. I interviewed him, thanks to you. Made my name.' The young enthusiast I recalled from the Hotel Scribe had turned into a lean, mannish, somewhat bitter, but respected journalist. She wore a short-jacketed denim suit and smoked small cigarillos more or less constantly. She makes up the contingent of 'Old Gals', here in Saigon. Not that Lily's old – she's in her late forties – but most of the dozen or so women journalists and photographers here in Vietnam are young, almost all in their twenties. Lily, Mary and I are relics from the past, from other, older wars. She suggested we go out on the town – have a meal and then show up at the Non-Com Hotel for some fun.

'Aren't we too old for the Non-Com?' I said as we headed there in a taxi.

'They don't fucking care,' Lily said. 'And we don't fucking care. The main thing is that they know what we need to know – the units that like journalists.' She was now writing for a magazine called *Overseas Report* that was perceived to be too left wing, and had found it difficult to gain new accreditation. 'They keep saying no to me,' Lily said, 'so I'm going to take matters into my own hands.'

I have to say I did feel a bit old in the Non-Com Hotel, however, as I wandered through its rooms, the music blasting out, the mood raucous and edgy – and self-regarding: the place was full of people burnishing or developing their own myths. A lot of these young men – they were mainly men, the stringers – seemed to be high on the war, excited to be relaying atrocity stories, weird GI rituals, and the sheer thrill of choppering-in to a firefight near the DMZ. The air was bulky with acronyms.

I stood in a corner of one room, lit with blue neon, sipping at a can of beer, smelling the pungent reek of marijuana, the Rolling Stones telling everyone to get off of their cloud, thinking – this is different, this is why you came, my dear. This is why you're not at the Northern Meeting in Inverness taking photographs of bagpipers.

'Hi.'

I turned. A young man stood there in a silk collarless shirt. It was blue, everything in that room was blue, including our faces. He was small and handsome, this blue man, with big candid eyes – something elfin about him.

'I'm John Oberkamp.'

'Amory Clay.'

We shook hands. He had a noticeable Australian accent, I registered, as he asked me what I did and who I was stringing for. He said he was a photographer himself, currently unattached to any magazine or newspaper, though when the conversation turned, as it always did, to cameras and techniques, I realised he was something of an amateur. He could load film and press the shutter release but that was about it, I concluded. He brought me another can of beer.

'Could you get me some kind of a job at Sentinel? I just need some validation.'

I said it was very unlikely; even I was deemed surplus to requirements.

'Surplus to requirements.' He repeated the phrase a few times. 'Story of my life.'

I lit a cigarette. 'Why can't you get accreditation?'

'Because there are too many fucking stringers in this town. Kids buy a camera, just jump on a plane in Europe, fly over, think they're "war photographers".' He shrugged. 'I've been here for over two years, my pictures have been published in *Life*, in *Stern*, in the London *Observer*, but I can't get accredited.' He looked at me closely. 'Do you mind if I ask you how old you are?'

'Not at all.' I told him.

'You don't look that old.'

'It's this blue light, takes years off you.'

He laughed at that.

'It's pretty fucking amazing that you're here,' he said. 'I mean that's really cool, someone like you.'

By now I realised he was very stoned, a thought confirmed when he touched my breasts. I gently removed his hands.

'You're not my type,' I said. 'Sorry.' But I was thinking: intriguing, wild, irresponsible, sexy.

He nodded. 'Surplus to requirements ... Have you ever seen action?' he asked abruptly.

'Yes.'

'Doc Tri, Rockpile? Highway One?'

'Second World War.'

'No shit?'

'Shit.'

'That is completely amazing. Amazing. Can I kiss you?'

The evening at the Non-Com Hotel did provide me and Lily with information about a unit that had a reputation of being journalist-friendly, even woman-journalist-friendly. Lily suggested we team up – print and camera – and put in a joint request to MACV as if it came from both Sentinel and *Overseas Report* and she might just be able to sneak in unobserved. We applied and were accepted and four days ago we were flown in a Caribou transport plane up to An Boa – 'Sandbag City' as it was known, a huge airbase and firebase up north by Da Nang.

Before we left, Truong drove me to a rackety emporium in Hy Kiy Street where I could buy, on the black market, a helmet and flak jacket that fitted me. '*Où allez-vous, madame?*' he asked. We tended to speak in a mixture of French and English. I told him. '*Ce n'est pas* good place,' he said. '*Beaucoup* dangerous.' I could see his concern. I told him it was my job but I wouldn't take any risks.

The night before we left, Lily and I had a meal in the Majestic Hotel, treating ourselves. She had been in Cuba and Algeria, she told me, and she wondered if it was the reports she filed from there that made MACV think she was some kind of communist. She was eager for our trip; I could see she still had that ardour and driven ambition of the true correspondent, driven also by the fear of being left out, missing out, somehow. I didn't have that kind of zeal, that much I was sure of, and I thought of Truong's anxiety and wondered again about my actual motives for coming. Now I was here in Saigon my vague thoughts about finding myself, needing a new war so I could reassess my old self, seemed a bit woolly and pretentious. Maybe, I thought, I was just as driven and ambitious as Lily Perette and was hiding it from myself. Did I want that adrenalin rush; did I still worry that I was missing something, just as much as Lily, I wondered?

An Boa is a 'firebase' – in so much as it is home to batteries of long-range artillery and vast numbers of helicopters – but that appellation gives a false impression. The place is huge, square miles of it, with its precincts and streets, just like a city, even though one constructed out of sandbags, cinder blocks, chipboard sheeting and corrugated iron. We queue for food in a giant cafeteria for T-bone steaks and a choice of six ice creams; shower in tiled bathrooms; sleep in bunkers – 'hooches' – with ceiling fans; buy six-packs of beer at the PX.

At night, though, the mood changes and the war comes calling, but distantly: we can hear the thud of far-off mortars, see multicoloured flares falling beyond the invisible perimeter. The *dugga-dugga-dugga* of helicopters passing over, low, wakes you in your 'rack'. Lily Perette has dysentery and is being flown back to Saigon to hospital. So I'm on my own.

I climb into the Huey helicopter and squeeze in behind the gunner. A section of 'D' Company, 1st Battalion, 105th Infantry Brigade, joins me. My hair is tucked up under my helmet and I'm sitting on my pack and my two cameras – a Nikon and a Leica – are in my musette bag along with six rolls of 35 mm Ektachrome film. We are going to a 'Country Fair', so called. 'D' Company choppers into a village in the Que Son Valley, surrounds it, searches for suspected Viet Cong amongst the inhabitants and any caches of weapons or ammunition that might be hidden, and then departs. Country Fair operations, as their name suggests, are routine and usually safe, which is why I chose to come along. The village is called Phu Tho, anglicised to 'Pluto'. 'Is there life on Pluto?' some joker asks as we take off. It is 5.45 a.m.

In the pearly morning light, mist evaporating from the meandering rivers and the creeks, the sky hazing into blue, Vietnam looks very beautiful. Only the scars, the bulldozed brick-coloured scabs on hilltops and ridge-ends of abandoned firebases and observation posts, mar the abundant, lush greenery. Looking closer I see areas of felled or flattened trees, and occasional clusters

Arriving at Phu Tho village, Que Son Valley, 1967.

of rimey, water-filled bomb or shell craters, like pustulant ulcers. The green landscape seems primordial, untouched – but of course it isn't.

Soon we swoop down with our reverberating clatter towards the rice fields around Pluto. The men leap out of the Hueys that then soar up and peel away, having disgorged their human load. As we hover closer to the earth I lean out past the gunner and – click – grab my first photo. Pluto's Country Fair has begun.

The men fan out, sloshing through the rice fields, plodding along the low causeways, and the village is quickly surrounded. Captain Durado goes into the village with the interpreter and the 200 or so villagers are led out – women, old folks and children are separated from the young men. They settle down on their haunches, patiently, uncomplainingly, waiting for this rude interruption to their daily lives to be over. The men of 'D' Company occupy the village, the dog handlers set their German shepherds loose, sniffing out tunnels and buried bunkers, for any sign of VC or NVA presence.

Off to the Country Fair. Que Son Valley, 1967.

Midday. It's hot and wet. Clammy and hot. All the village haystacks have been set on fire and the smoke curling from them seems reluctant to climb into the sky.

I ask Captain Durado why he gave the order to burn the haystacks as doesn't that rather signal our presence in the valley? He says he gave no such order – the men did it themselves, it's something they seem to like to do, almost a habit, a *rite de passage*, I infer. I wander away and sit on the edge of a drainage ditch and eat my C-rations – ham and lima beans and a can of fruit cocktail – then smoke a cigarette.

'Excuse me, ma'am, but – if you don't mind me asking – what the fuck are you doing here?' A GI sitting along from me cannot contain his curiosity.

I explain that I'm a journalist. It's my job. 'Just like you,' I add.

'Yeah, but I didn't ask for this job.'

General laughter at this.

'No, what I mean,' he goes on, 'is that aren't you a little bit—'

He never finishes his predictable question because all heads turn to look, turning to the sound of popping gunfire from the treeline across the rice fields from where we are sitting. Everyone starts swearing and grabs their weapon. I jump into the drainage ditch and scurry along it, heading for a wooden culvert. Shouts and orders ring out. Captain Durado is standing on the culvert ordering his men to take cover. *Whump! Whump!* The first mortar shells explode and Captain Durado leaps into the ditch beside me. The villagers begin to scream and scatter aimlessly, heading for obscuring vegetation – nobody tries to stop them. Now there's a steady rattle of enfilading fire from the treeline. Now we are firing back with more intensity. I think I can see where the shooting is coming from but I can't spot the enemy. Suddenly I'm back in Villeforte in the Vosges mountains.

Captain Durado is joined by his radio operator who twiddles with dials and switches on his machine. Hiss of static, voices.

'Maybe we shouldn't have set fire to the haystacks,' I say to no one in particular.

Captain Durado is young – twenty-five or twenty-six, I'd say – with a light moustache. He is swearing profanely as he unfolds a map and peers at it. Squinnying over his shoulder I see that it has various coordinates and names scribbled on it in capital-lettered blue biro: ANIMAL, ABODE, JUDY, BEER, PARIS, CITY.

'Twenty-five Judy,' Durado calls into the handset handed to him by his operator. 'Proximity to enemy three hundred yards. Twenty-five period one. D-three period two. Zone fire.' He blinks and shakes his head as if he's suddenly remembered something. He stands up and yells at his sergeant: 'Get some guys round the back by the bridge!'

The mortar shells are coming over with more frequency but landing short in the wet rice fields which robs them of their effectiveness, flinging up columns of muddy water, and spattering us with mud droplets.

I move away from the captain, heading further up the ditch, now filled with 'D' Company grunts answering fire with fire, blasting away with their CAR-15s at the invisible enemy in the treeline. Back by Captain Durado's position by the culvert the mortar fire appears to be more accurate. There are shouts of alarm as the blasts creep closer and erupt on the causeway. Stones and earth begin to fly around. A pebble pings off my helmet.

Then I hear our artillery going over, called in by Captain Durado from some distant firebase – a brake-screeching sound mingled with a vibrating swooshing in the air – and, in one giant rippling volley, the whole treeline across the fields is obliterated by the exploding shells. The mortaring stops abruptly. There's a few popping rounds from AK-47s then another salvo erupts. Smoke drifts away. There are no more trees. Silence. 'D' Company begins to whoop and shout; men stand up, light cigarettes, the mood one of sudden, relieved jocularity. Fuck, shit, hell, motherfucker, gooks, way to go, man.

The Country Fair operation at Pluto hasn't been quite the saunter in the park that was envisaged. I climb on to the banked causeway between the rice paddies and feel my legs trembling. My mouth is dry and I crave the syrupy sweet fruit cocktail that had been in my C-ration. The last accurate mortar rounds had caused casualties, it transpires. Three wounded in action and one killed in action. I walk over to join the group looking down on the dead man – the dead boy, I see – as we wait for the corpsmen to arrive. He has been blown out of his refuge in the ditch and his body lies awkwardly at the fringe of the paddy field. The blast has ripped his clothing and webbing from his body, leaving only his trousers and boots, and his skinny white torso is revealed. He has vivid ginger hair and this is what makes his body look so incongruous. A pale, freckled redhead lying by a paddy field in South East Asia, his back a small crater of mangled ribs, flesh and protruding organs. I think about taking a photograph but the idea revolts me. Somebody throws a poncho over him. I make a decision – no more combat missions. The men are right: I'm too old. One visit to Pluto is more than enough warfare for me.

I was sitting in the rooftop bar of the Caravelle Hotel with a dry martini, smoking a cigarette, looking through my contact sheets that I had produced in the small darkroom I had managed to create in a little-used lavatory on the top floor of the SPS building. Back to school – shades of Amberfield and Miss Milburn, the 'Child Killer'. We had been sending film off to labs in Hong Kong and Tokyo where they were developed, printed and transmitted by satellite to the New York office. But now we could print our own (black and white only) we could send them down the wire, with a short-wave drum printer, so we could be up there with AP and UPI in terms of speed. Even Renata Alabama was grateful. From my point of view it meant I could keep copies of photos I liked – I had my own record and my own little, growing archive. My book was taking shape.

I had a new plan, after my experience at Pluto's Country Fair. I was going to ignore the field – the combat zones and flashpoints, the search-and-destroy missions – and stick to the bases. My idea was to

South Vietnam, 1967. From Vietnam, Mon Amour.

take pictures of the soldiers, the grunts, off duty. When you saw them shed their carbines and flak jackets, their helmets and ammo packs, you suddenly realised how young these soldiers were – teenagers, college kids. They became youngsters again, not menacing, multi-weaponed warriors, anonymous in their bulky armour.

And I also started travelling out to the countryside with Truong, taking photographs of the people of this small beautiful country we were visiting as if I were a tourist and not part of the media sideshow of an enormous military machine. I was a war photographer but the book I had in mind would have no war in it.

I looked round at the screech of metal chairs being pushed back against terrazzo tiles and saw the large group of people who had been sitting behind me make their noisy, bibulous exit from the roof terrace. My eyes flicked over the messy detritus of their table – the bottles and the glasses, the ashtrays and the empty cigarette packs, abandoned newspapers – even a book.

I called out: 'Hey! You've forgotten—' but it was too late, they'd disappeared.

I wandered over to the table and picked up the book. It was French and I felt that shiver of ghostly shock run through me as I read the title and the author's name.

Absence de marquage by Jean-Baptiste Charbonneau.

Vietnam. The noise of frogs, deafening, in the back garden of the Green Tree coffee shop on Binh Phu Street. Truong introducing me to his family, bowing to me as if I were visiting royalty: Kim, his wife, his two tiny daughters, Hanh and Ngon. A thirty-foot high metal hill of malfunctioning useless air-conditioning machines in a field by Bien Hoa airforce base. The Saigon police in their crisp bleached uniforms – the 'white mice'. The press escort officer who looked like Montgomery Clift. Endless rain in August. The massive percussion of the B-52 strikes – felt ten miles away, a trembling, an uncontrollable flinching of the facial muscles. The tamarind trees in Tu Do Street. The rich Vietnamese kids in their tennis whites at the Cercle Sportif. Black-toothed women at the Central Market selling US Army gear. 'We Gotta Get Out of This Place', a song by the Animals. Motorbikes. Australian troops playing cricket. Beautiful villas on the coast at the foot of the Long Hai Hills – built by the French, decaying fast, empty. Women in conical hats sifting through the waste of US Army rubbish dumps. The smell of joss sticks, perfume and marijuana – Saigon.

I was walking past a bar in Tu Do Street, coming back from my tailor, when I saw a girl sitting outside a shack called the A-Go-Go Club. She was an ordinarily pretty bargirl, her hair teased and lacquered, but there was something about her pensive mood as she sat there dreaming of another life that made me stop and surreptitiously remove my camera. She was wearing white jeans and a white shirt – maybe ready to go on her shift. I snapped her – she never noticed.

'Shouldn't you ask permission, first?'

I turned round to see John Oberkamp standing there. He was in jeans and a tight, ultramarine, big-collared shirt.

'I suppose I should have,' I said. 'Do you know her?'

'She's my mama-san. Come and meet her.'

Her name was Quyen and she worked in this bar and also at Bien Hoa airbase as a cleaner. She seemed fond of Oberkamp; when she said 'John, he numba-one man,' she seemed to mean it. Oberkamp called her 'Queenie'. We strolled in and ordered a beer. It was mid-afternoon and the place was quiet, the bargirls sitting around in their tiny lurid miniskirts and bikini tops, chatting, smoking, reapplying their make up, waiting for the cocktail-hour rush. Oberkamp told me he finally had accreditation – he was now a recognised stringer for a Melbourne-based newspaper, the *Weekly News-Pictorial*, and was now spending much of his time with the 1st Australian Task Force at their base, Nui Dat, south-east of Saigon. He came up to the city as often as he could to be with Queenie. He kissed the top of her forehead – 'My little lady' – and she hugged herself to him. By coincidence

Two photos of Queenie. From Vietnam, Mon Amour.

I ran into her again two days later at Bien Hoa where she was polishing the boots of some Air Cavalry gunners. She looked different, hair wild, uncoiffed – a servant, not an object of male fantasy – humble and hard-working. 'You tell John I love him,' she said to me. '*Beaucoup, beaucoup* love.'

For some reason I can't bring myself to read Charbonneau's book. *Absence de marquage* has been sitting on my bedside table for two weeks, now. I know where this dread comes from: without thinking I read the blurb on the back – it was one of those large-format, pale cream, soft-covered French novels, just lettering on the front, no illustrations. *Absence de marquage* was the story of a young Free French diplomat – called Yves-Lucien Legrand – in New York during the Second World War, so the blurb informed me, and his doomed love affair with a beautiful English woman, a photographer, Mary Argyll.

I actually felt a squirm of nausea in my throat when I read this and dropped the book as if it were burning hot. Mary = Amory. Argyll = *argile*, the French for clay. A *roman à Clay*, then, I said to myself – not amused.

Of course it has to be read, and I have skimmed through it looking for those passages that concerned 'Mary Argyll', my alter ego, my doppelgänger . . . It's disturbing to read a fiction when you know all the fact behind it. I've been consuming it in small sips, as it were, reading a paragraph here, half a page there, only to realise that Charbonneau was recounting episodes of our time together wholly unaltered in any degree, apart from the names of Yves-Lucien and Mary. Here is Charbonneau describing Mary Argyll after their first night together:

Mary Argyll was one of those almost-beautiful women, a not-quite-beautiful woman. But, for Yves-Lucien, that was precisely what made her, paradoxically, more beautiful than anyone he had ever encountered. Beautiful women were boring, he thought; he needed something other than mere perfection to interest him. Her nose was a little too prominent and she should have paid more attention to her hair, which was dark brown and straight, and as a result of this negligence could often look lank and ungroomed.

He loved her body, naked, however. She was so slim that her ribs showed but her breasts were full and generous with small perfectly round nipples. Her feet were a little too large, another imperfection he cherished as it made her seem sometimes graceless and awkward, particularly when she wore her highest heels. Yves-Lucien found this ungainliness *un peu loufouque* and extremely exciting, sexually.[1]

---

[1] My translation. *Un peu loufouque* is hard to render exactly in English as it has many nuances: burlesque, extravagant, bizarre and droll, amongst others. It's very disconcerting to read such a portrait, with no disguise, in a published book. It's like overhearing other people discussing you, unaware of your presence. You are confronted with your *effect* – the last thing anyone knows about themselves.

My breakthrough as a photographer in Vietnam has occurred with the publication of this photograph of a Huey pilot waiting for his mission briefing. It made the front cover of three magazines and was syndicated to over forty other magazines and newspapers, worldwide. I have to admit I saw its potential as the image was printed. The suspended man, the shades, the 'danger' arrow, the can of beer – all perfect juxtaposition. Once again the photograph stops time (in monochrome); the historical moment, with whatever freight it carries, ideally frozen.

I garnered fees of over $3,000 at the end of the day but, more importantly, it saw my name being bandied about – requests came in for more, similar images – and I have suddenly become aware of the commercial dividend of working in a war zone with the eyes of the world upon you. Your accreditation was extra-valuable, not just because it gave you access, took you places other photographers couldn't go and made you sometimes a unique witness, but also because all that could be turned into cash. This was (I was learning fast) another edge to the stringers' hunger for action – there was money to be made for putting yourself in harm's way.

To my surprise, Lockwood was very excited by the response to my 'Pilot in his Hammock' photo. I received a rare Telex from him: more of the same, please, now, now, now. People were growing tired of towering GIs and cowering peasants; Zippo lighters firing thatch; muddied wounded being medevac'd – show us the hidden human face of Vietnam, Lockwood urged. I was way ahead of him.

But encouraged, and finding doors were opening as a result of my new reputation, I resumed my tour of the bases – Long Binh, Bien Hoa, Da Nang – and their backstreets and byways. I even went to visit Oberkamp at Nui Dat and saw the little sandbagged, cinder-block hooch that he called home, now, out on the airport perimeter – but he wouldn't let me take any photographs of the Australians. 'The Aussies are mine,' he said, and he wasn't joking.

I was in Hong Kong when the Tet Offensive broke out in January 1968. I watched the simultaneous mass assault on some thirty South Vietnam towns and cities as I sat in my room in a hotel – the Royal Neptune – that looked out over Kowloon Bay, seeing the faces of the TV reporters I knew, ducking and wincing, under the roar of incoming fire in Hué, in Khe Sanh, in Saigon itself. They were that close.

I had needed a holiday, a break of some sort, as I'd now been in Vietnam for nearly a year. In the GPW bureau in Hong Kong I could call my family and have a proper conversation – Annie was thinking of doing postgraduate work; Blythe was playing in London pubs in a folk group called Platinum Scrap.

I had a long conversation with Blythe and there was something about the flat tone of her voice that worried me.

'Is everything all right, darling?' I said. 'Boyfriend trouble?'

'How do you know I've got a boyfriend? Did Annie tell you?'

'Educated guess. Is he nice?'

'Tall, blond, talented, wicked.'

'Sounds good to me. Is he nice as well?'

'Only four adjectives, Ma. You know the rules.'

But she seemed to have brightened up, now she'd told me and we chatted on about her band and the awful pubs they played in.

While I was in Hong Kong I was also able to sort out the financial mechanics of the new success I was enjoying as a result of the prominence of my photographs of young soldiers. I was in almost daily telephonic correspondence with a counter-cultural Californian entrepreneur who wanted to license one of my photos to put on a T-shirt. His name was Moss Fallmaster.

'I'm thirty, tall, skinny, I have a beard. I'm pretty sure I'm gay.'

'I don't quite understand.'

'Of a homosexual persuasion.'

'Oh. Good for you. So's my uncle.'

'Well, isn't that wonderful! So, I'm on your side, Amory, I won't rip you off. If I win, you win. We'll make a fortune.' (I never made the fortune that Moss Fallmaster promised me. However, the deal still provides me with a diminishing but still welcome dividend.)

He bought the rights to the photo he was after for $1,000 with a ten per cent royalty for me on every $2 T-shirt he sold. He printed them up with an ambiguous caption that caught the mood of the time: 'Never Too Young To . . .'

The 'Never Too Young To . . .' photo.

I had vowed never to go back into combat again but, to our general consternation, after the cataclysm of the Tet Offensive seemed to have died down, so the Mini-Tet arrived in May '68 – and right on our doorstep. You could stand on the roof terrace of the Caravelle in downtown Saigon watching the gunships strafing the streets of Cholon a mile away.

Mary Poundstone, back in Vietnam, fully accredited to the *Observer*, said it reminded her of Madrid in 1936 when the Falangist forces were dug in right in the heart of the University district. You left your hotel – the Ritz, by preference – and caught a bus to the front line. Meanwhile, here on the roof of the Caravelle in 1968, we sipped our martinis, smoked our cigarettes, and watched the lambent roseate jewels of tracer arc into the evening sky.

I had Truong drive us into Cholon – Mary came with me, it was her insistence – as close as we dared. Truong would take us down narrow side streets, drop us off and we would creep forward to join whatever unit we could find, US or ARVN. I was very nervous but I could see all Mary's old war fever return, her passion fired again. Tracer, machine guns, mortars, RPGs – she loved it, perversely; her dander was up.

At one stage, a few days ago, we took shelter in a ruined house during an airstrike. The fetid air in the room seemed to physically shudder from the percussive force of the bombs. We huddled in a corner, backs to a wall.

'Mary,' I said, 'what are we doing here? Are we insane? We're two old ladies.'

'We're not old – we're wise. We've lived, we're experienced, that's why we should be here. Not like these potheads running around trying to get their million-dollar wounds. That's not for us. We see things clearly.'

After that I've only been up once again. I'm beginning to feel my luck is running out.

I was in a newish bar in Tu Do Street called Marlon 'n' Mick's – perhaps to lure in both rock fans and film buffs. It was always dark and only played American soul music, which was why I patronised it. I was becoming an uncritical admirer of Aretha Franklin.

Then John Oberkamp came in with a friend, a lanky Englishman, who was introduced as another photographer called Guy Wells-Healy. They were both stoned, but functioning, looking for 'poontang'. Wells-Healy found his tart but John Oberkamp was plainly more interested in talking to me, waving away the circling bargirls impatiently. I made him drink a quart of Coca-Cola and we went and found a booth where we, with an undergraduate earnestness, discussed the art form we both practised. I started with my usual broadside – that there were only thirteen types of photograph – but I could see he wasn't willing to engage.

He took out a pack of Peter Stuyvesant cigarettes – twenty immaculate ready-rolled marijuana joints that retailed for $3.50 on the streets of Saigon – and suggested I try one. I held up my Scotch and water and told him that this was my chosen means of intoxication. But he wheedled away at me so eventually I agreed to join him in his joint.

I did it, not because I wanted to smoke marijuana but, for the first time since Sholto's death, I was aware of being attracted to a man. How does this happen? I wasn't looking for it – but it creeps up on you and, if you're honest with yourself, you can't ignore it. From the first second of meeting Oberkamp in his Non-Com Hotel I had felt that little frisson of interest in him. There was something lithe and unpredictable about John Oberkamp that I responded to. It might have been his smile, or the way he'd touched my breasts that night (so I knew he was attracted to me). I wanted to get high because I fully intended that to be the excuse I would offer for making love with him, shedding all responsibility. Not my fault, Your Honour, he drugged me. I desired John Oberkamp that night and I didn't want to pretend that wasn't the case, didn't want to do the sensible thing and back off.

So I smoked his cigarette and felt good – but I had been feeling good with the whisky, anyway – maybe I felt better. Who knows? My theory about intoxication is that it all depends on mood and inclination. If you are thus inclined, a sip of Madeira will do the job for you. If you're not, a bottle of 70-proof bootleg gin won't work. And of course we had the added ingredient of the old war-zone aphrodisiac. If you stepped outside Marlon 'n' Mick's and listened hard you could hear the muffled thump of explosions as the Mini-Tet offensive played itself out in Saigon's distant suburbs. We were safe in our Tu Do bar but not far away ordnance was being delivered and people were dying. It concentrated the mind on the here and now.

We sat close together in our booth listening to Dionne Warwick walking on by and, in the way that two human beings who are sexually interested in each other – and in very close proximity – understand exactly what is going on, neither of us needed to say anything. Messages had been sent and received.

'I don't have anywhere to stay tonight,' John said, taking my hand.

John Oberkamp. Saigon, Vietnam, 1968.

'I have an uncomfortable daybed in my horrible flat, if you're interested.'

'I might well be. Can we check it out?'

And so we left, after a final drink, and wandered back to my place and one thing led to another, as we both intended it should, and John Oberkamp and I made love several times over the next twelve hours.

In the afternoon – we rose late – I had Truong drive me to MACV for the 'five o'clock follies' press briefing. John wandered off to pick up a plane heading for Nui Dat.

We kissed goodbye, chastely, and John said he'd be back in a week. I said fine – you know where to find me – and off he went, glancing over his shoulder, giving me a wave. I felt a warmth that I hadn't experienced in a long time. I had no illusions – it was the classic Saigon encounter – but I had needed it. John Oberkamp was the first man I'd slept with since Sholto. Some personal sexual Rubicon had been crossed, as far as I was concerned, and I felt pleased and strangely fulfilled. Sholto's ghost laid to rest.

As it turned out I was sorry that he'd gone back to Nui Dat because that evening I had a Telex from the New York office informing me that one of my photographs – that I'd called 'The Confrontation' – had won the Matthew B. Brady Award for war photography. It was an honour that brought with it a cheque for $5,000.

I went out on the town with Mary Poundstone and a couple of other photographer acquaintances – we went up one side of Tu Do Street and then back down the other, and wound up with a bunch of AP staffers in the bar of the Majestic – and in the course of the evening we duly drank ourselves into an agreeable state of quasi-insensibility. But all the time I was thinking: I wish John Oberkamp were here. It would have been altogether better with John.

Mini-Tet was more or less over by the end of May. As the fighting in the suburbs fizzled out I came to realise that what had disturbed me as much as the nightly show of flares, artillery and the throbbing pulse of helicopters passing over, had been the sense that the city had been surrounded by the Viet Cong and the NVA. There had been fighting in the north and in the south; in the south-east of the city and the north-west and so on round the compass. It seemed unreal – this is the capital, what's going on?

'The Confrontation', winner of the Matthew B. Brady Award, 1968.

– but a little further thought was destabilising. If they're everywhere, if they're this close, how long can we realistically hold out? What happens the next time . . . ?

I visited areas of Cholon where the street battles had been fiercest and took photographs – none of which were ever used. Restaurants were open; the streets were a honking gridlock of traffic and shoppers, and then you'd come across a shattered building, pitted, scorched and blasted apart; a gaping shell crater steadily filling with rubbish or the carbonised remains of an Armoured Personnel Carrier. And there was a strange reek in those streets that seemed to cling to your clothes and hair when you went home at night – like a sweet brackish perfume of smoke, cordite, charred wood, decomposing bodies, gasoline – that you could still smell when you woke in the morning.

Even in early June at night from the roof bar of the Caravelle you could see the flares going up and the nervy chatter of a machine gun sending its looping beads of tracer up into the black sky. First-time visiting journalists were very impressed as they sipped their drinks. I heard one Englishman say that he felt like Lord Raglan on the heights of Balaclava.

I was in my makeshift darkroom in the bureau checking my supplies of developer, stopper and fixer when Renata Alabama peered in the door and said, 'There's some crazy Australian out here insisting on talking to you.'

I hadn't seen John since our night together – a week ago – and I felt that breathless rush of anticipation as I went downstairs and along the corridor to reception, running my hands through my hair and wishing I'd put on some lipstick that morning. Fool, I said to myself – you're not sixteen years old.

But I could see at once he was in a state, ill at ease. We shook hands – Renata was hovering, curious – and he asked if we could go somewhere quiet where we could talk properly. I picked up my bag and we left, heading down the street to Bonnard's, a French-style café where they played American Forces Radio at low volume – you could talk without raising your voice.

We took our seats, ordered coffee, I lit a cigarette.

'I've missed you,' I said. 'Silly me.'

'Queenie's run away. Run away home.'

'Well, you know what these—'

'She's pregnant.'

'Bargirls get pregnant, John. Occupational hazard.'

'She says it's mine.'

'Come on—'

'It can only be mine, she says.'

I felt a weariness of spirit descend on me. Fool, I rebuked myself for the second time in ten minutes. You were a one-night stand, old lady. I tried to reason with him but he didn't want reason.

'You can't be sure it's yours.'

'Yes I can. She wouldn't lie to me.'

'What's it got to do with me?' I asked, letting some cynical steel into my voice. I was, I had to admit, a little hurt.

John explained. He knew where Queenie's parents lived, in a village called Vinh Hoa on Highway 22 north out of Saigon, on the road to Tay Ninh. He needed someone who spoke French to be able to explain the situation to them – Queenie's parents spoke French, she was proud of that, which was how he knew. I could see the panic rising in him so I said: whatever I can do to help, just tell me. He wanted to go directly to Vinh Hoa – he was sure Queenie would be with her parents – also he wanted me to bring my photos of her as a means of identifying where the family lived.

'Hang on,' I said, remembering. 'There's still fighting on Highway 22.'

'Very sporadic. They're mopping up. It's only thirty clicks up the road, anyway – an hour, max.' He wouldn't stand for any caution. 'Traffic is flowing. I checked.'

'I'll try and get hold of Truong.'

'We can't wait. I've got my bike with me. Come on, Amory – it's very important. You owe it to me.'

I bridled at this: I owed him for a fuck?

Then he leant forward and kissed me and I forgave him.

'She's carrying my child. I can't just let her vanish. I'll never find her if I don't go immediately. It's now or never.'

He was right, I supposed, or so I thought as we walked back to the bureau. I wanted to take one precaution – I insisted – we had to tape *BAO CHI*[1] in large letters to his bike.

'Of course, anything,' John said. 'We can tape it to the leg shields.' He pointed at a dirty old red and white motorbike, paint smirched and flaking.

'What kind of bike is this?' I asked.

---

[1] *Bao chi* is Vietnamese for 'journalist' or 'press'.

'Why do you want to know?'

'I just like to know these things.'

'It's a Honda Super Cub.'

'You meet the nicest people on a Honda.'

'Ha-ha.'

I went into the office and found what I needed – I also put my camera in my bag (a Paxette, a 35 mm miniature, a solid little thing) – and taped a piece of card with *BAO* written on it in black marker on one leg shield and *CHI* on the other. John kick-started the motor and I climbed on the small pillion behind him. There was an aluminium handhold between the seats but I felt safer with my arms around him.

'You don't mind if I do this?' I asked.

'I don't mind.'

We set off and I hugged myself against his damp sweaty shirt. It was cheap cotton and had a pattern of red clipper ships in full sail on it. I closed my eyes for a moment, feeling like a teenager again. It was proving to be the strangest day, with my emotions veering around from soft and silly to cynical and uncaring; and my sense of adult responsibility seemingly switched off – what was I doing on this bike with Oberkamp heading off to Highway 22? It was as if I was in some hallucinatory state.

John seemed to know where we were going. He had a street map folded up in a pocket that he consulted from time to time, pulling into the side of the road for a few seconds to get his bearings. We took back roads to avoid the traffic jams at Tan Son Nhut airport and finally pulled on to Highway 22 about four or five kilometres north of the city limits. I was very pleased to see it was busy – military and civilian vehicles going in both directions. 'Highway' was something of a misnomer, though: a two-lane strip of potholed tarmac with wide dusty verges heading through a scrubby landscape and the occasional grove of coconut palms. It was a hot and hazy day – I wished I'd brought a hat.

But half an hour up the road we were the only vehicle moving. I tapped John on the back and he pulled in.

'What's happening?' he asked

I pointed to my right where, about two miles away, a converted Dakota known as a 'Spooky' was flying in a tight pylon turn. Then there came a noise like a chainsaw as its Gatling gun opened up from its position in the gaping side door.

'There's a problem,' I said. 'Where's all the traffic? What's the Spooky shooting at?'

'They're just mopping up. I checked with CIB,[1] I told you. We're heading west. All the trouble's in the north.'

Then, as if to back up his reassurances two cars sped down the road towards us.

'See? We're only fifteen minutes away, I reckon.'

'OK, let's go.'

After about another mile the vegetation became sparser and over to the left I saw a flat expanse of semi-dried-out lake come into view, that had drained away or been half-evaporated by the heat. Parked on the near shore were three US Army personnel carriers, their crew sitting in the shade cast by their high sides. I was pleased to see them, made John stop and took a few photographs and gave them a wave as we puttered off. One of the soldiers jumped to his feet and shouted something at us, making crossing motions with his hands, but he was quickly lost to sight as we turned a corner. I tapped John on the back and he brought the Super Cub to a halt, once again.

'Those GIs,' I said. 'They were telling us not to go on.'

'We're almost fucking there!' he protested, pointing.

Up ahead, I could see a wooden shack by the roadside, roofed with palm leaves and with some rickety market stalls set out in front of it on the verge, ready to trade with passing vehicles — except there was no produce laid out.

---

[1] Central Information Bureau.

I slipped off the bike and stepped into the middle of the road, looking up and down the shimmering tarmac. All traffic had disappeared and we were quite alone on Highway 22 again. Far in the distance the Spooky was banking into its pylon turn, looking for targets. I shaded my eyes, feeling the sweat trickle down my spine, listening.

'Come on, Amory!' John shouted and just at that moment I saw something move in the roadside shack.

The first shots hit the tarmac about ten feet in front of me. I felt the sting of bitumen chips hit my forearms and as I turned and ran heard the flat firecracker noise of several AK-47s open up and sensed the burn and tug of something hitting my right calf muscle. We ran into the undergrowth and crouched down. The Super Cub lay incongruously on its side. A bullet pinged off its front fork and tall puffs of dust erupted around it.

I looked down at my right leg. My chinos had a tear at the calf and blood was spreading. I rolled the trouser up and saw a neat three-inch furrow torn along the surface of the muscle. I felt no pain.

John pulled off his shirt and ripped off a sleeve – with remarkable ease – and bound it round the wound, knotting it tightly. The gunmen in the shack were now spraying the undergrowth, randomly searching for us. We were safe for the moment if we kept our heads down. Then I heard the roar of engines from the APCs from the lake, heading up the road towards us at full speed. The firing stopped and I raised my head to see three people run from the roadside shack and pelt into the scrub, just before the palm-frond roof was shredded into a thousand swirling pieces as the .50 calibre machine gun on the lead APC hosed the building. Some internal structure must have shattered because the whole shack half-collapsed with a creak and what sounded like a sigh and a thick cloud of dust rolled across the road. We stepped out of the undergrowth, hands up, just in case, as the lead APC lurched to a halt and its commander, sitting in the turret with the machine gun, began to swear at us colourfully.

I had my little war wound – that was now beginning to throb. And, now we were safe, John pulled on his one-sleeved shirt, righted the Super Cub and declared his intent to drive on to Vinh Hoa.

'Are you completely insane?' I yelled at him.

APCs by the parched lake. Highway 22, Saigon, 1968.

He hugged me, kissed me quickly on the lips to halt my protestations and said, 'I'll be back tonight. I'll come to your place. I'll bring Queenie.'

'No, John, don't go,' I said, angrily and grabbed his arm. But I released it when I saw the look in his eye. Mad, unreachable.

'I don't advise it, sir,' the lieutenant commanding the APC squadron said, dryly.

'I'm a journalist,' John said. 'I'll be safe. Don't worry.'

'Oh yeah. One of those fuckin' crazy journalists. You'll be fine, man. Go for it.'

His men laughed.

John climbed on to his bike, started it, smiled, gave me a thumbs-up and motored off down the road, flinging out a final wave as he dwindled away into the wobbling heat haze.

I waited in for him that night, but he never came. The next day he was posted as missing in action – villagers in Vinh Hoa said he'd been taken prisoner by a cadre of retreating Viet Cong, no doubt the ones who'd fired at us from the roadside shack. I wasn't too worried: journalists were quite frequently captured but usually well treated and released after a few days, the reasoning being that they would speak favourably about their captors – good propaganda.

A week went by, and there was no sign of John Oberkamp and his Honda Super Cub.

Two weeks later I had a letter from his mother, Mrs Grace Oberkamp, from Sydney. John had written to her about her forthcoming grandchild and had given her my address, for some reason. It seemed to me a strange precaution, as if he had a prescient worry about what might happen to him. I was suffering from retrospective worry, also, recalling that moment alone on Highway 22 just before the shooting started. If those VC had been better shots I would have been cut down there and then, I was now realising. Annie and Blythe orphaned. I felt sick – genuinely shaken up – but these thoughts and images haunted me in the days after John disappeared. I could close my eyes and see myself fall, feel the bullets hit.

Mrs Oberkamp said that in his letter John had been concerned about his possessions and that if anything happened to him she was to contact me. Would I be so good as to gather up his bits and pieces and post them on to her? She would be eternally grateful and would reimburse me for all expenses incurred.

And just at that moment the first copy of my book arrived. *Vietnam, Mon Amour* (Frankel & Silverman, 1968). I knew the title wasn't original but it served my non-combat photos admirably. Moreover, its appearance caused something of a stir in the press corps. A good number of the photographers working in Vietnam had books planned, I knew – we often discussed them – but I was one of the first to be published, beaten only by Jerry Strickland of UPI and Yolande Joubert of *Paris Match*. Even Renata Alabama looked at me with new respectful eyes, asking if I could put a word in for her with Frankel & Silverman. I should have savoured the acclaim – and the overt envy – but I was suddenly aware that whatever 'amour' there had been between me and Vietnam was swiftly diminishing.

I kept thinking – and, what was worse, dreaming – about that moment when I'd stood alone in the middle of Highway 22, south of Vinh Hoa, in the eerie stillness, apart from the distant drone of the Spooky gunship doing its pylon turn. It stayed in my head like a film loop, a scene from an unfinished movie. I had my three-inch bullet graze, nicely scabbed, now, and I had my shiny new book with its glossy photos. I was aware of my good luck, the good fortune, that had led me to this position. But I knew I wanted to go home – to Scotland, to Barrandale.

However, there was a last task to be done, a final deliverance of duty to John Oberkamp. I managed to hitch a ride on a Royal Australian Air Force Hercules that was making the short hop from Saigon to Nui Dat where I showed Mrs Oberkamp's letter to the base's senior PEO.

'Oh, yeah, Oberkamp,' he said. 'Any news?'

There was no news, I said.

He drove me out to John's sandbagged hooch near the perimeter by the main runway and showed me in. He said he'd be back in thirty minutes to pick me up. Inside there was a metal bed with a Dunlopillo mattress, some half-drunk bottles of rum and bourbon, about a thousand cigarettes, an electric fan and a gunny sack filled with dirty clothes. Under the bed was a cardboard box that contained a dozen paperbacks, two cameras and John's trademark bush hat with its cryptic slogan – 'BORN TO BE BORN' – painted on the front in coral-pink nail varnish. Pinned to the wall above the bed, I was pleased to see, was one of my 'Never Too Young To . . .' T-shirts. That was it – he travelled light, did John; this was small cargo for a man who'd been in Vietnam since 1965. I dumped the dirty clothes on the bed and filled the gunny sack with the books and cameras and anything else personal that I could find (two Zippo lighters, an ashtray from the Hilton Hotel in Tokyo, a few rolls of undeveloped film). I kept the bush hat for myself and pulled it on my head, tucking my hair in under it.

I decided not to wait for the PEO and so set off, strolling back towards the control tower and the administrative buildings, John's gunny bag over my shoulder. It was mid-afternoon and the sun was burning through the milky sky, a blurry, brassy disk. I smelt rain coming.

I heard the chugging clatter of helicopter engines and paused to see a couple of RAAF Hueys coming in low over the perimeter fence to dust down next to a waiting ambulance with medics standing ready by a gurney with a drip rigged, waiting for some casualties. I wandered over.

The Hueys landed, the rotors stopped and the men inside began wearily to disembark. The medics ran forward and carried two body bags into the ambulance before returning with the gurney for another soldier, seemingly unconscious, both legs bandaged from ankle to thigh. A jeep pulled up by the ambulance and a senior officer stepped out. He talked to the medics as they carefully loaded their grim freight of suffering humanity on board the ambulance. I saw him touch the shoulder of the wounded man.

I was close to the disembarked soldiers now – some standing, some sitting on the ground, all of them smoking – and I recognised that air of filthy, blank exhaustion about them that comes upon soldiers after hours of combat, of being under fire. I'd seen it before – most notably at Wesel in 1945 – and once seen, never forgotten. Their clothes were damp and dirt-ingrained, the green cotton drill dark and blackened from the grime and sweat. They carried an assortment of weapons – FN rifles, M16s – I even saw one man with an AK-47 – enough to tell me that these men were not regular Australian Army; this must be the Australian SAS – the SAS Regiment, as it was known. John had told me that units were based here at Nui Dat from time to time. I edged closer – mechanics were checking the Hueys, and a petrol tender had rolled up so there was a fair bit of distracting activity going on – and I could see a couple of two-ton trucks heading out to pick the unit up.

I wondered if I could sneak a photo, then I thought, no, better to ask. I went towards one man, an officer, but stopped as soon as I heard the voices around me as they spoke to each other. These men weren't Australian – they were British. I heard cockney accents, Lowland Scots; one man was a Geordie. I crouched down and pretended to fiddle with my knapsack straps. Yet they were all wearing SASR unit patches, yellow and beige, and a couple of them even sported the regiment's caramel berets. As the men turned and made ready to climb into the approaching lorries I could see the shoulder flashes saying 'Australia'. These manifestly non-Australians were clearly making every attempt to be Australians.

The senior officer who'd been in the jeep, who was wearing neatly pressed olive-green fatigues, approached and the men climbed to their feet and straightened up in a notional stand-to-attention as he had a few words with them. I backed off, carefully. What was going on here? The two-ton trucks stopped, the men were dismissed and they hauled themselves on board. As the senior officer headed back to his jeep he passed close to me.

'Hello, Frank,' I said. 'Small world.'

Frank Dunn froze, then turned. I could practically hear his astonished brain working. He managed a thin smile.

'Amory,' he said. 'Bloody hell.'

He came over to me and kissed me on the cheek, to his credit.

'May I ask what you're doing here?' he said, stepping back and looking me up and down. 'Love the headgear.' I now rather wished I wasn't wearing John's bush hat.

I explained. 'Picking up a colleague's stuff.' I held up the gunny bag. 'He's MIA.' I paused. 'More to the point: when did you join the Australian Army?'

'I've left the army,' he said, bluntly. 'I've retired.'

I looked at him – he had no badges of rank, no identifying name above his breast pocket; he was dressed as a soldier, but that was all. Yet those men had stood to attention as he came up to them.

'Some retirement,' I said. 'Why are all those British soldiers pretending to be Australians?'

'They're on secondment to the Australian Army – as observers.'

'Come on, Frank. I've been out here for well over a year. I was married to a soldier. I'm not a fool – they're straight out of combat.'

Frank Dunn linked arms with me and walked me towards his jeep.

'I'm only going to say this once, Amory. Let me be clear. You came to Nui Dat, you picked up your friend's bits and pieces, and then you went back to Saigon. You didn't see them. You didn't see me. You certainly didn't talk to me. Understood?'

'Understood.'

'I'll drop you off at the CIB.'

'Thanks.'

Even though we made our fond farewells – Frank asking for news of the girls, how I was coping out here, kissing me goodbye – I knew I had made a mistake. I should have kept my mouth shut.

I was upstairs at my desk in the SPS bureau trying to draft a resignation letter to Lane Burrell. Seeing John's paltry collection of possessions had depressed me – a whole young existence subsumed by some dirty laundry, damp-swollen paperbacks and a couple of cameras. It had been no life for John and it was no life for me – and it was time I brought it to a dignified end.

Renata rapped on the door frame. She looked a little alarmed.

'You'd better come down, Amory.'

I followed her to the reception area to find a US master sergeant with an MP brassard on his arm and two smart ARVN military police acting as escort.

'Amory Clay?'

'Yes. What's this all about?'

He glanced at the sheet of paper in his hand.

'Your visa has been rescinded. You are illegally in this country. You are under arrest.'

I am writing this down, sitting on my suitcase, somewhere in Tan Son Nhut airport. This hut has a mud floor and no furniture. The door is locked and an ARVN MP is standing outside it. I'm being deported and I know exactly why – because of what I saw the day before yesterday at Nui Dat. Unwittingly, I now share a secret – but a secret no one wants me to share, hence this unseemly rush to have me out of the country.

The master sergeant who took me into custody told me the bare minimum as he allowed me to return to my apartment and pack up my belongings – following orders, highest authority. I sit here feeling frightened and glad. Glad to be leaving – that was planned – but frightened by this exhibition of absolute power. My visa had six more months to run – I had renewed it on my return from Hong Kong. My accreditation was solid. I was being rushed out of this country as if I had the plague. On whose orders? Frank's? I doubted it. No, Frank would have told someone important about our meeting at Nui Dat; then that information would have gone up the chain of command until a decision was made. Get her out. I'm waiting for a Pan Am charter to Hong Kong where I'm to stay in transit until I'm put on a BOAC flight to London. I am not being charged for any airfares.

FINAL THOUGHTS ON LEAVING VIETNAM

John Oberkamp had more scars on his body than Sholto. Maybe that was what attracted me to him – he reminded me of Sholto in some way. Not physically, but some quality of alertness, of curiosity.

Just the loose-limbed, supple way he carried himself. There is still no news. No reports of his capture.[1]

Truong returned just as I was leaving the apartment with my MP escort. He foolishly tried to grab hold of me and bundle me into his Renault. 'No, Truong, no!' I shouted. 'I'm all right. Don't worry. I'm going home.' He began to sob, his hands over his face.

The name of the master sergeant who escorted me out of the country was Sam M. Goodforth. He was burly, unsmiling, florid – as if he'd just stepped from a hot bath – with a close crew cut. I remember his name because it was printed on a plastic rectangle over his left breast pocket. Goodforth – go forth.

After John Oberkamp had motored off up the road to Vinh Hoa, one of the APC crew replaced John's makeshift bandage with a proper field dressing. 'You ought to get that properly cleaned up,' he said. 'I heard Charlie puts shit on their bullets.' The lieutenant called in a medevac helicopter for me – as a favour – and it was to be my last trip in a Huey helicopter in Vietnam. I was designated as a 'lightly wounded casualty (civilian)'. I was choppered back to base hospital in Saigon. That's how I feel now, on leaving – a lightly wounded casualty (civilian).

And as I sit here, worried, uncomfortable, a bit miserable, a bit angry at this summary, enforced departure, I ask myself if I'd done the right thing in embarking on this Vietnam adventure, leaving my home and my family behind to go on some half-thought-out mission to prove something to myself, to discover something of myself. What did I learn that I didn't already know? Quite a lot, actually. And I took some good photographs and made a book

---

[1] John Oberkamp was never spotted again after his capture by the Viet Cong in Vinh Hoa. No trace of his body has ever been discovered. His fate remains one of the many mysteries of the Vietnam War.

of them. And made some money. And I met and loved another man ... I don't think I can blame myself for wanting to do what I did – and I don't think Annie and Blythe blame me, either. It is my life, after all, and I have every right to live it to the full. Oh yes, you keep saying that to yourself, don't you?

I can hear voices outside the door – American voices. Is it time to leave? Am I finally going home?

★

And that was the end of my Vietnam Scrapbook, but not entirely the end of my Vietnam experience – it travelled with me a few thousand miles. I arrived at Heathrow on the Hong Kong flight early in the morning. As I crossed the tarmac apron towards the airport building two police officers intercepted me and led me to an unmarked car parked nearby. I reminded them that I had a suitcase on board; I was told it would be brought to me.

I was driven through early-morning London, the streets still pretty much empty, to St John's Wood, north of Regent's Park, to a block of mansion flats with its own underground car park. I was taken to a service apartment on the fourth floor where I was greeted by a sour-faced, heavily built young woman in a puce suit and sensible shoes. She showed me into a sitting room with brown upholstered furniture and a gas fire and offered me a cup of tea and biscuits. If I wanted to use the toilet, she said, I should ring this bell, pointing at a bell-push by the door. And then she locked me in.

I drank my tea and ate my digestive biscuits and an hour after I had arrived my suitcase was delivered. I waited. At lunchtime I was provided with a round of ham sandwiches and a glass of orange juice. I dozed on the sofa for most of the afternoon. I deliberately didn't ask my guardian what was going on. Supper was a round of cheese and tomato sandwiches and a glass of orange juice. I stretched out on the sofa again and slept for a troubled few hours.

Very late in the night I was woken by puce-suit and led down a corridor to another room with a dining table and six chairs. Another cup of tea was served. After ten minutes or so I heard voices at the flat's front door and moments later two young, suited men came in and introduced themselves as they took their seats opposite me: Mr Brown and Mr Green. They were in their thirties; one was dark and solid (Mr Green), the other languid and corpulent with fair, thinning hair (Mr Brown). Both of them were, no doubt, educated at expensive private schools and were graduates of excellent universities. They had polite middle-class accents. They could have happily read the news on the BBC.

MR BROWN: *Lady Farr. Your professional name is Amory Clay.*
ME: *That's correct.*
MR GREEN: *We won't detain you much longer. Our apologies for your wait.*
ME: *I'm keen to return home. May I ask why I was detained in the first place? I'm not aware of having done anything wrong.*
MR BROWN: *We had to detain you because of what you thought you saw at [consults notebook] Nui Dat airbase, Vietnam.*
ME: *I really can hardly remember anything at all.*
MR GREEN: *We will assume, for your own sake, that you will remember nothing at all.*
ME: *Of course. I promise.*
MR GREEN: *Nothing. Ever. For your own sake.*
ME: *I repeat – I promise.*
MR BROWN: *Because if you so much as breathe a word . . .*
ME: *I promise. Nothing.*
MR BROWN: *Excellent.*

And then they both gave tight little smiles and we stood up. Brown asked if I had any money and I said only American dollars. He gave me a £10 note that I had to sign a chit for and I was then shown back to the front door by puce-suit where my suitcase was waiting for me.

I travelled down in the lift alone and stepped out into the first glimmerings of dawn in St John's Wood. I hailed a passing taxi and asked to be taken to an all-night café. This proved to be in Victoria bus station where – beneath blazing fluorescent light — I ate, and hugely relished, a greasy breakfast and drank many cups of strong tea.

But I was feeling increasingly strange as I sat there in the refulgent cafeteria considering what had just happened to me in the last forty-eight hours or so and I realised I had experienced this sensation before but I couldn't remember when. That sense of fearful powerlessness; of other forces suddenly taking over the direction of your life that you had chosen; of being completely out of your depth in what you thought was familiar society. And then I remembered. My 'obscenity' trial over my Berlin photographs, all those decades ago — sitting in the Bow Street Magistrates' Court pleading guilty when I knew I was innocent; learning that my photographs were to be destroyed; being admonished and humiliated by the judge.

When you encounter the implacable power of the state it's a deeply destabilising moment. In an ordinary life it happens very rarely — maybe never, maybe once or twice. But your individual being, your individual nature, seems suddenly worth nothing — you feel expendable — and that's what frightens you, fundamentally, that's what makes your bowels loosen.

When the world was stirring I telephoned Blythe at her flat in Notting Hill but there was no reply. So I tried Annie at her student hall of residence at Sussex University.

'Ma! I don't believe it! You're back! How wonderful, why didn't you tell us?'

'Yes, it is wonderful and all very sudden, but I'm here to stay, my darling. No more travelling.'

We spoke some more and I told her I'd tried Blythe with no success. Annie said to keep trying — she hadn't moved. I had a powerful need to be hugged, close and hard, by someone I loved. I telephoned again, but there was still no reply so I hailed another taxi and was taken to Ladbroke Grove, to a peeling stucco four-storey house with twelve brimming dustbins outside it. I rang the bell for Blythe's flat and eventually a bleary, long-haired American came to the door. Was Blythe in? I'm her mother. Sorry. Blythe's been away for weeks. Gone on a long holiday. I couldn't take any more and began to cry.

BOOK EIGHT: 1968–1977

1. Room 42, San Carlos Motel

I checked in at reception to a bored gum-chewing young man with a middle parting and an acne problem and was assigned a cabin, room 42, out on the parking lot at the rear of the motel complex. I didn't care. The Californian desert sun was hammering down as I parked my teal-blue 1965 Dodge Coronet as close to my door as I could. I lugged my suitcase in, switched on the air conditioning and unpacked. I had a huge bed, an ice-making machine, and a clean white-tiled bathroom with a prophylactic polythene shield on the lavatory. I hoped I didn't have to stay here long.

★

THE BARRANDALE JOURNAL 1977

One of the most inexpensive joys available to almost everyone – if you're lucky enough – is to wake up in your warm bed and to realise that you don't have to leave it and that you can turn over and go back to sleep again. The first three mornings I spent in the cottage when I returned to Barrandale I didn't quit my bed until well after eleven o'clock. I needed that calm, that banal quotidian luxury of sleep.

I opened up the house, aired it, stocked up on food and drink, reclaimed the dog, Flam, from the farmer who had been looking after him. Flam's evident delight at seeing me again was another emotional high point – staccato barking, leaping up, face licking. It took him hours to calm down.

Very swiftly I put the pieces of my old life on Barrandale back together. I took long walks around the island; I visited my friends to let them know I was home again and all the while I was re-familiarising myself with this existence that I'd put on hold while I was in Vietnam – but of course what had happened in Vietnam and my precipitate return kept thrusting itself into my mind.

Even now, after so much time has gone by, I still wonder if I was only allowed to leave Vietnam because of my title, because I was the widow of Sholto, Lord Farr. God bless the British class system. What would have happened if I'd been plain Amory Clay? Without 'Lady Farr' I'm more and more convinced that on one of my trips I'd have gone mysteriously MIA and been found dead amidst the detritus of some firefight with the Viet Cong. Another foolhardy photographer caught out looking for a scoop. It would have been very easy to arrange. My title and the fact that Frank Dunn knew me and had served with Sholto in the war made the difference. My long wait in the St John's Wood mansion flat represented the time taken to evaluate the risk I posed, now I knew the secret. A meeting would have been convened. Lady Farr? Widow of Lord Farr MC, DSO? We can't really do anything to her, can we? Soldier's widow. Make her promise to keep quiet, see if we can trust her to keep her mouth shut. Mr Green and Mr Brown would have reported back: she's no fool, she knows what's at stake. We can let her go.

★

In that first week back Joe Dunraven's office sent me on a package of my mail – I'd had everything diverted to them so that bills could be paid, the house maintained, and so on. Once a month they had forwarded personal letters to the Sentinel bureau in Saigon. The package that arrived only contained the post of the last few weeks and was insignificant, except for one letter, postmarked in Los Angeles. Inside was a piece of card.

Darling Ma,

I just wanted you to know that I am well and happy and am living in America, now. I won't be coming home. I'm very happy and very well so please don't worry about me.

All my love,

Blythe

Under her signature was a small symbol: a Christian cross, with a stylised eye drawn above the upright.

I called Annie.

'I'm not sure if this is some kind of a joke but I've had a very strange card from Blythe.'

'So have I,' Annie sounded upset. 'I had a letter.'

'Posted in America?'

'Yes.'

'I didn't know she'd gone there.'

'Neither did I.' She paused. 'It's all very sweet and lovely and she keeps going on about how happy and well she is. But she says she's never coming back. Ever.' Now there was a catch in her voice. 'But it doesn't sound like Blythe. It sounds like she's taking dictation.'

'Is there a funny kind of symbol on it?'

'A kind of cross with an eye on top. I think.'

'It is her handwriting though.'

'Oh yes. But the tone seems wrong.'

Now I felt disturbed, a small shiver of alarm and worry. I told Annie I'd been to the Notting Hill flat and had been told she was on 'holiday'. Maybe somebody there would know something. I'd spoken to an American guy who was living there, I told her.

'I'll go this weekend,' she said.

'No, don't worry. I'll go myself.'

The journey to room 42 in the San Carlos Motel had not been straightforward, I reflected, as I unpacked my clothes. I'd already been two weeks in California and at times had despaired – but now, in theory, I was only a few miles away from Blythe herself; it couldn't be very long before we were face to face.

I had travelled down to London within twenty-four hours of speaking to Annie, and went straight to Blythe's flat in Notting Hill. There I met the man who had opened the door to me after my night in St John's Wood. He was affable and candid, not American but Canadian, he corrected me, politely – his name was Ted Lundegaard.

'Is anything actually wrong?' he asked me. 'Is Blythe in some kind of trouble?'

'We just don't know where she is.' I improvised. 'She needs medication, medicines, she left without enough supplies and I'm worried.'

'Oh, right. Jeez. I see what you mean. Could be nasty.'

Blythe had gone to America, he told me, with her boyfriend, Jeff – an American.

'Her boyfriend?'

'They played in this band together, Platinum Scrap.'

'Do you know Jeff's last name?'

'Bellamont. Jeff Bellamont. They were going to set themselves up as a duo, you know: "Blythe and Bellamont". Jeff said they had a booking at a club in LA.'

'Do you know the name of this club?'

'Sorry. I forget. I know he told me but . . . Wait a sec.'

I followed him from the sitting room with its two busted sofas and huge loudspeakers into a large bay-windowed bedroom at the front of the house looking on to a strip of untended public garden opposite. This was Blythe's bedroom, Ted informed me, Blythe's and Jeff's. In a way it was as dispiriting as John Oberkamp's hooch at Nui Dat airbase. There was a double mattress on the floor with grubby sheets and a blanket, a central light with a dusty paper globe-shade, a dressing table with a propped mirror and about a dozen cardboard boxes that functioned as a wardrobe, filled with clothes and shoes. There was no carpet. By the bed on both sides were ashtrays full of ancient cigarette butts. The smell of dust, mould and ash overlaid with some cheap deodorant permeated the air. What do we know of our children's private lives, I asked myself? Nothing.

Ted was searching a cork pinboard next to the dressing table. He held up a card and passed it to me.

'Hey. We got lucky.'

The card said 'DOWNSTAIRS AT PAUL'S', under a logo of crossed guitars, and gave an address on Fountain Avenue in West Hollywood.

So I bought a plane ticket, BOAC to Los Angeles, and left the next day, grateful to the gods of luck that I was sufficiently in funds to do this, spontaneously, thanks to my windfall from the Matthew B. Brady Award. On the flight I had many hours to think and I wondered about Blythe and whether I was (a) being a fool, or (b) doing the right thing, or (c) risking alienating my daughter even more by rushing after her in this panicked way.

Everything about her letters had been meant to reassure – I'm fine, Ma, nothing's wrong – but I had an unmoving apprehension that all was not that well with her and I reasoned that I would rather draw down Blythe's irritation and accusations than stay on Barrandale vaguely worrying about her and feeling guilty for doing nothing. But guilt was the issue, I realised. I was feeling guilty that I'd gone away and left her and my deepening guilt was driving me on to make this trip, however annoying and futile it might prove to be.

I was still fretting over my options when I arrived in LA, where I found a perfectly comfortable hotel, the Heyworth Travel Inn on Santa Monica Boulevard, just three blocks from Downstairs at Paul's.

And there my trail petered out and ended in a small jazz/folk club with a tiny stage and about forty seats. Yes, the manager told me, Blythe and Bellamont had played two nights at Downstairs, and they were really quite good. He checked the date – some seven weeks ago. Seven weeks, I thought – where had I been seven weeks ago? In the middle of the Mini-Tet Offensive taking shelter in a bombed-out house with Mary Poundstone, no doubt. I felt the stupid illogical guilt crowding in on me again, and told myself that if I'd been at home Blythe would never have gone gallivanting off like this without telling anyone her plans, despatching bizarrely anodyne postcards to her mother and sister.

And then I remembered that I'd missed the twins' birthday, their twenty-first. I'd sent cards and cheques. Surely that couldn't have – I stopped berating myself. Cheques. I'd sent them each £100 for their twenty-first birthday. A mere gesture beside their inheritance from the Farr estate that fell due on their 'maturity': £1,000. A fortune for someone like Blythe, living the way she did, and a fortune, it had just occurred to me, for Jeff Bellamont as well, no doubt. The money influx must have been the catalyst for the trip to America; it explained everything, I was sure.

I went back to the Heyworth and wondered what to do next. I needed some help, that was obvious; I'd done as much as I could on my own. I thought about calling Cleveland Finzi, my knight in tarnished armour, but I couldn't bring myself to pick up the phone – it wasn't the time or place or situation to increase my debt to Cleve. Who else did I know in Los Angeles? And then it came to me: my 'business partner', Moss Fallmaster.

I called him. He was delighted to hear from me, he said, and even more delighted that I was in town and invited me over to his 'factory' on San Ysidro Drive in the canyons above Beverly Hills. I drove my teal-blue Coronet over there, curious and hopeful.

Moss Fallmaster was tall, possibly the tallest person I've ever known – six foot five or six, I'd say – and he was wearing, in honour of my visit, a 'Never Too Young To . . .' T-shirt. He had a pointed sorcerer's beard tied at the end with an agate jewel and long hair held back in a ponytail. He was charmingly fey and loquacious and the only effect that was at odds with the whole carefully put-together persona was heavy black-framed spectacles that would have looked more at home on a lawyer or government official.

His canyon house had a fine, open view over the vast city and its coastal plain. Through the salt and smog haze I could see the blurred rectangles of the tall buildings miles away in downtown LA. Everywhere in the house – corridors, hallway, stacked against walls – were battered cardboard boxes with large, scrawled handwriting on them: Grateful Dead, Peace Sign, Marijuana, Naked Mickey Mouse, Ban the Bomb, Che, and so on.

'Ah. T-shirts,' I said.

He pointed at a box: 'Never Too Young To ...' He inclined himself apologetically. 'Not our best seller,' he said, 'but steady. In fact I think I may owe you some money.'

He went to a study and came out with a wad of cash from which he paid me several hundred dollars and had me sign for them.

'Let's hope these Paris peace talks drag on,' he said. 'An ongoing war is good business. Just kidding,' he added with a sly smile.

We sat down on his deck and he poured me a glass of red wine and I told him why I was here in Los Angeles.

'My God. English mother comes to California searching for her runaway daughter. I'll buy the movie rights.' He leant his long torso forward and topped up my glass. I lit a cigarette.

'You know, Amory – may I call you Amory? – I would just go home. She'll come back as soon as she's bored by her little adventure. How old is she?'

'Twenty-one.'

'She'll run out of money.'

'She has quite a lot of money. That's the trouble.' I explained about Sholto's legacy. I told him about the strange card sent to me and the letter to Annie with their pointed messages.

'You know,' he said, 'I can't really see why it might appear worrying ... She says she's happy—'

'It's not Blythe,' I said. 'I know her too well. Something's happened to her.'

'You know what?' he said. 'I think you need a private detective. I have just the man.'

★

THE BARRANDALE JOURNAL 1977

This morning, walking across the gravel to the car, I fell. There was no ice; I didn't trip, stumble or stub my toe – my left leg just gave way and I fell over. I sat on the ground for a while and counted to a hundred. Then I stood up again. All seemed well, but I knew what was happening – the neurologist had warned me. I tested my grip, both hands, on the door handle – fine. But my throat was dry and I felt frightened: it was as if something else was taking me over – this sudden loss of power, sudden loss of motor control is the significant sign that the disease is gaining ground. Calm, girl, calm . . . It comes and goes, chooses its own pace. It may be moving very slowly – don't panic. One day at a time and all the rest of it. You have the ultimate say, remember.

★

Cole Hardaway of Hardaway Legal Solutions Inc. was the private investigator who Moss Fallmaster recommended. He had an office above a nail parlour in Santa Monica. If you looked out of his window you could see the ocean reflected in the windows of the building opposite. He seemed a little unprepossessing at first, not at all what I'd hoped for or had been expecting in a private eye. He was wearing pale grey trousers and a checked lime-green shirt – a man in his mid-forties with a lean and thoughtful demeanour that was rather undermined by his hairstyle: his brown hair was cut in a Beatles fringe, snipped off straight at his eyebrows. It did make him look a bit younger, I supposed, but any man over forty who deliberately combs his hair forward in a child's fringe has something suspect about him, I always feel. Anyway, I tried to ignore it as we talked and, slowly but surely, I found myself coming round to a more favourable impression of Cole Hardaway. He had a reassuring deep bass voice and he spoke in a very measured way, always pausing to think, visibly pondering any question you might ask.

'I was in England in the war,' he said, explaining that he'd been an army engineer. He had taken part in the construction of several pontoon bridges over the Rhine in 1945. I told him my own experience of crossing the Rhine in '45.

'Wouldn't it be funny,' I said, 'if I'd crossed the Rhine on one of the bridges you'd helped build?'

It was a throwaway remark but Mr Hardaway thought about it silently for some moments, nodding, weighing up the probabilities.

'It would certainly be a remarkable coincidence,' he said, finally. I agreed and we pressed on with the matter of finding Blythe.

I gave him all the information I had plus the fairly recent photograph of Blythe that I carried with me. He informed me that he charged $100 per day not including expenses and advised me to return to my hotel. Relax, he said, see the sights – he would call me as soon as he had anything concrete.

I saw, by the door as I left his office, a photograph on the wall of a young soldier in fatigues sitting on a pile of sandbags, smiling at the camera. It was obviously Vietnam – it could have been one of mine from *Vietnam, Mon Amour*.

'I'm just back from Vietnam myself,' I said, explaining why I'd been there.

'That's my son, Leo,' he said flatly. 'He was killed in Da Nang last year. A traffic accident.'

I forgave Cole Hardaway his silly fringe.

I saw the sights, such as they were, in Los Angeles. I went on a tour of Universal Studios. I took some photographs on Sunset Boulevard. I watched movies (*2001: A Space Odyssey* and *The Fox*), I sat by the small hotel swimming pool and read my books. I was planning a trip to Anaheim to visit Disneyland when Cole Hardaway called, three days after my appointment with him. He had tracked Blythe down and I owed him $425. He suggested we meet up – it was a little complicated.

I returned to his office in Santa Monica where he offered me a drink. I asked for whisky but he only had bourbon.

'Shall we go to a bar?' he suggested. 'Would you mind going to a bar?'

Not at all, I said, excellent idea – I liked bars. So we wandered down the street to a bar a block away – Hardaway was obviously a regular – and sat in a curved red leatherette booth at the rear. A waitress in a silver miniskirt and a tight black halterneck took our orders.

'There you be, Cole,' she said with a warm smile, serving us our drinks. 'Nice to have you back.'

'May I call you Cole?' I asked.

'Of course, Mrs Farr.'

He told me that the key factor that had allowed him to trace Blythe had been her boyfriend, Jeff Bellamont, who had unwittingly and obligingly left a relatively easy-to-follow trail from Downstairs at Paul's – unpaid rental on an apartment, a car hire, a night in a motel, a run-in and a ticket from a traffic cop in Fresno – all the way to another hotel in Bishop, Inyo County. Cole had driven up to Bishop – over 200 miles north of Los Angeles. By now he had a photograph of Bellamont, a recent mugshot that he gave to me. It turned out Bellamont had a sizeable roster of crimes and misdemeanours and had even served time in Folsom prison for robbery. A certain amount of judicious asking around in Bishop (not a big place) had produced an accurate identification and a probable location.

'I'm pretty damn sure I know where he is,' Cole said. 'And if he's there, then your daughter will be there also, most likely. It's just ...'

he paused for one of his moments of cogitation. 'It's just a kind of weird situation. Not dangerous, no, no. Just prepare yourself for something not normal.'

★

THE BARRANDALE JOURNAL 1977

Hugo called and invited me to see how his new house was progressing so I walked round the headland and met him there in discussion with the contractors. The roof was now on and complete and I could see it was definitely going to be a fair-sized home. Once it was sealed, windows in and so on, they could work inside through the winter, he told me. He hoped to be in by spring next year.

'And we'll be neighbours,' he added.

'Which will be great.'

'You can pop over for a drink.'

'And vice versa.'

We wandered down to the rocks that the house overlooked – no bay. I had the bay.

'You know that I'm looking for a particularly close neighbourly relationship,' he said, taking my hand. He was always taking my hand these days – I didn't stop him.

'Hugo,' I began, 'I don't think—'

'Don't think. There's no need for thought. Nothing will be complicated.'

'Everything's complicated, surely you realise that by now. At our age.'

He sighed. 'No, what I mean is . . . We're not young, true, but we're not decrepit. Something like this – two houses, not so far apart – it can work, Amory. We can keep an eye on each other.'

That actually sounded rather appealing, so I untensed.

'Well, yes, I can see the advantages,' I said.

'And we can get to know each other better.'

I wondered when and if I should tell him about my particular problem.

'One step at a time, Mr Torrance. Can we go? I'm freezing.'

Some lists I made:

A list of the books written by Jean-Baptiste Charbonneau:

Morceaux bruts
Feu d'artifice
Le Trac
Cacapipitalisme
Avis de passage
Le Trapéziste
Absence de marquage
Chemin sans issue

A list of the thirteen types of photograph (plus an afterthought):

Aide-memoire
Reportage
Work of art
Topography
Erotica/Pornography
Advertisement
Abstract image
Literature
Text
Autobiography
Compositional
Functional illustration
Snapshot

Try it and see: all photographs fall into one of these categories or combinations of them. Actually, I now think there is a fourteenth category, as unique to photography as the stop-time device that is its defining feature, the snapshot – namely, the 'mis-shot'. It occurs when you make a mistake: you overexpose, you double-expose, the camera shakes or moves or the framing is wrong – the so-called 'bad-crop'. My most famous photograph, 'The Confrontation', is a mis-shot, a bad-crop. I suppose a mistake might function beneficially in other arts – the sculptor's hammer and chisel slips, the wrong tube of paint is selected, the composer unwittingly changes key – and it might enhance the whole in an aleatory way. But only in photography can our errors so easily become real virtues, again and again and again.

A list of my books:

Absences (1943)
Vietnam, Mon Amour (1968)

And the books I planned:

The View Down (shots from on high looking down)
Sleepers (images of people sleeping or resting)
Static Light (the final project – light stopped)
Bad-Crop (a deliberate selection of mis-shots)

And, crowning glory:

The Horizontal Fall: Photographs by Amory Clay

A list of my lovers:

Lockwood Mower
Cleveland Finzi
Jean-Baptiste Charbonneau
Sholto Farr
John Oberkamp
Hugo Torrance ...?

2. Willow Ranch

It was a 250-mile drive to Bishop from Los Angeles, north in the general direction of Death Valley. In the end it took me five and a half hours, with breaks. I set off on the Garden Park Freeway out towards Pasadena, then on to Highway 395 all the way to Bishop. The journey led me round the massive sprawl of Edwards Air Force Base – I saw B-52s climbing slowly into the air, training for Vietnam, no doubt – and then along the periphery of the China Lake weapons testing range. We were entering desert country, the land arid, caught in the rain-shadow of the Sierra Nevada mountains, whose long saw-toothed bulk – summits white with snow and ice – I could see as I drove ever northwards into the Owens Valley. On either side of the highway stretched flat steppes of desert scrubland – sagebrush, buckwheat, salt grass and creosote bush – and a lot of sand.

I pulled into a picnic area off the road at one stage to stretch my legs and I looked around at this great parched wilderness baking in the high summer heat. Away from LA's smog the sky was a crystalline blue – a perfect blue – and the few clouds that hung motionless there were cartoon-like in their whiteness, freshly laundered, ideally puffy, promising not one drop of moisture. I felt very alone all of a sudden and full of an unfamiliar trepidation. Cole Hardaway had insisted that I feel free to call him at any moment if I felt I needed some assistance but I stirred myself into a form of reasoned anger – something had happened to my daughter and changed her, she needed me, and I was going to find her on my

The San Carlos Motel, Glenbrook, California, 1968.

own. It occurred to me that those breezily robotic letters were actually a covert cry for help. I simply couldn't believe that Blythe had run away and foresworn us so casually, our small, close family of three. She must have been suborned, persuaded, turned in some way. I had to find her, talk to her, discover what had happened – and try to persuade her to come home, if that was what she really wanted.

I drove into Bishop and then out again, retracing my steps, finding the San Carlos Motel a few convenient miles down the road in the small town of Glenbrook, valiantly guarding its 'city limits' as Bishop's suburbs remorselessly encroached.

In my room, air conditioner thrumming, unpacked, I laid out my map on the bed and plotted my next move.

Cole Hardaway had told me everything he had discovered about Jeff Bellamont and Blythe. They had travelled from Los Angeles to Bishop, spent a night there, and then gone to a small settlement called Line Lake. At Line Lake they had paused at a convenience store and bought some provisions and made a phone call. Then they had asked directions to and then motored on to an abandoned dude-ranch complex called Willow Ranch and that was where their journey ended, he presumed, there was only one road in and out. Cole hadn't gone to Willow Ranch himself, but that was where the trail led. As far as he was concerned they were still there.

The problem was, he further explained, that Willow Ranch was no longer abandoned. It appeared that, according to the locals he asked, some sort of hippie community had taken over the existing buildings and had been living there for some two years, now, in sought-for isolation, 'Growing vegetables and weaving baskets and smoking pot, you know the sort of thing,' Cole had detailed in his matter-of-fact basso profundo. There were about forty people currently in residence, as far as anyone knew – Willow Ranch had a floating population, people were always arriving and people were always leaving. The place was the benign fiefdom of a charismatic Vietnam veteran called Tayborn Gaines. Gaines reputedly had served three years in Vietnam – and on his release from the army had joined the anti-war movement. He had been a prominent speaker at rallies and marches and had acquired some sort of minor celebrity reputation as he was an articulate and forceful debater. But, now he was installed with his community in Willow Ranch, Tay Gaines had gone off the media radar and rarely left the premises. There were a lot of runaways drawn there, a lot of girls, Cole said, the implication being that Blythe Farr was probably another of them.

There were more muted warnings from Cole, even though I had now received the message loud and clear. The Willow Ranchers kept themselves to themselves and they didn't welcome visitors. They sold their farm produce and would volunteer for community projects in Bishop and Line Lake. The locals seemed to accept them and respected their need for privacy.

'Just be cautious, Mrs Farr,' Cole had said. 'Up there you'll be in the middle of a very remote, hot nowhere. The local sheriff is miles away in Bishop. I talked to the cops. None of them had ever been out to Willow Ranch. Never been any trouble, they told me. But it's clear that the place, and what exactly goes on there, is something of a mystery.'

With that in mind, I had formulated a plan, of sorts, that I hoped would afford me entry to the place. Before I'd left LA I had ordered some business cards to be printed up. 'Amory Clay. Staff photographer. *Global-Photo-Watch.*' I was making the assumption that most people were flattered when professional photographers offered to take their photographs, for a fee, moreover – even, perhaps, publicity-shy people like Tayborn Gaines.

The next day I loaded up my two cameras with film, filled a gallon plastic container with iced water, bought a ham and coleslaw sandwich at a diner and drove out the few miles to Line Lake.

The lake itself didn't really exist any more, apart from some shallow briny pools. Like most of the water in the valley it had had its inflow diverted to feed the Los Angeles aqueduct and was now a dry alkaline flat, cracking up in the relentless sun like a pottery glaze in a furnace. The hamlet managed to survive on passing hikers and there was still some freelance mining going on in the deep incised arroyos in the foothills of the Sierra Nevada – miners needed food and fuel and a place to drink. Line Lake boasted a bar, a gas station and a general store on the one street of brick, wood and plasterboard shacks. It was the twentieth-century version of a one-horse town.

I pulled into the gas station, had the attendant fill up the Dodge's tank and asked the way to Willow Ranch.

'You don't want to go to Willow Ranch, ma'am,' the attendant said, a raw-boned, deeply tanned man who could have been thirty or sixty. 'You got nothing but pothead hippie freaks out there.'

'I'm a photographer,' I said and gave him my card – record of my passing. He read it carefully. 'Oh. You should be OK, then.' It always worked.

The dirt road out of Line Lake ran up the middle of a wide wash where the heat seemed even more intense. I saw a broken sign that said 'Willow Ranc—' and persevered. I was stopped by a pine log across the track and beside it sat a wheelless VW Combi with a tarpaulin awning rigged off its side to give shade to a ramshackle stall selling home-grown produce – pots of honey, squash, corn cobs, long thin avocados and an assortment of various-sized straw baskets. A young man, shirtless, stepped out, hands in his pockets, with the unfocussed, blinking gaze of someone just roused from sleep or massively intoxicated.

'Hey. Nothing down that road for you, ma'am. Ah ... Like private property, you know?'

'I've an appointment with Tayborn Gaines. I'm a photographer.' I showed him one of my cameras.

'Oh. OK. Sure.' He dragged the log away and I drove on to Willow Ranch only to pause, a hundred yards down the track, at a kind of crude gateway. On a rickety arch made of hewn timber and bits of planking there was a message, written in black paint, below the now familiar stylised eye: 'THERE ARE NONE SO BLIND AS THOSE WHO WILL NOT SEE'.

I drove on under it, slightly more apprehensive. And after a few turns in the dirt road, Willow Ranch was revealed to me. I paused to take a quick photograph.

Willow Ranch, Inyo County, California, 1968.

The abandoned dude ranch was bigger than I expected, with a strange assortment of ramshackle wooden buildings spread over a

420

two- or three-acre site, most of them semi-derelict, some roofless, with, at the centre, a three-storey western 'saloon' and a corral overgrown with mesquite bushes. Parked here and there in the shade of scrub oak or stunted cottonwood trees was an assortment of vehicles, sun-bleached cars and trucks and one ancient school bus. There must have been a water source as I saw a generator pump by a well head with black hoses winding out to those various buildings in better repair and to irrigate small vegetable allotments scratched out between the buildings. Here and there were other signs of semi-permanent habitation: a rubbish dump, washing hanging on lines – and graffiti, lots of graffiti. I slowed to take the slogans in – Ban the Bomb signs, flowers, and amongst them, carefully painted and stencilled messages: 'BRAINWASHERS ARSONISTS SADISTS KILLERS – ENLIST TODAY IN THE SERVICE OF YOUR CHOICE'; 'GIRLS SAY YES TO BOYS WHO SAY NO'; 'RICH MAN'S WAR'; 'WAR IS NOT HEALTHY FOR CHILDREN'; 'MAKE ART NOT WAR'; 'WAR IS GOOD BUSINESS INVEST YOUR SON'; 'GIVE PEACE A CHANCE'.

Young men and women looked on in vague curiosity from doorways, canvas awnings and porches as I bumped along the track in front of the saloon and halted the car in the shade cast by its facade and stepped out. There were advantages to being a woman in your sixties with grey hair – sometimes – you posed no obvious threat, but I noted that my hands were shaking and my throat was constricted. I smiled breezily at a couple of guys wandering towards me. They were smiling. The natives were friendly.

'Hello,' I said as calmly as I could manage. 'I've an appointment with a Mr Tayborn Gaines.'

'Tay!' one of the guys shouted towards a purple and white bungalow with an ex-army jeep parked outside, and more graffiti above the front door: the big stylised eye and the message 'CLARITY OF VISION = THOUGHT = PURPOSE'. Then he sniggered as he added, 'Old lady here to see you, man!'

After about a minute a tall, fit, good-looking man in his thirties emerged from the purple bungalow. He was bare-chested and wearing sawn-off jeans and had a red towel draped round his shoulders. His long, shoulder-length hair was damp, as if he'd just taken a shower, he was wearing sunglasses and had a droopy Mexican-style moustache.

'Hi there, ma'am, I'm Tay Gaines, what can I do for you?' he asked me in a friendly open manner, unfolding his towel and drying his hair.

'Let me give you my card,' I said. I had put my camera bag on the ground and as I started to rummage in it I covertly snapped a photo, quickly, hoping I'd managed to catch him in the frame. Evidence that might be useful. I stood and handed him a card.

'*Global-Photo-Watch*. I don't understand.'

'We have an appointment,' I said. 'Don't we?'

I don't know quite what I'd been expecting – some kind of low-life down-and-out, I suppose – but Tayborn Gaines was a handsome well-built man and clearly proud of his lean, muscled body. And something of a full-on narcissist, I suspected.

'No, I don't recall any "appointment",' he said politely, looking around at the small crowd that had gathered. 'I think you must have made some kind of mistake.'

'My editor told me to come here,' I said. 'He told me everything was arranged.'

'I'm sorry, ma'am, but I've had absolutely no contact with' – he glanced at my card – 'any *Global-Photo-Watch*.' He smiled. 'I stopped talking to the press a long time ago.' He handed his towel to another girl – a pale-faced black girl with a huge Afro hairstyle – as she wandered out of the bungalow, curious to see what was going on. He put his hands on his hips and stared at me, head on one side.

'Crossed wires, I guess,' he said.

'We're doing this piece on alternative Californian communities,' I said. 'You know, the Esalen Institute, Hog Farm, Drop City, the

White Lodge Commune in Marin County.' I smiled apologetically. 'I'm just a photographer, I go where they send me. I was told everything was arranged.'

Gaines smiled apologetically too, and then glanced again at my card.

'I was also told a permission fee of two hundred dollars had been agreed. Sorry,' I said and handed over an envelope containing $200. It was an old trick: cash usually overcomes the camera-shy. Gaines took out the money and riffled through the notes, $20 bills – I could see he was more interested now. I took the opportunity to turn and look around me. A dozen or so people had gathered, curious. All young, unkempt, grubby-looking. No sign of Blythe or anyone that looked like Jeff Bellamont.

'I'm afraid it's not convenient today,' Gaines said, smiling broadly. His smile revealed poor teeth with visible gaps and one incisor was black. The handsome, fit man revealed the malnourished youth when he smiled. 'Where are you staying? Close by?'

'The San Carlos Motel in Glenbrook.' I would have preferred not to tell him but there was no alternative.

'Well, if it's OK with you, I'd suggest you go back to your motel and we'll call you when we're good and ready.'

'Yes, of course. I apologise if there's been a mix-up but, as I said, I'm just the photographer.'

'Yes, sure, I know what it's like. Carry out those orders,' he said. 'And, by the way, would you mind telling me the name of your editor? You understand – I have to be a little careful.'

'Mr Cleveland Finzi.'

'I have to talk to my friends here – see if it's something we're prepared to consider – but I promise I'll give you a call in the next twenty-four hours.'

I climbed back into my car and drove away from Willow Ranch, my hands sweaty on the steering wheel. I felt a tremble of high tension in my body but also a curious sense that – however strange the set-up at Willow Ranch was – it didn't seem sinister. Perhaps, it struck me, Blythe was indeed safe and well, just as she had said.

Tayborn Gaines. Willow Ranch, Line Lake, California, 1968.

One day went by, then two. I spent a lot of time in my room waiting and hoping for Gaines to phone, not wanting to miss him. I went for a stroll on the morning of the third day, a Wednesday, and when I returned the receptionist told me that a Mr Gaines had called and it would be convenient for me to call on him at 4 p.m.

I prepared another envelope with $200 – just in case more financial incentive might help – but I drove back out to Willow Ranch with low expectations. Maybe Bellamont and Blythe had moved on and Gaines was just using this for what he thought would be an opportunity for more publicity. But there was no log across the track and no one in the VW Combi, nor any parched vegetables set out on the stall. I drove warily under the 'NONE SO BLIND' archway and parked outside the saloon again where a young guy with mutton-chop whiskers was waiting and led me into the purple bungalow.

He left me alone in what passed for the sitting room. The walls had once been white but were now smirched and foxed like old

424

parchment with that greasy handled sheen you find on much-thumbed banknotes. There were four stained and sagging mattresses pushed back against the wall and the worn emerald-green carpet made quiet sucking noises as I shifted about nervously. There was that incipient smell again of neglect: dampness, smoke, body odour. I was reminded of Blythe's room in Notting Hill.

Then Gaines pushed open the door and came in. He was wearing an olive drab field jacket with a grey T-shirt on beneath it and faded denim jeans. Over the left breast pocket 'US ARMY' was written, but over the right – where his name, 'GAINES', should have been – was a paler patch, as if it had been ripped off. As he shook my hand I noted the insignia on his shoulder: an embroidered red square containing a blue circle with AA curved into the diameter.

'Eighty-Second Airborne,' I said. 'All American.'

'Yes, ma'am. Third Brigade.'

'I was with some of you boys just a few weeks ago. That's how I know.'

'I've got nothing against the division,' he said, evenly. 'They just shouldn't be in this corrupt war.'

'So I noticed,' I said.

'I hate this game, war,' he said. 'Decided I didn't want to play it no more. So I moved to Willow Ranch. All like-minded folks seeking clarity are welcome.'

'Would you let me take some photographs?'

'I'm afraid not. We had a vote and you lost.'

'Oh. Right.'

'But before you go, I'd like you to meet someone.' He turned and called out. 'Honey? You there?'

We waited a moment and then Blythe walked into the room.

I felt a bolus of vomit rise in my throat. She looked very thin, her hair was longer than I'd ever seen it, almost down to her waist, lank and heavy. Her eyes were tired and she had a freckling of pink spots at the corners of her mouth. She was wearing a long white

425

T-shirt, almost down to her knees, with the number '3' on it. She had bare feet, filthy bare feet.

'This is my wife. Mrs Tayborn Gaines.'

'Hello, Ma,' Blythe said, calmly. 'What the hell are you doing here?'

'Hello, darling. Are you all right?'

'Never been better. I told you.'

'See, "Lady" Farr,' Gaines interrupted, sternly, all his polite bonhomie gone, 'your daughter is happily married to an upstanding American man. I resent your subterfuge, your duplicity. You are free to see Blythe any time you want. Assuming she wants to see you.'

I was hearing a kind of fizzing in my head, a constant effervescence as if my blood had turned to soda. I was, I realised, at a total loss.

'Do you think I'm so stupid, Lady Farr?' Gaines went on, almost pleadingly. 'Do you think I'm so dumb that I can't make a phone call to *Global-Photo-Watch* and ask if they've got some English lady photographer out on a shoot in California?'

I ignored him.

'Come home with me, darling,' I said to Blythe, gently. 'Everything will be fine. We miss you. Annie sends her love. We want you back home with us.'

'I'm happy here, Ma. Happy with Tay. I love him, he loves me,' she said with a small monotone laugh. I suddenly thought she might be drugged in some way. Gaines put an arm around her and squeezed her shoulder.

'You made what our Mexican friends call a *cálculo equivocado*, Lady Farr-Clay. A real *mal paso*. You thought there was something wrong going on but you can see there isn't. We're a close community here. Self-sufficient as much as we can be. We want nothing to do with the world out there—' He gestured, widely, grandly, as if taking in the whole of California, the entire United States. 'This is our world. Willow Ranch. Blythe was looking for it and she found it.'

Blythe opened her arms and I stepped into her embrace. She smelt sweaty, unwashed and her body seemed too thin as I hugged her, all ridged bones and starved muscles. I had the presence of mind to slip the small many-folded square of paper with my room number and the name and address of the motel into her hand. Gaines saw nothing and Blythe didn't react as her fingers closed around it. I felt a thrill of complicity – all was not lost. I stepped back.

'May I come back and see you again?' I asked, failing to keep the tremor from my voice.

'Of course,' Gaines said. 'You're more than welcome.'

I turned and left the room.

3. Mrs Tayborn Gaines

I felt cold, rather than upset. Inert, rather than panicky or angry, as if I hadn't fully taken in all the complex implications of what I'd seen – or didn't want to. Back at the San Carlos I called Cole Hardaway and told him I had found Blythe – but I couldn't see how I could extract her from Willow Ranch and her new life.

'She's married to this Tayborn Gaines,' I said. 'Or so they both claim.'

'I can find out in an hour or two.'

'It would be good to know for sure,' I said, feeling a little queasy. Then something else struck me. 'Gaines says he was in the Eighty-Second Airborne Division, Third Brigade. But I'm not sure I believe him.'

'I can check on that, as well.'

'Thank you, Cole.' I thought further. 'Is there any way we can get the police involved?'

'We'd need a reason.'

'What if I say I think she's being held against her will?'

'Sounds to me like that won't fly. Especially if she's married the man.'

'It just seems wrong, somehow. The whole place seems sort of fake.'

'Nobody's complained, that's our problem. Everyone who's there wants to be there, I guess.'

'So what can we do?' I asked, more plaintively than I meant.

'Why don't I come on up there tomorrow, talk to the sheriff in Bishop and see what I can set up. Any sign of Bellamont?'

'No. I didn't see him. I think he must have gone.' I had studied Bellamont's mugshot and I would have recognised his slumped resentful handsome face – long fair hair, with a General Custer blond moustache – had I seen it.

'Well that may help – could be our pretext,' Cole thought out loud. 'We could ask the police to locate Bellamont. Say he's stolen your daughter's money, or something. I'll see you tomorrow, Mrs Farr. Don't worry, don't do anything, we'll figure this out.'

I hung up and closed my eyes. Trying not to think of Blythe in her grubby '3' T-shirt and her filthy feet. What had happened to my little Blythe? What had led her down this road? I began to blame myself. Why had I gone off to Vietnam? Why had I thought only of myself? Stop. Think. Your children are free individuals – they can decide to become anyone they want and you can't prevent it. And she was twenty-one. It was no comfort.

I went into Bishop that night and found a diner where I ate half a plate of meatballs and spaghetti. I pushed it away; I wasn't hungry. I bought a pint of Irish whiskey in a liquor store and took it back to my room where I watched television in an aimless unfocussed way, changing channels back and forth whenever the advertisements appeared, sipping my whiskey from a tooth-glass. There was nothing I could realistically do, I just had to wait for Cole Hardaway to call back.

I was a bit drunk and unsteady by the time I took to my bed but I wanted unconsciousness and could hardly rebuke myself after what I'd witnessed today, so I reasoned. I lay in bed letting the room tilt and fall, listening to the hum of the air conditioner, and thinking how perplexing and strange life was, how complicated it was in the way it suddenly threw you these 'curveballs', as the GIs used to say in Vietnam. Sometimes it seemed to me as if my life had been made up entirely of curveballs and unwelcome surprises. No daughter expects her father to try and kill her by driving the family car into a fucking lake. No young photographer expects to be prosecuted

429

for obscenity – or beaten half to death by fucking fascists . . . I ranted on profanely in my drink-fuelled, self-pitying outrage, railing futilely against all the injustices; the mistakes I'd made and mistakes that had been thrust upon me . . .

I had fallen into a blank, dreamless sleep, thanks to my whiskey overdose, but I woke abruptly, fully alert, when I heard the rattle of the doorknob being turned. Thank God I had locked it and fitted the security chain. My head started to ache as I slipped out of bed – I was in my pyjamas – and, going to the window, pulled back the curtains an inch and looked out over the parking lot at the rear of the motel. The few arc lights dotted here and there cast a cold white gleam over the rows of cars and, as I peered out, I thought I saw a figure flit through the dark shadows. I pulled on my shoes and my cotton dressing gown, unlocked the door and stepped out into the warm, dry night. I walked away from my room heading towards where I had seen the figure, my eyes slowly growing accustomed to the gloom of the night.

'Blythe?' I called out, perhaps foolishly, but I was hoping she had come to me, had escaped from Tayborn Gaines, somehow. I ranged around the car park for another minute calling Blythe's name quietly but the place was empty, just the sleeping metallic herd of motor vehicles. I walked back to my room – the door had definitely been tried but it was probably just some tipsy late-homecoming motel guest mistaking the number.

I wandered back along the pathway to my room, feeling tired all of a sudden, pushed the door open and stepped in. It was completely dark and, as I felt for the light switch, I knew there was someone else in the room with me. I could hear breathing.

I clicked the light on.

Blythe was sitting on the end of the bed.

'Hello, Ma,' she said. 'I thought we should have a little talk.'

She was wearing a denim jacket and black jeans and tennis shoes on her feet. Her hair was pulled back in a loose bun, strands hanging down in front of her ears.

I gave her a kiss and sat down in a chair opposite her, my hands shaking, a feeling of breathlessness almost overwhelming me.

'You haven't a cigarette, by any chance, have you?' she asked.

'Of course.' I fetched my packet, gladly, taking time to rummage in my handbag, finding my lighter, telling myself to calm down, and offered her one. We both lit up and I sat down again.

'Tayborn prefers me not to smoke,' she said.

'Right. Well, he won't like me much, then.' I stood up again and went for my bottle of Irish whiskey. 'What's his position on drinking?' I said as I poured an inch into my glass.

'He'll have a drink from time to time. Just beer, though.'

'Thank God for that. Is he religious?'

'In his own special way. He believes in Jesus, but not really in God.'

'Fair enough.' I looked at her and felt my eyes fill with tears.

'You're not taking drugs, or anything?' I asked carefully.

'What? No, of course not.'

'Are you sure? You don't look very well, darling. You seem different, somehow.'

'Because I am different. I've changed.'

'You're not actually married to him, are you?'

'Yes. I love him, Ma – he's a wonderful, strong, fascinating man. Wait until you get to know him properly. He was a soldier, just like Papa.'

I suddenly remembered something my father used to say: 'We all see the world differently from each other; we all have unique vision.' I looked at my daughter and felt a bizarre pang that she'd never known Beverley Clay, her grandfather. I had a feeling they would have got on inordinately well.

And then I began to understand what had happened – or understand some of it – as she talked with a strange quiet passion about Tayborn's life as a soldier and the horrible things that he had seen, done and experienced in his Vietnam tour of duty and how it had altered him forever, made him see clearly how the world and its workings were; how it had made him hate the war and the forces that waged the war, the politicians, the industrialists, the generals. I thought about my father and Sholto and wanted to say, no, darling, your Tayborn Gaines is nothing like those men. But now I was beginning to feel slightly queasy and so forced myself to sit quietly and appear to listen to Blythe who was now going on about Tayborn's ambitions to make a new life, a new sheltered environment where people 'could see clearly' and so he had moved to Willow Ranch and created the Willow Ranch Community.

'But how did you ever wind up there, darling? I thought you wanted to be a singer, write songs, play your music. What happened to your boyfriend, Jeff Bellamont? You were living together in London, for heaven's sake – where did he go?'

'Jeff was a friend of Tayborn's. Was a friend. We went to Willow Ranch together and then, after about a week, Jeff just went away. Disappeared. Didn't leave a note. He took the car and whatever money I had in my bag and vanished.'

'Enter Tayborn.'

'He saved me, Ma.'

'I'm sure he did.'

'Don't be cynical.'

'Sorry.' I drew on my cigarette. 'Why on earth did you have to marry him, though?'

'Tayborn believes in marriage. As an institution.'

Feeling weak, suddenly, I poured out the rest of the bottle, just a few drops.

'How long have you been married?'

'About five weeks.'

'Where is he? Does he know you're here? Seeing me?'

'Of course. He brought me here. He's parked out front at the reception.'

'Come home, Blythe, come home with me.'

'No, Ma. Willow Ranch is my home. Tayborn's my husband. I've never been happier.'

We talked a little more and I didn't ask her to come home with me again. I had made the plea and it had been rejected. I walked back with her to the reception area, my arm around her thin shoulders. Across the street I could see Gaines's jeep parked in the shadow of the motel sign. We kissed goodbye and she promised she would write to me, let me know what she was doing, all the time reassuring me how happy and at peace she was, seriously, Ma, really and truly.

I let her hand go and watched her cross the moon-shadowed tarmac towards her new husband. She didn't look back as she gave me a quick wave.

Cole Hardaway, his face impassive, sat across from me in one of the curved red leatherette booths in the bar just down the street from his office. We were both drinking what Cole called 'highballs' but that I knew as Scotch and soda. I had an almost uncontrollable urge to reach forward and sweep his stupid fringe aside, off his forehead, but that was probably just a symptom of my frustration. I had come to like Cole Hardaway.

'You're sure,' I said, not hiding my disappointment – it had been my last desperate hope. 'A real marriage.'

'I'm afraid so. Married by the clerk of Inyo County about a month and a half ago.'

I felt that emptiness well up inside me, instinctively – then it subsided as I sipped my drink. Why was Blythe being so crazily stupid? Why Tayborn Gaines of all people? But I thought I knew the answer to that. And then I remembered how at her age I had slipped into the bed of my homosexual uncle and asked him to make love to me. We are not logical beings, especially when it comes to affairs of the heart.

'However,' Cole said, his expression unchanging, 'Tayborn Gaines never served in the US military. There are no records. Certainly not in the Eighty-Second Airborne.'

Now, I felt a little bloom of elation. Now I had my way in, my fifth column to destabilise this union. So Gaines was no soldier, as

I had suspected. What fantasies of warfare and warriorhood had he spun for Blythe?

Back at the Heyworth Travel Inn, in my room, the air conditioner at full blast, I took my time over the letter I wrote.

Darling Blythe,

It was both lovely and, I have to be honest, a bit disturbing to see you in your new life. Believe me, I understand better than anyone your desire to be happy and I understand that you are convinced that you have found that happiness with Tayborn. I love you and all I wish for you is to be happy – it's as simple as that. But I also wish you hadn't done everything so swiftly. It takes time to truly come to know a person and, I wonder, what do you truly know about this man you are so deeply in love with?

I ask because I've discovered that one thing he claims to be isn't in fact true. Tayborn Gaines was never a soldier. He was never in the 82nd Airborne. He never served in Vietnam. Now, I ask you – if a man can lie so convincingly about something he claims is of fundamental importance and significance to his being what then does that imply for—

I stopped. I felt that sickness in me again. It was a conscious realisation that I was wasting my time and the absolute knowledge of this fact made me want to vomit. I stood up and walked around the room taking deep breaths. Then I sat down at the table again. It was Blythe's life and she had every right to live it as she wished. Slowly I tore up my letter to her about the lies of Tayborn Gaines. As I arranged the shreds into a small neat square pile I found I was weeping inconsolably. I knew I had finally lost my daughter.

CODA IN BARRANDALE: 1978

My mother died in 1969. Greville died in 1972. The Clay family, diminishing.

Is it true that your life is just a long preparation for your death – the one thing we can all be sure of, all the billions of us? The deaths you witness, hear about, that are close to you – that you may cause or bring about, however inadvertently (I think of my dog, Flim) – are preparing you, covertly, incrementally, for your own eventual departure. I think of all the deaths in my life – the ones that left me riven, the strangers' deaths I happened to see – and understand how they have steered me to this position, this intellectual conviction, that I hold now. You don't realise this when you're young but as you age this steady accumulation of knowledge teaches you, becomes relentlessly pertinent to your own case.

But then I wonder – turn this notion on its head. Are all the deaths you encounter and experience in fact an enhancement of the life you lead? Your personal history of death teaches you what's important, what makes it actually worth being alive – sentient and breathing. It's a key lesson because when you know that, you also know its opposite – you know when life's no longer worth living – and then you can die, happy.

★

I met Blythe at a coffee shop down in Westchester, on West 82nd Street off Sepulveda Boulevard, near Los Angeles International Airport. I was on my way home so it was convenient even though I could see the neighbourhood was run-down and shabby. Our order was taking its time to arrive and Blythe left our booth and went to speak to the waitress. To me she sounded like an American,

437

now, her English accent all but gone. She was wearing a black and white striped shirt and jeans; her hair was cut carelessly short – there was a long untrimmed strand at the back – and she was wearing no make-up. She returned to our booth and sat down, managing a genuine smile, it seemed to me.

'Something's gone wrong in the kitchen. It'll be two minutes.'

'Doesn't matter, darling, seeing you again before I go is the main thing.' I reached for her hand and squeezed it and then let it go and turned the gesture into an airy wave, indicating the streetscape out of the window.

'So this is where you work.'

'Just round the corner. You have to go to the needy – they won't come to you.'

'Of course, makes sense.'

'There's nothing to see – just a room with a coffee machine and a few small offices.'

'Well, at least I have a picture of the neighbourhood.'

This was the third visit I had made to the US to see Blythe in the eight years since she crossed the road in front of the San Carlos Motel and went to rejoin her husband, Tayborn Gaines, who was waiting patiently for her in his jeep.

I suppose it was some private consolation to me that the marriage didn't even make its first anniversary. Some months after I'd left, the Willow Ranch Community was raided by the police and significant quantities of LSD and marijuana were discovered. Gaines was prosecuted but acquitted for lack of convincing evidence. He and Blythe moved to Los Angeles and then some weeks later he left. I don't know what happened – I had all this information from Annie who was more closely in touch with Blythe than I was – but I suspect that Blythe's Farr legacy had finally run out. Time for Tayborn to move on.

Curiously, Blythe kept Tayborn's name – she was Blythe Gaines from now on, not Farr. I think I understand. The name was all that remained of the dream-life she thought she had acquired and then lost so suddenly and cruelly. Or, now I come to think about it, maybe it was a harsh aide-memoire – don't get fooled again, girl. In any event she stayed on in Los Angeles and picked up the career in music she had abandoned; writing songs, playing in bands in and around the Los Angeles area.

On my first visit to see her she was living in a ramshackle house on Coldwater Canyon Drive with half a dozen other people – young men and women, all musicians, I think. She had dyed her hair auburn and parted it in the middle – I thought it didn't suit her. She smoked as much as I did. In the few days I spent with her we must have consumed a dozen packets of 'smokes', as she called them. The significant fact I remember about that trip was that she asked if I would mind if she called me 'Amory' rather than 'Ma'. I said it was fine with me.

She was better, more like the Blythe I knew than the Blythe of the Willow Ranch experiment, but she was more distant, cooler with me – hence my name change, I surmise – consciously treating me as an equal rather than her mother. I knew why: she was feeling a residual shame about the whole Tayborn Gaines period, for being so hopelessly duped by him. I tried to raise the subject in the hope of expiating it. I said she should forget all about that period of time, not feel ashamed. She was still very young; I started to list all the mistakes I had made at her age but she cut me off abruptly and said she never wanted to talk about it again. So I let it go. People are opaque, even those closest to you. What do we know about the interior lives of our children? Only as much as they choose to reveal.

Blythe came over to England a couple of years later to appear on a music show on television. She was one of three backing singers in a band called Franklin Canyon Park – part of that Californian soft-rock movement of the early 1970s – that had a couple of hit records in Europe. I remember watching the show when the band appeared on TV and feeling an absurd overweening pride when I caught two or three glimpses of Blythe in the background as the camera panned to and fro between the leading members of the group.

She came up to Barrandale to stay for a few days and collect her 'stuff', clearing out her bedroom, removing almost every trace of Blythe Farr from 6 Druim Rigg Road. Again I understood what was going on but in fact we were fine together during the time she was there. We went for long walks; she became very fond of Flam, the dog, and even opened up a little more to me, telling me of a man she had met (there was never any sign of Gaines – it was as if he'd disappeared off the face of the earth), a sound engineer, called Griffin, in a studio where she recorded. 'Don't worry, Amory, I won't be marrying him. I'm never going to marry anyone ever again.'

She never really achieved anything significant with her music. Annie told me that a song she'd co-written for Franklin Canyon Park had reached number thirty-six in the Billboard charts but that was the apex. Her life with Griffin the sound engineer ended also when his drug problem became too much to bear, Annie informed me.

On my second trip over I discovered that she was working as a volunteer at the Long Beach Memorial Medical Center. She was living alone in a small apartment in Anaheim but she did seem more contented. She played in bars at weekends, singing her own songs and rock standards to make something of a living. Luckily she had a small but steady royalty stream from the songs she'd written with Franklin Canyon Park (now long disbanded) but she was very happy to accept some money from me when I offered it. 'It's a loan, Amory. I'll pay you back.' I think Annie sent her money also and I arranged with Moss Fallmaster to divert any cash that came from the slowly diminishing sales of the 'Never Too Young To . . .' T-shirts into her bank account. She also insisted that these occasional payments were a loan – I would be repaid in full, one day. She seemed to survive fairly well, in fact: it was a modest life that she led but a busy one. She'd put on a bit of weight. There was another man in her life, Annie said, but Blythe told me nothing.

I knew in my heart she wouldn't come back to Britain. She changed job and stayed on in Los Angeles, working with former inmates from the Californian Institute of Women (a prison) at a drug-rehabilitation centre called Clean 'n' Sober in the Westchester district of Los Angeles. To be honest, I don't think we'll ever recover that old, unfettered, instinctive relationship we once had. Annie has seen more of her than I have and she says Blythe will come round, eventually, Blythe will see the reality of the situation, just 'give it time'. Well, time is exactly what I'm short of.

Our coffee finally arrived and we chatted about this and that – she told me more about her work with drug addicts and alcoholics and the appalling problems the poor and downtrodden of Los Angeles experienced. I told her more about Annie – about her teaching at CIDBS (the Conservatory for International Development and Business Studies), a private university near Brussels; that she had a boyfriend – whom I hadn't met – a Swedish colleague called Nils. Blythe didn't ask about me, or Dido, or the family – except to request a photo of Flam, whenever I had a moment. This was a good sign, I thought. I held on to it.

The coffee was strong – it had been stewing on a burner for ages – and I decided I needed it sweeter. As I reached for the sugar-shaker and picked it up my hand wouldn't grip and the shaker clattered on to the Formica tabletop. I righted it with my other hand but Blythe had noticed my expression.

'Maybe I won't have any sugar, in fact,' I said, resignedly. 'Curb that sweet tooth.'

'Are you all right, Amory? Is there anything wrong?'

'Just a bit clumsy in my old age,' I said, smiling brightly.

She looked at me searchingly, shrewdly.

'You'd tell me if anything was wrong, wouldn't you? I wouldn't forgive you if you kept something from me.'

'Of course, darling. But there's nothing wrong. I'm just happy to be sitting here with you.'

Eventually I said I'd better go and catch my plane and she walked with me out to where my car was parked.

'It was lovely to see you,' Blythe said. 'I did enjoy our dinner the other night. I'm sorry I've been so busy. I wish we could have spent more time together. It seems like you've flown all this way just to have a cup of coffee with me.'

'Oh, I have to come to California, anyway,' I lied. 'I have this sort of business partner out here. My T-shirt is still selling, amazingly.' That was true: I had dropped in on Moss Fallmaster and he had told me there was almost $400 owed to me. I asked him to send it on to Blythe's account. 'It's always a good excuse to see you, darling,' I said. 'We miss you, Blythe. But we understand.'

She frowned hard at this – I suspect to keep tears at bay.

'I feel I'm doing some good,' she said. 'It helps me – helping other people.'

We walked on towards the car – a cream Chevrolet Caprice. A plump young man in baggy green shorts, a Mothers of Invention T-shirt and a greasy baseball cap was standing there, smoking, as if he were waiting for us to appear. He had a droopy moustache.

'This your fucking car?' he asked me, aggressively.

'Yes,' I said. 'Well, I'm renting it.'

'You're in my spot, lady.'

'It's a parking meter,' I said. 'You can't reserve a parking meter.'

'I always park here, lady,' he said turning his small, pink eyes on me. 'It's reserved for me.'

'It's OK, sir,' Blythe said, very politely, stepping in, seeing I was about to explode. 'She's just going.'

'My sincere apologies,' I said as sarcastically as I could manage and he wandered off muttering to himself.

Blythe watched him go, her hands on her hips.

'Overweight, obnoxious, unwashed, insane,' she said, drily.

I laughed – feeling such a wave of relief surge through me that it made me shiver. I kissed her goodbye and she gave me a fleeting hug, a pressure of her hands on my shoulders. Somehow I knew everything would be fine.

★

I still feel a responsibility for her, however illogical that may seem. I keep wondering what would have happened if I hadn't left the girls and gone off to Vietnam. Would it have made a difference? It didn't seem to affect Annie ... Who can say? Life's unsatisfactory, half-baked, half-assed solutions are sometimes the best. Annie with her Swedish boyfriend in Brussels; Blythe helping junkies in Los Angeles. I really don't care what my children do with their lives – I have no agenda for them at all – I only want them to be as happy as they can possibly be, given life's stringent, sudden demands, on whatever road they choose to walk down. The desires of the heart are as crooked as corkscrews, as the poet says: not to be born is the best for man – only that way can you avoid all of life's complications.

I'm thinking about birth, I should say, because I'm in the process of arranging my death.

Last week I called Annie in Brussels to have a chat about something and she said, 'Ma, have you been drinking?' No more than usual, I said, I've had two glasses of wine. 'Well, your voice is slurred,' she said. 'Take it easy.' I was shocked because I had no idea my voice was slurred though I knew exactly what it implied – progressive bulbar palsy. My nasty little smiler with the knife that lurks inside me had inserted the blade again. So I decided the time had come. My birthday was approaching, my seventieth, threescore years and ten is good enough for me.

This is what I looked up in the Bible I borrowed from the Auld Kirk – I found what I was searching for quickly enough. Psalms 90.10:

The days of our years are threescore years and ten; and if by reason of strength they be fourscore years, yet is their strength labour and sorrow, for it is soon cut off and we fly away.

I know what's wrong with me and I know what I will become – a working, vital, thinking brain in a dead and uncontrollable body in which nothing works. No thank you. The days of my life will be threescore years and ten, I have decided. I will cut it off and I will fly away, myself.

Everything is in order. Here I am in my sitting room on 6 March 1978 waiting for midnight. The fire is banked up with peat bricks and I am ideally cosy. On the table beside my armchair is a full bottle of Glen Fleshan malt whisky, a glass and a jam jar full of Jock Edie's blessed 'sweeties'. Jock's capsules are a benzodiazepine – 'Librium' in this instance. Take them with alcohol, he advised: alcohol compounds the effects, leading to coma and then death. It's a tranquil feeling, he had added, consolingly. You won't be aware of anything. Flam lies by the fire watching me carefully. I think he knows something untoward is going on; he senses my troubled mind and it discomfits him. We're both animals, after all, so it's not surprising that he senses something's amiss. He knows me very well.

On the coffee table in front of me is my will, a letter for Annie and Blythe and my life story in a cardboard file and I will add the 'Barrandale Journal' to it before I fly away. Pinned to the front door is an envelope for Hugo with 'Hugo. Read this before entry!' written on it. I've arranged for him to come round tomorrow, ostensibly to travel to Oban to look for pots and pans and other kitchen utensils for his new house. In the envelope is a letter telling him what I've done – what I'm about to do. I don't want to shock anyone, which is one reason why I'm sitting in an armchair. I suspect I shall look as if I've dozed off when he pushes open the front door and comes through the hall into the parlour. He'll have been forewarned.

I don't like the word 'suicide' or 'assisted dying' or 'mercy killing' or any of the few other synonyms available. I prefer the expression 'by my own hand'. I will take my life by my own hand at a moment chosen by me – not by my disease. 'By my own hand' speaks to me of autonomy, of free will.

I feel very calm. I truly believe this option should be available to anyone who wants it. In fact I feel quite passionate about this issue now I'm about to put it into practice – it should be available to anyone who wants it as a matter of civil liberty, of human rights and human dignity. You go to your doctor, explain the situation, you sign all manner of affidavits testifying to your determination, clarity of mind, familiarity with consequences and so forth. You have the documentation witnessed, if required. Then you're given your bottle of pills, or, even better, one pill, and you go home, set your affairs in order, make your necessary farewells, if you want to, and gladly leave your life behind. End of story. I'm not going to give the lethal pill to anyone else. If I buy a kitchen knife no one asks me if I'm going to stab someone with it. With your purchase you are simultaneously handed the responsibility to use your knife as it was designed to be used – so too with my notional pill. Our lives are filled with potential lethal weapons, after all; a pill that will end your life painlessly is just another. If we're treated as responsible beings we tend to act responsibly.

There was a French writer – Charbonneau told me his name but I can't remember it now – who defined life as a 'horizontal fall'. It's a neat metaphor. I just want to end my horizontal fall now, before the bleak prison of my particular ailment closes in around me. What could be more reasonable than that?

Charbonneau's name coming to mind makes me think fondly of him – and all the people I've loved during my own horizontal fall. My threescore years and ten have been rich and intensely sad, fascinating, droll, absurd and terrifying – sometimes – and difficult and painful and happy. Complicated, in other words.

It's midnight. I take my first pill and wash it down with a sip of Glen Fleshan. I've decided to keep writing in my journal until my last moment of consciousness. Flam looks at me, his tail thumps on the carpet. I've walked him so he'll just have to wait until Hugo arrives in the morning. I've ordered Hugo to take Flam and Hugo can walk him, later, when he's been. And it'll be a fine day tomorrow, for a March day on Barrandale – a good day for a long walk. Clear skies have been announced, bracing sunlit weather. I should never have listened to the weather forecast. I take another pill.

My eyes flit around my sitting room, taking it in for the last time.

In a fruit bowl on the table in front of me are four oranges and a banana. And I think – without thinking – ah, breakfast tomorrow. The banana is freckling nicely. I could slice it into a bowl of porridge. I could have freshly squeezed orange juice and then a bowl of porridge with sliced banana and then go for a walk with Flam, down to the bay, round to the headland. Call Hugo, invite him for lunch. A bottle of wine . . . Except there won't be a tomorrow, I realise.

I take another pill, another sip of whisky. I won't feel a thing, Jock Edie said, just drift off to sleep and not wake up.

But, annoyingly, I keep thinking about freshly squeezed orange juice and the day ahead waiting for me. Sun on the wavelets in the bay and that cold bright weather that here on the west coast is about as invigorating as you can experience – cheeks numb, breath condensing, the light and shade razor-edged, the focus precisely sharp. I could take some more light-pictures by the rock pools . . .

Flam is standing now, as if he senses this new direction in my thinking, and he shakes himself, licks his chops and comes over to me and puts his muzzle on my knee and looks into my eyes. No, I'm not going to rub your ears, old dog, go and lie down.

I pick up another pill . . .

But I've put it back in the bottle and screwed the cap tightly on. Was I making another mistake, I thought, my last mistake? Was I being a little hasty . . . ? If I can plan my breakfast and look forward to the day ahead with its simple pleasures – isn't that a sign? Wouldn't it be wiser to experience the day ahead and savour it, as if it were my last, and postpone for a while my appointment with my pills and my whisky until the moment comes when I don't feel like coping any more and all anticipation has gone? I have the means so I can decide at any time of my choosing – Jock Edie says the pills will keep for years. I push the pill bottle away and pour myself a large dram of Glen Fleshan.

I am thinking – hard, concentrating. My life has been complicated, true, very complicated, and it seems to be entering another realm of complexity. But, then again, isn't everybody's and won't everybody's be just as complicated? Any life of any reasonable length throws up all manner of complications, just as intricate as mine have been. I pick up an orange and contemplate it. Remarkable fruit. I test its rind with my thumbnail. Like skin, porous, soft. What's waiting for me? A cold fine day, a dog, a walk, a white beach, the wind-scored ocean, a camera, an urgent concentrating eye, a curious active mind. I weigh the orange in my hand, sniff its citrus astringency. The singular beauty of the orange . . . The here and now. Seize the day, Amory.

Yes, my life has been very complicated but, I realise, it's the complications that have engaged me and made me feel alive. I think I should let my horizontal fall continue just a little while longer – keep falling horizontally until I decide to stop.

I know I won't sleep now that I've made my decision. I hold my glass of whisky up to the glow from the peat bricks in the fire and watch the small flames shuffle and refract through the golden liquid. Yes, I'll go down to the beach with Flam – now, in the middle of the moonless night and listen to the waves – and walk on the shore and look out at the darkness of the ocean, all senses dimmed except the auditory; stroll on my beach with the lights of my house burning yellow behind me in the enveloping blue-black sea-dark and contemplate this uncertain future that I've just bestowed on myself – me, Amory Clay, a certain type of ape on a small planet circling an insignificant star in a solar system that's part of an unimaginably vast expanding universe – and I will stand there in all humility and calm myself, with the ocean's endless, unchanging, consoling call for silence – *shh, shh, shh* . . .

AMORY CLAY

Photographer

Born
7 March 1908

Died
23 June 1983
(by her own hand)

ACKNOWLEDGEMENTS

Hannelore Hahn, Annemarie Schwarzenbach, Margaret Michaelis, Lee Miller, Gerda Taro, Trude Fleischmann, Gloria Emerson, Steffi Brandt, Martha Gellhorn, Constanze Auger, M. F. K. Fisher, Nina Leen, Gerti Deutsch, Lily Perette, Harriet Cohen, Greta Kolliner, Louise Dahl-Wolfe, Renata Alabama, Marianne Breslauer, Lisette Model, Edith Tudor-Hart, Françoise Demulder, Dora Kallmuss, Catherine Leroy, Edith Glogau, Dickey Chapelle, Margaret Bourke-White, Mary Poundstone, Diane Arbus, Rebecca West, Kate Webb, Inge Bing (and all the others).

A NOTE ON THE AUTHOR

William Boyd is the author of fourteen novels including
A Good Man in Africa, winner of the Whitbread Award and the
Somerset Maugham Award; *An Ice-Cream War*, winner of the John
Llewellyn Rhys Prize and shortlisted for the Booker Prize; *Any
Human Heart*, winner of the Prix Jean Monnet and adapted into
a BAFTA-winning Channel 4 drama; *Restless*, winner of the Costa
Novel of the Year, the Yorkshire Post Novel of the Year and a
Richard & Judy selection; the *Sunday Times* bestseller
Waiting for Sunrise, and, most recently, *Solo*, a James Bond novel.
William Boyd lives in London and France.

www.williamboyd.co.uk